Catherine Cookson was born in Tyne Dock, the illegitimate daughter of a poverty-stricken woman, Kate, whom she believed to be her older sister. She began work in service but eventually moved south to Hastings, where she met and married Tom Cookson, a local grammar-school master. At the age of forty she began writing about the lives of the working-class people with whom she had grown up, using the place of her birth as the background to many of her novels.

Although originally acclaimed as a regional writer – her novel *The Round Tower* won the Winifred Holtby award for the best regional novel of 1968 – her readership soon began to spread throughout the world. Her novels have been translated into more than a dozen languages and more than 50,000,000 copies of her books have been sold in Corgi alone. Fifteen of her novels have been made into successful television dramas, and more are planned.

Catherine Cookson's many bestselling novels established her as one of the most popular of contemporary women novelists. After receiving an OBE in 1985, Catherine was created a Dame of the British Empire in 1993. She was appointed an Honorary Fellow of St Hilda's College, Oxford in 1997. For many years she lived near Newcastle-upon-Tyne. She died shortly before her ninety-second birthday in June 1998.

'Catherine Cookson's novels are about hardship, the intractability of life and individuals, the struggle first to survive and next to make sense of one's survival. Humour, toughness, resolution and generosity are Cookson virtues, in a world which she often depicts as cold and violent. Her novels are weighted a̶̶̶ d̶̶ i̶v̶e̶n̶ by her own early experiences of illegitimacy a̶̶̶̶̶̶̶̶̶̶̶̶̶ ̶m power. In the speci̶̶̶̶̶̶̶̶̶̶̶̶̶̶̶ ̶ar fiction, Cookson has̶̶̶̶̶̶̶̶̶̶̶̶̶̶̶ Helen Dunmore, *Th̶̶̶̶̶*

D0830404

# BOOKS BY CATHERINE COOKSON

## NOVELS

Kate Hannigan ━
The Fifteen Streets
Colour Blind
Maggie Rowan
Rooney
The Menagerie
Slinky Jane
Fanny McBride
Fenwick Houses
Heritage of Folly
The Garment
The Fen Tiger
The Blind Miller
House of Men
Hannah Massey
The Long Corridor
The Unbaited Trap
Katie Mulholland
The Round Tower
The Nice Bloke
The Glass Virgin
The Invitation
The Dwelling Place
Feathers in the Fire
Pure as the Lily
The Mallen Streak
The Mallen Girl
The Mallen Litter
The Invisible Cord
The Gambling Man ━
The Tide of Life
The Slow Awakening
The Iron Façade
The Girl
The Cinder Path
Miss Martha Mary Crawford
The Man Who Cried
Tilly Trotter
Tilly Trotter Wed
Tilly Trotter Widowed

The Whip
Hamilton
The Black Velvet Gown
Goodbye Hamilton
A Dinner of Herbs
Harold
The Moth
Bill Bailey
The Parson's Daughter
Bill Bailey's Lot
The Cultured Handmaiden
Bill Bailey's Daughter
The Harrogate Secret
The Black Candle
The Wingless Bird
The Gillyvors
My Beloved Son
The Rag Nymph
The House of Women
The Maltese Angel
The Year of the Virgins
The Golden Straw
Justice is a Woman
The Tinker's Girl
A Ruthless Need
The Obsession
The Upstart
The Branded Man
The Bonny Dawn
The Bondage of Love
The Desert Crop
The Lady on My Left
The Solace of Sin
Riley
The Blind Years
The Thursday Friend
A House Divided
Kate Hannigan's Girl
The Silent Lady

## THE MARY ANN STORIES

A Grand Man
The Lord and Mary Ann
The Devil and Mary Ann
Love and Mary Ann

Life and Mary Ann
Marriage and Mary Ann
Mary Ann's Angels
Mary Ann and Bill

## FOR CHILDREN

Matty Doolin
Joe and the Gladiator
The Nipper
Rory's Fortune
Our John Willie

Mrs Flannagan's Trumpet
Go Tell It To Mrs Golightly
Lanky Jones
Nancy Nutall and the Mongrel
Bill and the Mary Ann Shaughnessy

## AUTOBIOGRAPHY

Our Kate
Catherine Cookson Country

Let Me Make Myself Plain
Plainer Still

# THE THURSDAY
# FRIEND

## Catherine Cookson

## CORGI BOOKS

THE THURSDAY FRIEND
A CORGI BOOK : 9780552144384

Originally published in Great Britain by Bantam Press,
a division of Transworld Publishers

PRINTING HISTORY
Bantam Press edition published 1999
Corgi edition published 2000

3  5  7  9  10  8  6  4

Set in 11/13pt Sabon by
Phoenix Typesetting, Ilkley, West Yorkshire.

Corgi Books are published by Transworld Publishers,
61–63 Uxbridge Road, London W5 5SA,
a division of The Random House Group Ltd.

Addresses for Random House Group Ltd companies outside the UK
can be found at: www.randomhouse.co.uk
The Random House Group Ltd Reg. No. 954009.

Reproduced, printed and bound in Great Britain by
Cox & Wyman Ltd, Reading, Berkshire.

The Random House Group Limited supports The Forest Stewardship
Council (FSC), the leading international forest certification organisation.
All our titles that are printed on Greenpeace approved FSC certified paper
carry the FSC logo. Our paper procurement policy can be found at:
www.rbooks.co.uk/environment.

# THE THURSDAY FRIEND

# One

Hannah Drayton got off the bus near Ealing Broadway. Three minutes later she was walking through a good-class district which gave abruptly on to a council estate. Yet this estate was different from the usual type, in that the houses were mostly terraced.

She turned into Buttermere Close, walked past a number of houses with well-kept gardens, then opened the gate of number 23, rang the bell and waited for the door to be opened.

A tall woman greeted Hannah with: 'Hello! What's brought you at this time of the morning?'

'Nothing, Janie. Nothing very much. Let me get in.'

'Let you get in? You look as white as a sheet.' Then, shaking her head, the tall woman led the way into the kitchen, saying, 'Oh, Lord! I haven't started to clear up yet. I was having ten minutes: Maggie's taken the kids to the park. The only good thing to say about school holidays is that she looks after the young 'uns.' Then, her voice changing as she half turned towards her sister, she said, 'You in trouble of some sort, Hannah?'

'Not . . . not what you would call trouble, Janie. Oh, may I have a cup of tea?'

'I don't see why not. And you've seen all this mess before, so what am I worrying about? Come and sit down while the kettle boils.'

Five minutes later, when they were sitting opposite each other at the narrow, crockery-littered table, Janie Harper said, 'Well, out with it.'

She watched her sister bite hard down on her thumbnail, an action, she recalled, which always meant Hannah was in some kind of trouble. It was some time since she had last seen her do it. But then she did not see her quite so frequently as she had before Hannah had married that stuffed shirt. Thinking of the stuffed shirt, she said, 'Is it to do with Humph?'

Hannah Drayton closed her eyes for a moment. Humph. Oh, how that term annoyed Humphrey; it had been Eddie who first used it on him. But she answered, 'Yes, in a way;' then, much louder, she said, 'Oh . . . more than in a way, Janie. I just had to talk to someone about it, and there's only you; but I know you don't care for him, no more than does Eddie. But it isn't his fault, I mean . . . but yes, it is in a way.'

'Look!' Janie's hand came across the table and gripped her younger sister's arm. 'Start from the beginning.'

At this Hannah's head drooped, and she muttered, 'It's . . . it's so personal, Janie.'

'Well, I'm a married woman, aren't I? and how! If there's anything you want to know about bed, here's your agony aunt looking at you.'

At this, Hannah said, 'I want to laugh at you as usual, Janie, but at this moment I can't. Well, it . . . it's like this.' Her head drooping again and her voice low, she began to talk.

She talked for fully five minutes before Janie burst out, 'The unnatural bugger! How long is it, you say, since you've had separate rooms?'

'About two and a half years.'

'And you've been married only four years altogether? Look, I had my suspicions of him at the beginning. Is he . . . is he the other way?'

'Oh, no! No, Janie.' Hannah's back was straight now, her voice loud in her husband's defence. 'Nothing like that. No! In fact, he's against them. There's a couple living further down the road, and I once said how nice they were, very pleasant and quite intelligent to talk to, and he actually went for me. I couldn't understand it. I'd never seen him in such a temper. You see, Janie, he's got such a kind nature.'

'Kind nature be damned! He couldn't keep you at arm's length for the past two and a half years just for an allergy. I never knew you were allergic to apricots. We used to have all kinds of fruit— Oh, didn't we!' – she laughed – 'from Eddie's stall! I don't remember you coming out with anything, apricots or no apricots.'

'We never had them, though, did we!'

'Have you had the allergy since?'

'Only once, and that was a few months ago. I ate some other fruit. I didn't know what it was then, but I think it was the fruit.'

'But you say he left you alone because you had the allergy?'

'No, not really. I happened to be scratching in the middle of the night and I had to get up and put on some soothing lotion, and I disturbed him. The next night he said . . . well, we would both rest better for a time if he went into the spare room.'

Janie put in quietly, 'And he's been there ever since?'

'Yes.'

'And you've done nothing about it, not spoken to him about it?'

'Oh, Janie, how could I? I'm not you, Janie, I can't come out with things.'

'More's the pity. That's what I say. How does he treat you otherwise, I mean at home?'

'Oh' – Hannah's voice held a lightness now – 'he's very kind. He discusses business. Well, I don't know anything about a broker's business, only that they buy and sell shares, but he tells me funny things that happen in his department. Including Humphrey, there are four men: Mr Wainwright is above him, and I don't think Humphrey likes him much; Hobbs, he says, is a quiet bachelor, but Brown is the butt of Wainwright. He calls him Windsor, you know, like the soup, Brown Windsor. And of course there's the big man whom most people seem to know only by name. He's called Manstein, or something like that. I don't know whether he's German or Russian, I only know that once a year they all go to different parts of the world for conferences and—'

'Has he ever asked you to go with him?'

'No. How could he? It's for men. And you know what happened last year. I went to Cornwall with Mrs Wainwright. You remember?'

They nodded at each other, and Janie said, 'Yes, you said you'd rather do a month's stint with my gang than another day with her. Yes, I remember. But anyway, about this other thing. You've got to do something about it, because something's happening to you: you've lost your colour and your spunk. You mightn't be like me, with plenty of get-up-and-go, but you were never a doormat; and that's how he's treating you.'

'Oh no, dear, no. It's . . . well, I was just wondering if you knew if this was usual or not.'

'Yes, it's usual, I should imagine, with queers; but he married you and you shared the same bed for more than a year and, as Eddie often says, he was damn lucky to get someone like you, because he's no oil painting. Oh, he's got a pair of long legs on him, I'll admit, but he's got a face that would sour milk at times, and he can give you ten years. By the way, what about his people . . . that aunt and uncle who live in Worthing? Have you seen them recently?'

'No; because, as I've told you before, they didn't approve of his choice. As his dear aunt said to me,

11

on the quiet of course, they were both surprised that their dear Humphrey, who up till then had showed no tendency towards marriage, should take someone so young, and she had glanced at my hair and stopped herself from saying, "with blond hair and likely bleached". No, I think we've been half a dozen times; but, as you know, he goes practically every weekend now, well, he has done over the past two years, because his uncle, who's getting on, is not at all well.'

'Well, what do you do with yourself? You don't always come here at the weekend.'

'No. I fill in: I go for walks; and I'm writing again. You know I used to dabble in children's stories.'

'Oh.' Janie moved her head impatiently. 'You don't want to carry on with anything like that. That'll keep you by yourself, if anything would. You want to get out and about. You know something, Hannah?' Her head moved slowly up and down. 'You can't have looked in the mirror seriously for years. I used to envy you, you know, your looks. I had what Eddie calls poisonality, but you had really what it took, and you still have, although it's lost its colour. Does he take you out? I mean, do you eat out and things.'

'Oh yes, sometimes we go to a restaurant.'

'Sometimes. Well, what does he do the rest of the week?'

'Every Thursday is definitely his night out because he plays bridge with Hobbs and Brown and another man. Apparently they've done so for years. They're all in some club.'

'Well, what about Monday, Tuesday, Wednesday, Friday, Saturday and Sunday?'

'Oh' – Hannah's head now moved impatiently – 'I suppose in that way we're just like everybody else, Janie. As I told you, we discuss work and what we've done during the day, and we often did the crossword in bed, but not any more, of course.'

'Oh, my God!'

'Janie, please!'

'All right. All right. But look' – she stabbed a finger at her sister – 'you came here to tell me something. Now you've told me something that's most unnatural, and so I'm putting it to you straight: If he isn't a homo, does he like women's clothes?'

'Oh, Janie; stop it!'

'Sit down. Sit down. You know me, at least you should do by now. There must be something wrong with the fellow.'

'No, there isn't, Janie; and I . . . well . . . he's none of those things. It was explained to me by a priest. But then I came to you . . . well, to . . . to ask . . . Oh!' Hannah put her hand over her eyes now but was immediately startled by Janie's voice exclaiming, 'You've been to a priest?'

'Yes.'

'A Catholic one?'

'Yes.'

'My God! What did he tell you?'

'He . . . he was very nice. He told me not to worry because some men were born . . .'

'Yes, go on: they were born what?'

'He called it celibate. He said Humphrey was

wrong: he should never have married, he should likely have been in a monastery or somewhere, or been a priest or something like that.'

'Or something like that be damned!' Janie was on her feet. 'Anyway, what possessed you to go to a priest?'

'Well, I thought he would give a sort of explanation.'

'And he did. By God! he did. Anyway' – Janie shrugged her shoulders – 'why am I asking why you went to a priest when we both had thirteen years under those bloody nuns?'

'Oh, Janie, please! Now just think: at one time you were jolly glad to be at the convent; it got you away from home and Mama and Papa.'

'Oh, yes, yes; Mama and Papa.' Janie pushed a group of dirty mugs to one side of the table before bending towards Hannah and saying, 'Your trouble and mine, Hannah, both stem from dear Mama and Papa. Remember the day when I dared address Papa as Dad, and then wanted an explanation why I shouldn't? The other girls all called their fathers Dad, not Papa; we weren't in the Victorian age any longer, and, too, why not Mam instead of Mama? Talk about snobs. If there was ever a pair they were, and you know it. I got out.' She put her head back and let out a high, merry laugh. 'Do you remember the day I got out?'

Hannah was smiling back at her sister, nodding her head, saying, 'Oh, yes; I'll never forget it. I can see you now coming in that dining room.'

'Yes, I can see myself, and Mama saying, "You're

14

late. Where have you been?" and my saying flatly, "With Eddie Harper, the barrow boy, as you call him. And he's not a barrow boy any longer; he's got a fruit shop and a flat above, and I'm going there to live with him. I'm twenty years old and if you try to bring me back then I'll come back, but pregnant. You believe me!"'

The tears of laughter were running down Hannah's face and she spluttered, 'And Mama fell flat on the floor.'

'Yes; and it was a real faint this time, not a Victorian lady's smelling-salts stunt. And I remember looking at you. You were all eyes and mouth and I said to you, "As for you, young 'un, stand up for yourself." But you didn't, did you? Anyway, you couldn't. They kept you at school until you were seventeen and brought you home when Nellie walked out one day. I laughed about that until I was sick; but not when I realised you were being used as an unpaid servant. You wanted to go in for nursing, didn't you? But no, they wouldn't even let you take a secretarial course. That would've cost money. Why they sent us to a private convent school, God only knows. Prestige, I suppose, to have one up on the neighbours. But you know, you never told me what made you go to night school to learn secretarial work. What was it? You must have been about twenty then.'

At this Hannah wiped her eyes and said soberly, 'You made me, Janie.'

'Do the secretarial course?'

'Well, in a way, because I told Mama that if I

couldn't learn a trade of some kind then I would likely follow you and do what you had done, walk out and go to live with another barrow boy. In any case I'd go and live with you.'

'You didn't!'

'Oh yes, I did; and so I had all those months at night school. Of course, then Mama died and the new freedom was marvellous, until Papa said he was going to marry again. And then it seemed to be heaven-sent when Humphrey took an interest in me. Quite honestly, Janie, I must admit I jumped at him. I think I would've jumped at anyone at that time, but I jumped at him because I loved him. He was so . . . well; gentlemanly.'

'Yes, not a bit like my Eddie.'

'Your Eddie's all right. I've come to like and admire him more than a little; from what you've told me he doesn't only look after you and his family, he cares for his own folk, and they're spread all over the place.'

Janie sat down again, and they both stared at each other for a while until Hannah said, 'Well, I feel much better now than when I came in.'

'But your opening up, has it solved any problems? What're you going to do?'

'Well, you know that he won't let me go out to work. When I once asked him plainly why, his answer was that he didn't want me to be exposed to clerical louts. I could do work at home, but that was all. And so I made up my mind I'd have a go at writing stories for children; not about po-faced ones, but about those more like your little tribe.'

'Oh, thank you very much. Thank you very much.'

But as Hannah looked across at her sister she knew she was pleased at the idea, and when Janie said, 'They're good kids, all of them, and we're trying for an addition: he wants another boy. Three of each, he wants,' Hannah exclaimed, 'Oh, Janie! Janie, you're the limit.'

'Oh, Hannah! Hannah.' They both laughed at the mimicry, and Janie, getting up, said, 'Let me get this kitchen cleared and prepare some lunch for the tribe; then we'll go down to the park and fetch them back.'

'You'll do no such thing, not with me you won't, because I'm off now, believe it or not, in search of a publisher.' Hannah lifted her bag from the floor and, tapping it, said, 'In there is a very well typed children's story. It's for five-year-olds, and I've done little drawings to accompany each piece.'

'Let me have a look.'

'No. No, look; I've got a thing about that. I saw an advert in the paper yesterday. It said Martin Gillyman, Publisher of odd books and buyer of rare ones.'

'Publisher of odd books and buyer of rare ones! Sounds someone dippy to me; real publishers don't advertise like that.'

'Well, this one does. And it was because it sounded so unusual that I'm going to try my hand with him.'

'Well, I wish you luck. I'll be interested to know the result.'

'You shall. You shall.'

'Anyway, where's this one situated?'

'Oh, it's in Bloomsbury, I think.'

'Oh, Lord! you've some way to go.'

'Well, I'll get the tube to Tottenham Court Road and step right out into Bloomsbury, or near enough. Anyway,' she added, on an almost sad note which she found impossible to keep from her tone, 'I have nothing else to do with my time. Mrs Fenwick sees to the house, as she did long before I came on the scene. In her eyes I'm sure I'm an intruder, and again and again she'll remind me she first saw to Mr Drayton immediately he stepped into London from that Worthing.' She smiled, 'It's always *that* Worthing, or *that* Brighton, or *that* Kent, where she used to go hop-picking at one time; that was when she was young, if ever she was young.'

As Hannah, now buttoning up her light grey coat, made for the door, Janie said, 'How are you off for money? I mean, we've never spoken about that. What's he like with his purse?'

'Oh, he's not bad, I suppose. Well, he sees to all the bills and everything.'

'Housekeeping an' all?'

'Oh yes. You see, he's always done it; I've just got to ask and he'll give it to me.'

'You've got to ask? Doesn't he give you an allowance?'

Hannah aimed to sound amusing as she said, 'Now who's going back into Victorian days? Allowance indeed! Anyway—' She put out her hand and squeezed Janie's, saying, 'You always do me good. I should've come and had a talk with you weeks ago, months ago.'

'If you want my opinion there should be no need for you to come and have a talk with anybody if things were as they should be, natural. Wait till Eddie hears of this.'

'Oh, no! No, Janie! Please don't tell Eddie.'

'All right. All right. Don't get yourself upset; I won't.'

Hannah stared at the tall thin woman who was so unlike herself and she knew that that would be the first thing she would speak of when her husband came into the house: she could hear his voice now, punctuating each sentence with bloody hell! or the bugger! and she wondered how it was that they had been so different in their choice of men and that now she could even envy Janie her Eddie.

They embraced warmly at the front door and kissed, and the last words Janie said, softly, were, 'I worry about you, you know. Funny, but I always have. You need looking after.'

'Oh! go on.' Hannah walked smartly away, but when she came to the end of the terrace she turned and lifted her hand, for she knew that Janie would still be standing watching her.

She came out of the tube at Tottenham Court Road, walked along the main thoroughfare, then, seeing a policeman on duty at the end of a side street, enquired of him if he could direct her to Jason Gardens.

'Oh, Jason Gardens. Jason Gardens.' He pulled

on his lower lip, then said, 'Oh, now, I think you've got a bit of a walk, miss. Do you know where the British Museum is?'

'Yes. Yes, I do.'

'Well, it's near there. I'm not sure exactly where, but someone will direct you if you ask them, I'm sure.'

She thanked him. They smiled at each other.

She found Jason Gardens before she reached the British Museum, and she was surprised to find it was made up of private houses, some three storeys, others two, but all well built and of a period long gone, for there were half-moon fanlights above some of the doors and nearly all had an iron-railed approach up three broad steps, at the top of which, on some, were placed urns full of scarlet geraniums, trailing nasturtiums and other seasonable flowers. Number 4, she noted, was slightly different. There were no urns, but in the place of one was seated a life-size stone dog. It, too, definitely was from another age, for the stone was very weathered.

On the wall to the right of the door was a brass plate stating simply, 'Gillyman: Publishers'. Why she smiled as she looked at the plate she did not know; it was only later she was to remember she had done so. She looked for a bell. There was no sign of one, but there was a letterbox, and to the left of it a large brass doorknob.

The door opened easily and there she was standing in a small hallway with, facing her, a door with a sign on it saying 'Private'. To her left was another door, by the side of which was a bell with a notice saying 'Ring and Enter'. This she did.

Slowly she opened the door, only to remain stock still and staring into what she imagined to be a warehouse.

'Come in! if you're coming in, and close the door.' The words were precise, but at the moment she couldn't see from where they were coming.

She turned and closed the door, then stepped gingerly between books piled in heaps on the floor and set in front of racks already full of others. She had taken five steps before she saw the owner of the voice. He was sitting behind a large, heavy mahogany desk, which was clear except for one stack of neatly piled books, and an opened book which he was apparently reading.

'Hello!' he said.

She stared at the man for a moment before she said softly, 'Good morning.'

'Well, sit down. Pull that chair up.'

She turned and looked behind her and there, its back legs stuck among more books, was a chair which she now pulled forward and then sat down upon, and they looked at each other. What she saw was a face topped by a mass of almost white grizzly hair. His face was long and clean-shaven and she noticed that his mouth was very large and full-lipped. He wasn't wearing a jacket and the sleeves of his shirt were rolled up above the elbow, and she further noticed and with some amazement that the shirt looked as if it were a silk one – white silk.

'Well, what can I do for you?' The voice startled

her, and she blinked rapidly and muttered something that she could hardly hear herself, and at this he said, 'You want me to buy some books from you?' Then, before she could answer, he added, 'You're very young and you don't look as if you've had a bereavement and have come to ask me to clear your house of all the rubbish.' The large head nodded violently now. 'That's what people call books, you know, rubbish, rubbish. It angers me. Well now, why are you here? What do you want?'

'I . . .'

'Yes, yes; go on, my dear, go on. I'm not an ogre and I'm not going to bite you and although you're very pretty, I would say beautiful, yes, beautiful, especially your eyes—' he was smiling widely now and showing two complete rows of short white teeth; then he went on, 'there has been no time as yet for me to have unseemly designs on you.'

She couldn't help it, she let out a burst of high laughter: he was the funniest man she had come across, not only in looks but in what he said. When she quickly took her handkerchief from her pocket and wiped her eyes, saying, 'I'm sorry,' he came back with, 'Sorry for what? You're the brightest spot that's happened in this day, because I've come across nothing exciting' – he flicked his hands towards the ordered books to his right – 'and your laugh goes with your eyes. Funny, that' – he leant further across the table – 'you laugh with your eyes, yes. So few women laugh with their eyes. I hadn't noticed that, you know, but David pointed it out to me. Oh, what am I talking about?' His head was shaking again. 'Let us get down to business. You know something?' His finger was wagging gently at her. 'You're a mesmerist.'

'A what?'

'A mesmerist. You could mesmerise a man. Yes, you could. Now, to business.'

She opened her bag, took out the little parcel and placed it on the table before her and said, 'I . . . I've written a little book for children and I don't think that . . . well, one of the big publishers would look at it; but I was . . . well, I was intrigued by your advert – I'm referring to you saying you published odd books – and I suppose my little effort could be . . . well, classed as odd.'

'Tut! tut! Well, well! So this is something. Let me see.'

She went to undo the brown paper parcel and he said, 'Leave it! Leave it! Let me do it.'

She watched him unwrap the parcel, turn to the first page, then flick through the rest of the pages with his thumb, before he said, 'Nice typewriter.'

Again he looked at the manuscript, lifted his head, and said, 'Well set.'

Her heart was thumping against her ribs as she watched him turn page after page without uttering a word. Twice he smiled, and once he gave a hic of a laugh. Then, when he could have been only half-way through, he stopped and, putting his hand flat on the pages, he said, 'What made you do it in this way?'

'Well,' she considered, 'I suppose I thought about it like that. Children's books are set more often than not so formally. I did the accompanying drawings myself.'

'Oh. Yes, yes, I see. Like the bird feeding its young.' He stamped his first finger down on the page. 'And the cat washing its face. I . . . I liked the one of the clothes line.'

She smiled widely at him now as she said, 'I liked that too. I think that's my favourite.'

He turned the pages; then, his eyes twinkling, he looked at her before reading:

'It's washing day! It's washing day!
My pi-jams are all soap.
They'll shrink and shrink, and shrink and shrink,
Oh dear! there is no hope.'

His voice gradually rose until he was almost shouting,

'It's washing day! It's washing day!
The clothes are on the line.
There's Daddy's things, and Mummy's
Things and next to them are mine.

'Nice, nice. And the drawings, very cute, very cute. And as yet you've not sent this out?'

'No.'

'No, of course. As you said, publishers . . . publishers. Oh! Publishers. They think they know everything.' He grinned now as he thumped his chest, saying, 'That's me too. I know everything, at least I think so. More than David, but not as much as my wife. Oh, that reminds me: David must see this.' He rang a bell that seemed to be under the edge of the desk and while they waited for it to be answered he said, 'David's got a very keen eye for the oddities, those that are going to work. Some oddities work, you know, and some don't. Most of my oddities don't, I must admit. But those that do, oh, those that do, they hit the headlines. I've got two best-seller oddities going at the moment, oh yes. Of course, they're about adults. Nasty adults.'

His face straight now, his lips tight, he nodded towards her before he said, 'There are a lot of nasty oddities about, you know: hidden ones; grabbing ones; money-minded ones. Aaah! There you are.' He turned towards what must have been a door hidden from her by more books, through which a man had appeared. He was tall, and tanned, as if he had been lying in the sun; but if that had been so his hair should have been bleached by the sun too, but it was dark, a very dark brown. It was thick and inclined to waves but was brushed back straight from his forehead. He was wearing glasses, but after looking at her for a moment he took them off, wiped them, and put them in his pocket. 'Good morning,' he said.

'Good morning,' she answered.

'Come and look at this.'

'What is it?'

'Don't be an idiot, man; you won't know until you look at it, will you?' The older man now grinned across at Hannah; but she was looking at the man who was holding her typed pages in their green cardboard cover. She watched him turn two or three pages before he looked up and glanced at her as if he were about to say something; but then he continued to turn the pages, reading a little, or perhaps reading them all, she thought, because some people were very quick readers.

He had got almost to the end when the older man said, 'Well, what d'you think?'

Hannah watched the man turn the last page, then hand the manuscript back to Mr Gillyman, saying with a wry smile, 'Well, I think it's odd enough to please even you.'

Her heart sank. What did he mean, odd enough? That children wouldn't understand it? Yes, they would; she was sure they would if it were read to them properly. When sitting in with Janie's lot she had read bits to them, and they'd liked them and laughed about them; but apparently they could not have held their interest enough for them to mention them to their mother.

The dark-haired man was looking at her, and his head was moving slowly as he said, 'They're very nice, and the way you've set them down is unusual. There're one or two similar on the market: Jessie Tyler and Florence Potts.'

She had never heard of Jessie Tyler or of Florence Potts. Perhaps she'd made a mistake in not reading other authors' writings for children. She had purposely not done this because she didn't want to copy anyone. Yet here he was saying there were other similar books already on the market.

'Would it sell in the right quarters, do you think?' Mr Gillyman was now asking of his assistant; and his assistant looked at Hannah. He looked at her for what seemed an embarrassingly long time before he said, 'Well, you've said it, Gilly, in the right quarters . . . if we could find the right quarters.'

'Oh, there must be one more sensible publisher besides myself.'

The two men were now looking at each other and laughing, and as she forced herself to smile the younger man said, 'Leave it here, will you? Just for a time, say a fortnight, and we'll try it around.'

'Yes. Yes.' Mr Gillyman was nodding now. He looked down at the folder. 'Hannah Drayton,' he read. 'Is that your real name, or a *nom de plume*?'

'Yes, I'm Hannah Drayton, Mrs Hannah Drayton.'

'Oh.' Mr Gillyman repeated her words slowly, 'Mrs Hannah Drayton.' He paused for a moment, as if the name were familiar. But he clearly did not want to waste time on it now, for he continued: 'Well, Mrs Drayton, there you have our verdict. By the way, this is my assistant.' He now thumbed back to the man standing at his side. 'He's Mr David Craventon. It will be up to him to put your book on the market. I leave all that to him, I have more important things to do.' He gave a chuckle as he glanced up at his assistant, but asked her, 'Where do you hail from?'

'Acton.'

'Oh, Acton. That's not so far away. We'd better have your address.'

'Seventy-two Beaufort Road.'

'Got that, David?'

'Yes, I've got that, Gilly.'

The man was smiling at Hannah, and she smiled back at him. 'Do you know anything about Bloomsbury?' he asked.

'No, nothing at all.'

'Well then, all I can say to you is don't come round here, or any of the neighbouring areas, by yourself at night in the dark.'

'She has a husband. Remember?' David reminded him.

'Oh, yes, yes; of course.' Then, quickly, Mr Gillyman bent half-way over the table and looked towards the tall window, half obliterated by books, and he exclaimed, 'It's raining! pouring.'

'Yes; it's just come on.'

'That's English weather for you' – Mr Gillyman was nodding at Hannah now – 'and you'll get drenched.'

'It'll only be a shower,' said David, now looking at Hannah; and she, smiling back at him, said, 'Yes, and I don't mind the rain.'

'I know of two people who reached their death-beds through being caught in such a shower.'

'Yes, but on the moors, Gilly . . . on the moors!'

'Anyway—' Mr Gillyman now looked up at David Craventon, saying, 'Well, the moors or Bloomsbury, I'm not going to have anybody on my conscience. Phone upstairs and ask Tishy to bring the coffee forward.'

Hannah noticed the younger man hesitate, then shake his head, and what retort he might have made was again cut off by Mr Gillyman's saying, 'Better still, as I don't want to waste any more time – time's precious you know –' he turned towards Hannah and emphasised this statement with a nod, 'go along with him, and you can sit with my wife until the rain stops. But don't' – his finger was wagging again as he watched her rise to her feet – 'don't keep sending letters to ask if your masterpiece is going to be published and how much you're going to get for it, and when and where, 'cos you won't get any answers. Understand?'

Under other circumstances she knew she would have been afraid to answer, or she would have felt indignant, or some such emotion, but now she answered him in much the same manner as he was speaking to her: 'I understand perfectly, sir, and I won't put in an appearance for a full fortnight. But I promise you, you'll see me then.'

The great mass of books could not mute the high laughter of both men, and David Craventon said enigmatically, 'And on your own ground too . . . how about that!' before adding, 'Come along, Mrs Drayton.'

For a moment she hesitated; then she nodded to the man who was now tapping each side of his mouth with the side of his forefinger, before following the assistant who, she thought, seemed to have a great deal of liberty, if she was to judge by the way he had spoken to his boss.

When they reached the pile of books opposite the window the narrow walkable space of floor turned sharply right and through a set of standing book-cases towards another door. David opened this door, then stood aside to allow her to pass into what she imagined could be described as a palace, after the room she had just left. It was a red-carpeted hallway, with large paintings hanging on the walls; leading the way again, he took her up a red-carpeted flight of stairs, the while calling out, 'Mrs Gillyman!'

'Yes? Yes, David?' A woman appeared at the top of the stairs, and when David Craventon brought Hannah face to face with her he said, 'This is a client, Mrs Gillyman. It's raining heavily outside and Mr Gillyman thought you might like to bring the coffee forward.'

'Of course. Of course.' Mrs Gillyman turned and led the way over a broad landing and into a beautifully appointed room, which Hannah recognised immediately was furnished with antiques. She knew a little about such furniture, because her father had indulged himself in buying an expensive magazine given over to antiques, so that he could confidently talk about such pieces. The carpet here was rose-coloured, the walls grey, and the hangings and upholstery all in a dull gold material.

'Do sit down, Miss . . .'

'It's Mrs.' The young man was smiling now as he added, 'Well, Mrs Drayton, do you like your coffee black or white?'

'White, please.'

Mrs Gillyman excused herself and as Hannah watched her leave through a door some distance up the room she thought, She's nice; but so much younger than him.

'Do you notice anything?'

'What . . . ? I'm sorry.' She had been looking round the room.

'I said, do you notice anything?'

'Only that . . . well, it's a very beautiful room, so very beautiful.'

'Yes, isn't it? All this floor is beautiful. But look around you: that table there; and that bookcase against the wall, what's in it? Miniatures and beautiful glass; not a book or a magazine in sight.'

She smiled. 'Well, it's understandable, isn't it? That place downstairs is like a—' She hesitated, and when he put in, 'Like a what?' she shook her head, saying, 'I nearly said dump.'

'Well, that's the right word for it, dump. And that isn't his only dump, I can tell you.'

Tentatively now she asked, 'What . . . what kind of books does he publish?'

'Oh, you'd be surprised. Not the kind of books that the majority of people read. I'd say they're similar to those that were published a hundred or so years ago. You see, he's a lover of such books, and so he's mainly a collector. You've seen proof of it downstairs. And so those he enjoys publishing are of a similar type: odd subjects, odd people with odd pursuits, odd travellers; in fact, a documentary was made out of one of his travel discoveries.'

'Really?'

'Oh yes, really. But Mrs Gillyman' – his head jerked back towards the door – 'she put her foot down many years ago as regards books in this part of the house.'

'She . . . she seems nice.'

He bent towards her now as he said softly, 'And, you're thinking, so different from her husband downstairs.'

'No, I wasn't. I found him interesting, amusing. You couldn't feel dull where he is, could you?'

'No, certainly not; you couldn't feel dull where Gilly is.'

He straightened up when the quiet voice came from a distant room, calling, 'David! David! just a moment.'

'Excuse me.'

As he went out of the room she looked about her again. At the far end there were two glass doors which obviously led on to a balcony, and she could see through them that the rain had stopped. Then her attention was brought to a door not more than three feet away. It was in the same wall as the door through which Mrs Gillyman had gone, and, when she saw it move, just the slightest, she thought: Someone is trying to come in.

Then someone did come in. The door, which must have been just ajar, opened further, and through the aperture an extra-large tortoiseshell cat with a magnificent tail and wearing a studded collar sidled in. It came straight towards her and jumped on her knee, and she smiled as she stroked it, saying, 'You're not shy, are you? Aren't you beautiful!' and when it purred and turned on its back and she scratched its tummy she couldn't help but giggle. She liked cats. There had always been a cat at home, but Humphrey didn't care for them or for animals of any kind, except in their rightful places, as he put it.

Then her attention was lifted from the cat as she heard a low voice say, 'Is it any good?' and another answer, 'I don't know. It's certainly an oddity as children's books go.'

The first voice came back now, saying, 'Well, as you and I know, children's books don't go, do they? Why did he send her up here?'

'Don't ask me. Don't ask me, Natasha. It's generally the lonely ones, or the literary down-and-outs, and then it's an extra cup downstairs.'

'Well, to my mind she doesn't look either lonely or down-and-out.'

'No; I agree with you there, and yet . . .'

'What?'

'I don't know. There was something. I just glanced through the book. It isn't the usual kids' stuff. Look, we'll talk about it after; I'll bring it up.'

She had the inclination to push the cat from her knee and get up and leave. Yet he'd been so kind and nice. But kindness could hurt, didn't she know that already? Humphrey's kindness hurt her. Oh yes. Oh yes.

'Well, Jericho, what are you doing in here?'

The cat now gently and slowly turned its head, looked up at its mistress and gave a gentle mew, as if to say, I was just entertaining the visitor.

When the woman lifted the cat from Hannah's knee it purred loudly and practically wound itself round its mistress's neck.

Hannah tried to forget all she had overheard and said, 'It's a beautiful animal.'

'She's a beautiful nuisance.'

'Why do you call her Jericho?'

'Well, just because from a tiny kitten she could climb any wall, get over any obstacle and even open doors. She can reach up to handles and turn them but she knows when they just require a small push. That one' – she pointed to the door through which the cat had come – 'must have been left ajar.'

As if a thought had struck her, she cast a quick glance at the assistant who was now pouring out the coffee, then gave a slight shake of her head as she added, 'She's a brat of a cat.'

During the short conversation that followed, which was about the weather and why they were having April showers in August and where she intended to go for her holidays, Hannah had refused a second cup of coffee. Now, getting to her feet, she thanked her hostess for being so kind, and said that she was sorry, too, that she'd put her to this trouble, to which Mrs Gillyman replied, 'Nonsense. Nonsense. It was a pleasure to meet you. So often the clients who brave downstairs' – she thumbed towards the floor with a laugh – 'are bearded, or grey at least. Isn't that so, David?' she said.

'Not quite. Not quite. I don't agree entirely with you. We had a man in his forties two days ago.'

There was laughter between them, to which Hannah added a smile; then she was going down the stairs again.

Mr Gillyman was not in the cluttered book room, and so David led her straight away to the front entrance.

His handshake was firm, his palm cool. Hannah looked up into his face. He was rather good-looking: his eyes were dark like his hair, and he seemed to have a kind nature, but she was no fool. After her secretarial training she had had at least four interviews, and on each occasion she had known whether or not the position was forth-coming. Today, she had the feeling that success definitely was not forthcoming. And so, looking straight into the dark eyes that were staring into hers, she said, 'Please don't be too kind. I know what you think about it. The only thing I ask is, in a fortnight's time, would you mind please returning it safely to me. I've got a rough but this is the only finished copy and . . .'

'I'm not being kind, Miss – I mean Mrs – Drayton. I meant what I said: he'll definitely do what he can for you, and,' he added, 'I shall too. Yes. Yes, I will. And, let me tell you, he's not as odd as he appears. He's a very sincere person, but he has a mania. We've all got manias, but his is books, books, books, books. He'll go to a sale to get one book and that one book might have come from a household where there's fifty, even five hundred, but he'll take the lot. And he's not so silly after all, because when you look through some of the rejected volumes you do come across a treasure here and there . . . so I can assure you, Mrs Drayton, he'll give his time and attention to your book, because, who knows,' he pulled a little face at her, 'it might turn out to be a little treasure in its own right. We all have different tastes.'

'Yes indeed' – she nodded at him – 'you've said it, we've all got different tastes. Well, goodbye, Mr Craventon.'

For a moment he seemed reluctant to let her go on that. He watched her walk down the three steps into the street and through the iron gate and on to the wet pavement, and he told himself that she wasn't dressed very smartly, but she walked well; and there was something about her face. It was her eyes, he supposed; she had strange eyes, sad eyes. No, no! he checked himself; her eyes laughed. Yes, when she wanted to laugh. Oh, well. He drew in a deep breath, turned about, and closed the door behind him.

# Two

The table was set for dinner, the first course of trimmed avocado already in place. Hannah gave a last glance at it, then left the room, closing the door behind her: Humphrey didn't like kitchen smells pervading the dining room. The main course tonight was to be a variety of cold meats and salad followed by a treacle sponge. Humphrey did not care for cold desserts and he was very fond of treacle sponge.

In the kitchen, she put the final touches to the bowls of salad and set them on a tray. Following this, she went into the sitting room.

There, everything was as usual. In front of the fireplace was a large bowl of flowers and leaves arranged to hide the empty grate, and when she heard herself repeating, 'Yes, everything's as usual here,' she bit on her lip and muttered, 'Oh, dear me!' Yesterday she wouldn't have thought along that sarcastic line. Well, perhaps she would, but she wouldn't have voiced it to herself; but something had happened today.

It had been a very strange day, right from the time

she had taken the bus to Ealing, when the young boy had offered her his seat. Now that had been strange, hadn't it? You could stand on a bus, she thought, for a hundred years if you were elderly or laden down with packages, and she had never yet seen anyone fold up his newspaper and offer a woman his seat. Then there had been that outpouring to Janie. That had been an act of desperation in order to erase this great gnawing want in her. The want had made her sit up in bed at night and start rubbing her arms from the shoulders downwards. Why she continued to do it she didn't know, because it didn't ease her at all. It was, she supposed, just something to do to turn her thoughts from the road of bitterness and condemnation which she was now walking most nights.

She had felt better after she'd left Janie's, quite buoyant, but the feeling hadn't lasted. By the time she had reached Jason Gardens she was her old self again. And look what had happened there. That had been a strange experience. She had expected to be shown into a publisher's office; and what had she seen? Something akin to the city dump; but really, looking at it another way, a wonderful dump. Those books, thousands and thousands of them. And the people. That odd man and his lovely wife, and the other one. Yes, the other one. She'd thought a lot about him since leaving him at the door. He had an unusual face.

The sound of a key being turned brought her round from the fireplace. But tonight she didn't hurry into the hall to receive the usual greeting,

'Hello, my dear,' then something along the lines of a sigh and, 'Oh, how nice it is to be home,' sometimes varied to, 'Oh, what a day it's been. Why does one have to work for one's living, eh? I'm dying for my pick-me-up. Just let me get tidied.'

Not until she heard her name being called rather sharply, 'Hannah! Hannah!' did she leave the sitting room and walk into the hall.

'Oh, there you are! Anything the matter?' He came towards her and bent down to kiss her on the cheek.

'No; nothing.'

'Oh.' He stood back from her and she wouldn't have been surprised if he had said, Then why weren't you in the hall to greet me? What he did say was, 'It's been a very testing day.' Another man might have used the word 'stinking', but not Humphrey; he rarely used slang. 'I'll be glad of that drink,' he continued. 'Just let me get cleaned up.' He turned now and glanced to where his briefcase leant against the hat stand.

When he turned to her again there could have been the slightest reprimand in his glance: usually she was there to take his case and put it in its place.

She now did just that and when she turned round he was still standing staring at her, 'You all right, dear?' he said.

'Yes. Yes, I'm fine.'

'Anything happened?' His head was bent slightly to the side, adding to the enquiry, and she answered almost frivolously, 'Lots. Oh, lots and lots.'

'Well, well! I must hear about the lots and lots.

Just let me sort myself out and have my life-saver.'

As he made his way towards the bathroom Hannah went into the kitchen and, lifting the tray with the salad bowls, took it into the dining room and placed the bowls on the side table. The meats she would bring in when they had finished their avocado.

She stared down at the table; but she wasn't seeing it, she was back in that mountain of books looking at the man across the desk reading her children's story. All of a sudden she lifted her head and said almost aloud, Shall I tell him?

Yes, and louder now in her mind, Yes! and if he's quiet and smiles at me and gives that little shake of his head I'll say something. Yes, yes, I will; I'll definitely say what I think.

'Hannah? Where are you?'

The dining-room door opened and he stood there for a moment before he said, 'What is it, Hannah? Is something troubling you?'

She actually laughed now, saying, 'No. No, nothing's troubling me, but something happened today and . . . well . . . I mean to tell you about it.'

'Yes. Yes, of course' – his head was bobbing – 'after I've had my drink and five or ten minutes' respite in the sitting room.'

'Of course. Of course.'

He approached her now but didn't touch her, yet his look was full of concern.

A few minutes later they were seated one each side of the flower-banked hearth, a glass of whisky and soda in his hand and one of sherry in hers; he took several sips from his drink before he said, 'Well, now! Fire away.'

Fire away, he had said. It wasn't exactly slang, but it wasn't his usual way of questioning.

She took a drink from her glass, not just a sip; then she placed it on a small side table before laying her hands palm upwards on her lap. She had felt inclined to press them between her knees as she always did when she was excited or troubled, but now her mien appeared quietly assured as she said, 'I took my book to a publisher today.'

'Your book?' He had been about to sip from his glass again, but he looked over its rim and said, 'The book? That book!'

'Yes, Humphrey.' Her voice had an unusually stiff note to it. She was surprised then to hear herself say almost tartly, 'The one that you condemned by your silence and a shake of your head.'

'Hannah, my dear. I did no such thing; but I couldn't say they were of any value when they were so childish.'

'Well, they were for childish children, five-year-olds. I told you at the time.'

'Have you altered them since?'

'Not really; only arranged them differently.'

'Arranged them differently?' He pronounced each word distinctly.

'Yes, that's what I said.'

'And it's been accepted; I mean, the book?'

'Well, he read it and liked it and he's going to consider publishing it.'

'He thinks it'll sell?'

'I suppose he must do, otherwise he wouldn't be considering it.'

He put down his glass on the little table that stood to the side of his chair, then he asked, 'Who is the publisher . . .' and he paused, then added, 'Who's looking at it?'

'A Mr Gillyman.'

'Gillyman?' He brought himself to the edge of his seat. 'Martin Gillyman?'

She didn't confirm this by saying yes, but just sat looking at him, for his face had suddenly become bright with interest.

'Gillyman, the collector of rare books?'

She now said, 'Yes, the same.'

'And he's taken your . . . your children's book?'

She rose sharply to her feet, saying, 'Yes; I've told you, he's taken my children's book, and what's more he seemed to find it interesting.'

'All right, all right. I . . . I was just surprised by the name, and Martin Gillyman is quite a name, you know. He's a very rich man.'

She checked herself from saying, Of course, you wouldn't have known him by name unless he was a rich man, would you? But then that is the work of brokers, isn't it, to know rich people? They never talk about anyone who hasn't money.

'He's known as a character. He buys books by the hundred or thousand and just stacks them away. And . . . and you spoke to him?'

She didn't move, but she turned her head to the side as she said, 'I've told you—'

'All right. All right, my dear. I'm being perverse,

42

I know I am, but' – he stood up and came to her side – 'the name was, well . . . so familiar. You see, we tried to do business with him at one time but we found his manner rather odd. What I mean is, he chooses the strangest people to see to his business. He owns a lot of property in the city, you know. His people used to be in shipping and mines. Well, you name it.'

She was looking fully at him now as she said, 'He doesn't use your firm as his brokers, then?'

She watched his mouth go into a small pout, then his lips move one over the other before he said, 'No. No. Unfortunately, no. He has three brothers, I understand, and they run different sides of the business for him. He's the eldest, and although' – he now bounced his head at her – 'he may be odd in some ways about books, he's no fool where money's concerned.'

They were walking to the dining room when she was stopped by the question he put to her: 'Did he ask you to sit down?'

She did not answer him, just stared at him until he said, now rather tersely, 'I'm only asking you how he received you.'

She took a deep breath before she said, 'He received me as any gentleman would, and he arranged that I have coffee with his wife in their beautiful house above his rather cluttered office.' She watched his long face stretch even further. His eyes were wide and his lips were forming a round O.

'Well, well!' he said.

They were in the dining room now and seated at the table when he said in a playful manner, 'Dare I ask you how you found his wife?'

'I found her, since you ask, to be a very beautiful woman and the room that I was in reflected her taste.'

'Oh! well, when you've got pots of money you can produce taste.'

'I don't agree with you there, Humphrey.'

His spoon was in the avocado. He left it there as he stared at her. What had come over her? His little blond pussy-cat, as he had at one time called her, had seemingly developed into a very large tabby, and all because of her visit to a publisher. Yes; but what a publisher! It was odd, when he came to think about it, that she of all people should form an association with a man like him, and with his wife. And all through her silly little book; and it *was* a silly little book, although he had never put it into plain words. To his mind it was the effort of some-one who was almost illiterate, for there was hardly a word of more than two syllables in it. Yet she had gained an audience through it, whereas his company had been snubbed time and again. He had never got to the bottom of it, but he understood it was some-thing to do with Mr Manstein, the mysterious chief whom they saw only once a year, and then only if their section was invited abroad for one of the four-day conferences. He himself had been twice, once to Germany and once to Greece, but their office had never been invited on to the yacht as some of the others had. But apparently it was their chief that

Gillyman would have no truck with. Why, nobody seemed able to find out.

He spooned up the avocado, chewed for a moment, then changed the subject entirely by saying, 'One of the fellows was selling tickets for a Mozart concert today, and I bought two. It's some charity affair. Then I noticed they were for tonight, and it being Thursday . . . well, it's a pity, otherwise we could have gone.'

She looked at him hard before she answered briefly, 'Yes; yes, of course it's Thursday.'

He was kind in so many ways, was Humphrey, but quite thoughtless in others. It never struck him to give up his Thursday nights at the club and his bridge session. The only times he had missed a Thursday night with his friends had been during the first two years of their marriage, when, in the first year, they had taken a fortnight's holiday in Worthing so he could be near his aunt and uncle, and in the second year when they went as far as Torquay. During the last two years he had spent two weeks of his month's holiday escorting his aunt and uncle to Torquay while she in preference had willingly spent her time with Janie and the family. The other fortnight of his leave he now took in odd days tacked on to weekends, and these he spent in Worthing, too. She had long since stopped enquiring what he did with the old couple during these long weekends – but there again he didn't look upon them as an old couple, more as parents, for they had brought him up from the age of four after his parents had drowned.

'Would you like the tickets? You could phone Janie. Perhaps she'd like a night out – a different kind of night out from what she's used to with that fellow; and it's not all that far away, Bailey Hall, just off Oxford Street. You could pop back here and have a bite, then send her home by taxi. I . . . I'll see to it.'

This was one of Humphrey's little kindnesses: he'd send Janie home by taxi. She smiled at him as she said, 'I couldn't see her sitting through a Mozart concert, Humphrey.'

'Oh, it's not all Mozart. Look, the tickets are in the form of programmes. There're several composers, but it begins with two Mozart sonatas.'

'All right; I'll ask her. But if she doesn't want to come, and I doubt very much if she will, I can always go by myself – I don't mind – and I'll take your offer of a taxi both ways.' She was smiling widely at him now, and he, smiling back, said, 'Yes, do that, and I won't ask for any change.'

'Well, if it's two journeys, one there, one back, you won't get much change out of a fiver. And I like to tip well.'

He laughed outright now, then said, 'Well, will a tenner fix it?'

'Oh' – she lifted her shoulders – 'just about.'

A tenner. He was kind. He'd hardly finished the sponge pudding before he said, 'I'll help you with the dishes, then I must get ready to go. I'm running a bit late.' He glanced at the clock on the mantelpiece, and at this she said, 'Don't be silly! I'll see to the dishes.'

He had reached the dining-room door when he turned and said, 'Well, you'll have to get a move on too, if you intend to do that concert. It starts at seven-thirty.'

He was in the hall when she called after him, 'Well, don't go without leaving the tickets!'

His laughing reply came from the bathroom, although she couldn't make out what he was saying . . .

Fifteen minutes later she had not only cleared the table but set it for the morning's breakfast and put the last washed plate away; then, after spreading a check cloth over the kitchen table, she glanced round the room before hurrying out, and was crossing the hall towards her bedroom when Humphrey emerged from his.

He was wearing a light dove-coloured coat over a grey suit, and in his hand were the two tickets, which he held out to her, saying, 'There you are, then! Hurry up, or you'll be late. Have you phoned Janie?'

'No . . .'

'Well, it's probably too late now. If you don't mind going on your own, I wouldn't ring her. You'd only miss half the concert. Anyway, I hope you enjoy it.' He paused, then added softly, 'I'm sorry it's Thursday; I'd have loved to come with you.'

'That's all right.'

He leant towards her and his lips touched her cheek as he said playfully, 'Be a good girl now.' Then he was gone.

In her bedroom she stood for a moment before the

cheval mirror and, nodding to it, said, 'Be a good girl.' He was sweet and kind; but, oh, dear me! If only . . . if only . . .

'Get changed, woman!' The order came from somewhere deep inside her, as was wont to happen these days. She turned smartly, opened the wardrobe door, took a summer dress and a jacket from a hanger, and within seconds she had changed into them. Then, moving to the dressing table, she bent down and looked into the swing mirror. She rarely used much make-up, a blusher and lipstick being about as far as she went. She had resorted to the blusher only this last year or two because at times her skin looked so pale, even transparent. She drew a comb through her hair, then took a clasp from a drawer in order to pin it up. More often than not she would let it drop over her shoulders, but she deemed it to be smarter when it was pinned up. She was crossing the hall towards the front door when the phone rang. She did not stop to think who it might be phoning at this time; she knew it would be someone from Worthing.

She picked up the receiver.

'Hello.'

'Is that you, Mrs Drayton?'

'Yes, it's me, Mrs Beggs.'

'I'd like to have a word with Mr –'

'I'm sorry, you've just missed him; you know, it's Thursday night and he goes to the club.'

'Oh, yes. Yes, of course. I'm so sorry, but I have a message for him from his aunt.'

'Is she not at home?'

'Oh yes; but, you see, Mr Drayton Senior has been in bed for the last two or three days. His gout has worsened and Mrs Drayton is sitting with him at present. She wondered if Mr Humphrey would be coming for a long weekend or just dropping in.'

'I couldn't tell you what arrangements he's made for the weekend, but he's usually there, isn't he?'

'Oh yes, yes. Oh yes; but . . . but sometimes he manages to make it a long weekend, coming on the Friday.'

'Well, all I know, Mrs Beggs, is that he has a few days of his holiday left, but I don't know what arrangements he's made.'

It sounded so pedantic, but she couldn't stand Mrs Beggs – the treasure, as Humphrey thought of her, in the Drayton Senior household.

'Thank you. I'll give his aunt the message.'

Hannah made no reply but put the phone down and for a moment stood looking at it. If he'd been going there tomorrow, surely he'd have said something; but then again, it was a foregone conclusion that he spend most of his Saturdays and Sundays in Worthing, and it was very rarely now that he asked her to accompany him, because he knew what her answer would be. On the Sunday night he would enquire how she had spent her weekend, and her reply would generally be, 'The usual way. I went to the pictures on Saturday, and I had lunch with Janie and the family on Sunday.' She never mentioned the time she spent writing and drawing, because that was how she filled up most of her weekends, that and walking in the park, even in the rain. She couldn't stand that Mrs Beggs. Hannah's dislike of Mrs Beggs was another reason why she avoided visiting Humphrey's relatives.

Mrs Beggs ran the house in Worthing. She had done so for years, apparently. When Humphrey was ten she had come on the scene as a young widow with a small daughter, who was boarded at her sister's. She was engaged as housemaid. Then, as the family was wealthy, there had been a cook and a kitchen maid in the indoor staff, a gardener and a boy outside. When the cook died (certainly not from over-eating, Hannah imagined, for Mrs Drayton, she had seen, was still an expert at weighing out ingredients), and as Mrs Beggs was of like mind to her mistress, she gradually took on the position of housekeeper. Later, when her master had his periodic bouts of gout she thought nothing of acting as nurse too. Oh, indeed Mrs Beggs was a treasure.

Apparently Humphrey had been twenty-four and in his last year of accountancy training when Mrs Beggs's daughter was brought into the house as her assistant. But Daisy must have been a great disappointment to her mother, for she went off and married the young gardener.

Whenever Humphrey spoke to Mrs Beggs on the phone, he would call her Beggie. He was almost deferential towards her. He had only once spoken about her and said she was a very good woman. He was very grateful to her because she had given most of her life to the old couple. She had worked for them for almost thirty years, and had looked after them and cared for them as few others would have done, because they were not everybody's cup of tea, being of high moral opinions and still very narrow in many of their views in this enlightened time . . .

Hannah hurried out of the house, and was in the street before she muttered to herself, and not without disdain, 'The *treasure*.'

Even the woman's voice put her on edge.

It was a lovely night. There were few people about; those who were seemed to walk leisurely. It would be different after eight o'clock, and more so after ten. Oh, yes. She was glad of the taxi money: the concert wouldn't likely be over until half-past nine or so and she didn't like travelling alone at night.

The hall was almost full. Her seat was an end one in the third row from the back. There was hardly time to look round before the performance began.

It started with two Mozart piano sonatas. It wasn't often she went to a concert of classical music. She classed her taste as middle-of-the-road music that would touch her emotionally.

Beethoven followed with the 'Moonlight' sonata. But what irritated her was a piece by a modern composer. To her it was all screech and discord, with odd silences suggesting it had come to the end. She heaved a sigh when the lights went up and there was a general stir towards the bar.

She would have liked a drink but she didn't feel like going into the bar by herself. She stood up to let some people move into the aisle; then she sat down again, and was comforted somewhat to see that there were lots of people remaining seated. She looked at the next part of the programme and as she did so she wondered whether to stay because, if she was truthful, the second half looked considerably less inviting than the first.

'Well, well!' A man had been passing her in the aisle, although she was only aware of his lower half because her head was bowed over the programme. It was David Craventon.

She looked up, then smiled widely.

'Now, isn't this strange. Are you on your own?' he said.

'Yes. Yes.'

'That's stranger still. So am I. To meet in the morning and then in the evening. I think it portends something. A drink, don't you think? Would you like a drink?'

'Yes; yes, I would, but I didn't want to go for one by myself.'

'Come on, then.' He bent over, then took her hand and raised her to her feet.

They were in the aisle when he asked, 'D'you often come to these concerts?'

'No. My husband bought two tickets, forgetting that it was Thursday night and the night for his weekly bridge session. He thought it was a shame to waste them, so here I am.'

'Have you enjoyed it so far?'

She paused a moment before she said, 'Mostly. I love some pieces, but when I suppose what you would call the real music begins I admit to becoming lost.'

'Don't express opinions without knowledge, madam.' His tone was playful. 'I'm a man who gets easily bored with all kinds of sounds from yapping dogs to endless birdsong. I've sworn never to hear another dawn chorus in my life.'

They were laughing together now as he led her to the far corner of the counter, where there was one stool free, and when she sat on it he said, 'What'll you have?'

'Oh.' Her eyes were laughing into his now as she said, 'I never get beyond sherry; that is, usually.'

'Which means, madam –' he was now bending close to her and whispering, 'you are asking for something stronger?'

And she returned his whisper, saying, 'No, not stronger, please! Just different.'

'Well, then, if you want something different, have you ever had . . .' – he straightened up and caught the attention of one of the young women serving behind the bar – 'Pimm's?'

'Pimm's? No, I've heard of it.'

'It's quite a fruity drink. Well, I say quite; we'll try you with a No. 1. Two Pimm's No. 1, please.'

A few minutes later she was guiding the half-slice of orange on its stick to the side of the glass as she sipped the drink, and her verdict came with a broad smile, 'It's lovely!'

They had both finished their drinks when the bell rang warning that the second part of the concert was about to begin.

He looked at her and asked, 'Would you like another drink?' and she answered, 'No, thank you; that was lovely.'

His eyes still on her, he said, 'Do you really want to hear the rest of this concert?'

The smile slid from her face as she asked, 'Don't you?'

And he answered, again playfully, 'I'm not overwhelmed by a desire to return to my seat, but how do you feel?'

'Well' – she cocked her chin upwards – 'I have no overwhelming desire either to go back in there.'

'That's settled, then. It was a beautiful evening when we came in; if it's still beautiful, would you like to take a walk? The city looks different at night; in fact all London looks different at night. It's like a child saying, "I've done my lessons all day, now let's play."'

She had slid from the stool and was staring at him. He was so different from anyone she had ever spoken to. The word was refreshing, like the drink she had just had. She felt warm inside, sort of daredevilish. If he had said to her, 'Take my hand and we'll run out of here and through the streets,' she would have done so . . .

They had been walking for some five minutes, and he had been pointing out places to her and explaining why they were there, and how long they had been there, or how they had changed. He was like a guide talking to a tourist, yet a personal guide . . . all hers.

Goodness! Fancy thinking things like that. She

said suddenly, 'What was in that drink, the Pimm's?' and he, turning to her, said, 'The Pimm's . . .? Well, orange juice, lemon juice, a little bit of this, a little bit of that.'

When he paused, she said, 'Yes, and what else?'

'A drop of whisky, I suppose, or is it rum? or is it gin? There's Pimm's Nos 1, 2 and 3, you know. I don't know how far they go on after that, but why do you ask?'

She bit on her lip and shook her head slightly before she answered, 'I suppose I could say I'm feeling nice, different.'

'Good. Good. Different from this morning?'

'Oh, yes; different from this morning.'

'You looked white and peaky this morning.'

'Did I?'

'Yes, and, I could add, slightly sad, a little wary and sort of lost.'

The smile left her face. Had she looked like that? Yes, she supposed, she looked like that all the time; that's what Janie often said to her: Do something with yourself; you're getting all skin and bone and you're losing your looks. D'you know that you're losing your looks? And I consider that a sin because they're not given out to everybody. Look at me.

Oh, Janie. Janie. Wait till she told her about this evening . . . about today.

There was silence between them for quite some minutes before he said softly, 'Shall we have a walk in the park? It's quiet there, at least more so than here in the streets. And look' – he pointed upwards

– 'there's a moon about to show its cheeky face.'

When she didn't answer, he said, 'Or would you rather have something to eat? Anywhere around here'll be pretty busy by now, but ten minutes on the bus and we'll be in Camden Town, and there's a little restaurant there where Monsieur Harold, otherwise known as Micky McClean from the heart of Camden, will supply us with a fine five-course meal or anything else you like, down to bangers and mash or beans on toast, and that's right up till two in the morning, mind you; and I can assure you that even if he's full he'll squeeze me in if it's only into the back kitchen.'

Oh, he was funny; so . . . so light. Yes, that was the word for him, so light; like somebody from another planet, he was bodyless. When she stopped and stared at him, he said, 'What is it?' and she didn't answer him for some seconds because she was thinking: His face, it was so appealing; not good-looking, yet . . . yet beautiful. His voice came again now, with some concern, 'What is it? Do you want to go back?'

'No! No!' Her denial was so loud that even he laughed, the while looking from side to side at the passers-by. Then again he said, 'Well, what is it?'

'It's only that . . . well, I ate earlier. But your description of Mr McClean's place has given me an appetite. Oh, if I'm truthful it's that I'm finding you very odd.'

'Really?'

She nodded at him as a child might have done after being naughtily frank. 'I've never met a man like you. I don't meet men like you. What I mean is . . . well, I don't meet many men, but those I do . . . well, are certainly not like you, or then again Mr Gillyman. Two strange men in one day is . . . rather overwhelming.'

He had to pull her to one side to allow a couple to pass them, and this brought her very close to him; his face now almost touching hers, he said, 'Would it surprise you if I told you something similar, that I find you very odd? Odd, I mean, in the same way that you find Gilly and me odd. For instance, you came into our lives this morning and caused some commotion. Mrs Gilly had never before been ordered to receive a client upstairs for coffee. Nor had Gilly and I agreed so wholeheartedly over a book. Your book.'

'Really?'

'Yes. Yes, really. For it's a very strange little book. It seems to have been written for children by a child. Oh, don't mind me saying that, please!'

She did mind his saying that: that's what Humphrey had said. But then she heard this different man saying, 'It was as if you had to get into a child's mind so as to put down what the child would understand and like, and you've succeeded. Perhaps not everybody would agree with us, but nevertheless you have.'

'Oh, thank you. Thank you.'

She felt she was going to cry, and he knew this and so, quickly taking her arm, he said, 'Come on, there's a bus.' And then they were running; and when he hoisted her up on to the platform they were both laughing, and ten minutes later, when they got off, they were still laughing . . .

The restaurant was beautifully clean but sparsely furnished. The tables had plastic-covered tops concealed mostly by tartan-patterned table mats. On each table stood a bottle of sauce, another of vinegar, a salt and pepper canister, and a stark notice that read, 'No smoking, with or after meals'. No 'please' or 'thank you', a bald statement.

'Aah! Mr Crav . . . enton. Nice to see you again; and you, madam.'

David Craventon, lowering his head, whispered, 'Come off it, Micky; she's a Londoner.'

'Thank Gawd for that.' The short, lean-faced and even leaner-bodied man grinned at Hannah, then winked and said, 'All in the line of business, miss.' Turning to David again, he said, 'What can I get you? I'll tell you what's on tonight, and they're good: lemon soles done in butter. They're so fresh we had to take the hooks out of their mouths.'

Hannah laughed outright and Micky, thoroughly shaking his head at her, said, 'It's a fact, miss. A fact.'

'All right, Micky, we'll have the sole. That's if it'll suit you.' David had turned to her, and she said, 'Yes, thank you. I like fish.'

'Now for a starter . . . Tell you what, there's lovely fruit, fresh as fresh? On a bed of melon, there's apricots, raspberries, peaches . . . you name it, you'll find it on that bed, and it's fit to be pictured and hung in the National Gallery.'

'All right,' said David; 'the art gallery it is.'

'Then for afters there'll be a sweet tray as usual,

but let me tell you' – he was bending towards them now confidentially – 'I've concocted a pudding. You'll be the first to try it, it's a cross between spotted Dick and crêpe Suzette.'

Hannah found it a most wonderful meal. She couldn't recall ever eating anything like it before. Humphrey sometimes took her out to dinner, but their usual first course was a prawn cocktail, sometimes followed by steak, sometimes by chicken; and the dessert always came from a trolley, with coffee to follow, and all very quietly eaten. Certainly no loud laughter, no hiccuping through merriment and no pudding that was a cross between spotted Dick and crêpe Suzette, which had turned out to be delightful. It was as well that Hannah had been too on edge to eat very much with Humphrey. They took almost an hour and a half over the meal, and when they left Micky McClean escorted them to the door, and there he said quietly to David, 'I was thinking about popping in to see Mr Gilly. D'you think it's about time?'

'Could be, Micky. Could be. The brothers are coming for a weekend, so there might be another avenue opening. Anyway, pop in and have a talk with him.'

'Thanks, Davie, thanks; I'll do that. And now what I'm going to say to you might be called tactless, being in front of your lady friend . . . if I'm not here I'll leave word that whenever you appear, twelve noon or midnight, it's on the house. Understand that? Now go on and get yourself away, because I'm not going to cross words with you. I've told you before and I'll tell you again, if I don't have me own way in this, don't come back here any more. Goodnight, miss.' He was grinning at Hannah now, and when his hand grabbed hers and shook it he nodded towards David, saying, 'Not a bad chap, when you get to know him. Not a bad chap at all.'

'I mightn't be a bad chap, but you're an impossible thick-headed Cockney. Always were and always will be. Goodnight.'

The last they heard from him was as they went down the street, when he shouted after them, 'I'll get one of my lads to split your nose next time.'

When David took her hand and ran with her, she was laughing again like a child; but then, suddenly pulling him to a standstill, she asked, 'What time is it? I haven't got my watch on.'

'Twenty-five-past ten.'

'Oh, my goodness! I'm always back by ten. And . . . and he comes in about half-past.'

'Your husband?'

'Yes. Yes, of course.'

There fell on them a silence, until he said, 'Well, I can get you a taxi.'

'Oh, would you? Oh, please do!'

'There'll be one at the far side of the square.' His tone rather flat, he enquired, 'Have you enjoyed yourself?'

'Enjoyed myself?' She paused in her walk; then, her head shaking, she muttered, 'You'll never know how much. It's been the most wonderful evening. I never knew there were such people. I should have done, though, because my brother-in-law is very like your friend Micky.'

'Really?'

'Oh yes. Very much so, he's in the fruit business. I . . . I must tell you about him some time.' She put her hand to her mouth now, saying, 'Oh! that sounds . . . well, a bit forward; but . . . but you know what I mean.'

'No, I don't really, but I want to. I suppose you're very busy at the weekends? I mean, you go out and such.'

'No. No. My husband goes to see his aunt and uncle – who are really his adoptive parents – in Worthing, that way.' She pointed, as if he could see Worthing from where they were.

'Well, what d'you do with yourself?'

'Oh. Oh, I scribble.' She smiled weakly. 'I walk, I go to the pictures; but on a Sunday I have lunch with my sister and her . . . husband.'

'Then you're alone most of the time?'

'Well. . . yes, most of the time.'

'Could we meet on Saturday?'

'Oh, I don't know.' She moved uneasily from one foot to the other.

'Well, if you've got nothing else to do and you go to the pictures alone . . . you go alone?'

'Yes. Yes. But I don't know.'

'I'll give you a ring; what's your number?'

'No. No. Please don't ring.'

'Well, where could we meet?'

61

He laughed now as he added, 'Don't say under the clock. And it wouldn't be proper for me to call for you, would it?'

'Oh, no, no!'

'Well, what about meeting at Micky's again? You know the way now: you could get the tube straight to Camden Town from your place and then . . . Look! here's a taxi. You'll do that?'

'No. Yes. I mean, I'll try, but if I don't turn up, will you understand?'

'I'll understand.'

'Something might happen, I mean at home.'

'I'll understand; don't worry. About one o'clock on Saturday, then?'

'Yes. Yes, all right. And thank you' – she was looking up into his face – 'thank you for a most wonderful evening; in fact, for the most wonderful day I've ever spent.'

He said nothing, but after stopping the taxi he opened the door, and after she had got in and sat down he took her hand and said, 'It's I who should thank you for this evening, for the whole day. But we'll talk about that later. Goodnight.'

'Goodnight.'

The taxi door was banged shut; then it was away out of sight, leaving him on the kerb staring after it. A wonderful day, she had said; yes, indeed, a wonderful day, a day marking a change in his life.

'Where on earth have you been? You've never been as late as this.' He stared at her, observing the brightness of her eyes, the strange look on her face, her colour: she was flushed.

'I was getting worried,' he said in a voice that had an edge to it now, and he was surprised when she replied, 'Did Eddie phone?'

'Eddie? Why should Eddie phone?'

'Well, I mean with us being late.'

'Oh, she went with you, then, after all?'

Hannah swallowed deeply before answering, 'Yes. Yes.' She'd decided to ask if Eddie had phoned because Janie herself might have phoned during the short time he had been back: there were times when she phoned in the evening when she wanted Hannah to go and mind the children the next day.

'But the concert would have been over hours ago.'

'I . . . I know, but . . . we went to a restaurant.'

'Which restaurant?'

'Oh, I don't know.' She walked past him now, pulling off her coat, and she was as amazed as he was at the tone of her voice; but, realising how she had spoken, she turned about and said, 'Well, you know I don't know restaurants, but she does. I don't know the name of it, but we had something to eat.'

'And something to drink, I shouldn't be surprised, knowing her.'

'Yes, Humphrey' – she now thrust her head towards him, that strange feeling of courage coming to her aid again – 'we had something to drink.'

'And not lemonade, by the look of you.'

'No; we had Pimm's.'

She watched his face stretch. 'Pimm's! You drank Pimm's? Pimm's has whisky in it.'

'Yes, some Pimm's has whisky, some Pimm's has gin, and some rum.'

'I'd go to bed if I were you; and, in future, I'd better be careful about sending you off to concerts.'

She had turned on him again; 'Yes, Humphrey, but perhaps I'll choose what I do for myself for a change.'

'What's come over you, Hannah?' He sounded hurt.

She suddenly sat down on a hall chair, muttering, 'Oh, Humphrey, I'm sorry; but it isn't often I go out to enjoy myself. You know that.' The next moment she was on her feet again, saying, 'How long is it since you bothered about me in any way; I mean, to give me any pleasure at all? I sleep by myself. Yes –' she was nodding her head now – 'yes, I sleep by myself.'

'Hannah!' There was a deep reproof in his voice. 'I thought we had passed over all that amicably.'

'You may have, Humphrey; but you've never asked if I have.'

His fingers now were moving around his throat as if he were trying to rub something off the skin; then he said, 'There are more things, more important things in marriage, than sex, Hannah.'

'Well, would you mind telling me one of them?'

She saw that he was aghast, not only at her question but at her whole attitude, for he turned from her now, saying quietly, 'I would go to bed, Hannah. Tomorrow, when you're quite sober, because I'm sure you're far from it now, you'll regret your attitude, for then you'll realise, I'm sure, that no husband could have been more caring or considerate of a wife than I have been of you. Goodnight.'

Hannah sat down again and leant back against the tall head of the hall chair. He was right. Yes, he was right. She must have been mad to go on like she had.

Good Lord! She hadn't given him the message from Mrs Beggs. Again she was on her feet, but her voice still sounded angry as she called down the hall, 'I forgot to give you a message, from Mrs Beggs. She wanted to know if you were going there tomorrow or Saturday.'

There was a moment's silence before his door opened and he came back into the hall and went to the telephone. She remained standing where she was until she heard him say, 'Hello, Beggie. I'm sorry to phone so late, but I've just got in.'

There followed a silence, and then he said, 'Oh, I'm sorry, I wasn't intending to come on Friday. What a pity! Oh, what a pity! But I'll be there on Saturday morning . . . No; I'll tell you what I'll do, Beggie: I'll come tomorrow night. I might get there rather late because we usually have a longer session at the office on a Friday; and so I may not see you till nine. But give my love to my dear folk.' Again silence. 'Yes. Yes, indeed. Yes, indeed. Thank you. Yes, yes, indeed, and please convey that to her too. Goodnight, Beggie. Goodnight.'

Hannah did not know why she had remained

standing there all that time, but he walked straight past her as if he weren't aware of her presence.

In her room she sat on the side of the bed and, her thin hands clasped between her knees, rocked herself backwards and forwards. It had been a most marvellous day and a wondrous evening. Oh, yes, a wondrous evening. But look how it had ended. She knew she had hurt Humphrey and that he was thinking her as common as her sister; but did that matter? No, no; it didn't, for she had met a wonderful man who liked her. Yes, he did. Yes, he did, otherwise he wouldn't have asked her to meet him again, almost pleaded with her to meet him once more. And she was going to do that. Yes, she was; she was going to do just that. She'd be there at one o'clock on Saturday, and neither hell nor high water would stop her.

Oh, dear me! She sprang up from the bed. She was like Janie; at bottom there was nothing to choose between them. How ridiculous to resort to clichés like that! It wasn't even appropriate to the situation.

She stopped for a moment in pulling her dress over her head. That's exactly what Humphrey would have said: it's not even appropriate to the situation. Oh, Humphrey. Humphrey. If only he were different. A little like the other . . . just a little like somebody other than himself. Yet that self was so good: he'd been right in what he'd said a while ago about his kindness to her, and she must never pay him back by hurting him.

As she was stepping into her nightdress, the voice almost thrust her round and threw her into the bed

66

as it cried at her, No! Humphrey mustn't be hurt; Humphrey must be considered. But, then, has he considered you every weekend, every single weekend for the last year? He had left her alone in order to visit his benefactors, his dear benefactors. Oh, she could have gone with him, yes. At least in the beginning. But had she continued, everyone would have felt discomfited. Very early in their acquaintance, she knew that her blondness had stamped her in their eyes as a flighty piece, even immoral, at the least a snatcher of innocent men like their dear Humphrey.

Tomorrow she'd go to see Janie again. She would tell her everything and see what she thought. She knew that there was a possibility her sister might not see eye to eye with her, at least about her proposed clandestine meetings with another man, because Janie still retained some of the moral values instilled at the convent: in her words, she had never had any hanky-panky with Eddie before they were married. On that famous day in the dining-room, when she had said she was going to live with him, she did not really intend to share his bed until they were married, which they were a week later, at a register office.

Hannah lay for quite a while staring up at the ceiling through the pink-shaded glow of the table lamp. Something had happened today; her life would never be the same after this.

# Three

It was about two o'clock when she reached Janie's. The house seemed very quiet. There was no one in the kitchen and when she opened the sitting-room door she saw Eddie lying on the couch and to the side of it Janie, sitting in the big chair, reading a magazine.

On seeing her, Janie jumped to her feet, saying, 'Oh! hello. You got here, then? You all right? You sounded odd on the phone.'

Hannah did not answer but looked towards the couch, asking, 'Eddie's bad?'

'Oh, very bad. Very bad; ready for his box. He had a tooth out this morning, poor bugger; and there's nobody had a tooth out before.'

Hannah looked at Eddie and was concerned by the sight of his face – one side was swollen to twice its usual size – and she said, 'Oh! Eddie; that's been a job. Was it a wisdom tooth?'

Before he could make a reply, his wife said, 'Couldn't be that with him, Hannah. Stupid question to ask.'

Her husband, rising to a sitting position on the

couch, muttered, 'One of these days, me girl, I'll take pleasure in knocking yours out one by one. I've promised you before, mind.'

'Yes, dear, yes;' then, smiling, Janie turned to Hannah, saying, 'Want a cup of tea?'

'I don't mind; but, oh dear!' She was again looking at her brother-in-law and she asked, 'Was it just the one?'

'Aye, Hannah, just the one, and more than enough, I can tell you. There was an abscess underneath or something. I've gone through hell the last fortnight with toothache, but I'd rather have stood another fortnight than go through this morning's business again. But she would have me there. Oh, yes; she loves torture, that one.' Then, his tone changing, he asked with deep solicitude, 'Are you all right, Hannah? I mean, not in trouble or anything?'

'Now what trouble could I get into, Eddie?'

'Oh, I don't know: still waters run deep, and Janie said you told her on the phone you were in a fix about something.'

'Yes, I did; and I am, Eddie. Anyway, I'll tell you all about it when we have our tea.'

Changing the subject, she got on to the topic that was nearest his heart: 'How's business?' she asked.

'Oh, that couldn't be better, Hannah; it really couldn't. I'm thinking about opening another shop in Forum Square.'

'No!'

'Oh, yes. I've got two good fellows running this one, but that's only because I'm smart. You know what I've done?'

'No, Eddie; what have you done?'

'Well, I shall have done it by the end of the year. I'm giving them a share in the profits. That's if they play their part: learn how to treat the customer; don't pass off any suspect fruit; don't overcharge some old girl who asks them to cut a melon in half because she's only got her pension; and, the main thing, that they keep their fingers out of the big end of the till.'

When Hannah laughed and he started to join her, he protested, 'Oh, Hannah, shut up! It's agony to open me mouth any further.'

As Janie entered the room with a tray of tea, Hannah asked, 'Where are the children?'

'Oh, Maggie's gone to a party; Winnie's next door playing with their boy; and the other two will be looking at television, although they'll both likely be sound asleep by now. It's funny' – she laughed – 'they always fall asleep when they're left alone to look at the television, don't they, Eddie?' He nodded at her, saying, 'Yeah; it's funny to see them, sitting on the floor, their heads nearly always stuck together, their backs against the couch.'

Janie now asked him, 'D'you think you can manage a cup of tea, Eddie?'

'If you put plenty of milk in it to cool it down.'

As she listened to this exchange it came to Hannah that they were one at heart, these two, no matter what they said to each other, and again she experienced a feeling of envy.

Presently Janie, looking at Hannah, said abruptly,

'Well, no more palavering, out with it! What's up? Is he going to leave you?'

'Oh, no! No; nothing like that—' Why, for a moment, had she wished it was?

She was about to continue when Janie, nodding towards Eddie, put in, 'He knows how things stand; I told him. So, let's have it!'

Hannah did not say, 'I knew you would,' but she looked at Eddie and he returned her stare as he said, 'Bloody morphrodite!'

Morphrodite? What was a morphrodite?

Then in his own way he gave her the explanation as he continued, 'Neither one bloody thing nor the other. You could get a divorce.'

'Oh! Eddie.'

'Never mind, our Hannah,' cut in Janie, 'saying "Oh! Eddie" like that. And you, Eddie, I'm sure morphrodite isn't the right word. You should look things up in a book before you get clever. Now, now! No more of your wisecracks; let her get on with what she has to tell us.'

Hannah considered for a moment, then related the events of the previous day.

A silence followed before Janie said softly, 'And all of this has happened since you were here yesterday morning?'

Hannah, head nodding, replied, 'Yes; I can't believe it, but all since yesterday morning.'

It was here that Eddie butted in. 'Wait a minute! Wait a minute! You mentioned a name, Micky McClean, who owned a restaurant. Are you sure it was Micky McClean?'

'Yes; and he sometimes pretends he's a Frenchman.'

'My God! That's him.' He turned to Janie. 'Remember! I've told you about him, the one who used to take his dad's suit to the pawn every Monday morning and get it out on a Friday night; and the time that it didn't come out because his mother had drunk the money. The old man wiped the floor with her and would have murdered her except that Micky hit him on the back of the head with a beer bottle and knocked him out. He thought he'd killed him. Anyway, he landed him in hospital. D'you remember?'

Janie was laughing now and nodding her head, 'Yes; yes; I remember you telling me that. Well, well!' She looked at Hannah now. 'Don't you think it's strange Eddie knowing that fellow?' she said.

'Yes, yes, I do. But he's a nice man, I must say, and doing very well in that restaurant.'

'Oh, yes; he certainly is, and coining money. He's no fool. It must be two years or more since I saw him last. When he first started he used to come to our stall in the market, but now we're too far out. Good grief! who'd believe it? We ran wild together, Micky and me, when we were lads.'

'You might have,' put in Janie, 'but that was years ago; if you meet him now you keep your mouth shut about what you're going to hear, or what you've already heard, understand? Because when men get together your tongues wag quicker than dogs' tails in season.'

'Well, go on now,' she continued, turning her

attention back to her sister; 'what was Humphrey's reception like, when you got back late?'

'Very cool; icy, in fact; and I didn't thaw it by lying, either, when I told him I'd spent the evening with you. I said you'd taken me to a café to have a bite.'

'My! My! you did? I can see you ending up in hell, together with your new boyfriend. By the way, is he married?'

'I don't know.'

'You don't know? Didn't you ask him?' put in Eddie.

'No, of course I didn't. You don't ask someone if they're married as soon as you've met them.'

'Under those circumstances, I think it would have been in order, girl.'

Janie's voice was low now as she said, 'If he's not married, jump at him; but if he is, and has a little wife around the corner, forget him, because you don't want to break up a family with a divorce.'

'Oh, I never would; and anyway I know that Humphrey wouldn't divorce me under any circumstances.'

'Has he said so?'

She looked at Eddie. 'Not openly,' she said; 'but he's very much against divorce, as are his aunt and uncle. I was in a conversation there once – well, I was a listener – when they were talking about it. Mrs Philippa Drayton gave her opinion that it was a pity that some marriages couldn't be dissolved. At the time she wasn't looking at me, but I knew what she was thinking. The gist of that conversation was

73

that, next to murder, divorce was the greatest sin anyone could commit. God had joined two people together and only God could release them. So, apart from everything else, if ever Humphrey tried to divorce me he'd be cut off without a penny, and Humphrey's no fool. So you can see' – she looked from one to the other – 'there would be no talk of divorce in our little household, even if I were to sin grievously.

'But what do you think? Is it wrong to think along the lines of "what the eye doesn't see the heart doesn't grieve over"? I know you both think he's prissy, but I wouldn't want to hurt him. He's always been very kind and understanding towards me – or so he told me last night.'

'He said that?' came from both Eddie and Janie almost simultaneously; and she looked from one to the other as, in his defence, she answered, 'Yes, but it was in reply to something I'd said, and for the first time that I can remember in our married life I had actually turned on him and told him what I thought.'

Now leaning towards Hannah, Janie said, 'About the other thing, the main business, was that it?'

'In a way, yes.'

'And what was his answer to that?'

Hannah lowered her head as she said, 'He didn't consider it the main thing in marriage.'

'Oh, hell's bells!' Eddie had swung his feet up on to the couch again and lay back. 'That really makes me sick. Look. Get to know how this other bloke stands – if he's married or not; then, if he's

married and living with his wife, finish it; but if
he's married and separated, and make sure it *is* a
separation, then go ahead and live your life on the
side.'

'Yes, once a week on a Thursday night.'

Hannah's voice had a dull sound and the futility
in it caused Janie to cry at her, 'There're the weekends, aren't there? And he takes long ones, so you
say. And you come here most Sundays, so, knowing
the way things are, we could stand in for you if
anything should transpire and he had to phone you
here. Anyway, I can't see that there's much further
you can go until you find out the lines his life runs
on, so get yourself to that restaurant tomorrow and
take it from there.'

And at this Eddie, aiming to grin, said, 'And we'll
be sitting here on tenterhooks, waiting to know the
rest of the serial. So you either come pell-mell here
on Sunday, or phone us. Understand?'

It was an hour later when Hannah rose to leave;
and again Janie walked her to the door, and there,
putting her arms around her, she said, 'If he's at all
free, go ahead, girl, the whole hog. It'll act as a life-
saver for you; you'll blossom again. But, then, I can
see by your face you've already started.'

'Oh, Janie. I'm all het up inside. I . . . I can't bear
the thought that after tomorrow I may not see him
again; and all this to have happened since yesterday
morning.'

'Oh, sis! That's the way it happens, whether he be
barrow boy or baron. Don't I know!'

# Four

She was fifteen minutes late. As she approached the restaurant she could see him standing on the pavement looking this way and that. When she reached his side she said, 'Hello! I'm sorry I'm late. There was some kind of hold-up on the tube.'

'Oh, that's all right, that's all right. You're here now.'

'I don't know what was going on; it was chaos.'

He had taken her arm now and was leading her through the restaurant to a far corner where a table was set for two. A card on it read 'Reserved'. The table also had the advantage of being more than half screened from the rest of the diners by a panel to the side of a flight of shallow steps leading into the basement.

As they seated themselves, he said, 'I phoned Micky this morning. He's not here today, he's out on business' – he made a slight moue with his lips – 'but he reserved this table for us. Wasn't that good of him?'

When she didn't answer but simply sat staring at

him across the small space he said quietly, 'I thought you weren't coming.'

'I shouldn't have come,' she said; 'I shouldn't be here.'

'Why? You're having lunch with a friend, what harm is there in that?'

'My husband wouldn't like it.'

'Do *you* like the fact he spends every weekend with his people?'

'I didn't like it at first, but now—' she almost said, I'm glad he does, but instead finished, 'it gives me time to myself.'

'My next question should be, why do you feel you need time to yourself? But I'll leave it till after we've eaten. That'll be one of the many questions I want to ask you. Anyway—' His voice changing, he picked up the plainly typed menu from the table and glancing down at it said, 'There's a variety, but it all depends on your taste. They're noted for their bangers and mash and their mutton stew and dumplings here. These head the list, especially on a Saturday. Then there's bacon-and-egg pie and stuffed tomatoes, or perhaps lamb chops with savoury rice, mushrooms and peppers.'

She was smiling at him now as she asked, 'What do you recommend?'

'I like the stew: it's very, very tasty, but it's filling; you want a long rest after it. You know the kind? The bangers and mash are very nice; and they're not just bangers and mash: nice little strips of bacon, button mushrooms, onion rings and bits like that.'

'I'll have bangers and mash plus, please.'

'Good choice. I'll have the same.' He beckoned the waiter, and when the man came to the table he said, 'Two bangers, Dick, please.'

'Yes, sir. Yes, sir. Two bangers it is.'

'Do you often eat here?' Hannah now asked David.

'No; not all that often. I have a very good cook of my own . . . Peter. He's my jack of all trades, my . . . friend.'

She knew he had been about to say 'my man', and this puzzled her. Manservants were a thing of the past. He had said he was going to ask her a lot of questions . . . well, she, too, would have a lot to ask . . .

The very tasty bangers and mash was followed by ice cream and coffee. Throughout, they chatted in a relaxed way, as if they had known each other for years. Things were going so well that Hannah dreaded asking him the questions that she knew might seal the end of their friendship. When, three-quarters of an hour later, they left the restaurant David had a quiet altercation with the waiter, who apparently had had his instructions with regards to the bill. 'If we are going to go there very often I'll have to take Micky to account,' he said. 'He embarrasses me. Now,' and he drew in a long breath, 'where would you like to go? To a matinée, for a walk or on a trip up the river?'

'Oh, a trip up the river. That would be wonderful. I've often seen people on the boats, but I've never done it.'

So they had a trip up the river. They boarded the

boat near Tower Bridge, and on the journey he pointed out places of interest she hadn't known existed.

After they had returned, they walked to a park and, espying a vacant seat, they quickly took possession of it; as they sat down he laughed and said, 'Would you like to make a bet that within fifteen minutes a down-and-out will come and sit at that end? He'll get his paper out as if he were going to make himself comfortable for a snooze; he'll look at me, and then depending on whether or not I'm wise, I'll press something into his hand and gratefully watch him move on to some other bench and some other likely victim.'

She turned a slanted glance towards him as she asked, 'How d'you know all this? Have you experienced it often?'

He leant towards her, saying softly, 'No, madam; I haven't experienced it often, I haven't experienced it at all, but I've seen it happening. I often walk in parks, it's my only form of exercise. I breathe in deeply, then puff out all the bookworms I've swallowed during the day.'

She smiled now, and he, still staring at her, said, 'Your face alters so much when you smile; your eyes are so bright. You look happy when you smile. Are you happy? I . . . I mean, when you're not smiling?'

She turned from him and gazed across an open patch of sunburnt grass to where some children were chasing each other amid high screeches, and she said, 'I never know what people mean when they say they're happy.'

'Well' – he pointed now – 'you're watching happiness personified: those children are jumping for joy; they're feeling the exhilaration of the chase and being chased; their minds are not looking backwards or forwards. At the moment they are expressing that phrase from *Childe Harold*: "Let joy be unconfined".'

Then she said, 'You can't judge happiness by children; as yet they haven't lived.'

They were half turned towards each other and staring questioningly into each other's eyes, when she startled him by asking, 'Are you married?'

She watched his shoulders hunch slightly before he answered: 'Yes; yes, I am married. I've been married for fourteen years, and separated for ten of them. Does that ease your mind?'

She nodded once, then said, 'Yes. Yes, it does.'

'If I had said that I had a wife and a family, well, what then?'

'I would have stood up and walked away.'

'You would? Without listening to any explanation I might be able to give you concerning them?'

'Yes, just that.'

'Then why, if you feel as strongly as that about married men with responsibilities, why did you come?'

'I don't know. Yes, I do. I thought . . . well, you were alone on Thursday night and you're alone today, so perhaps you weren't married. Then I thought, well, maybe you had free Thursdays and weekends, like I do . . . But I *am* married . . . Oh dear.'

She turned from him and slipped her hands once more between her knees. Then when her body made a slight rocking movement his arm went around her shoulder and, softly, he said, 'Oh, my dear, don't distress yourself, please. I'm not in any way tied to my wife. We're legally separated and I've barely seen her during the past ten years; nor do I have any desire to. It's you who has the stumbling block. As you say, you have a husband, and you're feeling very guilty about Thursday and today, aren't you?'

Her throat was full: she couldn't answer and when her head drooped further, he said, 'If you want my opinion, a man who could leave a woman like you on her own, weekend after weekend, doesn't deserve to have her at all, and to my mind if he had been any kind of a man he would have brought you himself to that concert and said to blazes with bridge for one night. Is it the same every Thursday?'

Before looking at him again she said, 'I . . . I'm sorry. I've spoilt what was going to be a . . . well, I will say it' – now her head went up – 'a beautiful day. I've been looking forward to it.'

'Well, it can still be a beautiful day.' He had now taken her hand and was patting it. 'And tomorrow, too, can be a beautiful day.'

'Oh, I don't know.'

'Oh, but I do.'

'I . . . I generally go to my sister's for Sunday lunch. Oh, and by the way' – her smile was wide now – 'a strange thing happened. My brother-in-law, who is also a Cockney, like your Micky, used

81

to have a stall in the market, and he knew Micky. We used to buy our fruit from Eddie. That's how Janie got to know him; and you know what?' She was still smiling. 'One day she bounced into the dining room – I was only sixteen at the time, but it seems just like yesterday – she bounced in and said, "Listen! I'm going to marry Eddie Harper. Well, I'm going to live with him at first, in his flat above the fruit shop – he's no longer a barrow boy, he's got a fruit shop." And to my father she turned and said, "If you try to bring me back . . . I'm twenty, but if you try to bring me back, I'll come, but I'll be pregnant. Just you think on that." And then my mother fell flat on her face in a real Victorian faint.'

He was laughing now, as she was too, and she went on, 'Janie'd been brought up in a convent school. We both had. She left when she was seventeen, but you wouldn't recognise the convent in her were you to meet her now. But . . . but she's a lovely girl; and he's fine too, great fun. But what I want to tell you is this . . . I visited them yesterday and told them what had happened.'

He stopped her here, saying in surprise, 'You told about us and our little night out?'

'Yes. Yes, I did. Well' – the smile went slowly from her face – 'she's the only one I can talk to. I've no one else to turn to, and lately I've . . . well, I've been troubled, very lonely.' She looked down and repeated, 'Yes, lonely. And . . . and yesterday Eddie was there. He'd just had a tooth out and I wouldn't have said anything in front of him, but Janie, in her own forthright way, said, "Oh, I told him about Humph." That's what they call my husband; his name is Humphrey. It annoys him; so we don't meet often, you know, as a family, I mean.'

'Yes, yes; go on. So you told them?'

'Yes, and I said it had been great fun. And I described your friend Micky, and when I mentioned the name McClean, Eddie bounced from the couch. Apparently he and your friend had been brought up together, and he gave me a vivid description of what that meant in the poorest quarter of London. When Eddie and his father had the business in the big market they used to supply Micky,' and she bounced her head towards him now as she emphasised the name, 'with vegetables,' and, adding a fair imitation of Eddie's voice, '"all first-class stuff, mind, no bruised fruit".'

David laughed again as he said, 'What a coincidence! And your brother-in-law sounds another Micky to the tee.'

'Oh, yes; just the same, and I'd love to hear them together.'

'Well, we'll have to take them down there for a meal one night.'

Again the smile slipped from her face. 'I don't think Humphrey . . .'

'Look here!' He took hold of both her hands and, shaking them gently up and down, said, 'I've never met your Humphrey and I have no inclination to do so but I'm going to ask you this: Are you afraid of him?'

'Afraid of Humphrey?' She jerked her head and made an attempt to withdraw her hands from his before she said again, 'Afraid of Humphrey? No, no! No, no! Only I . . . well, to be honest, I'm afraid of hurting him, if I can put it like that. He's so kind and thoughtful and I'd never want to hurt him. He's the kind of person you . . . you shouldn't hurt.'

'No matter how he's hurting you?'

She did take her hands from his now, and when she went to clasp them once more between her knees he stopped her, saying, 'Don't do that. It tells me you're worried. Look. You seem to be able to trust your sister and your brother-in-law, don't you?'

'Oh, yes. Yes. I could tell them anything and it wouldn't go any further.'

'And you went there yesterday and asked them what you should do, didn't you?'

Unsmiling now, she looked into his face and said, 'You're very astute, aren't you?'

'No, not really in this case. But in the short time I've known you, which, when I come to think of it, seems a very, very long time, I have come somehow to gauge your feelings by the tone of your voice when speaking of people.'

'Huh!' She gave a slight shrug of her shoulders. 'You're like Janie: she says I'm like a mirror.' She did not add, 'My husband says that my thoughts are so patent as to be almost childlike.' He had said this to her on many different occasions, and she had promised herself, of late, especially when he was criticising her writing, that she would surprise him one day with her response. But at the same time she had warned herself not to, for her apparent simplicity acted as a kind of shield behind which she could hide.

David said, and his tone now sounded business-like, 'I'll come out into the open. I would like to be friends with you, but only to the extent that you wish to be friends with me. You have this fear of hurting your husband, which I think is very commendable of you; yet you're far from satisfied with your way of life. I didn't need any mirror to be made aware of that. On Thursday, at Micky's, you were like a child let out from a hated boarding school.'

'Oh.' She turned from him, saying tersely, 'Please don't keep referring to me as a child. I hear enough of that. I'm twenty-nine years old and I'm no child.'

'I'm sorry. That'll be the last time I'll use that phrase to you. But I wouldn't have said you were twenty-nine: twenty-two, -three, -four . . .' This made her turn to look at him again, while saying, 'You're being extremely kind.'

'I am *not* being extremely kind.' His voice was so loud that they both turned and looked from one side to the other. Then he was laughing as he said, 'Don't worry. If they heard, they'd think we were a married couple having a row, Hannah . . . and I'm going to call you Hannah. So, would you like to be friends with me, and I mean on whatever terms you care to lay down? Once a week, on bridge night, or more, if possible?'

Again they were staring into each other's eyes, both unsmiling now. Hannah's lips were trembling and she felt her face burning, in fact her whole body felt as if it was burning; but when she heard herself say, 'Yes, I'd like us to be friends,' her words sounded so calm, utterly without emotion. So much for the mirror of her childish thoughts. Yet the expression of her real feelings became evident when she thrust out her hand towards him and found it gripped; and now they were both smiling at each other again, and when he said, 'Thursday-night friends, at least,' their smiles turned into laughter.

Following this they were quiet for a moment, until he pointed to the group of children again, saying, 'They've stopped their racing, they're off somewhere else.'

And when she put in, 'Yes, to grow up,' he responded, 'Yes; yes, perhaps,' and his voice had a faraway sound as he ended, 'And find happiness somewhere. I've always believed it was there – happiness, I mean – just waiting to be found and picked up; and that brings me to you again. I seem to know all about you, but not quite. Are your parents still alive?'

'Well, my mother died.'

'I'm sorry.'

'Oh, you needn't be. We were never very fond of each other and after Janie's escape with her barrow boy I had to leave school. I was nearly seventeen anyway. I became a non-paid help in the house, and I had to revolt before I was allowed to take evening classes in secretarial work. But after she died I was promoted to unpaid housekeeper until my dear Papa – I have to laugh at that now; there was no father and mother in our family, they were

86

Papa and Mama, on Mama's insistence, I may say – decided to give me another Mama, and that wasn't so very long after my mother had died. So I up and go to Janie's, and I worked as a temporary secretary. That's how I met Humphrey; and when he asked me to marry him I felt I was the luckiest girl alive. He already had a house and life promised to be good.'

She stopped speaking, and he did not question her further until she said, 'Perhaps I *was* very childlike at that time. I know only that I was so grateful to anyone who was kind to me. I'll always be grateful to Janie and Eddie.'

'What happened to your father and his new wife? Don't you see him now?' he asked.

'No; they live in York and I have no desire to see either of them.'

Now she turned to him, saying, 'Well, I've given you the events of my life, which would just about cover a postage stamp; may I ask about yours? Of course, I know you're in the book trade and a friend of Mr Gillyman's, and that you also have friends like Micky McClean.'

Here she laughed, and he with her as he repeated, 'Yes, I have a friend in Micky McClean; but I have others too, at least one who's like a father, mother and nurse to me. You must meet Peter. Look; I'll tell you what.' He glanced at his watch. 'It's just on four o'clock now. It's Saturday, the cafés will be packed, and the theatres not yet open, and I don't know about you but I don't feel like any more sightseeing. Now, would you like to come and meet my friend

Peter and also see where I hang out and how I hang out?'

For a moment she paused, then said, 'No etchings?'

He laughed briefly and turned to her. 'No etchings. I can assure you, no etchings. Right?'

'Right!'

They took the bus to Oxford Street. 'My flat's hardly a stone's throw from where you were the other morning,' he told her. 'It used to be one of Gilly's store rooms, which was such a waste because it's a lovely little flat, or a big one, however you view it.'

As they passed Jason Gardens he pointed along it, saying, 'You never expected to be this way again so soon, did you?'

'No, I didn't.'

They had walked on for what could only have been three or four minutes when he turned into a short road at the end of which was what looked like a factory. And that was exactly what it was: 'That's a dress factory,' he said, 'where they turn them out by the second. These four houses are Gilly's property, all rented like mine.'

He turned into the iron-railed enclosure leading to the first house. To the right, steps led down to a basement; ahead were three steps leading to the front door. He put his latch key into the door. The door open, he now turned round, put out his hand and drew her inside, and she was amazed to find herself in a large room. He was pressing her forward when a door opened at the far end of it and a white-haired man appeared, paused a moment, then said, 'Oh, you're back, sir. Good afternoon, madam.'

'This is Mrs Drayton, Peter.'

'How d'you do, Mr Peter?'

David laughed now, saying, 'Not Mr Peter, Peter. If you want to be correct, he is Mr Miller, but I'm sure Peter doesn't want you to be correct, do you, Peter?'

'No, sir; no. Not at all.' He had been gazing intently at the young woman; then he turned to David, saying, 'Shall I get you tea, sir?'

'Yes, thank you, Peter; that's what we've come for.'

Smiling, the man left them and now Hannah, looking about her, said softly, 'What a remarkable room!'

'Yes, isn't it? And to think this was stuffed practically to the ceiling with books of every size and description. But at that time it was three rooms, not one, as now. I had the partitions taken down. There were five rooms altogether on this floor: a small kitchen and a small bedroom, a dining room, a small sitting room and a larger sitting room. Well, the dining room and the two sitting rooms are now what you see.'

She was gazing around, looking from one colour to another. She had never imagined what a room would look like with doors painted a bright golden yellow. The walls between were a soft grey, and here and there were pieces of furniture, old furniture, very like those in Mrs Gillyman's room. But on the wall between what she supposed were the kitchen and a bedroom there was a painting of a huge bird. As she stood staring at it he said, 'D'you like it? It's what they call a roseate tern. They're beautiful in flight.'

She moved closer to the painting, saying now, 'Is it actually painted on the wall?'

'Oh yes. Yes. Higgledy-piggledy in parts, as you'll see on closer inspection.'

Something in his tone made her turn and say, 'You . . . you painted it?'

'I have the honour, madam. A latent talent from my schooldays. Never been developed. Stumped, I think at times, by the remark of my art master, who said, "Don't worry, Craventon, you could always take up paper-hanging with your painting. It'll get you by!"'

'How cruel!' She smiled as she made the remark, and he, looking back at her, said, 'Yes, how cruel. I was to find that only sadistic men took up school-teaching as a career. Well, I mean many of them, anyway. That's why I gave it up. I couldn't get the hang of real sadism.'

'You were a teacher?'

'For my sins, yes, for a time; but I'll tell you about all that later. Come and sit down.'

She did not immediately respond, but she said, 'Did you design . . . I mean, all the colours and furnishings?'

'Again I must confess: yes, I did.'

'Well, all I can say is, that art master didn't know what he was talking about. I find it incredibly diffi-cult to match colours. For instance—' She pointed to the long pale rose-pink curtains, with their fringed pelmets, draping the two large windows at the far side of the room, and she said, 'Now, I would have thought that that colour would scream at the yellow doors and the green carpet and black rugs, not to mention' – she was pointing now to a long Chesterfield – 'upholstery in what I suppose you would call light tan?'

'Its correct title, madam, is rosy brown.'

She laughed as she repeated, 'Rosy brown. Anyway,' she added, 'it's a most beautiful room. Mrs Gillyman's room I found . . . well, delightful, charming. I never expected to see again anything to come up to it, but this is different somehow. I can only think of the word "stimulating".'

'Oh, what a pity! I thought you were going to say "restful".' He now took her arm and led her towards the couch, saying, 'Would you be surprised if I told you that I took all these colours from one flower?'

'Really?'

'It was a huge poppy, almost six inches across, and it was dying, and its outer rose-coloured petals were all crumpled with yellow, like a fringe. There they were, drooping, one petal after the other, with the tiredness of life. At least, that's how I saw it, and I made notes and all the colours of that poppy are represented here. All except the roseate tern. I put him in because I was fascinated by his flight and, where all the rest were dying colours, he was full of winged white life.'

Hannah was sitting on the Chesterfield now and

staring at him. His way of describing the room was holding her spellbound, more so than the actual place itself did. His words flowed, making strange patterns. She had been so used to Humphrey's precision all these years that she felt she was listening to a man who had been bred in some distant place, one where they spoke a different language. He was saying, 'When decorating, one can very rarely imitate nature: the colours just don't work out. Even in my case' – he spread his hand widely, indicating the room – 'I feel it's a little bizarre at times.'

'Oh no, no!' – she was quick to contradict him – 'anything but. It's unusual and beautiful.'

'Yes, yes; but it isn't soothing. I had hoped, like the poppy, it had picked up some of that flower's benevolent drug potion, but apparently no. Ah!' – he turned – 'ah! here comes the cup that not only refreshes but gives you indigestion, heartburn and hiatus hernia.'

'Well, it's been a long time in killing you, sir.'

'It does its best, Peter. You know what happens after I've eaten meat.' He turned to Hannah: 'I daren't touch tea for twenty-four hours. It kills me.'

'That's because, sir, as I've told you, you drink it too strong with too little milk.'

'Oh, that's what you always say, but in me, at least, it acts as poison on top of meat. I'll have coffee now, after those sausages. Oh—' he pointed to a plate on the lower shelf of the tea trolley, saying, 'You've been baking?'

'A little, sir.'

He now turned to Hannah, saying, 'Peter makes

the most delicious scones. He's hopeless at pastry, it's like leather, but scones . . .'

Hannah exchanged a smiling glance with the white-haired man, whose skin looked so smooth until he smiled, when his real age was depicted by the myriad lines round his shaven lips and chin. He had no jowls and he was thin, almost as thin as his master, and almost as tall.

When he said, 'If you should need me, sir, just ring,' and David responded, 'I'll do that, Peter, I'll do that,' she noticed the sly grin that was exchanged between them. Then they were alone again . . .

When, a few minutes later, she bit into one of the scones she exclaimed, 'Oh, how delicious! And so light. If he makes scones like this he must surely be able to make pastry.'

'It's odd, I admit, but his pastry isn't good. I sometimes think he uses dripping in it, as perhaps his mother did years ago.'

'Is he old? His hair is a beautiful colour, and so thick.'

'No, not really. I don't know exactly what age he is, only that in the war he was my father's batman and, after the Army business, they stuck together. I remember first seeing him through a haze of an asthmatic spasm, and also through a feeling of real terror, for it was happening in front of my father. Apparently I'd had these bouts from early childhood, when brave fellows didn't give way to such things. I remember that particular day, for Peter – Miller as he was known then – rubbed the sides of my throat and my back, only to be told, "Now, none of that, Miller! No coddling! Get him on to a horse and get the air through him. That's what he wants."

'I was put on a horse!' – he smiled now – 'and Peter used to trot me smartly out of the yard; but, once through the wood, he would slow down the horses to a walk then amuse me by telling me some far-fetched tale about his travels. He wasn't widely travelled, but he made me think he had been all over the world.'

He looked away from her now and, taking up the silver teapot, he refilled her cup before he went on: 'Apart from the nanny I had until I was eight, Peter was the kindest person in my young life. I had a few friends about my own age, but even friends at the age of twelve or thirteen or fourteen aren't capable of being kind and understanding towards a pal who, for no apparent reason, starts to choke and can't get his breath. Well, it isn't done, is it? Anyway, as the years went on the attacks lessened but they didn't disappear . . . Another scone?'

'Thank you; they're lovely.'

He himself took another scone and there was silence between them as they sat munching them.

Hannah's voice was quiet now as she asked, 'Do you still have the asthma attacks?'

'Yes, but not very often. The weather sometimes plays havoc, but it's more often because of an emotional upset. Since I haven't had one of those for a long, long time, I've been pretty free of late; but of course they vary in severity. When the ceiling blew off my home – I mean when my father and mother broke up, he going off with a young miss half his age and leaving a pile of debts behind him, which only the selling of the house and stock barely covered – I went with my mother to her people in Dorset. And Peter . . . she brought Peter with us. I've always liked to think she did it for my sake, but I know it was mainly to get me off her hands, because Peter was very good with me, especially when I had my attacks. The fact that I'd been ready for Oxford went by the board: What was to be done with me?

'My grandparents, although not horse-mad them-selves, liked riding, the hunt and such, but their neighbours, the Busbys, they lived on their horses. I think they slept with them at times, led by their father. There were three brothers and the sister, and all about my age, so for about a year I entered into a different kind of existence. I didn't get to win rosettes at shows, but I learnt how to hold my port and dance until three in the morning. That spell was really very short, though, which when I look back now I realise was perhaps a good thing, because my mother, after her divorce, married again and my grandfather said, very wisely, "Young man, you've a living to earn. What can you do?" And the young man said, "Nothing, Grandpapa, really nothing."' David was laughing now as he looked at her. 'I actu-ally said that to him and he didn't think it was funny. Oh no, not a bit of it. What he said was, "Well, young man, we'll see about that. They're looking for a pupil teacher over at Blakey School, so I heard at a meeting yesterday. This is for children seven to ten, and, after your long education, I should imagine you will have enough left in that head of

yours to instil the rudiments of English into petrified youngsters, for that, from what I remember, is
the condition of all who experience the first year at
boarding school."'

Hannah was laughing now and he with her.
'Believe me, I'm not exaggerating one word,' he
said. 'That's exactly what he said. It became im-
printed on my mind, especially during the following
months. The only thing he was wrong about was
the petrified youngsters; I was the only petrified one
there, and they knew it. Following three months
among them, I went on to teach, if you can call it
that, at three other private schools, until I was
twenty-two. The only break was the holidays and
going mad with the Busbys for a few weeks.'

His expression and his tone now becoming sober,
he said, 'I was at home on holiday when my grandmother died. I was twenty-two. She was a dear old
thing, but had been ruled by my grandfather all their
married life, I think. Yet within six weeks of her
going, he too died. There I was, left with a house
and no money with which to keep it up, because
prep schools then were notoriously bad payers,
especially to untrained teachers such as I. Anyway,
my grandpa had left a will to the effect that the
house was to be sold and I was to be paid a monthly
sum for the rest of my life. Fortunately, it's enough
to satisfy my modest needs.

'In the mean time, Peter had been acting as yard
man to the Busbys, seeing to their horses and doing
odd things, for which he was receiving a good wage.
My relative poverty was quite a joke among the

Busbys, but I must say they were very kind to me during that period, so much so that I became engaged to Carrie.' He put his head back now and, shaking it, he laughed. 'I can't tell you to this day how that came about. Who proposed to whom . . .? I can't see myself having the nerve. Anyway, I was engaged to Carrie Busby, and after a suitable period of mourning, which was rather short, there were high jinks with parties and races and dancing until dawn. Then, often, racing again. It was very noticeable during this period that I avoided any contact with Peter. He tried to get at me two or three times, and somehow I knew what he would say and I didn't want to hear it. A year later I married Miss Clarissa Busby, and shortly afterwards I returned to teaching. Four years passed, by the end of which we were legally separated. So there you have my life story.'

As she sat looking at him in silence she wanted to say, Not all of it. She wanted to ask, Why did it last such a short time? Why did you separate?

'Do you still teach?' She gave a toss of her head now, saying, 'What a stupid thing to ask! Of course you don't; you work for Mr Gillyman.'

'Yes' – he nodded at her, smiling – 'I work for Mr Gillyman; and do you know what the first job he gave me to do was?'

She shook her head.

'To clear this very house of books. It was another one of his dumps, and most of the rooms were stacked from floor to ceiling; you could hardly get in, and he said if I could clean it up and stack all the stuff down in the basement flat, then renovate it myself, I could rent it. He had given me the post of assistant and I was living in semi-furnished rooms. It's odd, you know, how a small kindness can change one's life. His twelve-year-old son was at a day prep school where I was teaching, and he had the same complaint as I had when I was young; and boys can be cruel about it. Don't I know it! If you have an attack you're accused of trying to dodge a lesson, not only by the boys but very often by the master, and so I used to speak to him whenever I could. Then he was absent for some weeks, and during that time Gilly came to the school and asked to see me. It was to request that I visit his son in hospital. It seemed that the boy had told his father what I did for him at odd times, which was really nothing.

'Well, of course I went to see the little fellow, and was horrified to know that he was dying; not from asthma but from a defective heart. Gilly and Natasha were in a dreadful state, because he was their only child. Anyway, I must at one time or other have told the boy that I wasn't very fond of teaching, so a few weeks after the boy was buried I was both amazed and delighted when Gilly met me coming out of the school one day and in his abrupt way said that he had understood from Rodney that I wasn't very fond of teaching. He asked if I liked books, then offered me the post of assistant, which he assured me straight away would be very dusty and dull, for it would mean simply nothing but sorting books into categories. How did I feel about that?

'Without a pause I assured him I felt very well about it, and thanked him very much; and when he said, "Aren't you going to enquire what the wage is?" I said no, that I would leave that to him. He was very generous. That's how I came to be Gilly's assistant and met you one Thursday morning.'

'What a delightful story,' Hannah said, 'but such a pity and so sad about them losing their child.'

'But they're very sensible about him. For a long time they talked as if he were still in the house and growing up. At times it was a bit weird, but I think it helped them both to manage their grief. Anyway' – his voice was loud now – 'that's all the talking I'm going to do for the rest of the day, at least about myself. I'm now going to ask the questions and I want fully fledged answers and no evasiveness.'

As she looked at him she thought to herself: no evasiveness, he says; but he had evaded quite neatly talking about his wife and how Peter, the man who, she imagined, was now indispensable to him, had come back into his life.

'Look at that!' – he was pointing to her cup – 'you haven't touched it and it's stone cold. I'll give Peter a call.'

'No, no! please. I don't mind lukewarm tea; I often drink cold tea in the summer.'

'If you're sure?'

'Quite sure. Cold tea can be very refreshing.'

He smiled as she sipped at the cold tea. Then, bouncing up from the couch, he said, 'Let me see the paper and what's on tonight. What would you like to do?'

He had pulled a newspaper from an ornamental rack standing to the side of the fireplace. 'There's comedy and drama. Let's see what else. A musical or the ballet? Oh' – he looked over the top of the paper – 'don't say you want to go to the ballet, because I'm not very fond of ballet, I must confess.'

'You're missing something, then.'

'Yes. Yes, so they tell me.'

'Well, I'm not mad about comedies; interchanging bedroom scenes never appear funny to me.'

He was laughing down at her now as he said, 'You are an odd thing, aren't you? In this case, it's a pity one can't insert "little", but you're too tall for that.'

Her face straight, she said, 'What d'you mean by odd?'

'Oh, something nice . . . surprising, one could say.' He was sitting near her again when he added, 'I can understand your not liking comedy. But musicals?'

'Oh yes, I like musicals.' And before she could stop her thoughts, she voiced them by saying, 'Probably because I've never had very much gaiety in my own life.'

Her voice trailed away and, her head drooping, she said, 'What a silly thing to say.' Then jerking her chin up she faced him, saying, 'But it's true. Life can go on from day to day, so very . . . the word here is "mundane". That's why it appeared I stepped out of my world on Thursday morning when I entered Jason Gardens and walked into that book cave and

Mr Gillyman . . . then you, which is why I must have seemed so eager to accept your invitation to go out for a meal.'

'You didn't accept it eagerly at all, you were quite cool.'

'Oh no; I wasn't inside. I was so excited. I knew I was doing something that I shouldn't and that if Humphrey found out he would be aghast and—'

'Why on earth should he be aghast? Fom what you say, he seems very keen to keep his bridge evenings intact.'

'Yes, but on that occasion I knew I'd have to lie, because he was under the impression I was going to that concert with my sister. Instead, what was I doing? I was having supper, or dinner, whatever you might call it, with a man I'd met for the first time that morning and about whom I knew nothing.'

He caught her hand as he said, 'Well, by now you know a lot about him. Does that make you feel any better?'

'Not really. There'll be more lying to do tomorrow night about how I spent my weekend.'

'Does he go away every weekend?'

She paused a moment, as if thinking. Then she answered him, saying, 'Yes; well, it wasn't always every weekend; but it has been for quite a long time now, since his uncle' – she dipped her head with the word – 'has gout or something, which always appears worse at the weekends, and Mrs Beggs, that's the housekeeper, and apparently a treasure' – she pulled a face here – 'generally phones to give Humphrey the state of her master's health, which determines whether or not he spends a long weekend there.'

He drew back from her, his expression straight as he asked, 'And have you been there? To the house?'

'Oh yes; yes.' She smiled at him. 'He's asked me time and again to go with him, hoping, I'm sure, that I'll refuse, because in the early days of our marriage his aunt made it quite plain that dear Humphrey had made a great mistake in taking on one such as me. But I've told you all this: she looks upon me as a brainless blonde.'

'How dare she! Oh no! . . . Are they wealthy?'

'Oh, I think they're pretty well-off.'

'And no family of their own?'

'No, only . . .' she mimicked now, '"dear, dear Humphrey",' then added, '"He was always such a thoughtful boy,"' which caused David to chortle. The sound he made caused her to be immediately contrite, and she said, 'I . . . I shouldn't do that. I . . . I mean, say things like that, because he *is* thoughtful. He *is* still very thoughtful. That sounded so spiteful.'

'No, no; it didn't. It just points out that you're not easily hoodwinked.'

'What d'you mean?'

'Well, that you're not being hoodwinked with regard to his aunt's wrong opinion of you and of blondes in general.'

He glanced at his watch, saying, 'The time's going on, and it's Saturday and we haven't booked anywhere, but we might just get a seat if we get to something early. What did I say about musicals?' He picked up the paper again, but before reading it he said, 'Oh, what I should have said was, would you like to freshen up? Look; it's through here.'

He pulled her gently up from the couch and led her to a far door; and there he said, 'I'm sorry, you'll have to go through the bedroom to get to the bathroom; it was the way I altered the rooms. The only mistake I made, I think.'

After the expanse of the sitting room the bedroom seemed small, but the bathroom was very adequate and well appointed.

She looked in the mirror. Her hair was hanging loose about her shoulders and looked messy. It should be tidied up, especially if they were going out this evening. She had a hair clasp in her bag; she would go and get it.

She returned to the bedroom, then stopped when she heard Peter's voice. 'I'm so glad for you, sir', then David's voice answering, 'Oh, don't be too glad, Peter; she's an unknown quantity: there's a will behind that naïvety.'

'I see her just as you described her, sir, and the word is nice.'

'Yes, she is. But how nice remains to be seen.'

'Oh, it'll work out for you, sir. In this case, it couldn't not.'

She moved quietly back into the bathroom and sat down.

*In this case, it couldn't not.*

So there had been other cases, then, that hadn't worked out.

And she appeared naïve, did she?

Well, she wasn't that naïve. She had said to him,

'No etchings?' and she had meant it. Yet what had she expected to be the outcome of these get-togethers? Her inner voice came at her now, saying, Well, why don't you answer yourself? You know what will happen eventually.

I don't. No, I don't. She was on her feet now. Anyway, it mustn't; I couldn't bear to look at Humphrey.

Damn Humphrey! The voice was almost a scream in her head and so loud was it that she clapped her hand over her mouth and cast her gaze quickly about the room. What had come over her? Fancy her saying that – Damn Humphrey! Nothing before had ever made her react like that. Well – there was the voice again – nothing in your life has happened to make you fear his displeasure as you're fearing it now.

I'm not fearing it. I don't fear him; I just don't want to hurt him.

Then why damn him?

Oh. For answer she pulled open the bathroom door and closed it loudly enough to give notice of her return; when she entered the room again David was sitting on the couch; but he immediately got to his feet and he said, 'Did you find everything you wanted?'

'Not quite—' She made her voice light. 'There's a hair clasp in my bag.' She reached down to the side of the couch and picked up her bag, and then added, 'Nor could I find any lipstick on your shelf.'

'Oh dear! dear! What a pity. I usually have some . . . Wait a minute . . .' He made a pretence of groping in his pocket, but she was walking from him back into the bathroom; and once again the door closed on her. She did not immediately open her bag, but stood looking in the mirror again, and softly she said to her reflection, 'It'll pay you to stick to your naïvety.'

They could not find a seat in either a musical or a play that interested them, so they went to the cinema, and, after sitting for nearly an hour through a brain-chilling enactment of what happened to innocent people during a witch hunt in America, he glanced at her.

Her head was lowered and he whispered, 'Had enough?'

'Much more,' she said.

Quietly they went out, and in the street they laughed when he said, 'This is the second entertainment we've escaped from. I wonder what the third one will be. Well, now what? It's just turned half-past nine. How about a little bite somewhere?'

'Oh no; no, thank you. It'll be much too late by the time I get home.'

'Hannah' – he had taken her arm and was walking her along the street now – 'there's no time-keeper waiting for you, and whoever heard of anyone having to be home early these days? Come on!'

'No; I'd rather not.'

'Well, what about just one drink?'

She glanced at him now as she said, 'I bet you know a little place where we can get a corner seat.'

His high laugh again rang out, and he took her arm and pulled her tight against his side as he said, 'You think you've got me weighed up, don't you?'

'No, I don't.'

'Oh. Oh.'

'Well, perhaps about food and drink I do.'

'Well, madam, I can tell you there's much more to me than food and drink, and you'll not know what it is if you rush off so as to be home early every night. Now, if you were doing a Cinderella and making it twelve, there'd be some excuse for your hurry. As a last resort, can I offer you a cup of tea from a street stall?'

'You know of a stall open at this time of night?'

'This time of night? *All* night. All night.'

She laughed, then said, 'All right, lead on.'

Ten minutes later they were standing with four other patrons at the stall, drinking a cup of very strong coffee. He had chosen it from the offer of tea, coffee or cocoa, but when she couldn't get half-way through it, he finished it for her, saying, 'I can see you'll have to get used to a number of things.'

When she shivered, he asked, 'Are you cold?' And when she answered, 'No,' he said, 'Well, let's have a walk along the Embankment. It's lovely at this time of night.'

So they walked along the Embankment. At one point they stopped for a moment to watch a pleasure boat streaming down the river with couples dancing on the deck, and when the music came to them clearly over the water he turned to her and said, 'May I have this dance, please?'

His arms were held out to her, and she flapped them away with her hands, saying, 'You would too, wouldn't you?'

'Yes! Yes, of course I would, so long as I could hear the music.'

'And have the police after you for unruly conduct?'

'Oh, they couldn't have me for dancing. Now, if you were to scream they could have me; and I shouldn't wonder but you're now going to scream when I say, "How are we going to spend tomorrow?"'

She didn't scream; she smiled and she answered, 'I don't know what you're going to do, but I'm going to have dinner with my sister, her husband, and their four terrors.'

'Well, where do they live? Not down in Cornwall; surely it won't take all day?'

'No, not all day, but quite a bit of it. They live in Ealing.'

'Ealing? Oh, I know Ealing. I used to know someone in Northcote Avenue.'

'I have to pass there to get to Janie's,' she said. 'They live in Buttermere Close. It's only about three or four streets further on.'

'And is that where your brother-in-law sells his fruit and veg?'

'Oh, no, that's in the centre of town; and I've told you, he used to have a stall in the market; but now he's going to buy another shop.'

'And his name's Harper, is it?'

'Yes.'

'And he lives in Buttermere Close?'

She did not answer him straight away but said, 'You wouldn't!'

'Why wouldn't I?' He now struck a pose, saying, 'Good afternoon, Mrs Harper. I hope you've finished lunch. I'm a friend of your sister, her Thursday friend, and was passing this way. I have a friend in Northcote Avenue. Oh, thank you; yes, I'll come in for a moment;' and he held out his hand to the side, and it was apparently shaken by someone, for he said, 'Yes; and I'm pleased to meet you, too. I've heard a lot about you from Micky, you know, Micky McClean.'

'You wouldn't dare!'

'Oh, I would. Yes, really I would. I dare to do things like that. When I get an urge that I want something very badly I have a secret source of courage that I can call upon. At other times I'm a coward about most things and run away. It seems I've been running away all my life but then, just sometimes, I face up to things, and I think that tomorrow afternoon could be one of those times.'

'Please don't.'

'Why not?' His voice was sober now. 'If you don't promise to see me tomorrow it'll be the usual Sunday for me. I'll sleep in late. Peter will have ascertained earlier whether I'm having lunch out or in. If I'm in he'll make a splendid roast; if I'm out I generally go without eating until the evening, then I have a bite somewhere, and sometimes, just sometimes, I go to Trafalgar Square and to St Martin-in-the-Fields, and, after the service, go downstairs to see if I can be of any help. But just sometimes, mind, because I'm no do-gooder. Oh, no; far from it. But I happen to know someone there who is a do-gooder in the right way. So that is my usual Sunday. Gilly and Natasha frequently press me to go there on a Sunday, but I feel they should have that day to themselves, and they generally go to the cemetery to visit Rodney's grave. Now, for instance, if you decided to have lunch with me tomorrow, just think of the fun we could have. We could go up the river again, or I can hire a car and take you to far-off places. Since I've been living in London I've never kept a car, but I often hire one. We could go to the seaside or whatever you fancied. Now, just think of that. Wouldn't it be lovely?'

She smiled softly at him as she said, 'I mustn't . . . I mean, I can't do it.'

'You were going to say you mustn't do it. Humphrey again. Well, what time does Humphrey get back?'

'It varies, usually about nine-thirty.'

'Nine-thirty on a Sunday evening.' He clicked his tongue twice: 'Tut-tut . . . Tut-tut,' then said, 'If I don't see you tomorrow, I won't see you until Thursday unless you promise to have lunch with me one day before that.'

'I can't do that, no . . . no. Humphrey . . .'

'Oh, Hum . . . phrey.' He split the name now, and there was a sound of impatience in his tone as he said, 'I'm already beginning to dislike Humphrey, you know.'

She didn't say, You don't know him, and that's

unfair; but what she said was, 'I would like to go to a service at St Martin-in-the-Fields.'

'You would? Oh, that's good. We'll do that. And . . . and you'll come and have tea again at the flat before that, a proper tea this time? What about it? What time shall I meet you? You'll be going to your sister's for lunch, I suppose?'

'Yes; yes, I must. I . . . I could meet you about three or half-past at Tottenham Court Road tube.'

'Make it three, eh? Oh, that'll be nice. That'll be really nice. Now I can lie in and have my roast lunch.' He put his arm tightly through hers, and, walking her forward, said, 'You're very kind to me, and I'm grateful.'

What could she say to that? But there was no need to answer, for he was pointing up the river to a tugboat ploughing its way, and he was saying, 'Oh, there she goes, Old Fanny Ficklebottom!'

'What?'

'That old tug, I call her Old Fanny Ficklebottom. Listen to what she says. Now listen . . . listen to her. D'you hear? Can you hear her?'

Hannah shook her head, and he went on, chuckling, 'Take note of this: "Rut-a-tut, rut-a-tut, rut-a-tut, ya bergar you . . . bergar, not bugger, bergar. Rut-a-tut, rut-a-a-tut, ya bergar you."'

She had to put her hand over her mouth to control her laughter, and, leaning over the rail and wiping her eyes, said, 'You know, you're a bit of an idiot.'

'Am I?' He too was leaning over the rail now; he pushed a pebble off the end of the flags with the toe of his shoe, and when it dropped into the water with a slight *ping* he said quietly, 'It's a nice feeling knowing that someone thinks you're an idiot, but you can only be an idiot with a certain type of person.' Their heads turned towards each other now and they stared in silence. The tugboat had disappeared from view, and except for the sound of the wash beating against the bank the river was quiet and gave no sign of movement. Neither did her hand when his came out and laid itself gently on top of hers on the rail.

# Five

Hannah arrived at Janie's at eleven o'clock. It was much earlier than usual, but she wanted to have a talk with Janie before the business of Sunday lunch got under way.

However, in the hall she was greeted by Eddie, his head poking round the kitchen door, saying, 'Oh! it's you, Hannah. Lord! am I glad to see you; you were never more welcome.'

'What's the matter? Where's Janie?'

He was in the hallway now, drying his hands on a tea-towel. 'Upstairs; her back's gone again. I've told her till I'm sick – you've heard me – she will carry that fellow around, at least up the stairs, and he's quite able enough to climb them himself. If he's not at two and a half he never will be.'

'Hello there, Auntie Hannah! Oh, I'm glad to see you.' This was a voice from the stairs, and Hannah, seeing ten-year-old Maggie, said, 'That's nice: two people already glad to see me.'

'Mam's back's bad.'

Hannah had taken off her coat and was hanging

it on the stand as she said, 'So I've heard already.'

The ten-year-old now turned a sly glance towards her father, saying, 'Dad says it's with carrying John upstairs. That way he'll never want to walk, will he, if Mam keeps carrying him about?'

'One of these days, me girl, I'll clip your ear so hard . . .'

'I know, Dad. I know.' His daughter grinned at him, then asked him, 'Have you done the spuds?'

Eddie didn't answer her but, looking at Hannah, said, 'Go on up and have a word with her. I'll bring you up a cup of tea.'

'I'd rather have coffee, if you don't mind, Eddie.'

'Me too, Auntie Hannah. Among other things, I get sick of tea in this house,' Maggie said, before making a quick escape into the kitchen.

'She's turned up trumps,' Eddie remarked; 'she's as sensible as they come. She's been a real help, looking after her mother and the young 'uns. She's a good lass. But this is Sunday, Hannah, and you know what Janie is for Sunday: a roast and at least four veg. I tell her, if she had to buy them she wouldn't be so liberal in stuffing them into her family.' His tone changing, and his head jerking upwards, he said, 'Tell her everything's fine down here; she thinks the house'll fall about us if she can't get downstairs.'

'Have you had the doctor?'

'You mention the doctor to her. Now do that, Hannah, just mention the doctor to her and see the answer you get.'

When Hannah opened the bedroom door, she

saw her sister lying almost flat on her back, her head supported by a thin pillow. As she made her way towards the bed she said, 'Now don't start asking me questions or telling me what should be done downstairs, because I'm going to tell you, and straight away, that you should have that back seen to, or before long this'll be your permanent home.'

'Good morning, Hannah! So nice of you to drop in. I see you've had a talk with Father Eddie and Mother Maggie downstairs!'

All this was said in the polite convent-bred voice and Hannah, on a laugh, answered in the same vein, 'Yes; I met dear Father Eddie; he was most concerned for you. As for Mother Maggie, I understand she's been working wonders, and I should imagine by now the sirloin and the four veg are well under way.' Then, her tone changing, she said, 'That satisfy you?' She walked round to the other side of the bed, pulled up a chair and sat down close to her sister.

'All fun apart, Janie, you should have that back seen to,' she said.

'How can I? Don't be ridiculous, Hannah. I know what would happen; they'd push me into hospital and stretch me or something. They did that with Mrs Saunders down the road, and she's worse now. I only want a couple more days flat out like this and it'll be over once more. I know what it is, it's a sciatic nerve. Remember Sister Amnesia?'

'Oh, forgetful Florrie, Sister Florentine?'

'Yes. She used to give us biology lessons, you remember? There was a great linen folder she used to drop over the blackboard which showed one part of the body after the other, but with all the vital parts carefully blocked out. It's a wonder we knew where our backsides were! I never thought nuns had them. Nor legs. But look at them now, how they run around: skirts up to their backsides . . .'

'Stop prattling on, Janie. All right, it's a sciatic nerve, but dosing yourself with aspirins isn't going to cure it; you want medical advice. I don't know what Eddie's thinking about, not to override you and get the doctor in, no matter what you say.'

'He knows better than to override me.'

'Oh, big noise!'

'Anyway, why've you come early, if not to give me some news? Come on, let's have it. What happened yesterday? You met him?'

'Oh yes, I met him.'

'Well, go on, then.'

So Hannah told her what had transpired, from lunch at Micky's, on and on until they parted, with her promising to meet him again.

'When?'

'Oh, some time.'

'Today?'

She shook her head, then said, 'No; no, not today.'

'You're fibbing. You were going to meet him today, and because you see me lying here you think you should do the loving sister bit and stay on with that lot downstairs. Well, you're not.'

'Yes, I am!'

'We'll see about that!'

They looked at each other intently for a moment; then Janie asked, 'What's he really like?'

Hannah didn't answer her straight away; in fact, she looked towards the window, then moved her eyes around the modern bedroom that appeared unusually tidy at this time, until, her gaze returning to Janie, she said, 'I can't put a name to it. He's wonderful company: he's funny, he's kind.'

'Oh, my God! don't get on to the "kind" business again. You've got one already. Dear, dear Humphrey is kind. You mustn't hurt Humphrey because he's kind.'

Hannah's voice rose now as she exclaimed, 'It isn't that kind of kindness I'm meaning!'

'Well, what other kind is there?'

'I . . . I can't tell you, but he's different.'

'Is he good-looking, tall?'

'Yes, both those things.'

'Has he any money?'

'Well, not really, but . . . I think he lives quite comfortably.'

'Did you like his flat?'

'Oh yes, it's beautiful, what I saw of it.'

Janie grimaced as she tried to move in the bed; but then on a laugh she asked, 'Did he show you his bedroom?' and Hannah's voice was precise when she answered, 'Yes, dear sister, he showed me his bedroom, and his bathroom!'

'Nice?'

'Very nice indeed.'

'Pretty-pretty or a man's room?'

'Oh, Janie! you are the limit. It was a bedroom, a very ordinary bedroom. The only things I noticed were the small pieces of antique furniture he had in the big room.'

'Truthfully now, when are you seeing him again? I want to know.'

'I . . . I'm not sure.'

'Well, after all that paraphernalia yesterday, and if what you tell me is true, you'd have made some kind of a date.'

'Well, I didn't. I said I'd ring him.' . . . Did she know his number? No, she didn't. But she knew his address.

'I don't know whether to believe you or not.'

'Well, it doesn't matter, dear sister, whether you do or not. I'm here to stay for the rest of the day, and in payment receive my meat and four veg. I don't know what you ordered for pudding.'

'Fruit. There's a fridge full of it.'

'Oh well, that'll be nice: I could make a nice fruit salad. I don't suppose you thought to order any cream?'

'Get yourself downstairs, Miss Fancy Pants!'

Hannah was making for the door when, in a tone quite different from any other she had used so far, Janie said softly, 'You know something, Hannah? Whoever this fellow is, he's worked a miracle on you, for you've gone back to the way I remember you when you were in your early twenties. Keep it up.'

Hannah could say nothing to this. She only knew that she was blushing, on which Janie immediately

117

remarked, 'That's something else; I've not seen you blush for years.'

Hannah stood for a moment, biting on her lower lip. Janie was right. Something had happened to her in the last four days: she knew that within herself she had thrown off the years of dull monotony that were making her old before her time; she knew she must have become staid, and her not yet thirty. And who was to blame? Oh, she couldn't blame Humphrey for everything. She should have demanded an explanation from the time of the separate rooms; yet who could demand anything from Humphrey? You didn't demand when dealing with Humphrey, you asked politely and, as politely, he would give you an answer.

As she moved down the stairs she met Maggie.

'Auntie Hannah, are you staying this afternoon?' It was a loud whisper.

'Well, I . . . I don't really know. Why?'

'Only because, if you were, I could go to the party, Nanette's. She's always on about their house. I haven't seen it, but last week Mam said I could go. Mam's bought me a new bum-freezer, and it's lovely, and a silk blouse.'

'Which is lovely? The bum-freezer or the silk blouse?'

Maggie laughed, then said, 'Both. They've got this big house; I'm dying to see it. Dad says we're going to move some day 'cos this place is becoming like a matchbox, especially if Mam goes and does it again.'

'Does what?' Hannah looked down into the dark round eyes, so like Eddie's.

'Well, goes and gets herself pregnant again. She wants another boy. She said Dad doesn't like paying for staff, so he's going to use the family.'

The light cuff Hannah gave the girl across her ear made her pretend to stagger, and when she said, 'You're a dreadful child,' the ten-year-old came back, saying, 'I'm not a child, and, Auntie Hannah, I can't ever remember being a child, being the eldest. I was four when Winnie was born, then I was six when Mam had Claire, and eight when she had John, and I remember saying to her then, "Is that the finish?"'

'You didn't!'

'Oh, yes I did, Auntie Hannah. I was sick of looking after kids, and I remember once saying to Dad that other people have nannies and' – she burst out laughing now – 'I remember him saying, "There's no place to keep a goat here, and we're not keeping one as long as we have you." Anyway, are you leaving early, Auntie Hannah?'

Hannah again looked into the beseeching dark eyes, and when she heard herself say, 'No, not very; there's no need,' the inner voice warned her, Look! What are you doing? Don't be silly. But she went on, 'The only thing I must do is use the phone. I was going to meet a friend, but I can attend to that later.'

'You sure, Auntie?'

'Positive, cross my heart,' and she made a sign on her chest, saying the while, 'Spit in your eye and hope to die if I tell a lie.'

'Oh! Auntie Hannah. Fancy you remembering

that. Every time I told a lie I used to come out with it.'

'Yes, I know; you were an absolute imp. Still are in part.'

'Thanks, Auntie Hannah.' The young girl reached up and impulsively kissed Hannah on the cheek, then said, 'I can go up and tell Mam now that you're staying on so I can go to the party?'

'Yes; do that. But don't be surprised if she tries to put a spoke in your wheel; you insist that I said I'm not going anywhere.'

In the kitchen Eddie said, 'What was all that palaver about in the hall? Maggie getting at you to stay on? Well, here's somebody that's telling you you're not staying on. You're not wanted after the dinner's over, so get yourself away then. Likely, if I know anything, you've got a date.'

'Likely, if you know anything, Eddie, you're wrong. The only thing I need to do is use the phone, and I don't want any listeners-in.'

'As if I would!'

'As if you wouldn't.'

'Have you still got the telephone extension?'

'Yes. Yes, it's in the garden shed. That's my new office and the only place around here where I can find a little peace.'

Hannah made no laughing retort to this, but went out of the kitchen, through the scullery and into the back garden, at the far end of which was a wooden hut.

Sitting on a stool before the rough bench that

acted as a desk, she rang directory enquiries, gave them David's name and address and was given his number.

She did not immediately phone the number, but for a moment sat considering: she could see him this evening, and go to St Martin's with him. The only other time would be on Thursday, but then only for a few hours and by lying again.

She rang David's number. 'Yes; can I help you?' The voice was Peter's, and she said, 'It's me, Peter, Hannah Drayton.'

'Oh, hello, madam.'

'Hello, Peter,' she said. 'Could I have a word with . . .' she hesitated not knowing whether to say 'David' or 'your master', so on a laugh she said, 'the man of the house?'

'Oh, madam; the man of the house left about ten minutes ago. But he'll be back shortly, because he's having lunch at home today. Look; can you give me your number? Are you at home?'

'No, Peter; I'm at my sister's.'

After she'd read out the number to him he said, 'He'll be so sorry to have missed you, but I'm sure he'll contact you straight away. It's a lovely day, isn't it, madam?'

'Yes, very, Peter.'

After a pause his voice came again, soft and consoling: 'I hope nothing is wrong, madam. You're not in any trouble?'

Her answer came high and bright, saying, 'Oh, no! Peter. Nothing like that. My sister's hurt her back and is in bed, and she has four children and a husband who knows much more about selling vegetables than cooking them.'

He laughed and said, 'So you're going to be the ministering angel and take over, is that it, madam?'

'Something like that, but without the angel, Peter.'

'Oh, spiritual bodies always come in disguise. Anyway, madam, I shall tell Mr David as soon as he comes in that you've phoned, and I'm sure you will be hearing from him shortly.'

'Thank you, Peter. Goodbye.'

'Goodbye, madam.'

Yes; no doubt, now he had the number, she'd be hearing from him, and pronto . . .

It was just on twelve when she had phoned and it was half-past one before the six of them were seated around the table, Janie's meal having been taken upstairs on a tray. As yet the telephone had not rung. So she told herself that perhaps David didn't have his Sunday meal until two o'clock.

'It seems funny, Auntie Hannah, to see you sitting in Mam's chair.'

'It feels funny to me, Winnie, and I'm not going to sit in it much longer, I can tell you.'

Eddie turned to six-year-old Winnie, who was sitting next to John, and said, 'Cut his meat up for him, will you, pet?'

'Oh, hell's bells! Why do I always have to do everything for him?'

Winnie banged on the table, which bounced all their plates, and there was silence for a moment while all eyes were turned on Eddie, but his were concentrated on his daughter and he said, 'I'll hell's bells you across your backside until you can't sit if I hear any more of that.'

With an effort to keep her tongue quiet, Hannah now resumed her eating. Eddie, of all people, going for one of his children.

There was a tremor now in Winnie's voice as she said, 'Well, you're always saying that, Dad, and worse.'

'I might be, miss, saying that and worse, but that's not for you to repeat; and you know what your mam said; if she hears about you using language like that again she's going to your headmistress.'

When Winnie began to snivel Maggie said, 'That's it, Dad, set a match to oily waters. If she starts blubbering you know what happens, she never stops, and then we'll be having Mam crawling downstairs. Likely she's heard the banging on the table and is wondering what's happening down here.'

'And you, miss! when I want your advice I'll ask for it. Now get on with your meal and thank God you've got a meal to eat. That's what the lot of you should do.'

When Hannah said in a prim voice, 'Me included, Daddy?' there was a splutter from all those at the table. Even John recognised there was something to laugh about, so he laughed and beat his fork in the middle of his gravy, so causing more consternation now as Claire shouted at him, 'Look what you've done to my clean dress! You're a dirty so-and-so! John Harper.'

When Eddie did nothing now, only placed his elbow on the table and put his hand to his brow, a warning signal seemed to cover them all and, quite surprisingly, they all got on with their meal, even John.

It was just on three o'clock. The dishes had been washed and put away, the dining room tidied, the sitting room likewise. John, replete after a cleaned plate and a bowl of fruit salad and cream, was sleeping peacefully now by the side of his mother. Claire was watching television, and in their bed-room six-year-old Winnie was watching Maggie get ready for the party at the big house. In the hall Eddie was saying to Hannah, 'What are you going to do with yourself now until teatime? One thing I would do is put your feet up.'

'And what are you going to do?'

'Tell you what I'm going to do, Hannah, I'm going to soak in a bath in a quiet house. I've never heard it so quiet. You'd think it was empty.'

'Well, in that case I'm going upstairs to sit by your wife and have a natter.'

'She'll like that, Hannah. Oh, she will.' He was nodding at her. 'I'm going to tell you something on the quiet, Hannah. I've never voiced it before, but I know it's true. She misses out here. She's a good mother and you couldn't get a better wife, but she misses out. She misses you. She misses her own kind. The only ones she comes in contact with are my sort.'

At this Hannah put in quickly, 'Well, she could

do a lot worse, let me tell you, Eddie. A damn sight worse.'

He laughed. 'It's funny to hear you swear, Hannah. Better not let the kids hear else that'll be a signed licence for them. Yet it's nice of you, all the same; but I know what I'm talking about: she wasn't brought up among my sort; she fell into it, and let herself down a rung or two, I know, when she did it, and I shall never forget it. I love her and care for her and always shall; and you know something? Although she would never admit to it, she would like the kids, the girls anyway, to go to a convent school somewhere.'

'Well, that's easy, there're plenty about.'

'Oh, I think our Miss Maggie is past that now.'

'Don't you believe it! Maggie would jump at the chance to improve herself; she's made that way. Why is she dying to go to this house today? Because it's a big one and the young daughter has swanked about it. Now, as I see it, you can help in that way. You've been talking about getting a bigger house – you've got the money – oh yes, you have, I know you have. You needn't move to a different area; there are bigger houses around here. Buy one, don't rent it, and get a decent garden. And you know something, Eddie? Janie was pretty artistic in her early days, and she would be again if she had the space and time. And time will come. But what she'd like now is for her children to be given a sound education, like she herself had and does her best to hide.'

'Aye, you're right there, she does her best to hide it. Needs thinking about. Not that I haven't thought about it, but in a different way. However, thanks, Hannah; you've set my mind working. You see, it's a funny thing you came today and we had this bit of talk, because between you and me I've got the chance of a house up Grange Avenue – there's some lovely places up there – but being me I thought we'd stick out like sore thumbs, and I hate to be patronised. My God! I do; I can't stand it. But seeing how you've put it today, well, I know this house is on the market and it's sticking, 'cos they want too much for it, but by the next time you come she'll probably have some news for you.'

Pushing out her lips and wagging her head now, Hannah took her fist and knocked it against his chest saying, 'Good for you, Eddie, good for you,' and they smiled at one another.

And then it was his turn to punch her gently on the chest, saying, 'Yeah, I think so, you know. Anyway, here's one off to have that cleansing bath,' and at this he turned from her, singing softly, 'If you wash me in the water that you wash your dirty daughter, then I shall be whiter than the whitewash on the wall.'

He was still humming as he climbed the stairs, but when there was a ring at the doorbell he paused and looked down at her, and she up at him, and she said, 'I'll answer it, go on.'

When she drew open the door her mouth opened in surprise and she said, 'You! How did you . . .? Oh, why did you? Oh, dear me!'

'What is it?' Eddie was at her shoulder now, to see a tall man standing on the step,

'I . . . I've just called to pick Hannah up,' the man said. 'I presume you're her brother-in-law?' David looked from one to the other. 'We were to meet in town, but I thought I'd save her the journey. May . . . may I come in?'

Hannah and Eddie stood apart and David walked between them into the hall, saying, 'I hope I'm not intruding.'

'Of course you are! You should have phoned first!'

To Eddie she said, 'This is Mr . . . Craventon.'

'Oh, yeah? Well, let's shut the door and sit down for a minute and get to know each other. Would you like to come this way?'

Eddie led the way into the sitting room, adding, 'Though I don't think there needs to be any more introduction: I'm her brother-in-law, she's my sister-in-law.' Eddie was grinning as he pointed to Hannah. 'My wife's upstairs on her back suffering from sciatica, and I was just about to go and have a bath after a hard morning's work in the kitchen; and so I'll leave you to fight it out. I'll be down later, Hannah.' Eddie left the room, leaving Hannah red in the face as she stared at David, saying, 'I don't think this is very clever of you.'

'I wasn't meaning to be clever, I only knew that if I'd phoned you you'd have put me off until Thursday, and quite honestly I couldn't wait that long.'

She swallowed deeply, then began to cough, and

as he made to walk towards her she said, 'If you pat me on the back I'll hit you.'

At this he let out a smothered laugh, saying, 'I don't doubt it. But what's wrong in me coming here? And, by the way, I liked what I saw of your brother-in-law. May I hope to meet your sister before I leave? That's if I'm offered a cup of tea or anything like that. If we'd been at the flat, Peter would have had the tea tray in by now.'

'Oh, yes, Peter and the flat. You can joke about it, but I must tell you, if Janie'd been here to meet you, she'd have wanted things to be different. She's like that. He might appear rough and she might talk rough, but with her it's all on the surface, and she still feels she knows how things should be done.'

'Oh! Hannah, don't worry! I'm sure from what you've told me about her she's the least prim and proper person in the world.'

But upstairs the least prim and proper person in the world was struggling to raise herself on her elbows as, looking up at her husband, she said, 'He's downstairs?'

'That's what I said, and he's a smart bloke, as smart as any I've met. Quite the gentleman. No wonder she's fallen for him.'

'Ssshh!' Janie now looked at her daughter in her white blouse and short skirt, and then to the equally wide-eyed Winnie standing next to her, and when this little madam said, 'Who's that man talking to Auntie Hannah? Is he her boyfriend?' Janie almost screamed at her, only checking it in time by saying, 'Keep your tongue quiet, miss! Auntie Hannah hasn't got a boyfriend, he . . . he's just an acquaintance.'

'What's he look like, Dad?' Maggie was looking up at her father, and he said, 'Well, what you'd likely call the tops: tall, good-looking, and talks just like me, proper, like, you know.'

When Maggie pulled a face at him and thrust her hand into his arm, saying, 'Your lingo suits me fine, guv'nor,' Janie fell back on the bed saying, 'Oh, my God! it gets worse.'

'Mam . . . Mam' – Maggie was bending over her mother – 'if he's nice enough for Auntie Hannah to like him – and he'd have to be nice for Auntie Hannah to prefer him to Uncle Humphrey – well, he won't mind how we talk.'

'Listen to me, girl' – Janie was hissing into her daughter's face now – 'he will mind. If he's a gentleman he'll say nothing but he'll take it all in, and he'll reckon it up when he gets out of the house: Who are these people anyway? he'll ask. Why am I mixing with them?'

'Oh, hold your hand a minute' – Eddie was now wagging his finger down at her – 'if I thought he was that kind of a bloke I'd put my foot in his . . .' All eyes were on him while they waited for the word; and when he said, 'bottom' they spluttered. 'Anyway,' he added, 'he'll want to come up and see you.'

'You'll not let him in this room. Where d'you think you're off to, Maggie?'

'I'm just going downstairs, Mam.'

'You are not, miss. Just you leave them alone for a time.'

'Well, Mam; if they were going to have a row it's been very quiet, and it should be over by now, anyway, and I want to see what all the fuss is about and judge if he's the kind I should go after.'

'Oh, my God! What things come into her! I'll have to get out of this.' Janie was pushing herself up on her elbows again when Eddie, quite unceremoniously, thrust her back, causing her to squeal; then his voice was loud with contrition, saying, 'Oh, I'm sorry, love. I'm sorry,' and turning on his two daughters he said, 'Get yourselves to . . . get down those stairs before I help you down! Go on!'

The two girls ran from the room and down the stairs, but on reaching the hall they looked at each other and Winnie whispered, 'What shall we do? How will we go in?'

'Just knock on the door,' said Maggie pertly, 'like this,' and she walked towards the sitting-room door and tapped on it, saying, 'Can we come in, Auntie Hannah?'

When the door was opened, their Auntie Hannah glared down at them and said, 'Have you ever before knocked on the door and asked to come into your own sitting room?'

'N-n-n-no, Auntie Hannah. But we . . . we thought you might be . . . well, b-b-b-busy, like.'

The laughter that came from behind Hannah made her turn round and say, 'Please!'

'All right. All right. But would you like to leave it to me and let me introduce myself?'

As the tall man sidled round Hannah the two children backed away, all the time staring at him.

'So you're Maggie, the eldest?' David was addressing the silk-bloused, bum-freezered Maggie, and she, smiling widely at him, answered, 'Yes, sir; I'm Maggie and I've been in charge of the house for some days because Mam's in bed with a bad back; but Auntie Hannah made the lunch today and said she'd stay on. That's why I can go to the party. I was invited to a party, but I couldn't have gone if Auntie Hannah hadn't come.'

'What kind of party is it? A birthday party?'

'I'm . . . I'm not quite sure. I don't think it's her birthday, she just wants . . . well—' Maggie cast a glance towards Hannah before she added, 'I think she just wants to swank about her big house. She's always on about it. She says it's got a conservatory . . . I ask you! that's posh, isn't it?'

'I'd say.' David was nodding down at her now.

'Have you got a big house?' she went on.

'Are you going to that party or are you not?'

'Yes, I'm going, Auntie Hannah, but there's plenty of time. It isn't till four o'clock.'

'Well it's a quarter-past three now, and you've got to get there.'

'Oh, I'll do it.' Quite nonchalantly now, Maggie turned her attention from Hannah back to this tall good-looking fellow who, she had decided, was the type she would go for when she grew up, and she took up the conversation where she had left it by repeating, 'Well, have you got a big house?'

'I wouldn't call it big, but it's not small either. It has a large sitting room, but I have to use it as a dining room, too.' His descriptions were interrupted by Hannah almost bawling at Maggie now, saying, 'You needn't sit yourselves down there.'

'Only for a minute, Auntie Hannah, please.' It was such a polite appeal that Hannah closed her eyes, turned about and leant her forearm on the mantelpiece and stared down into the fireless grate.

'You were saying?'

David chortled and looked appealingly at Hannah's back; then rubbing his hand over his mouth, said, 'Yes, I was saying about my flat. There's another one above it – my friend lives in that – and, below, there's a basement flat, which is full of books. You see, the house is divided into three flats, so I suppose you could say it's quite big.'

'I . . . I like to look at houses, all kinds of houses and flats, because I think I might take up designing. You can do it at the technical college here and—'

She was hauled up from the couch by Hannah gripping her shoulder, and she cried out in her usual ordinary voice, 'Aw, Auntie Hannah, give over! This is a new top.'

Hannah did not reply, but, almost dragging her niece from the couch, she propelled her towards the door, calling to Winnie as she went, 'You too! Come on.' Once the door was open she pushed them both into the hall, from where Maggie turned on her and said, 'You're a spoilsport, Auntie Hannah!'

Without answering, Hannah stepped back into the sitting room and closed the door none too gently behind her; then she stood looking up the room to where David was sitting almost doubled up with suppressed laughter.

By now Hannah wanted to laugh too, but at the same time she was vexed that he had sought her out like this. What would happen, she thought, if for some reason Humphrey should come home and, not finding her there, take it into his head to find out if she was at Janie's and put in an appearance?

When the voice said, Damn Humphrey! she again chastised it and recalled that Humphrey had looked at her very strangely on Thursday night: he was no fool; he had sensed a change in her. What if he should make it his business to try to find out what had caused it? Perhaps she could put it down to writing her children's book – he knew she had been on that for some time – but now that it had been taken seriously, would he blame that for creating a change in her so quickly?

'Come on, Hannah; sit down beside me. Forgive me; but I have two excuses: I've already told you one, that I couldn't bear to think I wasn't going to see you until Thursday; the other is, I was lonely.'

'Well, what have you done on other Sundays till now?'

'Well, I've tried walking in the parks. I think I know every one. I'm suspect, I think, in one or two.' He grinned at her now. 'Sometimes I drop into a church. Oh, don't look so surprised, it didn't seem to matter what church so long as it was open. And not many of them are now, you know. I prefer them empty, although I've sometimes found myself in the middle of a service. I can't remember ever feeling happy on a Sunday. D'you know, if I were in the middle of the Sahara Desert and I'd lost my memory, I'd know when it was Sunday. Sundays have a queer knack of forcing themselves upon you, no matter where you are; but I have never enjoyed one as I have today, especially during the last few minutes. She's a bag of mischief, that one, isn't she?'

'She's a little monkey! Very good in parts, but only in parts. She'll take some handling in four or five years' time.'

'How old is she?'

'Ten.'

'No! Just ten? Well, well! I think she'll take some handling sooner than in a few years' time. I thought she'd be twelve or thirteen in that outfit of hers. Anyway, I hope I'll be allowed to stay until she comes back from the party.'

'Oh, I'm not sure about that.'

'Well, what shall we do? I mean, what shall *I* do, and what will you do if I'm put out? I'll just wander around waiting for you to leave, and you'll just hang around in here doing your good turn for the day and likely stretching it out to annoy me. Isn't that so?'

'No, it isn't.' Her voice was low and tired-sounding now. 'And you know it isn't.'

She lay back in the corner of the couch, and he, too, lay back and turned his head towards her, asking softly, 'What is it about you that attracted me from the first sight of you? because you were dressed very plainly that morning; not dowdy, really, but not to your age. That long grey coat puts years on you.'

'Thank you!'

'Oh, you're welcome. I can give you tips on what

would suit you for different occasions: you should never wear square necks, because you have rather broad shoulders.'

She sat up straight now, her body seeming to bristle with indignation; and she wasn't soothed when he added, 'But they're beautiful shoulders. Some women have nothing with which to prop up their dresses or coats; their shoulders slope too much, and they're often pigeon-chested with it. And you can bet your life they pad themselves out.'

When her body began to shake he pulled her to him and for the first time she felt his arms about her, and when she started to laugh loudly he became slightly concerned, saying, 'Shhh! Shhh! They'll hear you upstairs.' Then his tone changed as he said, 'Oh, don't! Why're you crying? Please! What have I said? I'm a fool; I'm an idiot; I keep trying to amuse you, to make you laugh. Now this. It's all right. Please! It's all right.'

She felt down the length of her dress, hoping to discover a pocket with a handkerchief. Then, when he held his out to her, she grabbed it and wiped her face quite roughly all over; and she did not return the handkerchief to him, but kept it in her joined hands, saying, 'Oh, David! I'm all mixed up.'

'I know that; I know that; and I know I'm the cause of it, but I must admit that I'm happy that I am. You know, I cannot take it in that we met only last Thursday; it seems that you've been in my mind for years. Your face, your manner, your voice, everything about you; and in this short time you seem to have emerged like a butterfly from its chrysalis; you become more beautiful though more fragile, more susceptible to hurt. Yet all the while I feel you're opening your eyes to love. Yes, I've had to say that, because, like a butterfly, you seem to have come to a resting stage to let your wings dry off in the sun; and once they've dried you'll give yourself over to life and living.'

She was staring into his face, thinking, Those words! all fanciful; yet . . . yet I know what he means, and I am, I'm coming alive. I know it, I know it; but what's going to happen when, like that butterfly's, my wings have dried? What about Humphrey?

She forced herself to get there before the voice, and she cried at it, Well! if I'm always where he expects me to be at a certain time, then things will go on as they are, at least between us, but . . . but not with this man here. Oh no, no! When the butterfly's wings are really dry, things will happen. It's inevitable. But . . . Fancy thinking along those lines!

Well, why not? Why not think along those lines? . . . she knew where the lines were leading, didn't she? And oh, how she longed that they would soon come together.

'What is it?'

'Nothing. Nothing.' She rubbed her hand across her chest. 'I had too much to eat; I always do when I come here. A slight touch of indigestion. Would you like some tea?'

'Did you have meat for lunch?'

'We did; sirloin.'

'And you're going to drink tea? All right, if you can drink tea, I can drink tea.'

'Did you have meat?'

'Yes, roast lamb. And that's meat, but not as heavy as sirloin, so I'm sure my delicate stomach will accept a cup of tea and gladly. Shall I help you make it?'

He was about to rise from the couch when she pushed him back, saying, 'No! Please stay where you are. If I'm not mistaken you'll be having two other visitors shortly, because I can hear John's voice. Then there's Claire: she's been watching television. She's four and a bit, but takes after her eldest sister and always wants to know the reason why, so prepare yourself if she comes in.'

David lay back on the couch and looked about him. Everything in the room reminded him of the high-street shop window. All the bits and pieces were modern, some the worse for wear, such as the couch he was sitting on. The accompanying armchairs and the other odd pieces of furniture set tight against the wall, mostly for safety's sake, he imagined: the sideboard and drinks cupboard; the cabinet that suggested it was a radiogram. And yet everything appeared very clean: polished where polish was needed, and the soft grey silk-ridged curtains framing the windows looked fresh; indeed, the room said a lot for someone with four children.

When the door opened he pulled himself up from his sitting position, expecting to see the children, but when he saw it was the head of the household who was vigorously rubbing his wet head with a towel he rose to his feet, saying awkwardly, 'Hannah's gone to make tea.'

'Oh, that's good. That's good. Sit yourself down; no need to stand on ceremony here.'

'I'm glad to hear that.'

Eddie stopped his rubbing and peered over the edge of the towel at the visitor. He did not know quite how to take that remark, so he gave no answering quip, but said, 'Tell me, is it a fact that you've only known Hannah since last Thursday?'

'Yes; it's a fact, but I can't believe it either.'

'I understand you're married but parted.'

'Yes; that's right too.'

'I'm not just quizzing you out of curiosity, you know; we're very fond of Hannah. My wife's only four years older than her but at times you'd think she was her mother, the way she worries over her.'

'Has there been need to worry over her?'

For a moment Eddie said nothing, but, taking a comb from his hip pocket, he began to comb his hair. Parting it at the side, he drew the thick wet mass across his head and away from his brow; then, folding up the wet towel neatly, he laid it over the arm of the chair before answering, 'The answer to that is yes and no. First, no, because there was no need to worry over anything untoward that Hannah had done in her life, except perhaps that she had been stupid enough to marry a stuffed shirt, and that on the rebound, because their father, a widower, was about to take on another wife. Hannah had been housekeeper enough to both her mother and him, expecting she would be there for the rest of her life, but one thing she wasn't going to do was to take on a stepmother. So she goes and marries the first man who proposes to her. At least, that's how I see it: any port in the storm, if you know what I mean. But, on the other hand, she won't have a word said against him. Well, not really. She keeps saying he's kind. But why is he kind and hurtful at the same time? Marriage, as you know, is a two-way business, give and take; from the bed to the breakfast, and from there to Horlicks or cocoa last thing.

'I'm going to ask you something. I suppose I shouldn't, you'll say it's none of my damn business, but, as I've just pointed out to you, we are her nearest and dearest, so to speak. I'd like a straight answer to my question and I'll know if I'm getting one or not. I've been about a bit; like your friend Micky McClean, I know the ropes.' He grinned at David, but David was looking him straight in the face, for he knew what was coming. 'What I'm asking is, is this just a passing fancy? You look the kind of bloke who could pick up anybody anywhere, and you've got the style and that, and likely she's already fallen for it, but I want to know how you feel. All right, you're married and you've been separated for a long time. I don't know anything about that part of it, the whys or the wherefores. But I want to know if this is an ups-a-daisy: We've had some fun, no hard feelings, eh? You know the line; it's done every day; and if the girl's unlucky there's a bun in the oven. Now you needn't bother getting up.' He put his hand out and flapped it slowly towards David's face. 'If that happened to her, she wouldn't have a leg to stand on, 'cos she couldn't stick it on him, if you see what I mean.'

David's mouth was slightly open and his eyes were wide. What he said now, and softly, was, 'No, I don't know what you mean; but I'll come back to that. However, first let me tell you, for my part this is not what you call an ups-a-daisy. I've never felt for anyone as I do for Hannah, and I can't understand it.' His voice was harsh now and he stressed each word. 'And I can't say I'm happy about it, but since I saw her last Thursday morning, as I've told you, I can't get her out of my mind. She seems to have always been there, somebody I've been looking for but just missed on the way, and now I've found her I don't want to let her go. That's why I risked pushing myself into your family today, otherwise I would have had to wait till Thursday, if then, in order to see her. I felt I just couldn't wait, so there you have my answer. And there's a faint hope in me that she feels the same way, but won't own up to it yet. This kind Humphrey whom she has on her mind all the time . . . dear kind Humphrey. I've never met the fellow, but I hate him already. Now I've answered your question, would you mind explaining what you meant just then?'

'What d'you mean? explain it. I thought I'd made it plain enough.'

'You said that if she . . .' he couldn't bring himself to say 'had a bun in the oven', instead he said, 'found herself pregnant, she couldn't blame it on her husband. What did you mean by that? Is he a . . .'

'Well, I'm talking out of turn here, but . . . I'll tell

you because I have a feeling I can trust you. As far as I can get out of my wife, somewhere along the line Hannah had an allergy, and whether he took that as an excuse to have a separate room or was really afraid of catching something from her, I'll never know, and she'll never know and she won't ask, but from—'

'Dear God!'

'What did you say?'

Leaning forward, David put his elbows on his knees, then covered his face with his hands for a moment before looking up at Eddie again and saying, 'I merely said Dear God!'

'Yes, well, that statement covers a lot of things, it saves a body saying what they really think. But I know what you're thinking at this minute – and another thing that's just struck me is if my wife knew I was talking to you about Hannah like this she'd brain me. At least she'd have a damn good try, 'cos what she told me was after Hannah had come to her in dire trouble and told her.'

Of a sudden, Eddie dropped on to the couch, and, looking towards the tall fellow who was still sitting with his elbows on his knees, his head bent down, he said, 'I bet when you were coming along here today you didn't know what your reception would be, either from her or from us. Knowing I was once a pal of Micky McClean, you wouldn't have been expecting someone with an Oxford accent, although at the same time you wouldn't have thought that your eyes would have been opened so wide, would you?'

David straightened up and drew in a long breath; then turning to Eddie he said, 'You're right. You're right. But I can tell you one thing: I'm very glad I came. I knew I was presuming, but I couldn't help myself, and I see now it had to be like this because she would never have told me anything about her personal life. How long has she been married?'

Eddie thought a moment, then said, 'Oh, four years. Yes, it'll be four years. She's twenty-nine.'

David nodded, saying, 'Yes. Yes, I think she mentioned it somewhere. Four years.' He shook his head, then again repeated, 'Four years. No wonder she had that look on her face.'

'What look?' Eddie was sitting up, attentive again.

'Oh, when she came into the office, Mr Gillyman's place, you know, with the manuscript of her book that he wants to publish, she had the most odd look about her, like someone walking in a dream. Her clothes seemed to be moving but not she herself. Then for a moment I changed my opinion when I realised she had a sharp wit; and Gilly, that's Mr Gillyman, and his wife, they both felt there was something about her. Natasha put a name to it, "lost", and I recall I added "hurt", and that's right, don't you think? She's been lost for a long time and hurt too.'

'You're right there, mate. Yes, you're right there. By the way, what's your name again?'

'David.'

'Well, I'll call you that, eh?'

'Please do. And yours I know is Eddie.' They

smiled faintly at each other now and nodded; then Eddie, bouncing up from the couch, exclaimed, 'Where's that bloody . . . excuse me, David! it's just a habit, tea. She's had time to go to the tea gardens and pick the stuff.'

'Shut up! I can hear you. Open the door!'

When Eddie pulled the door open there was Hannah, her arms spread wide, holding a large wooden tray on which was tea, set for the three of them.

David had followed Eddie to the door and was looking at the two children, Maggie carrying a cake stand holding slices of bread and butter and a large cake, and Winnie carrying a small tray on which there was a glass dish full of jam.

David saw that Maggie was determined to make her entry into the room, but the younger girl, looking up at him and handing him the tray, said, 'Be careful, it's runny. It's home-made, but me mam didn't boil it enough. She never does.'

The voice from the sitting room was loud: 'Winnie! Get upstairs and stay with your mother. Has she got her tea?'

'She's got everything she requires. It's been seen to.' Maggie was answering her father, although she was looking at David, and he, smiling at her, went as far as to give her a wink, at which she spluttered and almost upset the cake stand; and when her father said, 'What's up with you, girl?' she answered, 'Well, he winked at me.'

'What!'

'He did, Dad.'

'Are you going to the party or not?' Hannah's voice had no laughter in it. 'If you're not outside that door within the next minute there'll be no party for you. And what's more, I've had enough of you for one day.'

The girls gone, and none too quietly, as Maggie had made a point of banging the door, Eddie now turned to Hannah, saying, 'That girl needs taking in hand. I'll have to see to it.'

David enjoyed his tea. He talked quite a lot, mostly to Eddie and about Peter. Eddie was now saying, 'Well, I think you're damn lucky,' and David replied, 'Nobody knows that better than I do.'

Turning to Hannah, Eddie said, 'I don't know what you've got in mind to do, missis, but I know what I've got in mind for you to do. I'm going to take this lot in the kitchen and start the washing-up and you're going to take our friend here upstairs and introduce him to my wife.'

'Oh, no. You know what Janie said.'

'Yes, I know, she'd give me hell if I did any such thing. But what I also know about her is that she'd give me hell if I didn't, and this might be the only chance she has of meeting him.' He turned to David and said, 'I'm not giving you a permanent invitation to pop in here every Sunday, 'cos as far as I can see you'll cause havoc among my family, and I think one lot of havoc is enough for you to deal with. What d'you say?'

'Oh, on that point I think I'll leave it to your wife. If she invites me to lunch on a Sunday, well, then, I don't suppose there's anything you can do about it.'

'I'll be buggered! Here's another one can get away with murder.' At this he picked up the tea tray and marched out, saying, 'You, Hannah, leave those where they are and do as I tell you.'

And to this Hannah answered him sweetly, 'Yes, brother-in-law. Anything to make you happy.'

'I can see why you like to come here at weekends,' David said; 'it really is a home.'

'Oh,' said Hannah, 'you can say that again. You haven't been here when they're rowing: when Janie's not going to stand any more and when he's going to emigrate to Australia. Well, come on, let's get it over with. There'll be high jinks after you've gone, I know that.'

On the landing she tapped on Janie's bedroom door and called, 'Can we come in?'

'No, you may not.'

She opened the door and said, 'Thank you, sister.' Then she beckoned David into the room, and there he was looking down on the supine figure of the Cockney lad's convent-bred wife. 'Good afternoon, Mrs Harper. I'm sorry to see you laid low.'

Janie stared up at him, and what she said, and in a quite refined voice, was, 'It isn't fair. I hate to be taken at a disadvantage.'

Hannah turned away and looked towards the window. Oh dear, dear . . . this was Sister Veronica speaking on one of her do-or-don't mornings: 'You chew on your words with your teeth and spit them out through pursed lips. Each word you utter is born

145

in your brain. It should be special, whether it is to be used in praise or reprimand or merely ordinary conversation about the weather. It should begin, as I have told you, at the back of your mouth, and, no! Janette Baker, we are not going to say, The rain in Spain falls mainly on the plain – I can see your lips already mouthing this well-worn saying. Instead, you will say, I am here to learn how to speak the English language correctly, and Sister Veronica is going to see that I do so, if she has to keep the whole class in for a half hour later this afternoon, which means that hockey will be off.'

Hannah turned towards the bed. Dear! dear! One thing was sure, Mrs Harper was doing Sister Veronica proud.

'Hannah tells me you deal in books; a great number and variety of them, so I understand.'

'Yes, you could say that, Mrs Harper, a great number and variety of them. I think there must be at least three thousand in the rooms under my flat, and that's only one store room. My employer, Mr Gillyman, is what you would call a fanatic where books are concerned.'

'It must be an interesting position.'

'I don't know about interesting, but I can tell you it's very dusty and thirst-making, besides time-consuming and back-breaking, because my employer goes to as many sales as time allows. He might just go for one particular book but that book might be part of a lot of fifty or a hundred.'

'I used to read a lot at one time, when there was time, of course,' Janie said. 'I remember I was well into Hugh Walpole and the Herries series when I left school.'

'Oh, yes, the Herries series. He was given a title, wasn't he?'

'Oh, was he?'

'Yes; I don't know whether it was for his writing or not, but he wrote some smashing tales.'

Hannah was thinking: Hugh Walpole and the Herries series; she doubted if David had ever read such romantic books as those. Oh, she'd have to get out of the room, because if Janie kept this up she'd surely burst out laughing. And yet it was her true self Janie was showing, so why should she laugh?

Looking at David as she moved towards the door, she said, 'I'll leave you to find your way downstairs; I must go and see why the younger members of the tribe are so quiet.'

She noted that Janie didn't say, 'Oh, don't go, Hannah,' but smiled at her, a strange smile.

After the door had closed on Hannah, Janie let out a long breath, and when she spoke again it wasn't in her high-falutin' convent-bred voice, but in a low and serious tone. 'We may not have many minutes alone; one or other of the kids are bound to come up, but I want to ask you something.'

Before she could proceed further David put out his hand and, taking hers, said, 'The answer is yes: I'm serious about your sister, very serious. How it has come about in four days, I don't know; indeed, it came about in less than four minutes, I think, from the moment I first saw her, in fact. Oh, yes; I'm very serious about her.'

'So . . . so you won't hurt her in any way, I mean . . . just make use of her and then walk out?'

'Oh, please! You haven't had much time to form an opinion of me, but I'd hoped you wouldn't suggest that.'

'I'm sorry. But I love Hannah, and she needs looking after. She's still a girl. She's been married to that individual for four years and he's not playing fair by her, has never done so, it seems to me, yet she's so loyal to him it makes me sick. Just because he's kind and, she says, so thoughtful. As I see it, and from the very first, he's kind only to secure his own ends, and what those ends are beats me, especially given their present way of life. Has she told you anything about him, I mean personally?'

'No. No, but don't worry, your husband has.'

'Oh, dear me!' She screwed up her eyes for a moment. 'Trust the ambassador of diplomacy; yet' – she laughed softly – 'whatever he knows, it never goes any further than me, which is a good thing. But if only she'd met someone like you at the beginning. Anyway, she has now and . . . and you won't let her slip through your fingers, will you? You know, she just might, she's got an outsize conscience: she mustn't do anything that'll hurt Humphrey. Oh! Humphrey. I know what I'd do with that City gent if I had my way.'

He laughed, then said, 'Well, I wish you had your way; it would make things a lot easier. I keep telling myself to make haste slowly, but you see the result, I'm sitting here now, after tracking her down, just because she couldn't meet me where we had arranged. And, oh dear! the thought of not seeing her till Thursday . . .'

'Oh yes, Thursday. He mustn't miss his bridge. If it was a woman I could understand, but no, it isn't; it's bridge, all right.'

'Then he goes away at the weekend to stay with his supposed aunt and uncle—'

'Oh, they're real enough,' she put in quickly. 'I wish they weren't. No; they're alive and kicking, both of them, and as narrow as the slit in a jeweller's eye.'

'A what?' He was nipping on his lower lip.

'Oh, that!' she laughed; 'as narrow as a slit in a jeweller's eye – that's one of Eddie's. Apparently it was a favourite of his mother's because,' she smiled, 'I might as well tell you, because he'll come out with it one day, likely when we're in company. You see, his mother had to go to the pawn shop pretty often, as did everybody else in his vicinity, I think, and the last resort for a woman was her ring. They'd watch the old pawnbroker put his eye to his magnifying glass and sometimes, when he turned to say, "No go, the stone's paste and there's not enough gold in the ring to cover a holy tooth," they'd raise the shop on him until he came up with some kind of an offer, perhaps as little as two shillings. They must have been terrible days for those women, yet they survived, and I've never met an unhappy one yet.'

'No; you're right about them seeming happy. Those I've met have been through all kinds of trouble yet they come up smiling and keep at it.'

'Yes, that's what's put my Eddie where he is today. He has a fine greengrocer's shop, you know, and he's opening another.'

'Good for him. I'm glad to hear it, and I can understand your being proud of him.'

Her face was straight as she said, 'You're just saying that, I know, but the truth is, I *am* proud of him.'

'No, I didn't say it lightly; I meant it. I can tell by your every word when you speak about him that you're proud of him, and rightly so.'

When she endeavoured to raise herself on her elbows, he said, 'What actually is it? Your spine?'

'No,' she said; 'it's the sciatic nerve. All I get from the doctor is being told to rest, or asked if I'd like some massage or told to try cool compresses: a bag of frozen peas from the freezer is suggested as likely to bring relief.' She laughed as she slumped back on to the pillow, saying, 'All that bag of peas did for me was to give me frostbite; I couldn't bear it.'

'You won't believe me', David said quickly, 'if I tell you I can give you a certain amount of ease, enough at least to enable you to sit up.'

'Yes? You've had medical training?'

'No; but my grandfather was troubled with sciatica in his hip and our old doctor showed my grandmother how to ease him by putting pressure on certain of the nodules. Would you like me to try?'

'Well . . . it's . . . oh, all right, why not?'

He stood up quickly. 'Your husband will have to give the go-ahead, and Hannah will have to help to turn you.'

'Are you serious?'

'Oh, yes; yes, I'm serious, all right, and it's such a simple thing.'

'Well, then, if you say you can ease the pain, then carry on. Go to the stairhead and give them a shout.'

He opened the door and, standing at the top of the stairs, he called, 'Is there anybody there?'

Both Hannah and Eddie appeared quickly from the kitchen, Eddie enquiring, 'What is it? What's up?'

'Would you and Hannah come upstairs for a minute?' he called to them.

At the foot of the stairs Hannah and Eddie exchanged glances; then he pushed her before him and they were soon in the bedroom and Janie was saying, 'He says' – she nodded towards David – 'he can ease this pain of mine; he knows a trick or two.'

'No, they're not tricks, just simple pressure. Would you like me to try it on her?'

He was looking at Eddie, whose reply was, 'I don't know so much. What're you going to do?'

'Just apply pressure to various points. You find out where the real sore spots are. You place your thumb on one and you press and I can tell you it hurts like billy-o: you've got to hold that for thirty seconds. By the time fifteen seconds have passed the pain should be easing, and when you come to thirty it should be gone. Now, if it hasn't gone, you're either on the wrong spot or it's too deep for this kind of treatment; but in nine cases out of ten it seems to work. I've seen my grandmother work what I thought were miracles on my grandfather. How about it?'

Janie looked at Eddie, then they both looked at Hannah and Hannah turned her full gaze on David and said, 'If I was in as much pain as she is I'd try anything.'

'Oh, let's get on with it without holding a board meeting. It's my body and I don't suppose it's the first bare buttock he's seen, so hoist me over on to my side, will you?'

Janie was addressing Eddie, then, turning her gaze on Hannah, she said, 'And you keep my nightie in place.'

Within seconds Eddie had turned her over on to her side. She was now facing away from them and when he exposed her buttock and Hannah drew up the bedclothes around her legs he half turned to her and, his head bobbing, he said, 'You bring some things on us on a Sunday afternoon, don't you?'

'Don't blame me.'

'Who else?'

'Will you two stop jabbering and let the witch doctor get on with the job?'

David was laughing heartily. 'I'd better kneel,' he said; 'I can put more pressure on that way than I could bending over her.'

Both Hannah and Eddie stood towards the foot of the bed now and watched David's thumb move round Janie's hip as if he were searching for something; then with a quick movement his thumb dug into the flesh and they all knew he had hit on a tender spot when Janie gave a gasp and a cry.

'Oh! God, that hurts,' she cried, to which David answered by counting seven, eight, nine, ten, eleven, twelve, thirteen, fourteen, before saying, 'Is it easing?' There was a slight gasp before Janie said, 'Funnily, yes, it is.'

'Nineteen, twenty: is that better?'

'Yes; yes, it's nearly gone.'

When he had reached thirty seconds he took his thumb away from the point and asked, 'You're sure?'

'Yes. It was a bit hellish at first, but, my goodness! I wouldn't have believed it.'

'Well, then, are you up to my trying another?'

'Oh, yes; you go on. Shoot as many as you can of them if there are more there.'

'Yes; I'm sorry to say there are more there, and most of them'll probably be as painful. Well, here goes: get ready!'

Within the next ten minutes, of the six bad pain spots he had relieved her of four. Now looking up at Eddie, whose face was showing his surprise, he said, 'Come down here and you try it.'

When Eddie was kneeling by his side, looking very self-conscious as he gazed at his wife's buttock, as if he'd never seen it before, David said, 'Let me find a sore spot.' And when Janie gave another yelp, he said, 'Yes, here's one. Now just place the pad of your thumb tight on it; now press for all you're worth and count up to thirty seconds.'

When fifteen seconds had passed, Janie's voice came at them, saying, 'It's going, but not quick enough, you're not pressing hard enough.'

'Well, I'll be . . .!' Eddie swallowed, then added, 'Well, how's that?'

'That's better. Yes, it's going now.'

When Hannah burst out laughing the two men looked at her, and she said, 'Janie, you should see his face. By the look on it you'd think he was opening his third fruit shop.'

This caused general laughter, and when Janie slowly turned round, she said, 'I wouldn't have believed it.' Then, looking up at David, she said simply, 'Thank you. Oh, thank you!'

'You're welcome. I recommend a dose of the medicine every day for the next week. By the way, I send my bills out once a quarter. You understand?'

'Oh, yes, sir. Yes.' Janie paused and glanced towards Hannah before looking at David again and adding, 'I wonder, sir, if you'd mind being paid in kind. A meal a dose, say? Sundays only.'

They were all laughing as the door burst open and before their surprised gazes there stood Maggie, who had apparently been crying.

And this fact brought her mother up on her elbows again with a jerk and a groan. 'What's the matter? Now what is it? Come here.'

As the girl made towards the bed David and Hannah moved back, but her father reached out and pulled her close to him, saying, 'What's up, love? Somebody been at you?'

Maggie shook her head. 'No, Dad. No.'

'You went to the party?'

'Yes, Mam. Yes.' Maggie nodded towards her mother and went on, 'And the table looked nice. She had only invited three of us, Belle Smith, Barbara Brown and me.'

'And was it a big house?'

'Well, Mam, not as big as she'd made out; and her granny lives upstairs; and they have a lodger too. He isn't very young, but he seems a nice man, and he was going to show us tricks after we'd had our tea. It looked as if everything was going to be very nice, and the granny was funny, she made us laugh. She made me promise I'd lend her my skirt, and I said I would and she'd be able to wear it 'cos she was little and thin; then the front doorbell rang and her mother went to answer it.'

She now cast her glance from one to the other and her voice gave a little break as she said, 'Then everything seemed to happen so quickly. He came in. It was Nanette's father. He'd brought her a present; and . . . and he was drunk.' She looked up at Eddie now, then added, 'Oh, Dad! he was so drunk; and he went for the lodger, who tried to put him out 'cos . . . 'cos he mustn't live there with them, and they fought and the table went over and smashed the cake. And the cake had looked lovely. And Nanette kept yelling, "No! Dad. No! Dad. Come away," and Belle and Barbara ran out screaming.'

'And what did you do?'

She looked at her mother. 'I left too, Mam, I was frightened, but I stood outside the open door. I saw the granny take something . . . I don't know what it was, but she hit the drunken man on the back of the head and he fell on the floor; and then Nanette's mother came to the door. She was crying something

155

awful and she said she was sorry, and I said it was all right and that we'd see Nanette tomorrow at school and tell her not to worry.'

When her father's arm tightened about her, Maggie gave a big heave, then turned and buried her head in his waist, sobbing loudly now.

'Poor woman' – Janie shook her head on the pillow – 'and the poor child! It'll be all over the school tomorrow.'

Her face streaming, Maggie seemed to almost spring out of her father's arms now as she turned towards her mother, crying, 'No! it won't, 'cos I told 'em what'd happen: I'd knock their bloody heads together if they said one word; and what's more I told them they wouldn't come to our house-warming party when we get our big house—' She glanced quickly up into her father's spreading countenance, the expression on which was impossible to describe, and she stuttered on, 'You . . . you said we were gonna move soon or something like that. Anyway, I told her . . . them, and . . . and what's more' – her voice trailed away as she held her father's eye – 'I said it was going to be a . . . a big place, but it was a secret . . . well, as yet.'

There was a movement in the room: Hannah was making for the door and David was behind her, and they didn't speak until they reached the sitting room, and there, holding her by the shoulders, he said, 'Now don't you start or else you'll have me at it, because that was the finest piece of melodrama I've seen in my life, and it was real. Oh, yes, it was real, all right. There's character for you: "I'll knock their bloody heads together!"'

Hannah blinked at him through her wet eyes; then in a low voice he said, 'In a short while we'll be leaving. You won't let me get off the train and see you home, I know that without asking, and there'll not be another opportunity, at least today, to say what I want to say. I love you; I need you; I want you.' When he jerked her into his embrace she gasped and was about to protest, saying, 'Oh, David,' when his mouth fell on hers. The kiss was long and hard, and at what stage of it her arms went around his neck she wasn't aware, but he held her all the closer. It was from this moment their life together began.

# Six

Humphrey was later than usual arriving home. It had turned half-past ten when she heard his key in the door.

Hannah was seated in the sitting room in front of the electric fire. She was in her dressing gown and had been looking through the Sunday paper. A book and a magazine lay on a table to her side. She had purposely placed them there. She trained her eyes on the newspaper while she waited for him to go through his routine: she could see him setting down his weekend case at the foot of the stairs, before opening the cloakroom door and placing his overcoat on a hanger.

Next he would wash his hands, stroke back his hair, square his shoulders and then, and only then, make his way into the sitting room. The washing of hands, stroking of hair, squaring of shoulders was the same as the bathroom routine that had at first amused, then irritated her, for to her it was as though he were preparing himself for some distasteful task.

As he entered the room she looked at him over the

edge of the paper and immediately detected that he wasn't wearing his usual pleased and patient expression. His first remark was, 'You've got the fire on. It's warm outside.'

And to this she replied, 'I've only been in a short while and the room felt chilly. Have you any objection to my putting the fire on?'

She watched his eyes widen; then, his voice stiff, he said, 'Of course not. Of course not, except that you must be the only one in the street who's feeling chilly tonight.'

'I find the fire comforting.'

He stared at her a moment longer, but made no remark on her statement.

She was folding up the newspaper as she said, 'Did you have a nice weekend?'

When he turned to her it was to say, 'Would you consider it a nice weekend having to placate two grumpy old people? It is very noticeable in the elderly. They get more self-opinionated: they make laws for others to keep; they get bees in their bonnets about certain subjects.'

He was standing at the far end of the fireplace, one arm resting against the mantelpiece, and quietly she asked, 'Subjects such as what?'

He turned to her as if startled and said, 'What did you say?'

She pulled herself forward in the chair, laid the folded paper on the side table, then said, 'You were saying that your aunt and uncle were getting very opinionated and had bees in their bonnets about certain subjects.'

'Oh, yes.' It was as if he were surprised and had been caught thinking aloud.

He now sat in a chair and crossed his long legs and lay back, then rubbed his hand over his eyes for a moment before he said, 'Oh, they pick something out of the paper, such as divorce, and actresses having so many husbands, and the immorality of it all.'

Dear, dear! he was upset. She looked at him intently. Divorce? Oh no, no; he'd always known what they thought about divorce. He'd once said they considered it to be a sin next to murder. But something certainly had upset him.

'How's your weekend been?' Things were topsy-turvy, for this was generally his first question on arriving home, and put over with a kindly smile as if he really were interested in how she had spent the weekend; and so now, when she answered, 'Oh, fine. Fine,' she had his whole attention.

'It wasn't as usual, then?'

'Not quite.' She now stood up; but he did not rise from his chair, only pulled himself to the edge of it and looked towards her, which made her want to say, I had a marvellous time on Saturday, and a much better one today; instead she said, 'Oh, I spent Saturday looking at London, places I've never seen, but all day today I've been at Janie's; she's in bed with a bad back, and so I had quite a busy day.'

'And apparently you enjoyed it?'

'Yes. Yes, I did. I helped to cook the dinner and see to things, and where there's children there's always a lot of laughter. Yes, I enjoyed it.'

He was on his feet now, standing at arm's length from her, and what he said caused her whole attitude to change.

'Well, as you're so happy doing domestic work, why don't you take over the complete running of the house? I've thought for a long time you haven't got enough to fill your days, and I don't see the need for Mrs Fenwick.'

Her voice came loud at him, crying, 'Oh no, you don't, Humphrey. And anyway, I'd think twice about it: you might be needing someone to do your housekeeping, because I'm looking for a job, I might as well tell you.' She hadn't been, but it was a thought. For a moment, she imagined he looked afraid, but then he gave an odd laugh and said, 'It was only a suggestion; I . . . I was just thinking about something to fill your days.'

'I have plenty to fill my days, at least my week-days, Humphrey. The weekends are something different, when I have no one coming in to lunch or in the evening. I have no one to speak to at all. Well, that being so, I'm going to make use of my time in future. I've been meaning to broach the subject with you for some time, but you've not given me the opportunity.'

With some surprise she saw that he appeared upset and that her suggestion was in some way putting him out, for his hand came out towards her. He didn't touch her, but nevertheless it was held out towards her as if in supplication as he said, 'Oh, now, don't let's be silly or hasty. You see, I . . . there's the yearly conference coming up, and

I . . . well, it's only for four days, as you know, but I thought that if we were allowed to take our wives, then you might . . . er . . . well . . . er' – he swallowed deeply – 'like to accompany me.'

She stared at him. This invitation, she realised, was impromptu. He'd never before asked her to accompany him on the foreign conferences. He was saying now, 'Wainwright; yes, of course he'll be there. He's cock-a-hoop since he won over the Burgoynes. They're the hardware people, you know, shops all over, oddments and bags and things.'

At this point she had a desire to laugh, so she turned from him and picked up the book and magazine, and as she went to pass him she couldn't resist saying, 'Hardware; they're stooping low, aren't they? On a level now, I should imagine, with fruit stalls in the market and barrow boys.' She half turned towards him. 'Why doesn't your company have a shot at them; there's money there. Oh, yes.'

'Hannah!' She was walking towards the door and his voice came as a command for her to stop; but she didn't immediately obey it. She had opened the door and was standing in the hall before she turned and looked back at him and said, 'Yes, Humphrey?'

She saw his Adam's apple bump twice up to his chin before he could speak: 'Sarcasm doesn't suit you,' he said, and then got in his own shot by adding, 'especially if it's on the barrow-boy level.'

He listened to her going up the stairs and was troubled: something had happened to her; she'd changed. It was all since last Thursday, when she'd taken her damn book to that publisher, who was known to be so eccentric he'd publish lavatory rolls.

He shuddered. Dear, dear! And after such a week-end. One shouldn't have to pay right into middle age for kindness shown in youth, but he knew that should he in any way lessen his weekly payments his whole future would be at stake, not just bleak but black; and he'd worked too long and put up with too much to let that happen.

When Hannah's door banged overhead he looked upwards and a strange thought came into his head: His whole future depended upon her.

# Seven

David was waiting for her at Tottenham Court Road Station, and when he saw her he hurried towards her but did not speak until they reached the street where, hugging her arm tightly, he asked quietly, 'Is it you?'

'Part of me.'

'Oh, I don't want part of you; and you know something? We have only two hours. This is ridiculous.'

She pulled her arm slightly from him as she said, 'Well, don't spoil it at the beginning.'

'Oh, my dear; look, tell me what you've been doing.'

'Well, Monday I went across to Janie's again. Believe it or not, she was up.'

'No!'

'Yes.'

'Well, I'm not really surprised. It does work.'

'Well, it's worked in her case; and she had Eddie at it again on Monday morning before he went out, looking for pressure points. Anyway, we talked: she passed judgement on you.'

'Yes?'

'Yes, what?'

'Don't be funny. What was the judgement?'

'Oh, she thought you were all right, just.'

He was hugging her arm again. 'Tuesday?'

'Yes, Tuesday: well, I went to the British Library.'

'What were you doing there?'

'Looking up styles of writing for children for the past hundred years.'

He smiled at her, saying, 'Oh, Gilly'll be very interested to hear about that. By the way, he's excited about your book, you know.'

'Really?'

'And he's going to ask Ollie Swinburne if he'll do the cover. He's a fine children's illustrator. You'll have a lot to discuss with him when you next come to the office.'

'I really can't believe it.'

'Well, it's true. It's all part of the fairy tale.'

'Yes' – and in a more sober tone – 'the fairy tale. That's what it seems like; not real, a fairy tale.'

His tone too was sober as he said, 'It's no fairy tale, Hannah, not for me. It's a piece of reality: you are what I've been waiting for for a long time. Oh, look!' – he put out his hand – 'it's beginning to rain; let's run.' And so, like two children, they ran until they came to the iron staircase where the rain was now pinging from the steps, and he dived towards the door and fumbled for his key.

When the door was opened Peter greeted them with, 'My goodness! I thought it was the bums, sir.'

As Peter now helped her off with her jacket, she asked, on a laugh, 'What are the bums?'

'Bailiffs, madam. Come to clear us out, poor souls.'

'But it does happen, doesn't it? The bailiffs and clearing people out.'

He answered her in the same serious tone, 'Yes, madam; I'm afraid it does, all too often; and in this age too.'

'Is everything ready?' put in David.

'Yes, sir; everything's ready and waiting, piping hot.'

'You've made the dinner?'

'Of course, madam. This is a special night.'

'Daft old thing,' David said. 'It was his day off, but he insisted on coming back and making dinner. I told him we didn't want dinner. Do we?'

'Oh, yes; I want dinner. I haven't had a bite all day; I've been saving myself for tonight. It's true, really' – she was nodding at David now – 'I didn't have any breakfast and I had only a poached egg for lunch.'

'Dear, dear! Well, madam, we're starting with pâté. It'll be with you in a minute.'

The pâté was lovely. The rolled sole in sauce was delightful, as was the shoulder of lamb and its accompaniments; and the fruit fool that followed was the best she had ever tasted. In fact, she found the whole meal delicious, and she said so; and Peter showed his pleasure by saying, 'I'll cook for you any time, madam, any time.'

A little later, as they were sitting drinking their coffee, she said, softly, 'It isn't a fairy tale – a fairy tale has an end – it's a dream, and if a dream has an end it's not always pleasant.'

'This one will be. I've made up my mind; I have it all planned out up here.' He tapped his forehead. 'It will work out, you'll see. That's what I want to talk about. But let's have our coffee first.'

They had their coffee; then she thanked Peter again before he left to finish his day off.

As they sat back on the couch and heard the front door close, she said, 'Where will he go at this time? It's nearly nine o'clock.' Then she repeated, 'Oh, no! It's nearly nine o'clock. The time has flown by.'

'Yes, it certainly has, so come here.' He pulled her into a tight embrace and he said, 'To answer your first question: he goes to his club. Oh, it's open till all hours. He says it's for single butlers and batmen, and he always adds, while laughing, for anyone who can swear they've never used their boss's Christian name. And that isn't such a joke, because it's "Yes, sir," all the time. Several times I've tried to get him to drop the "sir" – he's Peter and I'm David, that's how I think about him – but no. It's use, I suppose. Still, I'd rather have him as a friend than any other man I know, and I know quite a few, high and low. But there' – he hugged her – 'enough of Peter and all his works. Let's talk about us, eh, Hannah?'

She was gasping from the tightness of his hold. 'When . . . I can speak, yes.'

'Oh, I'm sorry, my love; I'm sorry.' As he slackened his hold on her his face came close to hers and he said, 'And that's what you are . . . my love. My love. I can't believe it. I have no answer to the question that is constantly in my mind: Can it be only a week today since I set eyes on you? But, then, time isn't relevant to the emotions: you can die from fright in a split second, or you can be brought to life in a split second, as I was when I first saw you. I'll never be able to explain it, as I've already told you, and I don't want to, but I do want to know what our future is to be.'

She tried to release herself altogether from his hold, but he again pulled her to him, although more gently now, saying, 'Hannah, we've both found something that's very rare . . . at least to my knowledge.'

She was some time in answering, for he was holding her gaze and she could not find words with which to express her feelings of the moment. When she was apart from him she had only his image in her mind and then she knew that she had not only fallen in love with him, but that she really did love him. But hadn't this happened with Humphrey, too? No; this was different, *she loved this man*. It was just as he had said to her: she wanted him, needed him; and she always would. It was up to her whether he would be in her future or not. But there was still Humphrey.

Don't say it! Don't say it! Her mind was again barking at her, when she heard his voice overriding it, saying, 'What is it, darling? What is it? Have I upset you?'

She closed her eyes now to blot out his presence as she said, 'You could never hurt me, David, only if you stopped loving me. And yes, I love you, and I don't know how it happened, either. I only know that I've been waiting for it to happen for a long time.'

'Then we must be together, and always.'

His words brought her eyes wide and, her head shaking, she said, 'No! No, I can't. We can't, David, without hurting other people; but we can be together at times.'

'On the side, you mean: Thursday nights and an odd Saturday, perhaps Sunday, until Humphrey changes his routine.'

'Strangely, yes; I suppose that is what I mean; but listen, listen' – she put her fingers on his lips – 'I feel there's something happening. On Sunday night he came in really angry. He'd had a bad weekend: he'd found his aunt and uncle very testy; he talked about their narrow views and it came to me after some thinking that he wouldn't mind having a divorce tomorrow. The only snag is that they'd wipe him off their slate. On Sunday night he kept on about the narrowness of their views, and that, as he has more than once said, in their eyes divorce is second only to murder. If you're married, that's a life term, nothing less, and separation, I should imagine, is the next on their list.'

'Could it be possible that he's got a girlfriend on the side?'

'Oh no! no!' She shook her head and laughed.

'All his movements are checked. I think the old couple see to that; or, at least, their housekeeper does – their treasure would see that he kept to time. I should imagine that sometimes the old couple are more than fractious, and she feels she wants a break from them, and she asks him if he's coming for a long weekend or some such. That's why, except for a fortnight, he breaks up his holidays so that he can tag days on to his weekends with them. But I've never known him come back so irritable – almost miserable, I'd say – as I saw him on Sunday night, and it would happen that I myself was feeling on top of the world.' She put up her hand now and touched his cheek, and he held it tight as, smiling widely, she said, 'My manner with him was almost flippant, and when he adopted a superior attitude towards a new client, who was in the hardware business, I had the nerve to remind him that that was on a level with a stall in the market or a barrow boy.'

'You did?'

'Yes; and that'll tell you the change you've wrought in me, Mr Craventon.' But then she added with a nod of her head, 'I keep wondering why I haven't stood up to him in some way before, but then you can't go out to hurt someone who is continually kind and thoughtful—' Then, the smile fading from her face, she added, 'That is, in some ways.'

And when he repeated, 'Yes, in some ways,' she looked at him intently, but did not take the matter further, because the small voice in her was saying: No, no; Janie would never mention that, surely, nor could she imagine even Eddie bringing up the subject; that would be out of the question. And so she put in quickly now, 'I did give some thought to the idea of our meeting during the week: perhaps we could have lunch together at Micky's.'

'Oh, yes; good idea, every day.'

'Oh, no! That'd be noticed! Mrs Fenwick comes in two days a week; but then' – she pursed her lips – 'I've already told Humphrey I'm going after a job.'

'You did?'

'Yes. That was another shock he got, poor man. He doesn't deserve it, you know, because he's so . . .'

'If you tell me once more that he's kind I'll have hysterics and start to scream. I will; honest I will. If a man is supposedly as kind as your husband is while still being cruel, I feel there must be something odd about him.'

'Look; I don't want to talk about it, but the fact is he doesn't . . . we don't . . . share a bed any more.'

'I know, my darling. Eddie told me— Oh, don't be angry with him. It just slipped out. He really didn't mean to tell me. All I can say is that your Humphrey must be the biggest fool under the sun.'

Again she was pressed close to him as he said softly, 'And I want to love you, really love you. You understand? And it needs no talking about; it must just happen – and soon.'

As she gazed at him she did not repeat 'and soon'; but her whole body voiced the words for her.

She arrived home fifteen minutes before Humphrey and she was in bed when he came upstairs and tapped on her door before he called out, 'Are you all right?' And to this she said, 'Yes; but I was very tired so I'm having an early night.'

'Best thing. Best thing. Goodnight.'

'Goodnight, Humphrey.'

# Eight

It was Thursday again and she was sitting in the chair opposite Mr Gillyman, her mouth agape and her eyes wide, and he was saying to her, 'Two hundred pounds. You don't think that's adequate?'

She had to gulp before she brought her lips together and, her eyes blinking, she said, 'I'm . . . I'm sorry, but I'm amazed. I . . . I didn't expect anything like that.'

'What did you expect, then?'

'Oh, I don't know. Fifty . . .?'

Mr Gillyman, his eyes twinkling, looked towards David, who was standing at the side of the desk, and he laughed as he said, 'Why couldn't you tip me the wink that's all she wanted?'

'We . . . we didn't discuss it.'

'You've never been any good at business, have you?'

'It all depends, sir, on what business we're discussing.'

'Oh, go on with you!' Gilly was looking at Hannah again, and he said, 'Well now; two hundred it is; but you're not getting it all at once: you'll get half on acceptance, as now, and half on publication. This is what is called an advance on royalties, and if we don't sell enough to cover our costs then I'm sure I'll be able to put you to work in one of my store rooms!'

'I wouldn't be a bit surprised at that either.'

Mr Gillyman glanced quickly at David, demanding, 'What did you say?'

'Well, I had to do a similar chore, but I wasn't paid any royalties.'

Hannah looked from one to the other: they were sparring as only friends could spar; yet two hundred pounds! What would Humphrey say to that? Two hundred pounds for her childish thoughts. Should she tell him? No. No, she wouldn't. Well, not at present, not until she'd bought herself some new clothes: she'd been feeling shabby lately and she hadn't been able to bring herself to ask Humphrey for money. And David's words about her appearance had struck home.

A loud voice in her mind was telling her what she would do, but there was also a feeling rising in her that touched on glee. It was as if a little imp was suddenly sitting before her eyes and holding up a picture of an outfit she had seen in a side street that very morning on her way from the station. She'd stopped to look at it: an exquisitely finished suit – long, in gunmetal grey – trimmed with petrol blue and teamed up with such a beautiful soft silk blouse . . . It looked so sophisticated, so . . . beyond anything she could afford that she'd dragged herself away. But now there it was in her mind's eye, and the imp was looking round the side of the picture whispering, Why not? You didn't know you were going to get two hundred pounds. In fact, you'd have been really surprised if he'd offered you one hundred.

The imp and the picture vanished at the sound of Mr Gillyman saying to David, 'Go up to my wife and tell her I'll join you for coffee. I don't see why you should always have a break and leave me down here working.'

There was a slight upward movement of David's eyebrows before he said smartly, 'Yes, sir,' then, clicking his heels together, he gave a right about turn and marched from the room.

'Showing off.' Gilly was looking at Hannah now, and he added, 'Whether you know it or not, that was a ruse to get rid of him for a minute. I want to ask you something.'

She was looking at him in enquiry and saw that there was no gleam of merriment in his eyes: his expression was straight, so the smile slipped from her face as she said quietly, 'Yes?'

He placed his forearms on the table as he leant towards her, saying quietly, 'You'll likely be thinking: Why can't he mind his own business; even, perhaps, This has nothing to do with him, and so on; but it has something to do with me and my wife. You see, we're very fond of David. We lost our son, as perhaps he's already told you, and David has taken Rodney's place, much grown-up, of course. What's more, he had a very unhappy experience of marriage, since when his relationships have been of short duration; usually just theatre or dinner companions. But now, from what he tells me, and even after such a short acquaintance, he has become more than fond of you. You are still a married woman, Mrs Drayton, but, from what little I glean, not very happily so. Now, the point is this: from my knowledge of David, he's not taking this matter lightly and, to a certain extent, being legally separated from his wife, he's at liberty to go his own way. What I'm going to ask you, and I'd like a plain yes or no, is whether or not this association is merely a light diversion to relieve your boredom, just as the writing of your little book, I feel sure, was. So, yes or no to my first question.'

She did not ask herself if she was annoyed at this form of questioning, but she knew she was in a way frightened by it, so much so that she could not answer him until he said harshly, 'Well! you should know.'

'Yes. Yes, I do know, and the answer is no. I am not taking the matter lightly; far from it. But there is still my husband, and he has done me no harm, in fact he has been kind in his own way; but, apart from that, our marriage is not . . .' she swallowed deeply here as she slowly shook her head before looking at him again and saying flatly, 'not what it should be. It hasn't been for some long time, mainly because of the feeling of responsibility my husband has for his aunt and uncle, both elderly and sick people, with whom he spends most weekends, in fact, every weekend. They . . . they seem to demand it. They were never fond of me.'

She gave a little wry smile now as she added, 'His aunt doesn't care for blondes, seeing them as frivolous, dangerous people, in fact, and is convinced they should never marry steady men like her nephew.'

'Oh, ye gods!' He was sitting back in his chair now, staring at her. 'How long have you put up with this?'

'Oh.' She was looking from side to side as if she would see the number of weeks, days, nights she had put up with it, and she said, 'Oh; more than two years.'

'Was it all right before that?'

'Well, he's always visited his aunt and uncle a lot. At first I used to go with him, but, just as his aunt did not like blondes, I did not care for tall, thin-faced, sparse-haired elderly ladies.'

He laughed now, saying, 'I can see the portrait vividly.'

He was sitting forward again now and then he said quietly, 'I don't know what the future is going to hold for either of you but, in the meantime, if you can make him happy and he in return can do the same for you, we'll be glad of that. Do forgive me for being such an interfering old busybody; it's just that he is so dear to us now . . . Well!' – he stood up and waved his hands – 'Coffee! Let's get upstairs.' He held out his arm to her and when she put hers into it he drew her round the table, saying, 'He'll probably ask you what we were talking about; you see, were he to know he'd be angry and go for me and tell me to mind my own business. So we've been talking about children's poetry, haven't we?' He was now standing abreast of her at the edge of the desk, and, looking into his smiling face, she said, 'Yes, of course. That's what I'm here for, to talk about children's poetry.'

He nodded at her, then with an almost dancing step he pulled her along the room and through the end door and towards the stairs, chanting as he went:

> 'McGinty is the gardener
> And he sometimes swears,
> Pongo is the poodle
> With only half its hairs;
> Father is the parson
> Reading from a book;
> Says I'll take some saving
> By hook or by crook.'

She followed him up the stairs, smiling, and he turned to her and said, 'Think you're the only one who's ever written children's poetry? I wrote that when I was eight. I did. I did.'

Then off they went again, he repeating his chant and dancing to it and she aiming to keep in step with him, all the while asking herself if, like in *Alice in Wonderland*, she had dropped into a dream, because here she was dancing with the equivalent of the Mad Hatter. Nicely mad – kindly mad – or understandably mad, sympathetically mad, wisely mad, but above all childishly mad. Yes, that was the best madness, childish madness.

Then the dream would shortly jump from *Alice in Wonderland* to *Cinderella*, and there would be the Prince taking her to lunch, and he would tell her again she was the most lovely thing that had come into his life.

When they danced into the room, and she was plonked laughing on to the couch and he dropped down beside her, the two people standing at the coffee table just looked at them, and Natasha Gillyman, turning to David, said, 'It's a white-coat job again; I think you'd better phone them.'

'Yes, you're right.' David nodded towards them, then added, 'And a female attendant; she's become infected too.'

Lying back on the couch, her body still shaking, Hannah heard a voice at her side saying, 'She's got the most infectious laugh.' Well, that couldn't have been from the Mad Hatter, he must have turned into the White Rabbit. As the general laughter flowed around her she felt she was about to cry, and the room became strangely still. She knew she was still dreaming, and she prayed that she would never wake up, especially when the Prince sat beside her and drew her head on to his shoulder. Then the Queen made her sip some coffee before they both chided the Mad Hatter, who defended himself by saying, ''Tis the best thing that could have happened: she's let go.'

She liked the Mad Hatter; yes, she did.

# Nine

Hannah looked at the elegantly dressed, sophisticated stranger in the cheval mirror and could hardly believe it was her. No, it couldn't possibly be her.

She took off the jacket, the better to admire the line of the long skirt, and smoothed down the silk blouse, turning to catch a view of herself from behind.

The proprietress was hovering close by, obviously pleased with what she saw. 'You have your hair tied back, madam,' she ventured, 'but I think it would suit you better if you coiled it into a sort of loose rope at the nape of your neck.'

Hannah saw the figure in the glass nodding agreement with this, but it didn't speak.

'You have beautiful hair. Such a glorious colour.' She took three steps back and viewed Hannah, who had now turned from the mirror, from top to toe. With a dramatic gesture she clasped her hands in front of her and said, 'I haven't sold anything with such pleasure for a long time, madam. It really is as if the outfit was made with you in mind. And you can ring the changes by wearing the pieces separately and dressing them up or down to suit the occasion. Each piece has been made plain without fancy trimming with exactly that in mind.'

'Yes, it's . . . perfect . . .'

'And the cut gives such an elegant line. Turn round, madam.'

Hannah obeyed and when she felt the bottom of the skirt swish luxuriantly over her calves she closed her eyes. Yesterday she had been with Alice in Wonderland, when the joyful feeling had been too much and she had almost cried; today, she felt as if she were still in a kind of dream. 'Well now,' the proprietress was saying, 'I'll have it parcelled up for you. And you're taking the trousers too? *So* smart.'

Hannah had put on the jacket again and was moving her hand down the front of the lapels, and for a moment she did not respond. Then she said, 'Er, yes . . . Would you mind if I kept these things on?'

'Mind, madam?' She laughed, and Hannah, her face quite red now, said, 'That was a silly thing to say. I . . .'

'No, it wasn't, madam. No, it wasn't. Would I mind? I'd be delighted to see you walk out of my shop just as you are. I'll have your garments packed up for you.'

She didn't say 'clothes' or 'dress and coat'; no, they were garments. Hannah was glowing inside; she was buying an outfit that cost £125. She knew now why she had asked Mr Gillyman if it would be possible for her to have the half advance royalties in cash, as she hadn't a cheque book, and she might want to spend now that she felt so affluent. And he had laughed heartily as he counted out ten £10 notes, and now here she was counting out twelve to Madame Yvonne; she was about to add a £5 note when the proprietress said, 'We'll call it a hundred and twenty, shall we?'

As she thanked Madame for the discount she was very pleased to have been given it, for, without it, she would barely have had her tube fare home.

She was being handed the bag containing her clothes. It was pale blue on one side, on the other 'Yvonne' was picked out in large yellow letters.

Madame herself showed her to the door and expressed a wish that she might again have the pleasure of dressing her.

Even in the short distance to the main thoroughfare she found she was not walking unnoticed, yet she knew that around Oxford Street you could wear anything from a sack to an evening dress at any time of the day and no one would remark on it.

Knowing she would be seeing David later that evening, she had refused his suggestion of lunch, but now she was feeling a strong inclination to rush back to Jason Gardens to show herself off; and not only to David, but to those other two nice people, the *Alice in Wonderland* people, for Natasha too had become part of the dream.

But she resisted, and decided to go straight home.

She was relieved to find that Mrs Fenwick had gone and so she went straight upstairs. In her bedroom the first thing she did was stand in front of the long mirror. She was someone different, poised . . . someone so very slim and . . . elegant. Her mind hung on the word 'elegant'. Oh! wait till David saw her.

But she couldn't wear this outfit tonight; it'd be too risky. What was more, she must, for now, hide it. The only place she could think of was the back of the wardrobe, among her winter things.

After changing her clothes, she made her way to the kitchen but all she did there was sit by the table and drum her fingers on the edge of it while asking herself, What now? Where do I go from here? knowing quite well she would be going into his bed.

Good God! what was the matter with her? Why was she thinking like this? She was married!

The voice was speaking again, not so loudly now, but firmly: No, you never used to think like this, because then you hadn't the experience of spending two years sleeping in the next room to a sadist.

He's not! Such words. Such a description.

Well, you tell me what other description you can give to him, but don't come back with, He's kind, Humphrey's so kind.

When she found herself whimpering, she said aloud, 'Oh, come on, Hannah! Stop thinking like this!'

The rest of the afternoon seemed to drag. She longed to hear Humphrey's key in the door; and when it actually happened she went into the dining room and attended to the table as if putting the last touches to it.

When she turned round he was standing in the doorway and her hand immediately went to her mouth and pressed it tightly: he was streaming with cold.

His voice was a croak as he said, 'I don't feel like anything to eat; I've . . . I've developed a cold. I'll just have a cup of coffee and take some aspirins. I'm . . . I'm going to bed.'

She followed him back into the hall, saying inanely, 'It's unusual for you to have a real cold.'

'Oh, it's going round the office. They seem to be short sharp attacks. I hope so, because I've taken one of my extra days. I've only three left, but if I don't take them before the end of the month I lose them. Anyway, it'll probably be gone or settled by tomorrow.'

'Would you like me to phone your friends about tonight?'

He looked at her in surprise, saying, 'There's no need. Two of the players are in my department.'

'Oh, yes. Yes, of course.' She watched him as he climbed the stairs. Then she returned to the kitchen and for a moment stood thinking: Nothing ever goes smoothly. It had been a wonderful day and she had imagined it would finish more wonderfully still, when she told David of her decision.

She would have to phone him. That coffee, yes! She must make that cup of coffee, and it would probably be the first of many she would have to make tonight. And she'd ply him with hot drinks every half-hour, anything to get him away for his weekend jaunt as usual . . .

184

On the phone David said, 'Oh, Hannah. I've been looking forward to it so much. And the weekend . . .?'

'Oh, he has to be very ill before he gives that up.'

'Really?'

'Yes.'

'Well, I'll start praying. It's only hours since I saw you but it seems like years. What did you do with yourself all day?'

'I spent part of my advance.'

'You didn't!'

'Yes, and all in one go, and twenty pounds more.'

'What on earth did you buy?'

'Just you wait and see.'

'Can you phone me again later on?'

'No, I'd better not; he might hear the phone from his room. I'll phone you in the morning. Goodnight.'

'Goodnight, darling.'

She was in the kitchen when she thought of her granny's cure for coughs and bad colds – horehound, whisky, sugar, lemon and boiling water.

Odd about horehound. She'd always loved horehound candy. She'd been introduced to it by her granny. Then there was horehound ginger. That was always doled out for a cold. It was also the standard medicine for the children in Janie's house; for adults, too, but with something more potent added. Well, she had both horehound candy and horehound ginger in the house, so she set about creating the potion. Into a mug she poured a generous measure of whisky, two heaped teaspoons of brown sugar, lemon juice, a quarter of a teaspoon of horehound ginger, and a quarter-pint of boiling water. She gave the contents a good stir, sipped at the mug, coughed, blinked, and took it up to his bedroom.

He was lying on his back. His eyes were closed and a handkerchief was held to his mouth.

'What . . . what is it?'

'Well, I've always understood this to be an absolute cure for a cold. It was my grandmother's remedy.'

'What's in it?'

She told him.

'Your grandmother's remedy?' He pulled himself some way up in the bed and looked at her. 'I've never heard of it before.'

'Because neither of us has needed it. I've never known you to have such a cold, nor myself. The sniffles now and again, but that's all.'

He felt the mug, saying, 'It's very hot.'

'It's supposed to be, and you must drink it all, not just sip at it.'

He tasted it, then coughed, and his lids blinked as hers had done. 'It's . . . it's very strong.'

'Drink it up.'

He stared at her for a moment longer; then, putting the mug to his mouth, he began to drink, only stopping to get his breath now and again. When the mug was empty he handed it to her, saying, 'Thank you.'

'I'd settle down and go to sleep now. I don't think you'll need anything more tonight.'

As he lay back and pulled the clothes up to his chin, he said, 'Were you thinking about going to Janie's?'

'Yes, but that doesn't matter. I phoned her.'

He nodded at her in acknowledgement, which made her think it was lucky there was no extension in the bedrooms, because she was sure he would have listened in.

'Goodnight, Hannah, and thank you.'

'Goodnight.'

She had slept late. It was twenty-five to eight.

Sitting up in bed, she turned her head to the side, realising that she had been woken by someone moving about and a door opening and shutting.

Oh, dear! She rose hastily, put on her dressing gown, then went into the kitchen, to see Humphrey sitting at the table.

He was actually smiling, and when he spoke to her his voice was clear, 'Your granny's medicine should be patented; it's a miracle worker. I'm practically free.' Then he added, 'Shall I get you a cup of tea?'

'No, no.' She put a hand out to him. 'I'll see to it. I've slept. I—' She stopped; then, looking at him from across the table, she said, 'Yes, you do look better. Last night you looked as if you were in for a thorough dose.'

'I thought so too, but now I . . . I feel fine.'

She made herself say with concern, 'I'd be careful, though; you're not clear of it yet.'

'Oh, yes; I'm sure I am.'

Hesitantly now, she put in, 'Will you be going off for the weekend?'

Before he could answer the phone rang, and when she answered it a voice said, 'This is Mrs Beggs here. Is Mr Drayton in?'

'Yes. Yes, I'll get him.'

She went to the kitchen door and said, 'It's for you . . . Mrs Beggs.'

'Oh. Oh.'

He hurried across the hall and his voice came to her clearly saying, 'I had an awful cold last night but it's practically gone this morning, so you can put their minds at rest.' His voice was loud. 'I should be there about twelve.' Then, 'Thank you, Beggie, thank you. Goodbye.'

Hannah was standing at the kitchen door when he said, 'I'm not going to be let off, and I'll tell them it's only thanks to you and your granny's remedy.' He was smiling again, and she smiled back at him, and when she said, 'It very rarely fails,' he answered, 'I'll have to remember that for future use.'

He had gone a few steps from the door when he came back hastily, saying, 'You . . . you'll be going to your sister's?'

'Oh, yes; yes, later.'

'That's it. That's it. I don't like to think of you here by yourself every weekend, but . . . well, you know the position.'

He seemed to be waiting for an answer of confirmation to his statement, but when none was forthcoming he merely nodded and turned away.

He had left the house by ten o'clock. She watched

him from the window striding down the street. His long legs seemed almost on the point of a run, and she told herself he'd have to run to catch that particular train to Worthing; and again she wondered why he did not buy a car. She'd put it to him, only to be asked where he was supposed to find the money for a car; and, what was more, there was the upkeep. She recalled she'd answered by saying, 'I'd have thought your uncle would have seen to that,' and she remembered the strange answer he'd given her on that occasion: 'You have a lot to learn about my aunt and uncle,' he had said, from which she could only infer there was a meanness in them. This had seemed strange, because she understood he was their only living relative, and both the uncle and the aunt were each known to be quite wealthy through inheritance: he had been a partner in a family textile company and she had been a director. Apparently they had married late in life, and adopted the boy Humphrey, who was the orphaned son of George Drayton's second cousin; they both saw the boy as the child they would never have; and so in a way she could understand Humphrey's one seeming desire was to pamper them in their old age, both as a means of thanking them and with his eye on the future when they should die.

When she saw her husband disappearing round the end of the street, Hannah hastily went to the phone.

When the voice came to her, saying, 'Hello, who's speaking?' she answered, 'A certain Mrs Hannah Drayton, Mr Miller.'

A laugh came across the line, and he said, 'Good morning, madam.'

'Good morning, Peter. Is David in?'

'No; I'm sorry, he isn't. He's along at Mr Gillyman's, but I can reach him there.'

'Will you tell him that there is a person who would like to take lunch with him at Micky's around one o'clock?'

'I'll definitely pass on that message, madam; and may I be presumptuous enough to ask if I'll have the pleasure of seeing you later, perhaps for tea?'

'You may, Peter.'

'That's a pleasure to look forward to.'

'Bye-bye, Peter.'

'Goodbye, madam.'

She stood looking at the phone. He was wonderful: David was really lucky to have found someone like him, a companion and a friend, a housekeeper and cook, all rolled into one.

She now flew up the stairs and began her preparations to surprise the man who would once more take her into *Alice in Wonderland*, and not just today, or tonight.

She had made up her mind.

She came out of the station and into the street. It was busy. She looked about her: there he was, standing near the kerb about ten feet away from her. He looked in her direction, then past her, as though not seeing her; then, the next minute, he almost jumped towards her.

As he grabbed her arm, and none too gently, he

said quite loudly, 'I . . . I can't believe it. I . . . I didn't think it was possible for you to look . . . well . . . more . . . more beautiful. It's absolutely—' Now he let go of her arm, tried to step back, only to be pushed to the side by a man who said roughly, 'Look out! there, mate. Look out!' He had to turn and, looking at the man's companion, say quickly, 'Oh, I'm terribly sorry. Did I step on you?'

'No. No.' The woman was laughing and looking towards Hannah; then turning to her companion she said, and in no small voice, 'I wouldn't mind being stepped on if I looked like that.'

'Get on with you!' The man pushed her forward, and David, now taking Hannah's bag with one hand, put his other around her shoulders and guided her through the moving throng to where they usually got on the bus, only then to say, 'Oh, you're far too elegant today to be squashed up on a crowded bus.' He put up his hand and yelled to a passing cab, 'Taxi!'

The next minute she was being pressed on to the black leather seat and they were sailing north, towards Camden.

Except for the two reserved seats in the alcove the café was already full; but their entry didn't go unnoticed, drawing one or two discreet but appreciative looks from fellow diners. Micky himself greeted them, but he gave special attention to Hannah, saying, 'My! you do look smashing! Been to Paris?'

'Yes, Micky; I just slipped over.'

'Well' – he jerked his head – 'you found a nice

piece of material when you were there, I must say. My! what a combination. I'd better not let me wife see it.' Then, lowering his head, he said, 'Where did you come by it? In the city? I mean, here?'

'Yes. Yes. A little shop near Oxford Street. Small place, Yvonne's. Take her there. She'll come out very pleased, I can tell you.'

His face stretched as he said, 'Yes, but will *I* be glad?'

'Yes, of course you will, because you like a bargain; and I have a strong feeling I'd've paid twice as much for it if it had been in the main street.'

'No kidding?'

'No kidding.'

'And you say the name's Yvonne?'

'That's it. Madame Yvonne.'

Smiling, he was about to leave them, but he turned quickly and, punching David on the arm, he said softly, 'Thanks for Tuesday's phone call.'

'Oh, don't thank me; thank Gilly for having his big ears to the ground. It mightn't have come off. It was just a chance, because, you know, he won't recommend anything fishy, and, as he says in his own funny way, some shares just need the chips, salt and pepper and a newspaper.'

'Does he say that? He's a funny bloke. Ah, here's Oscar. He'll tell you there's something really special on today.' He made room in the narrow space for the waiter, whose real name was Harry Blyth, but who, from the time of joining this establishment, had been Oscar Demont; but Oscar Demont had one advantage over Harry Blyth: he could assume three foreign tongues, in broken English, of course . . .

When they had the table to themselves Hannah leant towards David, and her voice held a gurgle as she said, 'I'm in Wonderland again.'

'What?' he put his head closer to hers.

'I said, I'm in *Wonderland* again. I entered it the other morning when Mr Gilly danced me through the book-lanes singing his poetry; and I was in it in Madame Yvonne's. She stepped out of *Cinderella*: she was the fairy godmother and was dressing me for the ball; then immediately I came out of the station today I was back in *Alice*, because you were there; and now, during these last few minutes' – her gurgle turned into a laugh – 'I meet the Mad Hatter again. They're all here, and the only thing I'm afraid of is that I'll wake up.'

He did not immediately answer her, but leant back against the partition; then he said, 'If it rests with me, Hannah, you'll never wake up.'

They did not linger over their meal, anticipating the moment when they could be alone together, in the safety of David's flat. They left the restaurant and took neither a taxi nor a bus, but walked, saying little on the way.

The door to the flat was opened by Peter, who seemed so stunned by the new Mrs Drayton as to have lost his voice. When he did speak, it was to say, 'Madam, may I congratulate you on . . . well, all I can say is, beautifying beauty still further.'

'Oh, you would come out with something like

that: top the lot, you would.' David was nodding at him.

'Well, I'm sorry, sir, if your admiration has been unable to evoke eloquence with which to cap my simple praise.'

'Oh, go on with you!'

'You two stop it and let me get my jacket off, and then I'll be able to relax, I hope.'

Peter took the jacket from her and, stooping, picked up her case and walked towards the bedroom.

Hannah's eyes followed him; then she said quietly to David, 'I . . . I was hoping I . . .' Her head drooped – she couldn't finish, but she walked towards where the tea was set out before the couch, and sitting down and still with her head lowered, she muttered, 'It should be so easy to say it.'

He was sitting close by her now, his arm around her shoulders. 'What should be easy?' he asked softly.

'May I stay for the weekend?' Her head jerked round and she was looking into his eyes. She had expected to be pulled into his embrace and kissed hard, but what he did now was put his hand out and gently stroke her cheek, and, to her surprise, he said, 'Will you pour out the tea?'

His response was so unexpected that she appeared like someone winded, so much so that she lay back against the couch, closed her eyes and drew in a deep breath, and when she heard him say, 'All right, I'll do it then,' she looked at him as he calmly stirred the tea before pouring it out.

Peter was now standing by the side table, saying, 'Can you manage, sir?'

'I think so, Peter. Yes, I think so.'

They were alone when he handed her the tea, yet he still did not look at her, but in a low voice he said, 'My dearest, take no notice of me for the next few minutes while I make a fool of myself.'

She quickly put out a hand and caught his, and again the small voice within was saying, How strange life is. She'd been worried about how exactly she should put over her proposal. It must have sounded bold; crude, in fact. She had expected to witness his delight and to feel his arms about her holding her close. But what had happened? The tables were entirely reversed. It was as if he had become embarrassed. No; that wasn't the right word, and yet something was affecting him.

She experienced further bewilderment when, his voice apparently cool, he said, 'I'll tell Peter he may clear the table; he wants to get off early and do some shopping before going on to his club.'

When he called Peter there was a break in his voice and he began to cough.

Peter did not immediately appear, and this caused David to look towards the ceiling and say, 'I didn't hear him going upstairs, and those stairs creak.'

It was at this moment that Peter appeared – it could be said he scurried into the room – saying, 'You're about to have a visitor, sir.'

David was on his feet now: 'Who?'

'Pill, sir. I mean Lord Pillbeck.'

'Oh! Peter, never! Oh, no.'

195

'I caught a glimpse of him from the window. He was hesitating about which stairway to take.'

'Oh, well, let's get these things out of the way and then get yourself out.'

'Oh no, sir; I'll stay till he goes. If not, you may have a visitor for the night; he looks in need of help.'

'Oh! not again.' At this moment the bell rang, and Peter, putting down the tray he was now holding and straightening the front of his jacket, put his shoulders back, cast a partly smiling glance at David and made for the door.

The clear high voice came to them both, saying, 'Hello there, Peter! Nice to see you again. Is your master in?'

'Yes, sir; yes. Do come in.'

'Thank you, Peter. Thank you.'

As David walked towards the newcomer Hannah saw a man of medium height who could be sixty or more. He had a round, chubby face, but its colour could only be described as muddy. As he took off his hat and handed it to Peter, Hannah expected to see at least grey hair, if not white, but instead she saw a dark mass yelling forth its black dye, and the sight wiped from her mind for the time being the feelings that had been enveloping her since David's reception of her proposal. At this moment she was filled with a mixture of pity and compassion. What was more, the visitor was a lord, and the first lord with whom she had ever come in contact.

As he approached her she took in his whole attire at a glance. 'Seedy' was the right word to express it: the navy blue overcoat was of an old-fashioned cut;

his grey trousers still held the shadow of a crease down the front, but the ends, lying on top of the brown leather shoes, looked frayed; and the thought sped through her mind that no one these days need look as he did, because they could be perfectly well dressed for a few pounds in one of the many charity shops.

'Hannah, let me introduce Lord Henry Pillbeck; this is Mrs Hannah Drayton, Henry.'

'Delighted to meet you, my dear.' He had a pleasant, well modulated voice. She answered, 'How d'you do?' and let her hand be lifted to his lips but instead of looking at him, her gaze darted to David, who made a little motion of his head, the meaning of which was lost on her.

'Do sit down, Pilly; I'm sure you'd like a cup of tea,' David said, and added, 'Would you mind, Peter, bringing in another pot?'

'Not at all, sir. Not at all.'

Before seating himself in a leather chair Lord Pillbeck moved it slightly so that he could have a full view of the room, and, now looking round him, he said, 'What a remarkable place you have here, David. Who did this for you . . . Spencer?'

'No, of course not. How could I afford Spencer, Pilly? No, I did it myself.'

'My, my! you are a clever chap. I always said you were.'

'What are you doing with yourself these days, anyway?' David said as he sat down on the sofa again, but the old man seemed to study them both closely before he replied, 'Oh, getting about as usual; but nothing, you know, David, is as usual. The world's changed. Have you been anywhere lately, house parties, anything?'

'No; as you know, Pilly, I never was one for house parties.'

'Yes. Yes, I recall that used to annoy the Lady Clarissa. Do you see her at all now?'

'No; not at all.' David's tone was stiff; but the old man seemed not to notice it and went on, 'She doesn't change. In fact, I think she seems to get younger. Well, in that way I mean more rowdy. I called there last week. It isn't the same. It isn't the same.' He shook his head sadly now and, looking down at one hand, he seemed to examine his nails before he added, 'No hospitality. Oh! in those days' – he was nodding at Hannah – 'you know, a party could go on for a fortnight. And the food would be beautiful, delightful. Unfortunately, I wasn't one for horses, I never rode much, but I did amuse them in the evenings, didn't I, David?'

'You did, you did indeed.'

'Those wonderful charades. I could imitate any actor on the stage and the ladies, too. Oh yes, and the ladies, too.' His head was bobbing now at Hannah.

'Have you been abroad lately, to your cousin's?'

'Oh.' The clay-coloured face moved into a wrinkled mass: the lips pouted, the nostrils widened, and the voice held a note of annoyance as he re-marked, 'Not for six months. You know he married again?'

'Alec! married again?'

'Yes. Yes, I was as surprised as you are and he can give me half a dozen years or more. Silly old fool! And she wasn't a young piece either, well ... kicking fifty, I'd say, but she knew what she was about. I was amazed because he had always gone in for dolly-birds; but she came to nurse him when his back went.' His head now was moving from side to side and it was as if he were trying to find words with which to express his disdain. 'A nurse, you know. Just a nurse.' His forefinger was wagging at David now. 'Nurses are dangerous people. Oh, yes, much more so than the dolly-birds. You get something for your money there. But I suppose he'd reached a stage when he imagined he wanted mothering, petting up. Well, she does that all right, so much so that when she decided to go on to another post he proposed, and she was into his bed faster than was seemingly decent. I am sorry, my dear' – he now inclined his head toward Hannah – 'I'm sorry, my dear, if my explanation of her desire to become his wife sounded crude, but facts are often so. You see, the creature took a dislike to me and she convinced him that I was no longer a household necessity; and this after we had spent years on and off together. We had, hadn't we, David?'

'Yes; yes, you'd travelled together quite a bit.'

'And I'd seen to everything. I was very good at arranging journeys, you know. That was my forte. I knew the best hotels; I always got us the best seats on foreign trains; oh, I did everything for him, and what did I get? To put it crudely, the push.'

'Would you like to clear these sandwiches, Pilly?'

David was handing him the plate. 'It's a shame, they'll only go to the birds.'

'Anything to oblige. Anything to oblige.'

He obliged by clearing a plate of smoked salmon sandwiches, then another of bread and butter and another holding four cakes.

And Hannah noted that he had very little to say while he ate; the man was obviously hungry. She watched him now wipe his fingers with delicate precision on a small tea napkin. Then, looking at David, he said, 'How many rooms have you here, David?'

'Only the one that we're sitting in, and my bedroom.'

'What! in a big house like this?'

'Well, downstairs is a store room for my employer's books, and upstairs an apartment that belongs to Peter, and there's only one bedroom there.'

'Oh, that's a pity. That's a pity. I was just looking for some-where to stay for a few days.'

'Haven't you got any lodgings?'

'Yes. Yes. I'm in with another man, but he's not compatible. Oh no, not compatible at all.'

Whether Peter had been listening to this discourse Hannah did not know, but it was at this moment that he appeared in the room and, looking at David, he said, 'The time, sir,' and he pointed to the clock on the mantelpiece. 'You promised to be at Mr Gillyman's by half-past four. They've hired the car for then.'

David now turned an apparently astonished gaze

from Peter on to Hannah, saying, 'Good Lord! I'd forgotten all about it. Why didn't you remind me?'

'I was about to, but I generally leave these things to Peter.' Immediately she'd spoken she knew she'd said the wrong thing: it implied that she lived there; and so quickly now she aimed to rectify her mistake by rising to her feet and saying, 'At work, you know. I do part-time at Mr Gillyman's among the books.'

'Oh. Oh, I see.' The guest was nodding his head now. 'And you are, like me, merely visiting.'

'Yes; yes, I was merely on a visit for Mr Gillyman, bringing a message, and . . . and I was inveigled into staying for tea, which I must say was delightful.' She nodded towards Peter now as if in thanks. Then she added, 'I'll get my things and the papers I came for.'

'Yes, do.' David, too, rose to his feet, and his rising seemed to bring the visitor towards the edge of his chair. Then, his head on one side, he looked to see if the young lady had disappeared into the far room before straining his face up at David in order to say, 'You wouldn't happen to have a set of . . . well' – he nipped at his trousers – 'or anything in that line? You see, I . . . I've refrained as yet from patronising these so-called charity shops. It marks a fellow, y'know, David. It marks a fellow. I have a few changes, but they're all . . . well, showing time and wear, and it hurts a fellow, you know, to go around looking like every other . . .'

'Say no more, Pill.' David turned to Peter, and quietly said, 'There're some greys and a jacket to match and some oddments. You'll know. Parcel them up or put them in that small bag of mine. You know what to do.'

'Yes, sir. Yes, sir, and gladly.' Peter smiled into the old man's face, and Pilly returned the smile, adding to it a two-finger salute to his brow.

In the bedroom Peter silenced any remark Hannah might voice by putting a finger across his lips; then, sliding back a panel in a fixed wardrobe that ran the length of the room he fingered some trousers hanging on rails, selected a pair, then threw them on the bed. Next he opened another panel and examined a half-dozen jackets that were hanging there. Lifting out one, he looked at the collar and the cuffs before throwing this, too, on the bed. Then stooping quickly to where there was a rack of shoes, he immediately selected a black pair, turning them over once before adding them to the other articles. Then at the end of the wardrobe he pulled open the third drawer down and whipped out a couple of shirts. Lastly, he reached up to a shelf above and took down a large bag, into which he stuffed the articles; then he made for the door. Again motioning her to silence, he indicated by a movement of his hand that she should stay where she was.

She stood looking towards the closed door in amazement, for he had completed the whole process in less than two minutes. Presently she heard the visitor's voice saying, 'Oh, my dear fellow, that is most generous of you; and you always had good taste, where clothes were concerned, at least.' A short silence followed, then the man's voice came again, 'Oh, that is really too good of you, David, but

202

it's just a loan, mind, just a loan. There's four of them to go and I've sworn to see them all out, and then I'll come into my own. I've always said I would, I've always said I would, haven't I?'

'You have, Pill, you have,' and now there was laughter as David added, 'And, not wishing them to be polished off quickly, I hope you don't have to wait too long. By the way' – David's voice was low now and Hannah had to strain to hear the words – 'should you happen to come across a certain lady, Pilly, I would be very grateful if you didn't mention this present address. Anyway, I won't be here much longer as I'm moving, but in the meantime . . . well, as I said, I'd be grateful.'

'My dear boy, not a word, not a word . . . Well now, I mustn't hold you up. Goodbye, my dear fellow.'

'Goodbye, Pilly, goodbye. The best of luck.'

She heard the door being opened, and then the visitor's voice saying, 'I do hope the Gillymans haven't forgotten that you're visiting today. Goodbye, Peter dear fellow, goodbye. You really are indispensable. You always have been.'

When Hannah heard the door being closed, none too gently, she stood nipping at her lip. She had rather liked him and felt sorry for him; but that last quip . . . oh, dear me.

The bedroom door opened and David stood there. His face was unsmiling as he said, 'You can come out now.' He held out his hand to her, and as he led her back into the room he said, 'You have just met a man who has ruined more marriages with a final dart from his bitter quiver than there are days in the month,' and Peter, who was clearing away the tea things, said, 'If I'd followed my own inclination, sir, I wouldn't have let him over the doorstep, because he'll never change. He's been bad medicine all his life, and I don't think he's ever left a house of friend or foe without leaving ruin behind him.'

As Peter left the room with the tea tray David drew Hannah down on to the couch again and, laughing now, he said, 'It's funny in a way, you know, because where scandal is concerned he seems to have more power than the *News of the World*: people are afraid not to let him in in case he says something awful about them, such as recalling some misdemeanour long forgotten; but when they do let him in, well, you see what happened. He was aware all along that we wanted him to leave, yet knowing that one is being kind to him, the hope is that he'll spare you this once. But no, not Pilly. And yet, you know, he really was at one time the toast of the weekend parties.'

'I couldn't help overhearing what you said. *Are* you thinking about leaving here?'

'No, no. That's the last thought in my head. But if he sees my ex-wife again, it is doubtful whether he'd keep his mouth shut about this place or wherever I might be. Anyway, there's not too much chance of that; she's going to be spending a lot more time in France, and, from what I've been given to understand, she's hoping to stay for good and set up a stable there. She has three brothers; the eldest, who's divorced, lives in France permanently, and so

I suppose that's the draw.' He smiled grimly now as he said, 'And, by the way, that marriage didn't last as long as mine. He was divorced within the year. My wife saw to that. They're a deadly trio, the brothers; yet I don't know. Without her they wouldn't get up to half the things they do.'

Suddenly jerking round to her, he said, 'What am I yammering on about? This is a most wonderful day and I have to go and talk about things that are buried deep down and would never have been resurrected but for our visitor, and that after I had greeted your wonderful suggestion with an attitude that must have puzzled you, but which I'll explain later.'

He leant towards her and kissed her. Then, cupping her chin in his hand, he said, 'I really can't believe it, that you're here and you're going to be with me for the next twenty-four hours; no! longer. I've waited years for that Thursday morning at ten to eleven.'

She laughed now, saying, 'You really remember the time?'

'Yes; because I was in my cubby-hole and I recall looking at the clock and thinking, Ten to eleven and coffee already. It was then I realised it was Gilly's bell that had rung, and there you were, a blonde goddess in disguise.'

She said soberly now, 'I wonder how long you'll be able to hold that image.'

And he, as soberly, answered, 'Believe me, Hannah, when I give you the answer: as long as I can breathe, because I know that something very vital, very important, very wonderful has happened to me during the past fortnight. I had never thought it would happen, because my experience of so-called love and marriage has been disastrous. The only good thing about it was that it was short. But this feeling you aroused in me right from the beginning is different. I ask myself why I should feel like this, what is the explanation, and I get no reasonable answer, except that it's like a transcription of all the love one reads about from Abelard and Héloïse or Beatrice and Dante, right through to Edward the Eighth and Mrs Simpson. All right, she wasn't everybody's choice, yet she evoked in him such a passion that life would be, as he said, worthless without her. And when you look back and conjure up a picture of her she wasn't beautiful, and she was only smart through her expensive dressing, yet she evoked a great love. Now you, Hannah, are both beautiful and smart and you evoke in me something beyond description. Perhaps those names, those couples I've mentioned, also experienced something like it. That's why they've been remembered down the ages, because all their deeds were prompted by love. Love that didn't turn sour. I feel the same with regard to you. You . . . you don't believe me, do you?'

She heaved a deep sigh and, her face still un-smiling, she said, 'Truly, I can't take it in. I know how I feel, but I have no words to express my feelings. I only keep asking myself if it's real and how long it'll last, how long can it last?'

'Oh, doubting Thomas.' He was holding her

close again, and she answered, 'No; just fearful Thomasina, who keeps wondering what she did before you came into her life.'

There was the sound of a door opening, a loud 'Ahem! Ahem!' and there was Peter standing before them smiling broadly and saying, 'Well, I'm going now, sir, and quickly, because I don't intend to open that door, not for the Mayor and Corporation. And by the way, sir, I may be a little late tonight; the club's putting on a shindig.'

'A what?'

'A shindig, sir. And don't ask me to explain, it's a bit of everything. If I were forced, I'd say it's a cross between an Irish jig, a Scottish reel and the can-can. That's for those who're able to get to their feet.'

'Go on with you!' David waved him away, saying, 'I'll have seen everything when I see you at a shindig.'

'Sir, you never know what one gets up to when one's off duty. It's that feeling of freedom, you know, of release.'

'D'you want me to push you out or lock you in?'

Taking two steps backwards, Peter smiled at Hannah and, bowing slightly, he said, 'Good evening, madam.'

'Good evening, Peter. Enjoy yourself.'

'I intend to, madam. Yes, I intend to.'

He did not add, as he could have done, And you, too, madam; but again inclining his head, he turned from them and left the room; and David said, 'A shindig. Could you ever imagine him doing anything like an Irish jig, a Scottish reel or a can-can? Can-can, indeed!'

'Yes; yes, I could' – she nodded at him – 'all three put together, and making a very amusing job of it.'

'Really? Well, if that's the case, all I can say is that you've discovered something in him that I haven't even had an inkling of in all the years I've known him. Anyway, what would you like to do? What time is it? . . . Half-past five. Well, if we're going to see a show we'd better get a move on.'

'D'you want to see a show?'

'Me?' He laid his head back on the couch and turned his face toward her, saying, 'No, but I thought you might want to.'

'No. I have no desire to see a show tonight. Of course, we could have a bit of a shindig here.'

At this he threw his arms around her and, his body shaking, they rocked together for a moment. Then, sitting bolt upright, he said, 'You've given me an idea, madam. We've never danced together. What's your preference?'

She considered a moment, then said, 'Anything easy – I can manage a sort of waltz, even a Gay Gordon, but I'm not much good at standing alone wobbling my body like a dog shaking off fleas.'

They were joined together, rocking in laughter again.

She was spluttering now as she said, 'I can't stand discos. Eddie goes one better: if Maggie puts on her music, he says something along the lines of: "There go the hounds again, let out for a delousing session." Poor Maggie, she won't bring her friends in just in case her dad comes out with such a comment. You can hear him, can't you?'

'Oh, yes; I can just hear him coming out with that, and more. But, you know, I liked him. There's a solidness there, as in Micky, and they're what the old boys in their clubs used to call the salt of the earth. The salt of the earth. Yet let the salt of the earth give them any backchat and it was stepping out of their place . . . Those fellows! What are things coming to!'

Suddenly he jumped up, pulling her with him. 'What are things coming to when we're sitting here like two idiots discussing all the things that don't matter a damn to us? All I want to do is to talk about you, and, yes, have you talk about me.' He now rubbed her nose gently with his as he whispered, 'And tell me that you love me and that you can't ever live without me and don't ever want to live without me.'

Obediently she said, 'I can't live without you, and don't ever want to live without you—' She paused, then added, 'And I'm not going to.'

'Oh, my dear.' He held her gently to him and looked towards the bedroom door, but the voice inside his head warned, Don't rush things, take it slowly. Let it happen naturally. Dance. That's it, dance.

They danced, they waltzed, they even attempted a Scottish reel, and at intervals they drank a glass of wine; and lastly they went to the fridge and, there, saw a covered plate holding sandwiches, another bearing minute sausage rolls; these they put on to the trolley that was all set for coffee . . .

It was a quarter to ten when they pushed the trolley back into the kitchen; then, as they returned to the sitting room, a silence fell on them as they stood looking at each other; and now he said softly, 'Would you like to wash?' and she answered as softly, 'Yes, please.'

He stood aside and allowed her to pass, and when she reached the bedroom she found she had to grip the foot of the bed-rail to steady her trembling limbs. Her case lay on the bed – Peter had tactfully not opened it – her jacket hung on the back of one of the wardrobe doors. After a moment she opened her case and took from it some trousers and a light pullover, and a couple of blouses. These she hung in the wardrobe, along with her jacket. Her dressing gown she laid across the foot of the bed, and lastly she took from the case a pair of soft slippers and a silky nightdress. The nightdress was one she had never worn while sleeping with Humphrey; in fact, she'd worn it only once before. It had taken her fancy in a sale, where it had looked elegant, but there was so little of it that it lacked comfort, and earlier on, as she packed it, she had wondered if it had been made for such an occasion as she was bound for.

After she had washed she returned to the bed-room and had just taken her case from the bed when David entered. He was wearing a plaid-patterned dressing gown, and when he saw her pick up the case and place it against the wall under the window, then stand for a moment looking out, he went to her and put his arms about her and pressed her to him, saying as he did so, 'It isn't a very pleasing view, is it? That's the extension of the dress factory from the bottom of the street, and you'll note it only has windows in the roof. I understand that's to stop the girls wasting their time looking out.'

Loosening his hold on her, he lifted the ornamental ropes from the hooks that held the curtains looped back; then, after pulling the heavy drapes closed, he turned her about to face him and said softly, 'What is it? You're not worried . . . regretting?'

'Oh, no, no.' She smiled into his face. 'But I feel, oh—' She gave a little toss of her head, and to this he said quickly, 'I know. I know, my darling. But it's going to be all right.'

Slowly now he again turned her about and when she felt him unbuttoning her clothes she closed her eyes. When the last of her garments had fallen to her feet she was facing him, and he was without his dressing gown. He did not take his eyes off her as he turned back the bedclothes. Then, stooping, he picked her up in his arms and gently laid her down.

The next moment he was lying beside her and stroking her face tenderly as he said, 'This is the beginning, Hannah. If I could marry you tomorrow I would do so, but I will one day. Oh, yes, I will. There'll come a day when we'll be man and wife, you'll see, but until then we must be together as often as we possibly can, night or day; it doesn't matter which as long as I can see you and know that you love me.'

'Oh, David. David. This feeling I have for you, if it's not love I don't know what name to give it, because it's partly pain – at least, a constant ache; and you know something? a few moments ago I was extremely nervous. If it had not sounded like something out of a bad play I'd have said, "I'm not used to doing things like this."' They both laughed a little and their bodies fell together; and then as his lips were about to meet hers she said, 'You know something more? I seem to have been like this with you before. At this moment, David, you are neither new to me nor strange, but it seems like a continuation of something. That might sound silly, but . . .'

'No, my love; there's nothing silly about it; it only confirms what I thought those few short days ago, that we had met before. I'm a firm believer in re-incarnation and if ever I wanted proof of it I've had it in the feeling I had that morning and what has grown on me ever since . . .'

Their love swept them both into realms neither had hitherto experienced, and she knew that she was loving, and being loved, for the first time in her life; also that it was something unbearable and could be endured for only a matter of seconds. When again she was resting in his arms, her breathing coming in gasps and her face strewn with tears, he became alarmed, saying, 'Hannah! What is it? I'm sorry.' And at this she put her wet fingers across his mouth as she murmured, 'Never, never say that word to me, David. Never be sorry for loving me. I'm . . . I'm so happy, it became unbearable, and I know that my tears have washed the last four years away as if they had never been.'

At half-past eight next morning, when Peter awoke them with a bedside tray of tea, it was as if he were carrying out his usual morning routine. 'Good morning, madam,' he said.

Hannah opened her eyes, blinked, was about to sit up, then realising she was naked she pulled the bedclothes under her chin and answered, 'Good morning, Peter.'

'Tea, sir?'

'Oh! what? Oh.' David blinked, shook his head, then said, 'Oh, hello, Peter. What time is it?'

'Just turned eight-thirty, sir. It's a very nice morning: the sun is shining and it promises to be a warmish day. May I ask if you will be in to lunch today, sir?'

David pulled himself up on the pillow, ran his hand through his hair, then thought a minute before turning to Hannah and asking, 'Shall we eat out?' and she, unable to find words with which to meet the situation, simply nodded her head.

'Very well, sir. Very well. Drink your tea while it's hot.'

When the door had closed on him they turned to look at each other; then quickly he bent and kissed her, and she said, 'Is he used to seeing strange women in your bed?'

His expression serious now, he replied, 'It appeared like it, didn't it? but I can assure you, my darling, that even when I was married I can't remember his bringing us tea, and never, never at any other time. He's a card, is our Peter.'

Turning quickly on his side, he pulled her into his arms, asking softly, 'How d'you feel?'

She answered as softly, 'Believe me when I say I don't know. I can only tell you that I don't belong to the person I was yesterday at this time. No; it's true I can't tell you how I feel because I feel neither embarrassed nor awkward, and I certainly don't feel sinful; in fact, I suppose I'm really feeling wonderful.'

He pushed her on to her back, and now his hands were running through her already tousled hair, and he was laughing as he said, 'You're wonderful, simply wonderful.'

This was followed by another long kiss, and when he turned from her to get the tea she heard that voice loud in her head saying: When are you going to wake up? because wake up you must. There is still Humphrey, and there is still David's wife. Of the two, the more awesome is his wife. You must get him to talk about her.

Oh, why? Why couldn't her conscience leave her alone on this wonderful morning of all mornings? Anyway, whatever might happen, nothing would be able to separate them now, so why worry?

Yes, why worry?

# Ten

Hannah was to remember the following six weeks as an oasis in which she neither looked back nor ahead, living only for Thursdays and the weekends. Thursday night seemed as important as the weekend, for it bridged the empty days from Sunday evening, when he set her on the train, until about seven-thirty on the Thursday evening, when he himself always opened the door to her. Only once had they taken lunch together, and that was in the week following their first lovemaking.

She had reached the stage when she didn't care whether or not Humphrey was aware of her escapade; but on that particular night, when he came home in a kittenish mood and started to tease her about her double, she knew she would be unable to bear the thought of him knowing about her relationship with David.

He had hardly got his coat off when, wagging his finger in her face, he had said, 'Aha! What is this I hear? A beautiful girl lunching out with a handsome man. Could it be Mrs Drayton? No, no; of course not, I said to Brown. Well, it was her double, if ever he saw one, he said.' Now it was his head that wagged at her. 'There you were, in a well-known restaurant dressed up to the nines. In style, he said. And let me tell you' – his head was still wagging – 'your double must be of some import because the proprietor came out and spoke to her and her escort, and they had a reserved corner to themselves. He saw them leaving, too. The only difference, he said, between you and your double was that she was a little taller, but he'd never seen such a likeness and he swore you could have been twins. Of course, it made food for a lot of chaffing. You know what they are, but I quashed that: I told them it just possibly could have been you, as you were having lunch with your publisher. Oh' – his head really was wagging now – 'that changed the whole situation. My wife's publisher, well! well! She's having a book published? Yes; yes, she is. Dear, dear; they didn't know that my wife was an author. I said there were lots of things that they naturally didn't know about my wife. One of them was that she could wear *haute couture* when the occasion demanded it.'

She could not prevent herself from saying, 'Did they not wonder where I got the money from for French fashions? or were they putting it down to your generosity?'

His expression changed, as did his voice as he said, 'Now now! you know that I couldn't possibly afford to dress you that way. Anyway, you, being an author, would make your own money.'

'Out of a silly little children's book – because that's all it is, isn't it, Humphrey?'

'Don't be nasty, Hannah. I thought you would see the funny side of this.'

'Well, to tell you the truth, I don't see the funny side of it, Humphrey. I'm only jealous of a woman who looks like me who could be enhanced by a fancy outfit. It makes one think.'

And it certainly made Humphrey think, because he watched her march away towards the kitchen; and she was marching: her head was up, her back was straight, and her step was very firm, noisy in fact, on the parquet floor. What was the matter with her these days? She'd been acting somewhat oddly, but then . . . His eyelids blinked rapidly, he rubbed his forefinger hard across his lips, and said to himself, 'She's used to it by now. Couldn't be that.'

Towards the end of September Hannah received a phone call of the most surprising kind.

'Hello! Hello?'

'Is that Mrs Drayton Junior?'

Hannah actually pulled her face back from the mouthpiece: she recognised the voice and it was some seconds before she said, 'Yes, this is Mrs Drayton . . . Junior.'

'Oh. Good morning, Hannah.'

'Good morning, Mrs Drayton.'

She was about to ask if anything was wrong when Humphrey's aunt said, 'No doubt you will be surprised that I am phoning you.'

'Well, it is a little out of the ordinary.'

'Yes; yes, you could say that, but it is important to me and my husband. We are seeking some facts.'

'Facts?'

'Yes, facts.'

It was as well Mrs Drayton Senior could not see Hannah's expression, because she was thinking: Well, here it comes, and, after I've told her to mind her own business, I shall tell her what I really think of her and her dear boy.

'Hannah! are you still there?'

'Yes, Mrs Drayton; I'm still here.'

Mrs Drayton's next question startled her. 'Have you any idea, Hannah, where Humphrey is this morning?'

Hannah's face was a picture as she replied, 'I can only say that I expect him to be where he is every Saturday and Sunday and sometimes on a Friday, too. He should be with you by now.' Her tone had become tart.

Hannah was now about to say, 'Are you there?' in her turn, when Mrs Drayton's voice came to her: it was changed and rather small – a cross between a whisper and a whimper, she would have said: 'You are telling me, Hannah, that you think your husband spends most weekends with us?'

'Not most, Mrs Drayton, but all, as he has now for years.'

There was a short silence, then the voice said, 'And what do *you* do with *yourself*, Hannah?'

Again some seconds elapsed before she answered, 'I've filled up my weekends with writing and shopping, and have often just passed the time with window-shopping. That is on a Saturday; but on a Sunday I have a lie-in; sometimes I then go to my sister's for lunch. Not too frequently, though, because I consider it their family day; it's the only day my brother-in-law is off work. There are other times when I babysit for them. This may be on a Saturday night.

'Anyway, Mrs Drayton, I'm sure you registered my surprise when you asked me where I think my husband is: of course, I assumed he was with you. And I may tell you truthfully that I've at times felt bitter at being left alone, not for the last weeks or even months, but for the past two and a half years, because you and your husband were demanding his attention. I know that you brought him up from a boy, but I've always considered it very high payment that I, too, have had to pay in order to recompense you and your husband for the kindness you showed him then.'

When there was no word from the other end of the line Hannah thought, with slight panic, Oh dear me! I've said too much, and she's an old woman. Or is she an old woman? How old is she? Seventy? Well, that isn't really old today.

'Mrs Drayton?'

'Yes, Hannah?' The voice was still small.

'I . . . I'm sorry if I've upset you.'

'No, no, Hannah; you haven't upset me. I mean you've not upset me, not at all, in fact I feel I owe you an apology; both my husband and I owe you an apology. At the present moment we are in the nursing home: my husband's leg needs constant attention and so we have taken a suite of rooms here. I . . . I'd like to talk further with you. Would you be able to come here one day next week? I must ask if you could make it as soon as possible.'

'Yes. Yes, Mrs Drayton, I could come and see you.'

'I would ask something further of you. On no account . . . on no account,' the words were repeated, 'will you mention to your husband that I have phoned you.'

It wasn't 'dear Humphrey' now, Hannah noted, and she said, 'I'll do that, Mrs Drayton; and I'll be pleased to come and talk with you, because I think there's something here that needs clearing up.'

'Indeed. Indeed it does, Hannah. Indeed, indeed it does.' The voice was no longer weak nor that of an old woman; it was strong and full of bitterness.

'Can you give me the address and at what time you'll expect me? I have a notebook here.' As she listened to the voice on the phone it was as if someone else were speaking, for there was no trace of the tentative old lady.

After she had taken down the address she repeated it: 'Pine Nursing Home, at eleven o'clock, Monday.'

'Thank you, Hannah. I'm looking forward to your visit. Thank you again. Goodbye.'

'Goodbye, Mrs Drayton.' Hannah sat back on the hall chair. To say that she was amazed was putting it mildly. Could she tell Mrs Drayton where Humphrey was this morning?

My God! She found herself now on her feet and

walking up and down the hall. All those years and her lying alone while he was having it off – for there was no other way to describe it – with someone else. What else would he be doing with his time? She couldn't wait for Monday.

She couldn't even wait until she saw David, and that would not be until eleven o'clock. She was already dressed for outdoors, and within another five minutes she would have left the house and missed that call. Yet such was the state of Mrs Drayton Senior that she would definitely have had that call sooner or later.

At quarter-past eleven she was seated on the couch in David's flat, and he was saying, 'Come on; come on, tell me what it was impossible to tell me outside.'

'Well' – she swallowed deeply – 'I was afraid that in the telling I might shout.'

'Shout? With pleasure or . . .?'

'No; certainly not at the moment. I've only been told the mere outline of the story. I'll know more on Monday, and I can't wait till then.'

He put his hands on her shoulders, saying, now, 'Can you take time to kiss me?'

She laughed shakily, and put her arms around him, and after they had kissed she pushed him away and said, 'Humphrey's aunt phoned me.'

'His aunt? The old girl he visits every weekend?'

'None other, she and her husband.'

'Well, go on.'

And so she told him all that had transpired on the phone. After she had finished he said, 'I'm going to say this: I've known all along in my heart that it would be impossible for any normal man to lie next door to you when he had a right to your bed, unless he was being . . . well, what should we say, fed from other quarters.'

'I feel wild inside, David.'

'Oh, I can understand that, because I've heard nothing about him since we first met, other than how kind and thoughtful he is and that he must not be hurt.'

'Hurt him! If I had him here this moment I would go crazy, I really would. I wouldn't be able to resist hitting him with something that would leave a mark. He left a mark on me.' From being bitter, her voice changed to almost a whisper now: 'You've no idea, David, what it felt like to be rejected. How I filled in all those weekends I don't know, except that the strain was beginning to tell on me. I was feeling old and, in a way, someone of little consequence, because I had a husband who didn't want me.'

'Oh, my dear' – David drew her into his arms again – 'it might seem strange to you, and I hate to think of those lonely years that I could have filled, but I'm glad that he acted as he did, otherwise you wouldn't be here now. But if I could get my hands on him now I'd floor him. If only you'd brought your little book to Gilly's much earlier. Although I have dear friends like Gilly and Natasha and, of course, Peter, and some acquaintances like Micky, the last few years have been arid for me too. Oh yes, I've known different women, but they've come and gone: met at a party or some such, a dinner or two, then goodbye. At times I'd feel a bit of a swine because they were nice women; but I seemed to be waiting for someone. I didn't know who until, on Thursday the seventeenth of August, a young lady brought a children's book to Gilly and wondered if it could be published. Well, the disturbance flared up immediately, and I couldn't push it off. This was serious. Then I looked back and asked myself if this was as it was the first time too. The answer was a firm No! Then I was literally carried into marriage on the back of a horse, you could say.

'Well, not quite literally, but very near it, because they were a mad family. Truly mad. Oh yes, truly mad. On her side, anyway; the boys are different. We call them boys although they're men. The father and the three brothers lived in the stables, and she did too. Where horses were concerned, she was madder than they.' He turned his head away now, saying, 'And in her case, Hannah, I mean mad, insane mad. I can say this now, but then I did not know anything about the insanity in the family. That was kept secret until we'd been married some weeks, when she had her first tantrum in a hotel, and the cost of the breakages ran into hundreds. It was then I discovered that she had a sister in a psychiatric hospital in Wales. She'd been there since she was about five years old and was now in her thirties. Her mother, I knew, was delicate and had long spells in a nursing home. That's the name they put to the private mental home; yet no ordinary person would have had an inkling of this, so I can't really blame myself; and yet I can, because Peter tried to warn me. I can recall him giving me hints which I threw aside. After my father died, my wife's family took him on, and they took me on too. They were so kind, so jolly, so full of hospitality, you have no idea.

'But looking back, I know now, in my case anyway, there was method and preparation in all their madness, because they pushed Carrie at me. The idea, I think, was to shift some of the responsibility for her which had fallen on the shoulders of Tony and Max. Alex was in France, as Pilly said. And at that time, as I had very little money except that which I earned by teaching, I couldn't set up a home of our own, so I lived at The Manor. Except for the hotel attack and one other, when there was a scene with a taxi driver, we got by for the first year. But then I became her personal target. And she was a big girl, a big woman, and often the result would be a wrestling match from which one or other of the brothers would try to extricate me. Oh—' He turned his head to the side and shaking it slowly he said, 'No one knows, has any idea of what life was like during the next three years. Without Tony and Max I think I would have been in an asylum too. In any case I had a breakdown. I had said I wanted a divorce but she threatened to shoot me if I humiliated her through the process of a divorce, and she would be in her sane moments when she came out with that.

'When, eventually, I became ill both my doctor and my solicitor said that there must be a separation. Her brothers told Carrie that if she didn't agree I'd take her to court and chance going through with a divorce, too, and so, after four years, I was what you call free. Yet, during that period, I was physically ill and my asthma attacks returned; but I managed to go back to teaching and through Gilly's son my desire to live returned because I found there were different people in the world, even people who didn't like horses' – he smiled – 'and those like Gilly and Natasha who repay small kindnesses with life-long gratitude. So there you have my history. Life went on, bearable, but only just at times until, as I've impressed on you, the seventeenth of August.'

Hannah put her arms about him and brought his head onto her shoulders, and in a soft voice she said, 'And here am I, moaning about *my* life.'

'Oh' – he put in quickly now – 'you certainly had something to moan about with that man. He's a sadistic individual, and that's putting it mildly.'

She in turn now asked, 'Have you seen her since the separation?'

'Only once. I was about to board a train, at the Gare du Nord in Paris. Apparently she and Alex were waiting for the arrival of some friends when she caught sight of me, and anyone who didn't know anything about her would have imagined from her greeting and the way she spoke that she was the most sane and charming person alive. "Why, darling!" she effused, "how lovely to see you again. Are you arriving or leaving?" And when I said leaving, she came back with, "Oh, can't you put it off for a day or two? It would be lovely to have you to stay. We're waiting for the Parkinsons . . . you know them. Wouldn't it be lovely if he stayed, Alex?" And Alex said to me very quietly, "Hello, David." And when I answered, "Hello there, Alex," she cried at her brother, "Make him stay! It's ages since we had a talk. What about it? Come on. Come on, David."

'She'd gripped my arm, and I recall saying quietly, "The train's about to leave, Carrie; I must go." And at this her charming attitude changed and, her voice rising, she almost yelled, "In one of your moods, are you? When did you ever do anything I wanted?"

'It was a good job that Alex had fast hold of her at this point, for as I went to step up into the compartment she screamed at me, "Coward! Sadist! I'll get you one of these days for what you've done to me."

'You can imagine the interest I aroused in that compartment. There was a long journey before me and I spent it mostly in the corridor.'

'She . . . she sounds dangerous.'

'Oh, she's dangerous, all right. If it wasn't for her brothers she would have been in a psychiatric hospital long before now, like her sister. When she's normal there could not be a nicer person; the trouble is one didn't really know when she was in a normal condition, for a wrong word or any fancied slight could trigger off one of her so-called turns.'

'How long ago was that meeting in Paris?'

'Oh, four years, and I'd hope it'll be another four, or fourteen before I see her again. But then' – he now caught hold of her hands – 'from what you've told me today you could apply for a divorce tomorrow, and you wouldn't feel any compunction in divorcing him now, would you?'

'Oh no. Compunction indeed! I'd gladly do it tomorrow.'

'Well, then, in that case I too would have to brave the elements, and file for a divorce. The time we've been parted would surely make things very easy, and there'd be no need to bring up her insanity as a plea, because I wouldn't want to hurt the family unnecessarily. Just think' – he jerked her towards him and held her tightly – 'this time next year we could be together; no short weekends, no fleeting Thursday-evening hours. We could be together for good and the days would be our own. We could do what we liked with them.'

Her gaze was cast downwards, and no matter how she tried, her imagination wouldn't follow his. But she could see them together, though as yet only in this room . . . in this house. The inner voice on this occasion remained quiet.

Of a sudden she snuggled her face into his neck and when she murmured, 'I love you, love you, love you,' in answer he put his hand gently on her head, saying, 'And I you, and every hair of your golden head.'

# Eleven

At just on eleven o'clock on Monday morning Hannah found herself walking behind a nurse down a long narrow corridor, and the nurse was saying, 'Mrs Drayton is expecting you. They're in the annexe.'

She was now ushered into the small but well-furnished sitting room that gave on to a double french window and a private stretch of garden.

The nurse went to one of two doors at the far end of the room and, tapping on it, she said, 'Your visitor has arrived, Mrs Drayton,' and the answer came clearly to Hannah: 'Thank you, Sister, I'll be there in a moment.'

When the nurse who had now become a Sister had left the room, Hannah stood looking out of the french window, but when she heard the far door opening she turned to see Mrs Drayton, dressed in a smart blue two-piece suit, entering the room.

'Good morning, Hannah. Are you admiring our garden?' Before Hannah could give any reply Mrs Drayton went on, with a slight laugh, 'We call it *our* garden because over the past few years we've seen such a lot of it and it's so pleasant to sit in, quite private.'

'Yes, it looks a lovely garden, and so sheltered.'

'Yes, it is, very sheltered. Do sit down, my dear. Do sit down.'

Hannah sat down on a two-seater couch, and Mrs Drayton took a chair to the side of it. They were within an arm's length of each other, which they hadn't been for years, and Hannah noticed that although the older woman hadn't seemed to age, what had altered was her voice. It had a less stringent tone; in fact, she told herself, it could almost be called warm. She now watched Mrs Drayton lay her hands palm on palm on her lap, then look towards the tall windows as she said, 'D'you know, Hannah, as one gets older one's opinions rarely change. If they were strong in one's young days they remain strong, perhaps' – there was a wry smile on her lips now as she added – 'through perverseness if no longer through conviction. Another thing that seems to become more solid with the years is your opinion that nothing can surprise you . . . or no one. You've dealt with all kinds of people through business and pleasure; you tell yourself that no facet of another's character have you ever judged wrongly. Oh, no; you know people. Well, Hannah, I must admit that the reason you are sitting here now is that I have definitely been proved wrong, as has my husband. There's an old-fashioned saying that I could quote that describes our feelings: we are cut to the bone by our discovery that we have been wrong, so terribly wrong.'

She now changed the position of her hands before going on: 'I think I'd better start at the beginning of how this has come about. You see, Sister is leaving' – she nodded towards the door through which Hannah had entered the room – 'and she has been so good to us over the years. This is the annexe, you know.' She now lifted one hand and spread it outwards before returning it to its place on her lap. 'It has two bedrooms and this very comfortable little sitting room. The bathrooms are adjacent to our bedrooms, and then there is the addition of this very sweet garden; but topping these, the nursing here is very good. The Pines is noted for the professional staff it always employs, so I thought it would be very nice to give Sister some personal effect, such as a piece of jewellery, as a private going-away gift. But on Friday, when we arrived for this present stay, I found that I had come away without the piece. It was still in my jewel box. Now, as you know, Mrs Beggs is my housekeeper and she holds all the keys, except for the one to the safe, and my jewel box was in the safe, so there was nothing for it but for me to go home on Saturday morning. Now it hasn't been a rule, it has just happened, that once we're settled here we don't go back to the house until my husband is well enough. If I want anything I just phone for Mrs Beggs to bring it. But in this particular regard I had to go home myself. So I ordered a taxi; but I was somewhat surprised when, outside our gates, I saw another taxi waiting there. I therefore asked my driver to drive round to the back of the house. Looking back I don't know why I didn't get out of the taxi and just walk straight up to the front door, because Mrs Beggs rarely goes out on a Saturday morning. It is in her routine to do a little baking and as the daily woman doesn't come on Saturday she's always there to take any phone calls. And so I was made to wonder.

'I always carry a set of spare keys in my handbag, the habit of a lifetime, so it was quite easy for me to unlock the garden gate, then the conservatory door, and enter my house that way; but I must confess that, being intrigued by the taxi and whoever might be visiting, I went in very quietly. Our conservatory is L-shaped and the farthest door leads into the hall. Well, I heard a voice coming from there and I made my way towards the door, but I didn't go through into the hall, I stood and I listened, and as near as possible I will tell you what I heard. It was Mrs Beggs on the telephone. She said, "I had to get a taxi because, besides the odds and ends I baked today, there's enough other stuff to keep you going for a week."'

Mrs Drayton now took from her cuff a handkerchief and dabbed at the moisture on her upper lip before continuing. 'There followed a silence. Someone at the other end was talking; and then Mrs Beggs said, "It's this postnatal business. You know what it was like last time and you also know it goes. Anyway, I must go, too. Tell Humphrey to be at the gate in about fifteen minutes. I won't come in because you never know when she decides that she wants something. Anyway, dear, it can't go on for ever. And, Daisy . . .'"

Mrs Drayton now spread out both her palms towards Hannah, saying, 'I couldn't hear what was said next. It must have been in a very low voice or a whisper, but it ended with, "His leg's in a bad condition, so you tell Humphrey what I said. Bye-bye, dear. Bye-bye."'

Hannah said nothing. She sat looking at this elderly woman who might be nearing eighty but certainly didn't look it, except that the expression now on her face was one of pain when she said, 'Your husband, my dear, when he was a boy, was *our* dear Humphrey. He was the son I was never able to give my husband, so therefore it has been with great difficulty I've had to make my husband realise that his dear boy is a liar, a cheat, an immoral man, and I can say that at this moment I think of him as every inch a scoundrel.'

'Please don't distress yourself, Mrs Drayton.'

'Distress myself, my dear? I am dumbfounded; yet I've had my doubts for a long time. You see, I know Daisy. D'you remember Mrs Beggs having a daughter named Daisy?'

'Yes, I do; and I remember she married your gardener, the younger one.'

'Mrs Beggs', said Mrs Drayton now, 'was supposedly left a widow with a very young daughter when I engaged her as housemaid. I soon found out that she was lying; she'd never been married. The child was illegitimate. But in spite of our views of them, as you know, I kept her on because she was

232

a good worker and she needed a home. At first she repaid my kindness with her work and loyalty. That was until her daughter came on the scene at seventeen. In the meantime, she'd been brought up by an aunt. Now at that time Humphrey was a young and impressionable man, and Daisy was a flirtatious girl. I didn't know that an association between them was being encouraged by Mrs Beggs, but when we saw how things were shaping my husband decided that Humphrey should do another year of accountancy training before joining a firm in London, a firm with which my husband had been associated.

'Well, in the meantime, Miss Daisy was lost for male company and she set her sights on the gardener, just to pass the time, I think, until Humphrey returned. But being who she was and the young gardener who he was, she became pregnant. He married her, but when she lost her baby he walked out on her. I can't tell you whether or not they were divorced, but Mrs Beggs was very indignant about all this and supposedly cast off her daughter for good and all. One thing was very plain, though – Humphrey was greatly distressed by the girl's marriage, and for a time we thought he was going to have a breakdown. Then time passed and he took a post in London, and it was there that he happened to meet you. Now you are a very presentable girl and I could understand his being attracted to you, but' – she smiled here – 'I had, as I think I made plain to you and very tactlessly, my dear, I am sorry to say, something against blondes.

You see, at one time I was director of our company, and if there was ever any trouble it was always' – she smiled again – 'with a blonde. The blondes seemed, to my mind then, to break up marriages as a yearly pastime, so we weren't at all pleased with Humphrey's choice, although at first there was nothing in your manner or bearing that gave us cause to dislike you. Not until about a year after you were married did Humphrey's weekend visits become chequered. Before this he had been so glad to come home and spend time with my husband, mostly talking business, I must admit, and so we used to look forward to the weekends. Then it emerged that Humphrey's wife was, as all blondes are, a flighty piece.'

She now leant forward to Hannah, saying, 'Forgive the assumption, Hannah, please, but if you're told a thing often enough you can't help but believe there's no smoke without fire. Whereas he had seemed to keep you in control, you were beginning to demand all his time, and he was obliged to entertain you on a Saturday. The only time he could call his own was his Thursday evening bridge game with his associates at the office.'

Hannah had now pulled herself to the front of the couch and was holding her face with one hand.

'Then there were the Sundays,' Mrs Drayton continued. 'Sunday mornings apparently were spent at your sister's. Sometimes he managed to avoid having lunch there, when he would come on to us. But then he would have to pick you up at about six o'clock because by that time apparently you had had more than enough of your coarse brother-in-law and their four children.

'And then, my dear, there was your extravagance. Now, he never asked after the first loan, which quite truthfully he said he could not see himself ever being able to pay back. Of course, in the first place my husband had pooh-poohed the idea that he should ever think about paying him back. But following this there would be times when he was very worried about your extravagance. You had a habit of running up bills. You would order goods, unnecessary articles for the house. You were always changing curtains and things like that and at the best shops; so on such occasions a cheque was always pressed into his hand, from my husband, I may say, because I did not agree with his loaning or giving, and there were times when I dared to suspect something wasn't right. And lately, of course, you have been buying the most expensive clothes, and he's been receiving the bills. Now, my dear, don't mind my saying this, but that is a very expensive suit you have on, may I ask – and please forgive me if I'm wrong – whether he bought that for you?'

Hannah was on her feet. 'Mrs Drayton, he has never bought me a single decent thing to wear during our marriage. I've had to beg him for enough money for a summer or a winter change. He didn't want me to go out to work, but he didn't give me money for clothes or anything like that, and he saw to all the housekeeping. What money I had was from my occasional spare-time secretarial work; and just lately I was paid two hundred pounds advance royalties on my children's book, which is going to be published.'

Mrs Drayton was now on her feet. 'You're having a book published, my dear? Oh, my dear. May I ask you, Hannah' – Mrs Drayton was now holding Hannah's hand – 'would you come into the bedroom and repeat this to my husband, as well as all that you have told me?'

'Yes. Yes, I will if you think it wise and won't upset him too much.'

'He cannot be more upset than he is already, my dear. Come along.'

Mr Drayton was propped up in bed, and over his legs was a cage supporting the bedclothes. He was very thin and certainly looked his age, which she understood to be about eighty-five.

'Here's Hannah to have a talk with you, George.'

'Good morning, Hannah.'

'Good morning, Mr Drayton.'

'Sit down here, my dear.' Mrs Drayton drew a chair up to the head of the bed, adding, 'He's slightly deaf in his right ear.'

'George, Hannah has been telling me that she's going to have a children's book published.'

'A book published? My dear, my dear; this is amazing. When did this happen?'

'Oh.' She smiled at the old man now, saying, 'I can give you the exact date; it was on Thursday the seventeenth of August. That is when it happened; at least, when I took it to the publisher.'

'Oh, that's surprising. That is surprising.'

'And she was given a two-hundred-pound

236

advance, George.' George Drayton looked up at his wife, saying, 'Two hundred pounds! That's very good for a children's book. Who's the publisher?'

'It's a Mr Gillyman. He only publishes a few books, as he says, and he is—'

Before she got any further the old man's interest was obviously aroused, because he pulled himself up on the pillows and said, 'Martin Gillyman? Oh, I know him well; in fact, a lot of people know of him because he's not only a bibliographer but a biblio-phile. He's got a mania for books.'

'I could endorse that, Mr Drayton: his office is like a great warehouse. It's stacked with books from floor to ceiling. He lives above the business in a lovely flat; but it's noticeable that his wife won't have a book or a magazine anywhere. She's laid down the law on that.'

'You've met his wife?' This was from Mrs Drayton, and Hannah turned to her and said, 'Yes; and she's a very charming lady.'

There was an exchange of glances between the husband and wife, and then George Drayton said, 'I understand, Hannah, that we have grossly mis-judged you, and I for one wish to apologise. We have been given to understand that you are a most selfish individual, but my wife tells me that you have spent over two and a half years entirely on your own at weekends.'

'That is true,' Mrs Drayton said.

'Yes, it was perfectly true but not so now, not since the day of Thursday the seventeenth of August. My life seemed to change when I met Mr

Gillyman and his assistant, Mr David Craventon.'

'Oh. They've befriended you?'

'Yes; yes, you could say that; and Mr Craventon and I have become close friends. As Mrs Drayton', she turned and looked at the older woman, 'has been honest with me, I will now be honest with you both. My loneliness ceased from that time, because it was on that evening that Humphrey had two tickets for a Mozart concert, but, it being Thursday, he couldn't possibly go; there was his bridge.'

She looked from one to the other. 'Humphrey suggested that I go on my own, and, as I was feeling lost at that moment, that's what I did. And whom should I see there but Mr David Craventon, and he was on his own too. During the interval we got talking, and since then we have become friends.

'I feel you should know, though it is a very delicate subject to raise, that Humphrey and I have been sleeping in separate bedrooms for well over two years now. This was Humphrey's desire, not mine. I would also like to tell you, Mr Drayton, that I have never caused Humphrey to get into any debt, ever. He saw to all the bills and anything to do with money. What little he gave me for clothes bought me only the barest essentials. This,' she now stroked her hand down her suit jacket, 'as I have explained to Mrs Drayton, I bought out of my advance. I may tell you, and I feel no compunction in telling you this, that on occasions I have had to visit Oxfam shops for a change of clothes.'

Mr Drayton was looking down towards the bedcover and his fingers were picking at the quilted pattern on it as he said, 'You have no idea, Hannah, how distressed I am, and not only with my great, great disappointment in that man, but with the fact that you have been maligned for so long, while all the time you were left to suffer an unnatural marriage.' He was now looking fully at Hannah as he said, 'May I ask you a very personal question?'

'Yes; yes, Mr Drayton, ask whatever you wish.'

'What excuse did he give you for such an odd separation?'

'None whatever. I had an allergy, after eating some fruit, and this he took as an excuse to sleep in another bedroom; and he never returned to my bed. He also stressed that marriage was made up of all kinds of things, and that sex wasn't important. I . . . I went to a priest and asked his advice, but he wasn't very helpful. On the very day I took my book to the publishers I had earlier been to my sister and un-burdened myself, pouring out on her my loneliness and rejection, and she upbraided me for putting up with it for so long and told me I should leave him and file for a divorce.'

Again the couple exchanged glances, and now Mr Drayton said, 'Knowing this about Humphrey – and this is only part of it, for I am sure there is much more to be uncovered – how do you feel towards him?'

Hannah's face was straight and her voice grim as she said, 'If I'm to be honest, I must say I hate him. I hate him for his duplicity; I hate him for the fact that I've defended him when my sister and brother-in-law insisted I was being badly treated: I've told them how kind he was, how good I thought he was, because not everybody would come every weekend and sit with you both.' She turned her head away now, saying, 'Yes, I hate him for so many things. I don't know how it's going to be possible to stay in the same house with him.'

'Oh, you must, my dear.' Mrs Drayton was on her feet. 'Do, please.' She turned to her husband. 'She must, mustn't she, George? Try to leave things as they are, my dear, until James looks into this matter further. James is our solicitor and a very old friend. I went straight to him on Saturday when I had use of the taxi, and he was astounded, even though he had told me twice before that he thought he had seen Humphrey in Worthing on a Saturday. The first time it was only from a distance so he wasn't sure. The second time he seemed more sure, and this created an uneasiness in me, or, I should say, it increased the uneasiness that I was then experiencing. On occasions I came across Mrs Beggs using the phone and looking guilty about it. She always said she was ordering something, but I guessed it was a private call to someone. Well, now—' She went quickly to the bed and, taking the sponge from a bowl on a tray, she wiped her husband's brow, saying, 'I think it's time for coffee, dear, isn't it?'

'Yes; yes, Philippa, yes.'

They drank their coffee, over which they talked, mostly about the garden and the kindness of the staff at The Pines Nursing Home, and also about how wonderful it was that Hannah was writing books for children.

The conversation jumped jerkily from one subject to the other; then when Hannah noticed that the old man was beginning to sweat profusely she rose to her feet, saying, 'I'll go now; but may I call and see you again?'

'Do that, my dear. Do that, please.' Mr Drayton was holding out his blue-veined hand, and when she took it he shook it slowly and said, 'You've blossomed with the years, Hannah. You deserve every happiness, and I'm sure it'll come to you in the end.'

As his voice faded away his hand became limp in hers, and she laid it back on the counterpane before saying softly, 'Goodbye for the present,' and being followed from the room by Philippa Drayton.

The older woman's first words were, 'Thank you. Thank you, indeed. You have convinced him where I'm sure I never really could, and my husband's no fool. He'll repay Humphrey in kind; oh, yes, he will; but you'll do as we ask and not mention this matter to him?'

'It's going to be difficult, Mrs Drayton, very difficult; and there'll come a time soon when I'll find it impossible to live with him.'

'Oh, I'm sure of that, my dear; I'm sure of that, and for more reasons than you give. Our solicitor will be seeing to the matter, but I don't think we can all go ahead until we've found out what Humphrey's really up to. One of James's clerks, I believe, is a brilliant researcher and a sort of amateur detective – perhaps he can help. However, if anything further transpires during the week concerning this matter, I'll get in touch with you; but of course not in the evenings. Goodbye, my dear; and thank you, not only for your co-operation, but for your honesty. We are very moral-minded people, but there are circumstances in many cases that allow for leniency, and neither my husband nor myself would blame you for continuing a friendship, considering the position you have been placed in by your husband, not just for these past weeks or months, but for years.'

'Yes; that is what I say to myself, Mrs Drayton, not weeks or months but years. Anyway, goodbye. We'll be meeting again, I'm sure.'

'Yes, my dear; we'll certainly be meeting again.'

As Hannah walked towards Worthing station the words she would keep repeating to herself were 'postnatal condition'. *Postnatal condition.*

Oh, how, during that second year, she had longed for a child. Someone to really call her own, someone to love. Someone who needed her. *Postnatal condition.* She knew that if he appeared before her now she would be unable to keep her hands off him: she'd want to claw at him, use her feet, hurt him . . .

Her mind was still in the same condition when she was met by David at Victoria and he, immediately noting the change in her, said, 'What is it? What's the matter? Has something happened?'

'Yes; yes, you could say something's happened. By the way, is there any place nearby where we could . . . I mean, I could have a drink, a proper drink? Gin, not sherry. Gin, brandy, whisky, anything you would advise. Something that will calm me down, at least for the present.'

'Yes, I know a place, and it's back in the flat. You may have your choice of gin, brandy, whisky . . . oh, not sherry, although I have a good one.'

'Yes; let it be the flat.'

On opening the door Peter showed his surprise at seeing them, but any remark that he might have made was checked by David's saying, 'We're parched. D'you think you could make up two good Pimm's?'

'At your service, sir. At your service. Pimm's it is.'

David helped her off with her coat. Then he took it into the bedroom and laid it on the bed, and when he came back she was sitting on the couch, tucked into the corner as if she were pressing herself away from something; and that's what she was doing, against those words, *postnatal condition*, and all they meant.

'There you are, sir and madam.' Peter was pushing a small trolley towards them. 'I hope they're to your taste.'

'Thanks, Peter.' David picked up a glass and handed it to Hannah. She didn't thank him or Peter, but immediately put the glass to her lips, and it wasn't a sip that she took but a long drink, after which she took in a deep breath, but did not return the glass to the trolley; and Peter, looking at David, said, 'Would you like something to eat, sir? You missed lunch. Madam? There's plenty of food in the fridge.'

'That would be nice, Peter, thank you.'

She had her second Pimm's. This one she sipped at while eating; but she didn't really start to talk until the table was cleared and they were alone again. As she spoke he uttered: 'The swine!' and 'The pig of a man!' Then he asked softly, 'And they think he's with this Daisy?'

'Oh, yes, they're sure of it. But they want proof; they've got to know where he goes, and with whom he spends the weekend.'

'You can't stay in that house with him.'

'I . . . I don't want to, but I must play this game as he's played it. I want to see the outcome of it. I don't know how long that'll be, not very long, I hope, but then, David, I'll come, yes. In the meantime, if I could gradually bring some of my things, where could I put them?'

'Oh; upstairs in Peter's place; he only uses the bedroom. It's a proper flat, you know. There's an extra boxroom up there. Oh, don't worry about where you'll put your things.' He now took her face between his hands and said, 'I'd push them under the bed myself as long as I knew you were coming to stay; and you will be; oh yes, now you will be. But what you'll do with what's left of this afternoon is rest: either have a lie-down on the bed or on the sofa here. Look! put your feet up.'

'No.'

'I say yes, and lie down there; I must go and talk to Peter. I'm going to tell him you're going to live upstairs with him,' and he laughed now; 'he'll like that.'

Suddenly she pulled his head down towards her

and kissed him, after which she said, 'If this had come about without my knowing you I'm sure I couldn't have stood it. I'd have done something desperate. Don't shake your head like that, I really would.'

'Well, I am here and always will be, and you'll have to learn to do what you're told, so lie down. I'll get a cover for you.'

Obediently she lay down, and he went into the kitchen. Here Peter met his gaze, which told him he knew everything that had transpired, and he gave evidence of this when he said, 'Bloody hypocrite of a man! and to get away with it for years. It's as she said, sir, if she hadn't had you, God knows what she might have done.'

David did not reprimand Peter with, you didn't miss a word! but just said 'Let's go upstairs and see where she can put her things.'

# Twelve

Hannah knew that she would be unable to sit opposite Humphrey for their evening meal and look at him without exploding her knowledge in his face. She set the table for one, and, as soon as he came in, planned to say, I've had my meal; now I'm going out for a while. To this he would likely want to know where she was going, so she prepared her response beforehand.

But events turned out differently. She was in her room when she heard his key in the door. Then she was more than surprised when her name was bellowed out.

'Hannah! Where are you, Hannah?'

She came slowly down the stairs and walked along the corridor into the hall, to see him standing there, still in his overcoat. His long thin face was flushed and his voice matched his expression as he demanded, 'What d'you think you're up to, making a fool of me?'

When she did not answer but just stood staring at him, he said, 'Answer me! You've been laughing up your sleeve at me, haven't you? It was a joke to you, wasn't it, when I told you that Brown talked about your having a double dressed up like a *Vogue* model? And then again, when he was coming out of St Martin-in-the-Fields there was that same model walking in with a man. And he tells me that he greeted you and you smiled back at him, saying, "Good afternoon, Mr Brown." Well, what've you got to say?'

'Nothing. You said it all.'

'Don't you stand there defying me.'

He sprang at her and gripped her arm, only immediately to jump back with a painful cry as she brought her doubled fist down on his wrist, almost screaming at him, 'Don't you dare touch me! I'm telling you, don't you dare come near me or it won't be my hand I'll hit you with.'

He was staring at her open-mouthed while rubbing his wrist with his fingers. She saw his teeth chattering with fear, and when he did speak, it was with an effort. 'I want an explanation; you're not going to make a cuckold of me.'

'But what if I don't care to give you an explanation, at least not just yet? You'll have your explanation all in good time. Oh yes, all in good time, Humphrey.'

'You're beside yourself. What's come over you, anyway? You were never like this before.'

'*You* came over me, Humphrey; years of empty weekends.'

'You know why,' he put in quickly; 'it's important that I visit the old people. And, anyway, you wouldn't come with me: you didn't like them, and they didn't like you.'

She did not answer for a moment, but then she said quietly, 'Perhaps they were given the wrong impression of me.'

'You gave them the impression, not me: going there with your hair all over the place and your short skirts; you looked a type.'

'Oh. Oh, I looked a type, did I? Then that was the kind of person you married.'

His head wagged back and forth before he said, 'Yes, and that, I know now, was a mistake.'

'You're not the only one, Humphrey.' Her voice was quiet. 'You say that you know now, but I've known for a long, long time. Anyway, I'm going out. Your meal's ready; enjoy it.'

'Oh no, you're not!' He took a step towards her again. 'You're not going out of here until we have this thing settled.'

'Well, Humphrey, from where I stand it's going to take some time, perhaps weeks. But in the meantime I'm going out when I like; that is, before I leave altogether.'

'Don't you dare talk to me like that! Acting like a slut!'

He had hardly got the last word out of his mouth before her shout, verging on a scream, made him jerk to the side as if trying to escape a blow. She cried, 'You don't know how near you are to being brained. Yes, I mean brained! You dare use that word on me again and you won't know what's hit you, I promise you, as big as you are. But, then, how big are you? You're a worm inside, an empty, blown-up hypocrite of a man. I'm going out now; and don't you dare speak to me again until I'm calmer, for God knows what'll happen to you. And, Humphrey,' she spat his name at him, 'I mean this' – she was now speaking through her teeth – 'I mean every word I say: if I don't get you from the front I'll get you from behind.'

She asked herself what she was saying. Oh, my God! She swung round and dashed up to her room. She had never felt such anger. While she was listening to Mrs Drayton telling her how she had been maligned all these years she had thought she could never feel worse, but this feeling exceeded all other emotions she had ever experienced because she had meant what she had said; she could see herself, see herself with an implement in her hand hitting him on the back of the head. What had he done to her?

She was shaking as she rummaged in her wardrobe for a jacket. She must get to David's. If he was out, there'd always be Peter to talk to or to listen to. Peter had a calming effect on one.

When she returned downstairs he was standing in the hall. He still had his coat on, but he made no move towards her as he said, 'You might find the door locked when you come back.'

And to this she replied, in as flat a tone as she could render, 'Lock it, by all means. It'll be of some help when I file for a divorce.'

She opened the door as she said this, and as she stepped outside she was aware that he was hurrying towards her, and so she quickly pulled the door closed and almost ran down the street.

David was in and he immediately comforted her, but it was some time before he could calm her down, when she said, 'Phew! I could have spat it all out, everything I know now. If only I hadn't promised Mrs Drayton to keep quiet for the next few days; but it seemed most important to her that I should do so.'

Later, David insisted on taking her back in a taxi and waiting to see her safely in. When she inserted her key in the lock and the door opened she turned and signalled to him, then went indoors.

Immediately Humphrey appeared at the sitting-room door. He did not approach her but waited until she was about to pass him to go up the stairs, then said in a placatory tone, 'Hannah, let's talk. There's . . . there's something I must say to you.'

When she passed on without answering him, his tone changed and he cried, 'Hannah! I've got to talk to you. All right, all right, this might be the breaking point, but I . . . I've got to say something.'

Half-way up the stairs she turned and walked slowly down to the hall and confronted him.

'Come into the sitting room,' he said.

There, she sat on a chair; he took his stand with his forearm on the mantelpiece, and he did not look at her as he said, 'Well, it's about divorce. I . . . I'd give you a divorce tomorrow, yes, yes, I would' – he turned and nodded at her as if emphasising his desire to divorce her – 'but it's them, you see. They're so dead set against divorce or the breaking-

up of a marriage that if I were to mention it, well . . .
it would—' He stopped here as if lost for words, and
he took his forearm off the mantelpiece, thrust both
hands into his trouser pockets and began to pace the
hearthrug.

When he still did not continue, she said quietly,
'What you're trying to say is that you must keep in
their good books or you'll be cut out of their will,
and they're pretty wealthy, from what I understand.'

He stopped in his walk and nipped on his lower
lip before he said, 'That's putting it baldly; but who
else have they to leave it to? I mean, if they were an
ordinary couple without these prejudices . . . and I
*have* looked after them.'

'What?' The word seemed to suggest she hadn't
heard, and he repeated, 'I've looked after them. I
mean . . . well, that's why I've had to leave you at
the weekends.'

She could not sit and listen to this. She stood up,
then asked very quietly, 'Is that the only reason,
Humphrey?'

His tone was emphatic. 'Why else would I want
to leave you on your own, *have* to leave you on your
own? They're a very demanding couple. You've no
idea how trying it is. By Sunday evening I feel worn
out.'

Her reactions to this remark were twofold: first,
she wanted to laugh, to turn it into a sexual joke by
saying, 'I bet you are, Humphrey'; second, she experienced again the terrifying desire to spring at
him, to tear at his face. She had to get away. Quickly

she turned and walked towards the door, where his voice checked her, crying, 'Hannah! Hannah! Wait a minute. All I'm asking you is, you'll . . . you'll not do anything about . . . I mean, about a divorce yet. All right. All right, have your fling, if that's what you want, but as a special favour will you please, for the time being, keep it on the side?'

'How long is the time being? Until they both die?'

He had the grace to droop his head here as he said, 'The old man is very near his time, and I . . . I know she's really not well. She had cancer some time ago.'

'And you're waiting for them both to pop off.'

'Don't put it like that.'

'How else would I put it? I must wait until they're both dead before I can put in for a divorce? What grounds will I have then, Humphrey? You might change your mind.'

'Oh no. Oh no, I won't, Hannah. I promise you. I promise you.'

'But if you've done nothing to cause me to divorce you, how can I get one?'

'These things can be done amicably. Oh, yes; yes, they can. I promise you, as soon as they're gone.'

'So I must wait until they both die before I can get a divorce, is that it?'

'Please don't put it like that.'

'*Is – that – it?*' Each word was distinct.

'Well, I suppose so.'

'Thank you. Goodnight.'

'Hannah.'

She took no notice of the last plea and went up to her room. There, for the first time, she locked her door for, the state he was in, she could see him going to any lengths to try to placate her.

She needn't have worried. He didn't approach her; neither did he make any comment when she did not get up the next morning to see to his breakfast.

However, he had hardly left the house before she was up and dressed, because she knew this state of affairs could not continue. She would have to see Mrs Drayton.

It was shortly after nine when she phoned the nursing home. Mrs Drayton answered immediately, and straight away said how strange that Hannah should ring at that time because she herself had been about to contact her to tell her she had news. And yes; yes, of course, any time. Half-past eleven? Yes, yes . . .

So here she was again facing Mrs Drayton and she was surprised at the difference in the older woman's appearance. Apparently Mr Drayton had had two bad turns since last she was here, and now that lady was saying, 'I don't know what your news is, Hannah, but I'll give you mine while I can, because any moment I may be called next door. The nurse is sitting with my husband all the while. It's like this. You know that I got in touch with my solicitor after discovering Mrs Beggs's duplicity, and I told you that one of his clerks was a very good sleuth. Well, James gave Tom Frint, his clerk, all the details about Humphrey, one of the main ones being that he visited us only on a Sunday. Last Sunday it should happen that Mr Frint was in the vicinity and he saw

Humphrey coming here. Knowing that he leaves about five he made it his business to spend some time in the park opposite, and when Humphrey emerged he followed him.

'First Humphrey took a bus to the near end of the town, and after alighting he seemed to disappear for a time, until Mr Frint saw him on a rough road that crossed the open farmland. Having lost sight of him again, Mr Frint found himself in a farmyard that he remembered having visited many years ago. It had then been owned by an old couple named Johnson. A man was crossing the yard, and Mr Frint asked him if Mr Johnson still ran the farm, and the man laughed and said, oh no, he'd been gone for years; in fact, there had been another buyer before he himself had taken it over. And now Mr Frint realised he must fabricate his reasons for being there: Did he think that the old couple were living hereabouts, or any of their relatives, because his firm was making enquiries about them. He was from Morgan the solicitors.

'The farmer appeared very interested and said, well, he didn't think so, but there was a couple living in a cottage a quarter of a mile further along the road. Perhaps they were relatives of the Johnsons. They were called Beggs, just a young couple; at least, she was young. She was called Daisy and he was Humphrey. He was older, he would say, perhaps in his forties, and he worked somewhere in the City, and only got down at the weekends. They'd just had their second child, the other one being only eighteen months. They have them fast these days.

'As you may imagine, Mr Frint had heard all he wanted to hear.'

Mrs Drayton now spread her hands out wide, and, looking at Hannah, she said sadly, 'This time last week I . . . I was just sad that he had betrayed our confidence and treated us in this way, but with this new knowledge I feel angry, not only for myself but for you, because you had indicated you wanted children and he deprived you of them. Perhaps you might have been, like me, unable to bear them, but he didn't give you the opportunity.'

Hannah did not answer. She was too consumed with anger and bitterness, and again to such an extent that it amazed her that she was capable of such feelings. Of love, yes, and of hate also.

Mrs Drayton's hand now came on to hers, for Hannah's index finger had been unconsciously scraping at the material of her coat and the older woman's voice was soft as she said, 'Try not to take it to heart so much, my dear; yet I know exactly how you're feeling, you want to do something desperate.'

At this, Hannah nodded, saying, 'He . . . he was waiting for me last night when I returned at about ten o'clock. We'd had words, very strong words, before I left the house and just as I was closing the front door I mentioned divorce, and this is the word that I'm sure he's afraid of. In fact, I know he is because there he was, all placating, wanting to talk to me quietly, and so on, and the gist of it was—'

She closed her eyes and turned her head away, and when she didn't go on Mrs Drayton said, 'Yes, my dear? Tell me exactly what he said.'

'Well, he wanted me to promise to hold all talk of divorce until—'

Again she couldn't finish, but Mrs Drayton did so for her: 'Until we were both dead, is that it?'

Hannah did not answer but looked down at their joined hands. Mrs Drayton said quietly, 'Somehow, I know he's been waiting for that for a long time. Before his double life was exposed I had a very odd feeling about him and his supposed caring for us. As he has made you aware, we are against divorce: we feel that couples should work it out between themselves and try to reconcile matters. He knows that if the talk of divorce were to arise, one of your main points would be his neglect at weekends, and where would he be then? Oh, he knows he's in a tight corner, does Humphrey; but he doesn't realise just how tight. We're not going to be made out the doddering old fools that he imagines we are. Oh, no. And a business like this makes you think of the past, and I definitely recall finding him out in lies when he was a boy, and my husband explaining them away because he was very fond of him. This business has really broken George up, but as I want justice to be done I had to make things plain to him and show Humphrey in his true colours. I'm sure now that he has had his suspicions for some time about Humphrey's very curtailed Sunday visits. It's nearly always the same time, early afternoon . . . then, this Sunday I don't know how my husband contained himself when Humphrey told him that you—' She patted Hannah's hand now, saying, 'Now don't get upset, but we were informed that you had run up a bill for an expensive outfit that neither he nor you could in any way afford.'

'Oh, no!'

'Yes, my dear; and it proves how much my husband now realises his duplicity that he said nothing, but just looked at this man he had treated as a son for so long. He had educated him and tried to instil his own values into him. I think this is what's hitting him now: the fact that this man who has been in his house for so many years has what are virtually criminal tendencies. The fact that he's living a double life should, as you know, be enough, but that he has been enabled to live that double life only by blackening the character of his wife has got through to my husband as nothing else could; and I feel now that you wanted to see me today to ask to break your promise and come out into the open. I know how you feel, but could you just hold on for a few more days, because—' Her voice broke here, and taking her handerchief she pressed it over her mouth.

Hannah rose quickly from her chair and put her hand on Mrs Drayton's shoulder, saying, 'Please! Please don't upset yourself. I'll do whatever you wish.'

There was a silence between them for a short while, then Mrs Drayton said, 'Thank you, my dear. It . . . it won't be for long. And there is another thing. When my husband goes, I . . . I don't intend to inform Humphrey at his office. No matter when it is, I shall wait until the following Sunday. Nor will I inform Mrs Beggs, because she would be bound to get word to him. She only visits here when I invite her, as I've made it plain to her that I would rather she remained in the house to take calls from friends and such and then to phone me here. But most of my friends already phone me here and, you know, you would have thought, being supposedly such a faithful servant, she would have got in touch every day to see how my husband is. But no; if she has to ring, she asks after him, certainly, then she always finishes up that everything is all right at home: our budgerigar is still very happy and the goldfish in the garden pond are all still intact since we had the wire netting put over to save them from marauding cats. I think of you, Hannah, every time I hear that woman's voice, or Humphrey emphasising what a treasure she is. I don't remember his being so fond of her when he was younger; in fact, after she had allowed her daughter to marry the gardener he was incensed.'

The door opened and the nurse appeared saying quietly, 'Mrs Drayton.'

At this the older woman got hastily to her feet, and still holding Hannah's hand she said, 'Keep in touch, my dear. What . . . whatever transpires at this end, I'll phone you.'

Hannah's voice was full as she said, 'I'm terribly sorry.'

'I know you are, dear, and I only wish that we had previously become as well acquainted as we are now. My husband regrets this deeply. Anyway, goodbye for the present, my dear.'

Hannah stood in the room for a moment longer

trying to compose herself. The feeling of bitterness and hate was still in her, but also a deep compassion for this woman whom, over the years, she had been made to dislike.

She did not return home, but went instead to Janie's. And when she had finished telling her of all that had taken place, Janie said, 'I won't mention this to Eddie yet.'

Hannah could believe her this time, because she knew that Eddie, with the help of his friends, would be quite capable of settling this matter in his own way. And Janie confirmed this when she added, 'I wouldn't dare mention this to him 'cos I know what he'd do. I feel like doing it myself, the dirty bugger. Anyway, he'll get his come-uppance if your mother-in-law, or whatever you call her, knows anything about it, and, oh, I wish I could be there at the time. D'you think they'll cut him out of their will altogether?'

'I don't doubt it, the way she's feeling. And her husband too, I now understand. And, you know, to think that he might have got away with it all if Mrs Drayton hadn't happened to phone me on that particular Saturday morning.'

'You've taken to her, then?'

'Yes; strange, but I have, and she to me, I think, and the old man too. Oh, he was really nice; he even apologised to me for the way I'd been treated. I've only been there twice, but each meeting has been very emotional. I've wanted to howl my eyes out.'

'Well, get on with it while I go and make a cup of

tea. But you haven't said anything about your life and the bookworm. I've still to hear about how that's progressing.'

'There's only one word for it – wonderful!'

As Janie left the room she exclaimed, 'Oh, how I wish I were young again, and hadn't four kids, and a fella who thinks of nothing but fruit.'

Hannah lay back in her chair, chuckling at this beloved sister, yet at the same time knowing that what she really wanted to do was cry.

As she always did, Hannah had felt a little lighter as she left Janie's; but the feeling was soon dispersed as she entered her own house, because the whole atmosphere now portended strife.

The feeling did not lessen over the Wednesday and Thursday. She and Humphrey had not exchanged a word; not even as he went out for his Thursday bridge did he make any comment.

No sooner had he left the house than she ordered a taxi to take her and a large case of her belongings, which she had already packed and waiting, to David's.

It was half-past ten before she returned from David's, again by taxi. Humphrey had already arrived. His coat lay over the back of a chair, which in a subtle way expressed his state of mind. They did not exchange any words until after she was in her room, when he came to her door and said, 'I'm taking a day off tomorrow. My uncle . . . er . . . isn't at all well.'

She made no reply.

It was some seconds after speaking that he left her door. And immediately after she heard his own close she got out of bed and locked her door; but again she needn't have worried on that score.

At ten o'clock the next morning she phoned the nursing home and asked to speak to Mrs Drayton. She told her that they might get a visit from Humphrey, as he had taken an extra day off because he understood his uncle wasn't at all well.

To this Mrs Drayton simply said, 'Well, we'll see, Hannah, we'll see.'

When Hannah asked how Mr Drayton was there was a pause before his wife said, 'He's resting peacefully. He's not in any pain and he's quite conscious of all that's going on around him; however, he's very low.'

'I'm sorry.'

'I'm sure you are, my dear. Goodbye. I'll keep you informed.'

'Goodbye.'

Hannah could have slept at David's on the Friday night but she didn't, because she felt that Mrs Drayton would soon be phoning her; and so when the phone rang around ten o'clock on the Saturday morning and she heard Mrs Drayton's voice, she knew what she was about to hear.

'My . . . my husband passed away yesterday at half-past three, Hannah. And, no, we had no visit from Humphrey; and as I'm not supposed to know where he is I can't inform him, so he won't know anything about my husband until he calls tomorrow afternoon. Could I ask you to keep silent until after the funeral, Hannah? It'll be on Tuesday morning.'

'Yes, of course, Mrs Drayton. Yes, of course. I'll do whatever you ask.'

'Well, you won't have long to wait, because the will will be read in the afternoon. From then on things will begin to move your way.'

'Don't worry, Mrs Drayton. Don't do anything that's going to upset you any more than you are at present. I can wait.'

'Thank you, Hannah. Thank you.'

What Hannah did before she left the house was to get in touch with the nursing home again and ask to speak to the sister. And of her she enquired where the funeral was to take place and to where one should send flowers . . .

It was around half-past two in the afternoon and Hannah was sitting at one side of a small card table, David at the other. She was in the process of taking a lesson in the game of chess, and at this moment she was laughing, saying, 'I'll never get the hang of this; and why did you take that pawn when you told me I could just move up?'

'But I didn't tell you where you could move up to,' David replied. 'You left yourself open.'

'Sir . . . madam.' They both swung round, almost upsetting the ivory pieces, as Peter came rushing into the room. His sleeves were doubled up and he was wearing only a waistcoat over his shirt. 'I'm sure it's *her*, sir. I'm sure it's *her*.'

'What are you talking about?' David was on his feet.

'Down the road, sir. I was putting the' – he gulped – 'the rubbish out in the yard, and there was a taxi stopped further down the street. Two men were on the pavement and they were handing a woman out of the car. It was *her*.'

'Who? Who?'

'Who else, sir? Carrie. Your wife.'

'Dear God! no.' David put his hand to his head, then said, 'Pilly! I knew he would. I knew he would.'

They both now turned towards Hannah. Then Peter, running past them, rushed into the bedroom, picked up the coat and bag from the bed and came flying out again, saying, 'Come on! madam. Upstairs. Upstairs.'

David was already pushing her towards the kitchen door, urging her: 'Stay in the sitting room.'

When Hannah reached Peter's sitting room it was to see him agitatedly waiting for her. 'Don't lock the door,' he said. 'If she should come up here, then I'll be with her. You can be reading a book or something, and I'll say you are my cousin . . . even my daughter. Yes. Yes, I could say that.' He gave a momentary grin, then said, 'But don't move about, or you'll be heard downstairs.'

When he was gone Hannah, still in a daze, went to sit down in what looked like a rocking chair but changed her mind. Instead, she sat on a chair that was placed between the door and the window, and waited.

Downstairs, David had already cleared the chess table and had gone into the bedroom to see if there were any signs left of Hannah's presence. Immediately he found evidence: her slippers under the end of the bed. He doubled them up and thrust them to the back of the top shelf of the wardrobe; then went into the bathroom. There, he whipped up a small bottle of perfume from the glass shelf above the washbasin, and lastly her dressing gown from behind the door. Once more he was scrambling to the wardrobe. The dressing gown could be hung on a hanger: it was of an indescriminate colour, and could be taken for one of his; the perfume he thrust into the top drawer of the chest. Then he returned to the sitting room.

Peter and he stood looking at each other in silence for a moment. As David was about to make a comment, the bell rang.

It wasn't until it rang a second time that Peter moved towards the door. When he opened it he was confronted by three people: two tall men and a very well-made woman who was of the same height as the men.

'Good afternoon, Peter. You were about to say, "Good gracious!" weren't you?'

'No, madam.'

'Is your master in?'

'Yes; his master is in.'

The voice had come from somewhere to the right of the door and neither she nor the men saw David until they were fully in the room; and it was with a loud exclamation that she cried, 'Well! well! Davie-boy. After all this time. So this is where you've been hiding out. Well! well!' She started towards him, then stopped and looked around her, and, flinging her arms wide, she said, 'Almost arty-crafty. And you never liked art, did you now? Oh' – she pointed to the wall – 'that's yours, isn't it? That's one of your roseate terns: you had them all over the bathroom at The Manor. I blacked them out with tar, you know, after you went. Didn't I, Tony?'

The tall fair man did not answer her, but, looking at David, he said quietly, 'Hello, David.'

'Hello, Tony.'

Then the other man spoke: 'Hello, David. How goes it?'

'Very well, Max; very well. And with you?'

'Oh, fine. Fine.' The man smiled a pleasant smile as he said, 'We had three winners in a week. Now wouldn't you say that was well?'

'Yes, indeed.' David nodded at him. 'Where was this?'

'Two in France and one here; but our stable's mostly in France now, you know, with Alex.'

'Yes, yes.' David nodded again. 'I understood Alex was making his home over there.'

'And it'll be ours permanently when we get rid of The Manor.'

'You're selling, then?'

'Yes, yes; if we can get the right price.'

'And if I decide to leave.' This came from Carrie. As she spoke she divided her glance between her

265

brothers, and it was Tony who answered her, saying, 'Well, it's up to you. If you don't come, you must stay here by yourself. Now don't start again.' He lifted his hand in warning to his sister. 'We've come to say hello to David; we're just passing through; so, please! woman.'

'Can I offer you a drink?' David now looked towards Peter, who was standing waiting as if for an order, and the men shook their heads. Tony said, 'We've just had lunch; and we had an hour to spare. Pilly, you know, had told us where you're hanging out.' He laughed now as he added, 'He's well named as Lord Gap in the Gob, isn't he?'

'He didn't tell us all, though.' It was Carrie speaking again, and she was looking at David. 'He just said you had a bachelor flat, and when I asked, "How much bachelor, Pilly?" his reply was to wink and say, "Aah! Aah!" And you know there's never smoke without fire with anything that Pilly says, don't you, David? So is it a bachelor flat?'

'Now what d'you take David for, an ass?' It was Max speaking again. 'You, of all people, he's likely to tell if he's got a girlfriend? Don't be stupid, woman.'

It was obvious that, of the two brothers, this one had at least some control over his sister, because again she changed her tone as she said, 'You were asking if we'd like a drink. Let them speak for them- selves. I would, and I'll have a whisky, Peter . . . large; well, you know my size, you should do.'

'You'll have nothing of the sort; and stop it! I warned you, didn't I? Mind, I warned you.' The man was shaking his finger at his sister, and then he turned to David, saying, 'I'm sorry, Davie, but you know the pattern. You've been through it so often.'

'Oh, you!' The woman turned on her brother now, saying, 'So understanding, so sympathetic, you know nothing.'

'I know this much: you're not having anything more except coffee or tea. Now that's your choice, coffee or tea.'

'Well, you know what you can do with your coffee or tea, don't you?'

'Yes, I've a good idea, sister. Well, now—' The man looked at his watch. 'We have half an hour to get to the station; so if we want to get seats I think we'd better be going.' He turned his attention back to David now: 'We could have a meal together some time when we're over this way, couldn't we?' he said.

'Yes; yes, we could, Max.'

'How many bedrooms have you?'

Carrie was looking straight at David, and he said, 'One.'

'Oh, just one. Does your henchman live out, then?'

'No; he doesn't live out, he has a flat of his own upstairs.'

'Oh, there's another flat? Well! well! We'll have to have a look round.'

'You'll do no such thing.'

'Who's to stop me, Tony?'

'I for one, madam.' It was Peter speaking; and they all turned to look at him. 'That is *my* flat and it's private property.'

'I'd have thought it's only private if you've bought it. It likely belongs to the house. Does it?'

'Yes, I suppose you could say it's part of the house, but it's also part of my salary, and my entitlement to privacy.'

'Don't talk to me like that, Peter. Who d'you think you're speaking to? A yard man's entitlement to privacy! That's what you were, you were our yard man.'

'I was never your yard man, madam. I was the yard man of the master of the house at that time, and it was only at the request of the master himself that I stayed on.'

'Don't you dare use that tone to me, Miller. Have you forgotten to whom you're speaking?'

'No, madam. Confronting you, I could never forget to whom I'm speaking.'

'Tony! say something.'

'What is there to say? You've said it all, as usual, sister. Now, come on. You promised to behave, but you just don't know how to behave. I'm sorry, David. We would never have crashed in if it hadn't been for . . .'

'Because we all wanted to know if you had a woman here. Didn't we?'

Carrie looked from one brother to the other. At this, Max bowed his head and muttered, 'I still wonder why we bother, David. We're both fools. We'll find it out one day.'

'How dare you! It's you who gets me wild.' She was now standing in front of her brother, her fist punching at his chest. Then, with the suddenness of lightning, her hand dropped away and she turned and, addressing David in a voice unlike any she had so far used and which didn't seem to belong to her, she said, 'Forgive me, David. I'm sorry, but they get on my nerves, the pair of them. If they would only leave me alone and let me go my own way. I've told you this before, haven't I? I'm sorry. I didn't mean to cause any upset.'

She smiled at him now, but he didn't return her smile; he just looked at her. Then she said, 'Of course, we did think you might have a girlfriend, and they said, who'd blame you; but you know what I said?' Like a child she thrust her face towards him. 'I said to them what I said to you years ago: "All right! good for him. He can have as many girlfriends as he can manage, but once he mentions divorcing me, that's going to be another kettle of fish." Because, David, you remember what I promised you then, don't you?'

Still he didn't answer, nor smile, and she was unsmiling now as she added, 'I said I would shoot you if you ever approached me for a divorce. I wouldn't let you divorce me, David. Till death us do part, definitely. Well, now.' The sweet tone had returned. 'We'd better be on our way. But we'll look in again; perhaps you'll have company next time.'

As Peter went to open the door her arm shot past him with a force that almost overbalanced him, and she turned on him a look so full of disdain that he had to prevent himself from reacting to it and doing what he had wanted to do many a time: strike her.

She opened the door herself and went out on to

the grid, where she stood a moment looking about her. She hadn't bidden David goodbye, but the two men had turned to him, and it was Max who said, 'We really must be as mad as her to keep this up; but you know what the result would be otherwise, and we just still can't bear the thought of that.'

David's voice was low as he said, 'I can understand, but she doesn't improve, does she?'

'Improve?' Max said. 'Improve? It's hell at times. Alex wants us to do what should have been done years ago, but we haven't the heart; yet both doctors, Clark and Ainsworth, will section her at any time, because she's becoming really unpredictable.'

Their voices were low, but the woman called from the pavement, 'Come along, boys; don't tell tales out of school; I can hear you.'

'Goodbye, David. Goodbye.' They shook hands with him. Then Tony leant forward and called, 'Sorry, Peter'; and Max, too, put his head round the door and muttered, 'And me too, Peter, me too.'

'I understand, sir. I understand. It's all right.'

'What about a taxi?' David said.

'Oh, we told the fellow to wait; he's just round the corner. We knew we wouldn't be able to stay long.'

David followed the two men down the steps to the street; then, as he said later, he almost jumped out of his skin when he saw Hannah coming round the corner. The men moved aside to let her pass, but Carrie remained where she was, eyeing this elegantly attired beauty with her mass of golden hair tied loosely at the back with a ribbon.

The taxi had now drawn up beside them, and it was Max who looked at his brother and laughed as he said, 'French, I'd say,' and Tony, laughing back, said, 'No, no, no! Italian.'

Carrie's remark, however, brought their attention back to her when she said, 'Tart. Who does she think she is?'

The brothers looked at each other. David said nothing, until his wife turned back to him and said, 'Goodbye, Davie; but you know I have a feeling we'll be together again before long. Yes; yes, I have.'

'I wouldn't bank on that, Carrie,' David said flatly.

'Why not? Why not?' And, as her voice rose, Max gripped her by the shoulders, turned her about and pushed her into the taxi, saying, 'Enough! Enough! we'll miss that train. Goodbye, Davie.'

'Goodbye, Max.'

The last David saw of her was her face glaring at him through the taxi window. She's madder than ever, he thought.

David waited until the taxi had disappeared round the corner; then almost ran to catch up with Hannah.

'What in the name of heaven has brought you out?'

'I' – she was gasping as if she had been running – 'I thought she'd be coming upstairs. Somehow, I was afraid to meet her and I could imagine her thrusting Peter to one side; so I quickly put my jacket on and went down the back way, only to walk straight into you all.'

271

'Well, I can only tell you that you caused some comment . . . whether your clothes came from France or Italy. They thought Italy.'

She did not laugh, but said, 'She . . . she's very big, isn't she?'

'She is indeed big, almost as tall as her brothers; and, what's more, even at ordinary times she has the strength of a man; but when she's having one of her turns it's taken all three brothers to hold her.'

'I heard her voice.' She shook her head as she stopped herself from saying, Why on earth did you marry her? That wouldn't do; he had married her likely under persuasion from all sides. He had said as much.

Back in the flat, Peter said, 'Oh, madam, I thought I'd die when I saw you passing them outside. But I know why you went out, because she really could have forced her way up the stairs.'

As David drew Hannah down on to the couch, he said, 'I love this flat, but from now on I'll feel uneasy, imagining she might drop in at any minute.'

'Oh, I shouldn't worry too much about that, sir; I think the boys will keep her in France; most of their stock seems to be over there already. Anyway, you wouldn't get a place as suitable as this –' and he added on a smile, 'for both of us. I've got to like my little nest up above.'

'There's one thing for sure,' said David, now nodding at Hannah; 'she'll recognise you if she ever sees you again, and if she were ever to find you in here . . . Oh, Lord! Oh, Lord!' – he shook his head – 'It's unthinkable what could happen. She told me to have as many girlfriends as I like but not to talk of divorce, or else. But were she to see you again she wouldn't see you just as a girlfriend, a temporary pastime, as it were. Oh, no. So that has to be considered too.' He looked up at Peter, and he, nodding, said, 'Yes; perhaps you're right. But not for the moment; and the moment could be weeks or months away. It'll be a while before they're back this way again.'

Yes, it could be weeks or months, or it could be tomorrow, Hannah thought; and to her emotions was added a wave of fear. The woman's voice, as it had come to her upstairs, had spoken of a weird strength, and the first glimpse of her had created a fear, for she looked mannish.

David broke in on her thoughts now, saying 'What are you for? Continuing the chess, going for a walk or just sitting here brooding on what's going to happen on the lady's next visit?'

'I plump for the walk.'

'Same here.'

But no amount of walking would dispel the uneasiness that Hannah felt after that day's visitors.

# Thirteen

Humphrey was later than usual returning home on the Sunday evening; it was well after eleven. Hannah was already in bed and when she heard the knock on her door she drew in a tight breath before calling 'Yes? What is it?'

'I want to talk to you.'

'It's late and I'm tired.'

'I know it's late, and I'm tired too. I've something to tell you: you either get up and come out or I come in.'

She could tell by his tone that he was disturbed, and no wonder. She said, quite lightly, 'I'll be down in a few minutes.'

She was adjusting her dressing-gown collar as she entered the sitting room: her whole attitude appeared casual, and when he said, 'I've news for you,' she looked straight at him and said flatly, 'Yes?'

'My uncle has died.'

'Oh. Oh, is that so? Well, that should make you happy; you're half-way there, I mean, to your fortune.'

'Shut up!'

Now her tone did change: her back straightened, her head went up, and she said, 'Don't tell me to shut up, Humphrey Drayton, nor speak to me in that tone.'

He flung round and made for the mantelpiece, and automatically adopted his usual stance. But this time both hands were gripping the edge as he muttered, 'I'm sorry, I'm sorry, but I'm in a bit of a stew.'

She said nothing, but waited; and now he turned and, facing her, said, 'There are complications.' He now ran his forefinger over his lips. 'Everything will be explained to you later; but, at present, I would ask you to do something for me.'

'Yes?' She waited.

'Well, it's just this. I can't understand why my aunt has asked that you come with me to the funeral on Tuesday.'

'Oh, that *is* nice of her, to invite me at last to the house. Didn't she give you her reasons?'

She saw that his Adam's apple was motionless in his throat, as if it were choking him; then he went on, 'No. No; that's it, she just said, "I . . . I'd like you to bring your wife to the funeral." Now it's . . . it's this way, Hannah: you can't go.'

'Why not?' Her voice was high with enquiry.

'Well, I've told you, there's something to explain and I'll explain it all later, after this business is settled.'

'You mean, after the will is read?'

'Oh.' He tossed his head now and his eyes closed

for a second before he brought out on a growl, 'Oh, yes; yes. I suppose that's it, after the will is settled. In any case, you must not come with me on Tuesday, you understand?'

'No, I don't; and if she's invited me, I'm going.'

'You're not!'

When he stepped towards her she remained exactly where she was, and her voice was quiet but her tone deadly as she said, 'Don't tell me what I have to do and what I haven't to do. Get it into your head, Humphrey, that you cannot control me in any way at any time, now or in the future. I go my own way, you go yours.'

'Hannah' – she could see that he was trembling – 'please do this for me, this one thing. It would be quite easy to say that you're not well or that you've got a cold.'

She stopped herself from saying, One of the hundreds I must have had over the last three years, I suppose; that is, when I wasn't being frivolous and getting you to take me out to wine and dine.

As her temper rose, she asked, 'Can you really give me a reason why I shouldn't go to your uncle's funeral with you on Tuesday?'

He came back swiftly, saying, 'Not at the moment, Hannah. I can't give it to you at the moment, but . . . but I will after Tuesday, say on Wednesday. Then I'll explain everything to you and I hope you'll be able to understand.'

'Understand what?'

'Oh, dear God!' He turned from her, clutching his head. 'If I could answer you now I would not be begging you not to come to the funeral.'

She stared at him. 'All right, Humphrey; I won't go to the funeral, but I'll phone and express my sympathy and tell your aunt why I can't come.'

'No. No!' But then his hand went to his brow and he said, 'Well, yes; yes, you could do that. Yes, you could.' She watched him take in a deep breath, then slowly let it out and, for a moment, his body appeared to be like a large, deflated balloon perched on top of two stilts.

'Is that all?'

'What? . . . I mean, yes . . . yes, and thank you, Hannah. I hope when all this is over you'll be able to understand, and you'll welcome the news, I'm sure, as it will mean you'll be able to go your own way.'

'Oh' – she allowed her face to stretch – 'that sounds interesting. How long have I got to wait for this?'

Again he was showing impatience before he said, 'I told you.'

She broke in here, saying, 'Oh, yes; the will will be read. After the will is read. Yes; yes, I understand.' She now walked past him, saying, 'Goodnight, Humphrey.'

He stared after her, and it wasn't until she had passed into the hall that he answered her. 'Goodnight, Hannah.'

On Monday morning, as he was loading his brief-case, she said, 'You're going to work?'

He had his back to her when he spoke, 'Yes; I may

as well. She's staying at the nursing home. I've left the number by the phone. I offered to go and help with things, but apparently everything has been arranged. She wants to be left alone, and so I won't go until tomorrow morning.'

'Oh.' Hannah added nothing to this.

She allowed half an hour to pass before she phoned Mrs Drayton, and when she told her of Humphrey's demand that she should not come to the funeral, Mrs Drayton said, 'Well, don't, my dear, don't come to the funeral; but see that you are here when we come back; that is, at the nursing home, you know. The funeral will be very quiet; there'll be only James Morgan, my solicitor, his clerk, Tom Frint, Humphrey and myself, and a few others; then you'll be there afterwards.'

Hannah was puzzled. 'You want me to be there to hear the will read?'

'Yes, Hannah.'

'Oh! Well, if that's your wish, Mrs Drayton, I'll be there.'

Mrs Drayton then asked, 'What was his attitude to you last night when he got home?'

'Well, to put it briefly, he was very disturbed.'

'Yes, my dear; I should imagine he would be. I've learnt over the last few days, my dear, that one is never too old to learn the lessons of life: never trust anyone, wholly; no, never wholly. And that's a strange thing for me to say, because I've lived with a wonderful man for nigh-on fifty years, but I now have to accept that none of us knows what's in the other's mind. I'll go now, my dear; but if I don't manage to get a private word with you on Tuesday, I want you to get in touch with me, wherever you are. I'd like us to meet again. Are you of the same mind?'

'Oh, yes, Mrs Drayton. Yes; yes, indeed.'

'Goodbye, my dear.'

'Goodbye, Mrs Drayton.'

Hannah's eyes were moist. Never trust anyone, never, no matter who they are. What an awful thing to learn at the end of one's life. Would it be better to learn it early on and not be hoodwinked? She didn't know; she had not yet acquired the experience of age . . .

She was waiting in the sitting room of the nursing home when the small company of mourners returned. Three directors from Mr Drayton's firm, together with the solicitor, his clerk and Humphrey himself had gone off to take refreshments, and a nurse came into the sitting room, saying, 'Mrs Drayton asks you to excuse her; she'll be with you very shortly.'

Hannah inclined her head and smiled at the nurse, continuing to wait. Some ten minutes later Mrs Drayton appeared. 'My dear, have you had anything to eat or drink?'

'I've had a cup of tea, Mrs Drayton, and that's all I wanted, thank you.'

'Me, too; that's all *I* wanted. Well now, I think we'd better get going. Be prepared.' There was the semblance of a smile on her face now as she repeated, 'Be prepared to assist your husband to a chair when he sees you are here.'

Hannah smiled but made no remark; then Mrs Drayton rang a bell and asked the nurse who responded, 'Will you please tell the gentlemen we are ready?'

Humphrey was the first to appear, strutting as though he were already in ownership; but he stopped the progress of the others by thrusting out his hand and gripping the doorpost. Every vestige of colour went from his face as he saw his wife sitting next to Mrs Drayton on the small couch at the far end of the room.

A slight push from the solicitor's clerk and he seemed to stumble into the room and glance about it before he made his way towards the end of a row of five chairs. This brought him almost opposite Hannah. His eyes were fixed upon her; from the expression on his face it could be said that he was absolutely flabbergasted. His mouth was slightly agape, his eyes were wide, and his nostrils were quivering.

The solicitor and his clerk seated themselves at a table on which lay several folders, while the three directors took the seats next to Humphrey.

Mr Morgan now opened a file, cleared his throat, straightened his tie, then began: 'For such an important person as Mr Drayton,' he said, 'you may consider this a very short will, but you'll see the reason for it as I go on.' He looked up and smiled around the small company, then continued: 'It's usually the most important people who have the least to say, and we remember that Mr Drayton was a man who came straight to the point.' He went through the usual preamble, then continued, '"It would take many reams of paper to hold all my wishes for the future of our company, and so this I have left in the good hands of my wife, an excellent businesswoman. It is she who has made it her business to change my views on suggestions that I had previously rejected, suggestions made by you, Mr Ferguson, for our Manchester works, and you, Mr Petty, for our two factories in the West Country. These suggestions will now be acted upon.

'"There may be people whom I should mention as beneficiaries, but again I've left this in the hands of my good wife. There is only one I wish to mention, and I'm doing this at the behest of my wife, for we think that this person has been very unfairly treated. We wish to make amends for the treatment she has received from her husband over the past three years and for the defamation of her character. I am speaking of Mrs Hannah Drayton, the wife of Humphrey Drayton, the son of a man who was thought to be my second cousin but who was no blood relation, his own father's parent being my stepbrother. I therefore leave to Mrs Hannah Rose Drayton the sum of fifty thousand pounds, although no sum of money can compensate her for the loss of character and loneliness through neglect over the past three years."'

There was a stillness in the room. Hannah could not look at Humphrey. She could only see his hands, and they were hanging limp over the wooden arms of his chair. It was as if he had fainted. No one in the company looked towards him, apart from Mrs Drayton, and there was not a shred of pity in her gaze. Although Humphrey's body was limp, the muscles of his face were tight; his eyes were stretched wide and his jaws were clamped tight, pushing his thin mouth out into almost a long pout. His features were absolutely colourless.

Hannah could scarcely believe what she had heard. Fifty thousand pounds! A fortune. No, no; she couldn't believe this; and now as she looked at the man opposite her she knew that, although she had wanted justice, she would have rather had it in some other way. Exposure, yes, oh definitely, but not for him to be stripped, as he surely had been, by his uncle and would be by the woman sitting next to her. The sensation she was now feeling was that of faintness. She heard a thin voice say, 'May I have a glass of water?' She was pointing along to the carafe and glass standing at the hand of the solicitor. Then she knew it was Mrs Drayton who was holding the glass to her mouth, and as she gulped at the water she heard the solicitor say, 'Gentlemen, we could adjourn for the present. Anyway, the main business of today is at an end, I think.' Then he added again, 'I think.'

'Take some deep breaths.'

Hannah did as she was told.

When the wave of faintness had passed she was aware that, apart from Humphrey, all the men had left the room. He was still sitting and staring at her in a most odd way. It wasn't so much that he looked shocked, but greatly puzzled. Then she saw him pull himself up and speak. 'Why have you done this to me, Aunt?'

After a few seconds Mrs Drayton said, 'I can answer that by using your own words: Why have you done this to *us*? Treated us as imbeciles while you've lied and cheated and thought nothing of defaming your wife, making her out to be an extravagant, demanding slut of a woman. Don't remind me, please, that we didn't take to her at first. That is quite true, but that would have changed with acquaintanceship, I'm sure, from what I know now. But one thing I can say with assurance, we would never have come to hate and despise her as we did, were it not for your weekly description of her selfishness, her demands, her profligacy and her thought for no one but herself. You gave us the impression that you would have divorced her, had it not been that we did not hold with the idea; and you sit there and ask why we have done this to you? I shudder to think that you could have come into a great inheritance; yes, a great inheritance, because my husband thought much of you. Time and again I had doubts, but he squashed them; and, I repeat, I shudder to think that it was only a Saturday-morning phone call that revealed you for the lying, despicable creature that you are, and disclosed how, for three years, you have been associating with the illegitimate daughter of my housekeeper. Yes, that surprises you, too, that this girl to whom you have given children is herself illegitimate. Your Mrs Beggs, I now find, has been stealing from me for years, while you have been insisting what a treasure she is: she was filling your bags from my store cupboard and helping to sustain your family. Unfortunately, I have never bothered much with household details; I have paid the bills, but at times I did think it was taking quite a lot of money to feed three people. Anyway, you will now have the pleasure of joining her and her daughter and your two illegitimate children. One last thing; I do not wish to see you again under any circumstances. Do you understand me, Humphrey?'

'No, I don't understand you.' He was on his feet now. Gone was the limp, amazed and even frightened-looking individual when, bending down towards Mrs Drayton, he cried, 'What I understand is this! I could make a case of it. You have brought me up to believe that I was to be your heir and now I'm to be cut out of the will for the simple reason that I take care of the only woman I ever loved. I wonder how Uncle's good name would appear if it were splashed across the papers, and yours too, with your narrow-minded ideas about divorce and separation and infidelity. How would it look if I were to tell my side of the story? Here was a woman deserted by her husband – your gardener, someone you had inveigled into marrying her so as to keep her from me. And when I find her destitute – years later – what do I do? I look after her. That's all I do, just look after her, because, by then, I was married. If I were to tell such a story, I wonder where the

sympathy would go then? It's so unfair. And she' –
he now thrust out his arm, his finger pointing at
Hannah – 'she's not without blame; oh no, if you
only knew.'

Mrs Drayton had put out her hand to press the
bell. When the nurse appeared, she said, 'Will you
please see Mr Drayton out, Sister, and I do not wish
for any more visits from him in the future. You
understand?'

The nurse said nothing but stood looking at the
tall man whose face was now no longer pale but
scarlet.

He turned to Mrs Drayton and said, 'I'm not
through. I'm not through. A surprise is waiting for
you, and you'll hear from me.'

Mrs Drayton said nothing, but she watched him
take three backward steps, then stand glaring at
her before throwing himself around, almost over-
balancing the nurse in the process as he left the
room.

Hannah was sitting with her back pressed tight
against the corner of the couch. Her eyes were
closed and one hand was cupping her chin as if to
stop her jaw shaking.

It was some moments before Mrs Drayton spoke.
Then it wasn't to Hannah but to the nurse, who had
appeared again after she rang the bell. 'D'you think
we might have a tray of tea, please?' she said.

'Of course. Of course, Mrs Drayton.'

Then Mrs Drayton's hand came on to Hannah's
and she said softly, 'Are you feeling sorry for him?'
Hannah opened her eyes; but it was some seconds

before she answered, 'In a way; but . . . but only in a way.'

'It is the same with me – but only in a way. Of course, if I was leaving him without sustenance, it would be a different matter; but he has a very good job and he has accommodation, and now, since you will be leaving it, my dear, he will likely take his new family there.'

The house: she must get back there and clear her few things out. Her typewriter, the little chair she had bought second-hand.

As if she were reading Hannah's thoughts, Mrs Drayton said, 'It would be best if you don't meet up with him for a time. He is, I would say, in a dangerous mood. Now, you will keep in touch, won't you?'

'Oh, of course, Mrs Drayton. I'll come here as often as you like. In the meantime, I can give you my new address.' She opened her bag, and from it took a piece of paper on which she wrote David's address and phone number.

And then she said, 'I shall never get over the fact of being left all that money, Mrs Drayton. I find it impossible to take in. Yesterday I hadn't tuppence, so to speak, and now—'

'To my mind, you deserve every penny of it, my dear. Now come along: drink that tea, then get yourself back as quickly as possible. I'll be anxious to know you're safely out of that house.'

Ten minutes later Hannah was saying goodbye to the older woman; and when she placed her lips on the pale, wrinkled cheek and found Mrs Drayton's arms going around her she could not withhold her tears. No further word of goodbye was exchanged, only a long look, which cemented their growing friendship.

The taxi driver had taken the box of books and another of papers and placed them inside the cab. Now he had picked up the typewriter from the seat of the revolving chair when a voice bawled at him, 'What d'you think you're doing?'

Startled, the man turned, then said, 'Putting these in the cab, as me passenger asked.'

'Put it down!'

'Do no such thing!' Hannah was standing in the doorway now. 'Put it inside with the other things. Please do as I say, it's mine!' Then, turning to Humphrey, she said, 'I bought that and this chair together, if you remember. They're my property, and I'm taking them.'

'Like hell you are!'

He picked up the chair and almost flung it back into the hall; the taxi driver, who had put the typewriter into the back of the cab, returned without hesitation to collect the chair, only to have the door slammed in his face.

'Think you're clever, don't you?' Humphrey was glowering at Hannah. 'For two pins I would throttle you, you scheming bitch! You think you're clever, don't you? laughing up your sleeve at me; but I'll have the last laugh on you, you'll see. Give me some of that money or I'll let the cat out of the bag; then see how far you'll get with her.'

Let the cat out of the bag? He was indeed mad;

but she couldn't see anything funny about it; he was dangerous. At this moment she knew he was capable of what he had threatened, that is of throttling her. She was thankful that the taxi driver was still outside.

She watched Humphrey making an effort to control his temper as he said, 'I'll . . . I'll strike a bargain with you. I'll keep my mouth shut about where you're going now, and your carryings-on. She doesn't know anything about that, does she? No, by God! or you wouldn't have got a penny from her. A fornicating wife. Huh! My double life would have paled before it. So there you are: I'll keep quiet if you'll share what is rightly mine.'

She managed to keep her voice steady and therefore more aggravating to him as she said, 'She's aware that you have a fornicating wife.' He stepped back from her, screwed up his eyes and said, 'Oh, no! You don't put that one over on me too. I know her better than you do. I lived with her, I lived with them both. For two narrow-minded individuals it would be hard to find their equals. Well, what about it?'

'My answer to that, Humphrey, is, if I had fifty thousand pounds in my hand and there was a fire in the grate, I'd burn every penny of it before I'd let you touch it. And as for my standing with Mrs Drayton, get on the phone and tell her. Go on, see what happens.'

'You think I wouldn't?'

'No, I'm sure you would if you thought it would blacken me.'

He stared at her, not knowing how to take her. Then he said, 'You're putting me to the test, aren't you? Because I'd do it, you know; but if you're sensible we can both come out of this with something. All right, I did the dirty on you, but there was no other way. I always wanted Daisy, and they knew that, and they stopped me. So I took the only way out, and you were the price; and later my alibi. And in a way I'm sorry; but I was always decent to you. You seem to forget that.'

'I forget nothing that you did, Humphrey, nothing. Nor what you didn't do.'

His eyes narrowed as if he were searching in his mind, but when she said, 'Will you move and let me take my chair out?' he reverted to his original manner and cried, 'No, I won't! Neither you nor the chair goes until we come to an understanding; and I tell you, I'll get on that phone and show you up to her for what you really are.'

'Do that, Humphrey. Do it.' Her voice was emphatic. He began, 'You . . .' then he stopped. Instead of continuing, he picked up the phone and rang the number of the nursing home.

The receiver pressed to his ear, his eyes over the top of it holding Hannah's, they waited. Then his head jerked and he said, 'This is Humphrey. I'm going to tell you something you didn't know, and it's this. My maligned wife, as you think of her, is hoodwinking you as much as I was, for she's got a man on the side and is now packing her things to go to live with him. How about that?'

Hannah watched him as he said, 'Are you there?'

What he then heard made his jaw drop, for Mrs Drayton said, 'Oh, I thought that Hannah would be gone to join her friend before you reached home. And yes, Humphrey, I know all about Hannah's friendship. She told Mr Drayton and me exactly what had happened. Of course, it took a long time for her to take this step, almost three years, because she only met this gentleman recently. Mr Drayton was greatly touched by her honesty, for she kept nothing back. Don't you think it remarkable that she didn't take this step for nearly three years? Is there anything more you'd like to tell me, Humphrey?'

As if it had become alive, the receiver was replaced in the cradle. Then Humphrey turned his amazed gaze on Hannah. His whole body was trembling, and she knew a moment of intense fear. It was then, thrusting the revolving seat to one side, that she sprang for the door; but he was there before her, and when she felt her coat being ripped from the collar downwards and heard the accompanying volley of oaths and curses she thrust out her hands and clawed at his face. The next moment his hands were on her throat, and she could only emit a stifled scream as he dragged her roughly to the wall and held her there. It was as the door burst open that she brought her knee up into Humphrey's groin and he fell backwards, almost colliding with the taxi driver who, seeing the bent figure with blood covering his face, said, 'Serves you bloody well right, I'd say. Come on, missis.'

Hannah was sliding down the wall as the bracing

voice demanded, 'Look! stand up! Here, let me help you.' He lifted up the shredded garment and wrapped it around her shoulders. Then, with his arm around her, he led her to the taxi, where he said, 'I don't think I'll go back for your chair, missis, because I don't want to meet him when he comes round. From what I heard, he's a bloody menace.'

When Peter answered the bell, the taxi driver said, 'I've a visitor here for you, but she's in a bad way.'

David pushed past Peter, and when he saw Hannah trying to lift herself from the taxi seat he ran down the steps; then with the help of the taxi driver he carried her into the flat and laid her on the couch.

The taxi driver now turned to Peter and said, 'Bloody menace of a man back there! It's a good job I had me ear to the door. He could've done for her. He was trying to throttle her; and by the look of it she must have clawed his face to bits. You never know what you're going to come across in this business!'

'Well, thank you very much for seeing to her; and I'm very glad you were there,' said Peter. Then he added, 'Wait a minute. Has she any luggage with her?'

'Oh, yes. There's bits and pieces on the back seat.'

Later, looking at the bundle of notes in his hand, the taxi driver said, 'Thanks very much, sir. I'm only glad I was there at the time. I hope she'll be all right.'

Hannah did not remember much that went on after she lay down on the couch. Although she was aware that Peter and David were nearby, and hazily that her throat was sore and that she was sore about her shoulders, she was also aware that she was consumed with fear.

The extent of her injuries became plain when David was able to take her into the bedroom and undress her, to reveal two large bruises on her shoulderblades, but more severe were those on her neck.

By evening, the swellings had darkened so much that David suggested calling in the doctor, but Peter said, 'I think, in her state, it would only distress her the more; but I have some ointment upstairs. We used it on the horses, you know, marvellous for grazes and bruises. I use it myself from time to time for my rheumaticky knee.'

As David applied the ointment to Hannah's swollen neck he wished really heartily that he could have five minutes with that man . . .

The next morning when the phone rang Peter answered it, and when a female voice asked to speak to Mrs Drayton Junior, he asked who was speaking, and was told it was Mrs Drayton Senior. Saying, 'Would you mind waiting a moment, madam?' he softly called to David, who was about to enter the bedroom, 'It's Mrs Drayton. I think you'd better deal with it.'

'Good morning, Mrs Drayton,' David said. 'I'm Hannah's friend David, David Craventon. I'm sorry she can't come to the phone at the moment; she's still in a very low state after what happened yesterday.'

'What did happen?'

'Her husband beat her up and tried to throttle her, and had it not been for a taxi driver he would probably have succeeded.'

'Oh, no! Surely he wouldn't go to those lengths.'

'He did, I'm afraid. When the taxi driver brought her here she had to be carried from the cab. He'd torn her coat off her.'

'Oh, dear me! dear me! I never imagined, no, never, that he'd stoop to that. I'm terribly sorry. Will you tell her so? May . . . may I come and visit her?'

'Yes; yes, of course. I'm sure she'd be very pleased to see you.'

'May I say tomorrow?'

'Yes; that'll be fine.'

'Thank you. Goodbye.'

'Goodbye, Mrs Drayton.'

Before making his way to the bedroom, he hurried to the kitchen and there he said, 'Damn silly not having a connection in the bedroom. Will you see to it, Peter?'

'Yes, of course.'

David turned about quickly and crossed the hall to the bedroom, and there, smiling down on Hannah, he said, 'That was your friend Mrs Drayton on the phone.'

'Oh. Oh, that was nice of her.'

'She asked if she could come and see you tomorrow.'

'Oh, then I must get up.'

'You'll do nothing of the sort. There's no need for

you to get up; but if you do get up it'll be only to lie on the couch, all right?'

Hannah swallowed painfully. 'Could you do something for me? Ring Janie to tell her where I am? I couldn't bear her to ring the house and get Humphrey in his present state.'

'Yes, of course, of course. Oh, and I've just remembered: Gilly and Natasha will be popping in tomorrow as well, so I'll have to stay there to hold the fort. I can do most of the correspondence from here, but when he's out he insists on somebody being in his place. Time and again I've told him we need another assistant, and the answer is always yes, when we make some money then we'll be able to afford someone else. That's the biggest joke going; when he makes some money.'

'Is he all that rich?'

'Well, let's say he's very rich. No; they say very rich men don't know how much they're worth, but Gilly does; and to the ordinary person he's the kind who counts every penny, yet nobody knows how many people he supports on the quiet. Oh, he's a strange man, is Gilly.'

She put a hand on his cheek as she said softly, 'And you like him?'

And at this he whispered to her, with his lips close to her ears, 'I'll let you into a secret; I've never told it to anyone else, but . . . but he's my third love.'

'Your third?' She let her lips rest against his for a moment; and then she said, 'Who is your second?'

'That fellow in the kitchen; and the first is the most beautiful woman in the world.'

'Oh, David. David. What would I have done without you, and what would I do without you, and what will I do without you if ever I lose you? I read a poem once about a woman who said that love was three quarters pain and a quarter anxiety, and I think she's right: I'm learning that it is like that.'

'Well, you must unlearn it, because love is full of pain only when it concerns the pain of the loved one. If they both love together, it's joy. I would admit to a little anxiety, that is, being anxious about the welfare of the beloved, but who would want to love if they knew it was to be all pain?'

'I would.'

And she was right, that poetess, because the actual fact of loving is like a pain in the heart. 'Look.' He took her face between his hands and gently stroked her cheek. 'You're not to think like that. Whatever happens to us, as long as we're together it'll be love. Painless love, joyful love, happy love.' Laughing now, he said, 'And how many more adjectives can I apply to it: glorious love, exquisite love, everlasting love, *ad infinitum*.'

'Don't make me laugh, my neck still hurts.'

'Oh, your poor neck. Your poor neck.'

When he kissed it she put her hand on his head and, looking across him and into the future, there was still that feeling of anxiety tinged with dread. About what she couldn't tell, for she couldn't see Humphrey doing her any more harm; yet there it was, and the feeling was strong.

# Fourteen

Mrs Drayton arrived about three o'clock in the afternoon, by hired car, and the uniformed chauffeur followed her into the flat, carrying in one hand a huge basket of flowers and in the other an ornamental basket of fruit. When she bent over her and kissed her on the cheek, all Hannah could say was, 'Oh, Mrs Drayton. They're beautiful, beautiful. You're so kind.'

Peter placed the chair close to the couch head and Mrs Drayton turned to him and surveyed him for a moment before saying, 'Thank you'; and Hannah smiled to herself as she thought, Peter is being dismissed as being not the chosen man; he is too old.

'How are you feeling?'

'Oh, much better. Much better, thanks.'

'Your . . . your friend tells me that Humphrey tried to throttle you.'

'Yes; I'd say he did his utmost; and he might have succeeded if it hadn't been for the taxi driver. I'll always admire taxi drivers after this.'

'Let me see.' Mrs Drayton's hand gently pulled

aside the turned-up collar of Hannah's dressing gown, then exclaimed, 'My goodness! I can't believe it. He must have had his thumbs on your windpipe.'

'I'm not sure where he had them, Mrs Drayton, I only know that things went very misty in my mind after my contact with the wall.'

Mrs Drayton now sat back in her chair and, shaking her head slowly, said, 'I don't want to believe this of him. I could understand his shouting and bawling and threatening when his double life was exposed – it must have been a colossal shock – but that's no excuse for using such force on you. Anyway, where do we go from here, my dear?'

'Oh.' Hannah clasped and unclasped her hands, which were lying on top of the rug, before she said, 'David has put it in the hands of his solicitor; the application for my divorce, I mean.'

Mrs Drayton said quietly, 'Considering that we are now friends, may I ask what Mr Craventon is intending to do about *his* marriage?'

'He too is seeking a divorce. They've been separated for so long it should be quite easy in his case.'

'Yes; yes, I should say so; and very easy in yours too, because Humphrey hasn't got a leg to stand on . . . Oh. Oh, that is nice.' Mrs Drayton now turned to Peter, who was pushing a trolley which held a silver tray on which there was a silver tea service with two delicately patterned china teacups, both resting on lace mats in their saucers; and, on the shelf below, there were two plates, one holding very thinly cut bread and butter, the other an assortment of small cakes.

It was the teacups about which Mrs Drayton remarked, saying, 'It's the height of bad manners, I know, to remark on your hostess's house and contents, but I must say that it is a lovely sight, such a pretty sight, to see cups resting on lace mats. I haven't seen that since I left home. My mother always had afternoon tea at half-past three, when friends would be invited on certain days.' Smiling, she turned back to Hannah, saying, 'And they all wore hats, as I do still. The teas were gossip sessions and we children were never allowed in on them, and I may tell you that we hadn't lace mats under our cups up in the nursery! We hadn't even cups; we had mugs.'

Peter was smiling as he said, 'Rightly so, madam. Rightly so.'

'What d'you mean, rightly so? That we should have mugs?'

'Yes, exactly that: children should have unbreakable mugs, for they play awful havoc with cups and saucers.'

As Peter walked away, Mrs Drayton, leaning forward towards Hannah, said softly, 'A very nice person, I should imagine.'

'Yes, he is indeed, Mrs Drayton, a very nice man. David is very lucky to have him as a friend; in fact, he's been more like a father to him for years.'

'Yes, yes; I should imagine.' Mrs Drayton was now nodding her head.

She had drunk two cups of tea, eaten a slice of bread and butter and one small cake. She was now wiping her mouth with a dainty tea napkin. Her whole manner seemed to have changed, and when she made no effort to speak for some time, Hannah leant forward and asked her, 'Are you all right, Mrs Drayton?'

'Yes; yes, my dear. I'm all right. Except for those times when I feel emotionally disturbed, which generally occur at night-time, I could say I am all right. It's in the night when one misses one's partner, and strange things happen to one's mind. You know, he was only buried on Tuesday and yet I seem to have been feeling his loss for years. I can't understand it. Just over a week ago he was alive and we were talking. He was ill, yes, but he was alive; and now it's as if he'd gone from me aeons ago. At nights I . . . I find that I have difficulty in conjuring up his face. I have to take up his photograph and look at it. He told me, before he went, that we would never be parted, that when I went he'd be waiting for me and we'd start life again together; where, he didn't know, but he seemed to be sure of that. I wish I could be sure of it. My friends, both business and personal, always tell me how wonderful I am in bearing up as I have done, but, Hannah, they know nothing about it, for I ask you, who knows what goes on in another's mind? We're all living behind a façade, and in my case people imagine that the façade is steel-plated. I am a businesswoman, I'm known as a businesswoman, so businesswomen don't think as other women do. They don't feel as other women do or else they'd be howling their eyes out all day. If they only knew, Hannah, that's what I want to do, howl my eyes out; but I'm a businesswoman, so the charade must be kept going.'

Hannah found herself quite unable to say a word. All she could do was hold the hand extended to her and smooth the long, blue-veined fingers, and as she did so Mrs Drayton went on, 'I know that tonight in bed I will ask myself why on earth I poured my heart out to you, showing you my true self, and I won't be able to give myself an answer. I only know that your fidelity to that rip of a man has shown me the side of a human's character that I would have said one only came upon in novels. You know what my husband said about you? He said there was a simplicity in you that overstepped that character-istic known as naïvety and touched on a truthfulness that could only be derived from wisdom, sub-conscious or otherwise.'

Hannah was now shaking her head, and she smiled as she said, 'I would have to work that one out, Mrs Drayton, but about the word "wisdom", I'm afraid that he was being more than kind; in fact, imaginative, because I know myself and I know that although I'm not a bird-brain, I'm a very mediocre person inside. I've wished, oh, how I've wished, I could be different, even like Janie, my sister. Now *she* is vivacious. Full of personality. Beside her, I've always felt like a mouse, but nevertheless I do thank you for telling me what Mr Drayton said. One regret I have is that we didn't really come to know each other earlier.'

'I too, my dear. That's another thing I could never forgive Humphrey for. Anyway—' She jerked in the chair as if throwing off her morbid feelings of the moment and, now smiling, she said, 'Talk about visiting the sick to cheer them up, and what do I do? pour my troubles over you.'

'You can do that any day in the week, Mrs Drayton. You know that, any day in the week, but please' – now she was wagging her finger at the older woman – 'don't expect to have any wise answers to your problems. It would be much better if you went to a fortune teller.'

They were both laughing, and as Mrs Drayton got to her feet the front doorbell rang, and now she hurriedly bent forward and kissed Hannah on the cheek, saying, 'Likely that'll be another visitor. Goodbye, my dear, I'll keep in touch.'

'Do. Do, please.' Hannah put her hand on to the fine-boned cheek. They stared at each other for a moment before Mrs Drayton picked up her bag and turned about to where Peter, who had now moved the trolley to one side, was making his way towards the door. Just then the bell rang again.

On opening the door, Peter was confronted by Mr Gillyman and his wife, and the gentleman's greeting was, 'My! it's taken you some time,' to which Peter answered, 'I'm sorry, sir, but my wings are at the workshop being refuelled.'

'Now you watch it, laddie!'

'Be quiet! Let's get in.'

'Oh, I'm sorry.' Gilly's voice and manner had changed, for now he was addressing Mrs Drayton. 'Good afternoon. Mrs Drayton, isn't it?'

'Yes, Mr Gillyman, it's Mrs Drayton.' She smiled gently at him.

'We've met before; it was in Germany – Frankfurt, wasn't it? At the conference. Oh, and this is my wife. Natasha, this is Mrs Philippa Drayton.'

Smiling, the two women shook hands.

Again Gilly's voice changed as he said, 'I was very sorry to hear about your husband. We were well acquainted, he and I. We seemed to meet up at least every year.'

'Yes; yes, I know you did. He often mentioned you.'

She now smiled and nodded her goodbye before moving to where Peter was holding the door open, and to him she said softly, 'Thank you for that most lovely tea.' Then, her voice dropping still further, she said, 'Will you please tell Mr Craventon I am looking forward to meeting him?' Peter did not close the door until Mrs Drayton entered the hired car.

'Oh, what beautiful flowers! And look at that fruit!'

As Natasha greeted Hannah, her husband said, 'Yes, some people can afford to bring such presents, but we're not up to it, I'm afraid.'

As she sat down by the head of the couch, Natasha exchanged a smiling glance with Hannah before saying, 'We're really not on speaking terms; the man's impossible. D'you know where he's had me this afternoon?'

Hannah shook her head.

'The river.'

'No! He knows you don't like the river and he takes you there?'

'Yes, Hannah, he knows how I hate the river, all

rivers, all water, but he takes me there. We were driving along an ordinary side road when he stopped by a high wall. At a green wooden door he said, "Get out; I've got something to show you here. Close your eyes." Yes, he did; he said, "Close your eyes." I closed my eyes thinking he was about to lead me into a secret garden or something, and after a dozen or more steps he said, "Look at that!" I looked, and there, before me, was a very green lawn leading down ... sloping down, not a nice flat croquet-looking lawn, no, it was sloping down to the river. And going past was a pleasure steamer full of people! D'you know what he did? He handled me – that's the word they would use in court, handled – and not gently, and got me into what he called the house; and it was nothing more than a bungalow, a straggling bungalow.'

'Your informant is wrong, Hannah. There is a beautiful verandah leading off four rooms on the upstairs floor. The bungalow, as your informant misinforms you, is a large house with four main reception rooms as well as kitchen quarters and an annexe for staff. It's a lovely place.'

'Yes,' put in Natasha, 'and all looking on to water: milling water, boats going up and down, up and down.'

'Are you thinking of buying it?' asked Hannah of Gilly, trying to keep her face straight.

'Of course, my dear; of course I am. Now I put this to you.' Unceremoniously, he pushed her feet to one side at the end of the couch and sat down, only to be chastised by his wife: 'What d'you think you're doing?' she cried at him. 'She's all bruised.'

'Her feet aren't.'

'Anyway, my dear; to answer your question further, I'll put it like this: if you happen to see a marvellous outfit in a shop window, you know, something like your last lovely one . . . Oh, I'd better not go on. As I was saying, if you were to see this outfit and, just to make it simple, say it's original price was a hundred pounds and because the shop was closing down it was going for seventy-five, what would you do?'

'Go in and ask what size it was.'

As both she and Natasha spluttered their laughter Gilly turned his head away, saying, 'This is no time for frivolity. Houses on that river cost a fortune.'

At this Natasha bent towards Hannah, again saying, 'You see, Hannah, he's being offered it at a bargain price—'

'And you know I can't resist a bargain! The house is owned by Oscar Overton, a friend of mine, and he's off to America. And he's asked me if I'd like to buy it before he puts it on the market. And as my ungrateful partner knows, I love rivers and always longed to live near one, but for years, to please her, I've buried myself in the midst of bricks and mortar right in the heart of the city.'

Natasha put in quietly, 'And at least fifty thousand books.'

'Oh, here's tea,' Hannah said, and as Peter pushed the trolley towards them Gilly, peering down at it, said, 'My, my! that looks elegant.' Then glancing up at Peter he said, 'Were you expecting royalty?'

'Yes. Yes, sir, we were.'

'Well, well!' Gilly was looking at the trolley again. 'Dinky mats under cups. Good gracious!' Then, again glancing up at Peter, he said, 'You'll be putting socks on the table legs next. Shades of Victoriana.'

'No, not quite, sir; it's just that madam prefers tea set like this in the afternoon.'

As he walked away unsmiling, Hannah put her hand to her face to avoid the look that Gilly was bestowing on her, and then, glancing at Natasha, she said, 'I never ask for afternoon tea, not like this: a cup on a tray does me as a rule, but he's so good, so kind.'

'Yes, he is.'

'Some people are lucky.' This disgruntled remark came from the far end of the couch; then added to it was, 'Well, who's going to pour the tea, then?'

Without further words, Natasha rose to her feet and went to the trolley to officiate, and immediately her husband moved up the couch to take her place beside Hannah, and quietly said, 'How are you feeling, Hannah?'

'Much better, thanks, Gilly.'

'Your back easier?'

'Oh yes, quite a bit.' He leant closer to her now and, taking her hand, he whispered, 'When you're on your feet again I'll take you out and show you this house.'

And she whispered back, 'Sounds intriguing; I'd love to see it.'

'Do you like rivers?'

'Yes.' She glanced sideways towards Natasha, but that lady, with head bent, was busily pouring tea. 'David took me up the river on a pleasure steamer recently. It's amazing how different the city looks from that perspective.'

The whisper was not quiet as it said, 'D'you think you could put a word in for me?' Gilly's head was jerked towards his wife, and Hannah, adopting his tone, said, 'I'll do my best. I can't promise results, but I'll try.'

'Well, anyway, I feel I've got someone on my side. That big stiff-neck back in the office is in sympathy with people who are obstinate about rivers.'

A few minutes later, when they were well into the tea, Gilly looked at the two pieces of bread and butter now left on the plate and said, 'If nobody wants those I'll finish them; I never get bread and butter like this at home.'

As Natasha shook her head, Hannah reached over and, lifting the other plate, said, 'Look, there's only one cake left; it's a shame to let it go back into the kitchen.'

'I'm with you.' Gilly picked up the cake and put it on the side of his plate; then, leaning towards her, said, 'Can you hear anything?'

'What do you mean?'

'Well, can't you already hear the echo of the telling-off I'm going to get once I get out of this flat?'

She nodded at him, saying, 'Yes; yes, I can.'

'And what d'you think?'

'I think you rightly deserve it.'

And so the banter went on for another fifteen

minutes until they, too, were about to take their leave. It was then that Gilly, putting his hand into his coat pocket, brought out a narrow box, which he handed to Hannah, saying, 'A pre-engagement present.' Then he immediately turned to his wife and said, 'Well, come on; dust the crumbs off yourself. You always were a messy eater.'

For answer, Natasha breathed more deeply, and said to Hannah, 'Open it.'

Slowly Hannah undid the pretty wrapping, to reveal a deep-blue velvet-covered box, with a gold emblem of hands on the lid. When she opened it, she continued to stare down at the gold-linked wrist-watch lying there; then looking from one to the other she asked, 'Why?'

'Haven't I just told you, woman!' Gilly's voice was loud. 'It's a pre-engagement gift.'

'But . . . but I'm not . . . we're not, and this is too—'

'Listen!' It was Natasha bending over her now, saying quietly, 'You may not be engaged at the moment, but you will be shortly. Your divorce will take no time, nor will David's, when he gets down to it. The only snag with his is that maniac of a wife he has. She fought against the separation and likely she'll do the same about the divorce. But we'll deal with that when the time comes.'

'Oh, I don't know what to say—' Hannah's voice broke now as she clasped the small box to her. 'Your kindness overwhelms me.'

'Well, all I can say is, it's about time you were overwhelmed about something. To my mind, loneliness is a thing apart, and that man imposed it on you. Oh, he was a brute. Goodbye, then, my dear; we really must get back to the house, because himself will be tearing his hair to get back here. That man is inordinately fond of you, you know.'

'Yes, yes, Natasha, I know. But even so, it can't be more than I am of him.'

'What are you two whispering together? Come along, Tishy, don't take all day.'

Natasha flicked a glance at her husband, smiled grimly, then stood to the side to allow him to take her place; and when he looked down on Hannah and said one word, 'Well?' she replied, 'It's silly to say I'm lost for words but I really am, Gilly, I really am. It's so good of you.'

'You like it?'

'Oh, how could I do anything but love it?'

'Well, put it on.'

'Oh, oh! Oh, yes.' Hannah took the watch from its case and Gilly helped her to adjust it to her wrist, muttering, 'Why do they make such fancy snappers, one would have been enough, not two. But there, that's fixed.'

'It's beautiful. Oh, really beautiful.'

'She chose it.' Gilly jerked his head towards his wife. 'Good taste in some things.'

'Oh, Natasha, I could never have imagined having anything like this in my life.'

'Why not, with the fortune that's been left to you?'

'Oh, yes' – she put her head back and laughed – 'I . . . I forget about that. That's another thing I can't believe.'

'Well, to my mind you earned that.' Gilly was nodding to her now. 'What d'you say, my dear?'

'Yes, indeed; indeed you've earned it; but there's something or someone you'd rather have at this moment than all the money in the world, if I know anything, so we'd better get back to my husband's right-hand, left-hand and brains man.'

'That's a new one, that is' – Gilly was nodding at Natasha now – 'right-hand, left-hand and brains. Well, well! we'll have to find out how you've come to that conclusion.'

'Yes, dear. Come along, and we'll discuss it on the way.' They both bent over her and said their good-byes.

Peter was waiting to see them to the door, where there was another exchange of banter.

After closing the door on them, Peter went to the couch, saying, 'A lovely couple.'

'Yes, aren't they? And I'm sure, Peter, he looks forward to the sparring match.'

'Yes, I'm sure he does. He had it all planned out what he was going to say.'

'You think so?'

'Oh, yes, yes. It was almost a verbal boxing match when we were clearing this flat out.'

Hannah sat back on the couch and said, 'It's been a lovely afternoon. And, Peter, look at this.' She held out her wrist, and he, taking her hand, stared at the watch, and after a moment he said, 'My! that's beautiful. It's a Cartier, studded with diamonds.'

'What!'

'Oh, yes, madam; Cartier wouldn't use glass,

madam. And Mr Gillyman is not the kind of man to give anyone he likes a cheap present; and apart from his liking you for yourself, he's also grateful to you for bringing happiness into Mr David's life, because between you and me, madam, it's been pretty barren over the last years and very uncomfortable into the bargain; we seem to have been hiding, as it were, going from one place to another, and you know the reason.'

'Oh, yes; yes.' She nodded, her face no longer smiling. 'From the little I've heard of her, and the very sight of her, I think she could be a dreadful woman. She must be very dominant.'

'You've said it; you've said it, madam. Very dominant. Even her two brothers, and they're no weaklings, need help with her at times. Oh, more often than not. And you know, since her visit here, he's more uneasy than ever and wonders if we shouldn't make yet another move.'

'Oh, that'd be a pity because he's made the place so comfortable.'

Peter now straightened and looked around the room and, as if reckoning up, he said, 'It would take her about three minutes to devastate the lot: bedroom, kitchen and upstairs too. A whirlwind is nothing to her when she gets going. She should have been put away years ago. Everybody says that about her. But then there are the brothers, and she could have no better guardians inside a psychiatric hospital than she has outside with them. But I can't understand, never have been able to, why they put up with her. They let their mother go without a qualm, and their other sister was there long before they had any say in the matter.'

When the telephone rang he smiled at her and said, 'Well, here we go again.'

A few moments later he came back to the couch, exclaiming softly, 'It's your sister; she seems in a bit of a state. Apparently she's been getting the wrong number.'

'Oh; I'll get up.'

'No; you'll stay where you are, madam. The wire will stretch to the couch.'

Janie said, 'Hello! Are you there?'

'Yes, Janie; I'm here.'

'Oh, my! woman, how *are* you? I've been worried to death since David phoned me. I've not had a minute when I haven't been surrounded by kids . . . and he told me you had visitors this afternoon. What's happened? Can you talk now?'

Hannah sighed. 'Well, now,' she said, 'I could if you'd let me get a word in.' She then related all that had happened since the day of the funeral, ending with her encounter with Humphrey.

'I went straight back to the flat to collect my things, but Humphrey came on the scene and tried to kill me. He'd have succeeded too had it not been for the taxi driver waiting for me outside. He heard me scream, and rushed in and just managed to stop Humphrey from throttling me. Things went a bit dim after that, and the next thing I remember is lying in bed here.'

'Wait till Eddie hears about this.'

'Janie, as I've told you before, if Eddie organises

any rough stuff it's only going to upset me more. Humphrey's paid enough already, and he'll go on paying because he knows that when his aunt dies he'll not get a penny.'

Janie was silent for a moment; then said, 'I'd love to come and see you, but there's the tribe.'

'Well, bring them.'

'The lot?'

'Yes, the lot; of course, the lot.'

'When?'

'Well, whichever day suits you. I'll be here taking things easy for the next few days; it's only when I try to walk, my shoulders won't move, they're so sore. Make it any day you like, but give me a ring first.'

'Saturday?'

'Yes; yes, Saturday.'

'What time shall we come?'

'Well, say, any time after two; come for tea.'

'Oh, I'll be glad to see you, Hannah. I worry about you, you know; I'm daft, but you never could look after yourself.'

'Goodbye, big sister. See you on Saturday.'

Hannah lay back and drew in a deep breath.

She had a family; she had a lover, and what a lover; she had Peter; she had friends, like Mr Gillyman and Natasha; she had a book about to be published; and strangest of all she had a friend named Mrs Drayton. It was a strange world, but a beautiful world with such kind people in it. She lifted her wrist and admired her new watch. Peter had said there were diamonds on its face!

A diamond watch and fifty thousand pounds in the bank and a life before her with David. She should be the happiest girl on earth. Yes, she was, and she would heed no longer that voice in the back of her mind that kept hinting she was still living in Alice's dream. Everybody was real now.

The children were sitting on chairs. There was John with his head bowed. Claire staring straight ahead, as was Winnie; only Maggie gazed about her.

Janie was sitting near the head of the couch. She was smartly dressed in a blue outfit, and her hair showed it had been attended to as recently as that morning, for the thick brown waves were uniformly taken back from her brow and behind her ears.

Eddie sat an arm's length away from the couch, and Hannah smiled to herself as she thought that the most expensive suit in the world couldn't alter Eddie's pose, nor his voice – although as yet he hadn't said anything untoward.

She turned to look again at her three nieces and her nephew. How long they would be able to remain in those statuesque positions she didn't know, but she was sure it wouldn't be for much longer. It was too much to expect of any of them, especially Maggie, as was demonstrated almost immediately as David, leaning over the end of the couch, said, 'You're looking very smart today, Maggie.'

When Maggie suddenly crossed her legs as if remembering something, uncrossed them and almost clapped her heels together, David emphasised, 'Well! you are.'

The bright gaze was turned up to him, and the voice came clear and sharp, 'Because I look dolled up?'

Hannah, realising immediately that Janie was about to say something to her daughter and that it would be in the form of a reprimand, put out her hand and gently slapped her sister's, then shook her head; and so Janie took a deep breath and waited.

'Dolled up? I don't think you look dolled up.'

'You said you liked me in my bum-freezer.'

'Yes; yes, I did; but you see . . . well, you're out visiting.'

'What's that got to do with it?'

Before Hannah lowered her eyes, she saw David rub his chin hard with his hand; then he said, 'I understand' – he swallowed – 'that bum-freezers are on the way out.'

'Not up our way, they're not. Peggy Stains—'

'We don't want to hear what Peggy Stains has to say, Maggie.' Her mother's voice had been low and firm, and her daughter answered, 'Well, I was just going to say—'

'I know what you were going to say, you told me this morning what Peggy Stains said. Now, if you repeat it . . . well, you know what'll happen.'

When the chuckle came from behind Maggie's chair, Maggie put her head back and looked at Peter, and he, bending down to her, whispered, 'Hung, drawn and quartered?' and she, shaking her head, replied, 'No; skinned alive.'

There was a suppressed gurgle round the room now, but when Maggie added, 'But that's only after

I've been starved for days . . . bread and water,' the laughter broke loose.

Peter's voice was controlled as he looked along the line and asked, 'Now, would you like a drink? Orange juice? Pineapple juice? And I've got an idea: I think we'd all be better off in the kitchen. I have a special chocolate meringue cake there just crying out to be eaten. How about it?'

It was Maggie who got up first and, reaching in front of her two sisters, she pulled John to his feet. Then, as if she were quite used to the flat, she made for the kitchen, with Claire and Winnie following, one on each side of Peter.

David sat down on the chair Maggie had vacated and, laughing again, he looked up the couch to where Janie was sitting with rather a straight expression, and he said, 'You've got a girl there, Janie.'

'Yes, I have, and don't I know it; she's getting out of hand.'

'There's a pair of you.' This came from Eddie. 'I've told you before it's no use arguing with her, she'll have the last word if it kills her; and she's way ahead of you every time, you know that.'

Hannah looked from one to the other. She had just witnessed a new side to Eddie Harper. She would have expected that, being the man he was, he would have blustered and yelled at his daughter to do what she was told; but he only had to speak one word and Maggie obeyed him. Odd, yet they were both alike.

When there came a high screech of laughter from the kitchen, Janie said, 'That's John.'

Then when other hysterical voices joined John's, David sprang up from his chair, saying, 'I'm missing something, I must see this,' and almost ran to the kitchen leaving Janie to comment, 'Well, really! boys will be boys,' but she was smiling.

Almost immediately Eddie, too, stood up and went to Hannah's side and said quietly, 'Let me see your neck, girl.'

'Oh.' Hannah put her hand up to her neck, saying, 'There's nothing there now.'

'Just let me have a look.'

Slowly, she unbuttoned her dressing gown; then he was exclaiming on the discoloured flesh and in a most strange way, for he was saying, 'He didn't do a bad job. He has big thumbs.'

'Oh, Eddie, shut up!' When Janie pushed him he took no notice, but said, 'What about your shoulders?'

'Now, Eddie' – Hannah wagged her finger at him – 'I'm not going to show you my shoulders. Anyway, you have to make an appointment to view, and the fee's double.'

'I've seen enough.'

He was solemn-faced as he sat down, and Hannah, now leaning across Janie towards him, said, 'Oh, Eddie, please! please forget about it. It's all over. Don't take anything into your own hands.'

'Oh, I wouldn't. How could I? He's a big fellow, is Humph.'

Hannah now lay back; her gaze on Janie was pleading, but Janie shook her head as much as to say, I can't do anything about it. Then, changing the subject entirely, Eddie said, 'Fine flat, this . . . well, this room, anyway. Never been in one like it. Wouldn't mind taking a pattern of it for our new place. You know we're moving, don't you, Hannah?'

'Yes,' added Hannah, laughing. 'I have been told.'

'Well, just wait till you see it. It's a fine house, with a big garden.'

'And in a posh neighbourhood, too,' added Janie.

Hannah suddenly laughed, saying, 'I thought you'd come here to commiserate with me' – she pursed her lips here for a moment – 'and also to congratulate me on the fact that I'm engaged to be married.'

'No!'

Eddie hitched a chair nearer to Janie's now. 'When did this happen?'

'And what about the divorce?' put in Janie.

'Oh, I'm told the divorce will be plain sailing: Humphrey has a ready-made wife and two children. As for the engagement, how long before we marry depends on David's divorce. That's going to be a bit more difficult. What I've seen and heard of the lady is not good. First, she's as big as a house-end and as strong as a horse. And secondly, there's a psychiatric problem on her mother's side of the family which seems to have touched her. Both her mother and sister are permanently hospitalised.'

A series of high squeals and laughter came from the kitchen; then Peter appeared, pushing a laden trolley, which brought from Janie a smothered 'Oh! Just look at that.'

'Now would you believe that.' Eddie was addressing Peter now, and he said, 'You'll understand this, Peter, but the last words she said to me before leaving the house today were, "Don't you go remarking on everything you see or telling them where you could get things for half the price," and what does she do?' He laughed now, then pressed his lips tightly together, before adding, 'But she's right. It's a very nice sight.' Then it was impossible for him to resist the next quip, 'Just like we have every Sunday.'

Hannah was laughing as she looked at Peter and said, 'Thanks, Peter.'

'And what was all that noise in the kitchen about?' put in Janie.

'Oh; your daughter is a very good mimic, Mrs Harper. I left her demonstrating the different ways people attack a plate of jelly.'

Eddie shook his head and laughed, but Janie drooped hers and for a moment she shaded her eyes with her hand and muttered, 'Oh, not that! Not that!'

'And I think I'd better warn you, Mrs Harper, that you've lost your daughter, and you, madam, your future husband.'

'Is that so?' said Hannah now. 'But how has it come about in such a short time?'

'These things happen, madam. You know they do.'

'Yes, yes' – Hannah laughed up at him – 'you're right, Peter; I know they do. But what has the lady to say about it?'

'She hasn't given her opinion as yet, madam, but I'm anxious to get back and hear more.'

They all laughed as Peter hurried from the room . . .

An hour later Maggie gave her the answer to the question, and caused not a little embarrasment. It was as they were ready to leave that David, paying special attention to Maggie, took her hand and, shaking it, said, 'Thank you, Maggie, for a delightful afternoon. I don't know what you're going to be when you grow up but—' only to be interrupted by Maggie, her tone definite, her eyes holding a deep twinkle as she gazed up into his face and said: 'Oh, I do. Oh yes, already I do. I'm just going to hang around like Aunt Hannah did with the wrong man until somebody like you comes along, and then grab him on the hop.'

It was her father who almost lifted her off her feet by gripping the collar of her coat and dragging her towards the door, where Peter was standing, his expression a mixture of amazement and amusement.

During this embarrassing declaration Janie had stood perfectly still, her eyes riveted on her daughter; but now she sprang back to the couch and, taking her sister's hand, she said, 'What can I do with her? I'm sorry, Hannah. I mean, she's never heard us . . . we've never discussed anything in front of her. I don't know what to do with her.'

'It's all right. It's all right.' Hannah was smiling now, although at the same time she was thinking, That girl wants taking in hand. But she reassured

Janie: 'What would life be without her? Go on. Go on. It's been a lovely day.'

'Yes; but what an end! Oh, he'll give it to her, and I'm glad; it's about time. He's been all for her but he's seen her antics for himself today.'

'Will you go on! They'll be waiting for you.'

'She's spoilt everything with that stupid comment; upsetting you like that.'

'Don't be ridiculous; she hasn't upset me at all. Look, this is how much she's upset me,' and Hannah thrust her arms up quickly and pulled Janie down to her and, kissing her hard, she said, 'There you are. Go and plant that on Maggie for giving us a really jolly afternoon.'

Janie said nothing more; she only looked down on Hannah, then shook her head before hurrying away.

But as Hannah waited for David to return after seeing them off, and Peter to come from the iron stairhead where he was standing looking down on them, she repeated Maggie's words to herself, 'grab him on the hop', and they no longer seemed funny.

# Fifteen

The weeks that followed took in Christmas and the
New Year and nothing happened to mar Hannah's
happiness. Only one incident made her thoughtful,
and something else brought her joy, but for the rest
she was mainly back living in Wonderland where,
once a week, she met up with Mrs Drayton for lunch
or had her to tea, and once a week she and David
had dinner with Natasha and Gilly. If they went out
for a meal themselves it was always at Micky's.

It was just before Christmas when they were
shopping in Harrods that she first met Alex Busby.
After David had introduced her, Alex said, 'Let's go
and have a coffee. I was hoping I might run into you
in London; there are bits and pieces I'd like you to
know.'

And so it was over coffee that they heard that
Carrie and her two other brothers were in America,
and that Alex had planned this so that he could
arrange the disposal of The Manor before they
returned. It was impossible, he had told them, to
keep up two places, for it was he who was having

to foot the bills for The Manor and the two racing stables.

He knew there would be skull and hair flying when she returned, which would be some time in February, he thought, but by this time he hoped the new owners would be settled in and she could do nothing about it.

At one point he had looked from David to his very attractive companion and asked with a wry smile, 'How are things going?'

And to this David had answered, 'Very well indeed; couldn't be better, except for one thing: Hannah's divorce will be through in the New Year, and I must, Alex, I really must press for mine.'

At this, Alex had bowed his head, saying, 'Oh dear, dear. Well, you know as well as I do what'll happen. She swore she'd never give it to you.'

'She can't withhold it,' said David; 'we've been apart for so long. I could claim it on those grounds alone, but if she puts up any opposition, as I know she will, then I'll be obliged to mention the subject that nobody likes to mention: that she's insane. You know it, Alex, better than anyone. How the boys keep things going in order to protect her beats me. Of course, it could be said it is their pastime that keeps them going. You know, Alex, I can't understand why she wasn't put away years ago. You all kept me in the dark until I experienced for myself what was wrong with her, and afterwards heard about your mother's delicate illness that kept her in the nursing home. And her sister, too, supposedly preferring to stay with another branch of the family. My God! I must have been dim . . .'

At this point Alex put in, 'I know we've been over all this before and we still haven't got over the shame of what we did, but, believe me, we did think that marriage would settle her down. Apparently, as I've explained before, it worked with Mother. After she married and had us lot she was as right as rain for years. It was Father's taking a mistress that shot her back.'

'But *I* didn't take a mistress,' said David. 'The first experience of her madness I had was on our honeymoon. Just imagine, on our honeymoon! and all because she found me laughing with a young girl who was staying in the same hotel. From then on, as you know, my life was a nightmare. So, if anyone has worked for a divorce I have, and it is already in the hands of my solicitor.'

Alex now bit on his lip and shook his head before he said, 'It's asking favours of you again; could you hold your hand until . . . well, the New Year, because if she were to have to return now for any reason the sale of The Manor could fall through: she has threatened to set fire to it rather than let it be sold. It's been on the point of being sold so many times of late but this time we're exchanging contracts early in the New Year. As soon as it's clinched I'll give you a ring. Would you do this for me, David?'

David had looked at Hannah, but she had turned her head away: she wasn't going to make a decision about a matter that was, as she saw it, going to change her life.

She heard David say, 'I'm sorry, Alex, but I can't promise you anything definite; all I know is I want to marry Hannah,' – he put his hand across the table and gripped hers – 'and as soon as possible. Her divorce could come through at any time.'

Disappointed, Alex said, 'Well, don't forget, David, Carrie always said she would shoot you before she'd give you a divorce. She's crafty in her madness, you know, even though in her really sane moments she's the most unhappy creature on earth.'

'You say she's to be pitied; well, so are those who come into contact with her,' said David grimly.

Their parting had been amicable, and that's all that could be said for it, but Hannah knew that the meeting had worried David.

It was the third week of January, and a Thursday. Hannah was in Gilly's office working with David in sorting out books. It was Gilly's suggestion that she should come in part-time and help David in his never-ending job of cataloguing the hundreds of volumes of old books lying on the floor of the office. Hannah was delighted by the offer, and the fact that she could spend half the day with David made it more pleasurable still.

On this particular morning, Gilly's younger brother, who was in his late forties and had been widowed three years previously, called with his new wife, a young woman of twenty-five, and their recently born baby daughter. They were on their way to her family in Devon and had just looked in.

The look-in almost turned into a party, for the baby's health had to be drunk, then drunk again, and if it wasn't that the younger Gillymans were due to get the train at one o'clock and had their seats booked, the admiration party would have continued all day. Neither Natasha nor Gilly showed any distress at the sight of the new baby.

That afternoon, there was little work done, and Hannah and David went home early. It was as Hannah stretched out her hands to the warmth of the fire that she said quietly, 'I hope ours will be as healthy and as bonny.'

There was silence in the room for a moment; then David's voice came in a whisper, 'What?'

Hannah turned from the fire, a soft smile on her face . . . 'You heard.'

'You mean . . .'

David rushed towards her and, gripping her shoulders none too gently, he said, 'Did . . . did I hear aright, you mean . . .?' He tossed his head much in the manner that an impatient horse might have done, then again he said, 'You're . . .?'

Sighing deeply, Hannah said, 'May I have your attention, Mr Craventon? I'm going to have a baby; would you please tell me what you think about it?'

For answer he pulled her into his arms and waltzed her around the room.

When she cried at him, 'Stop! Stop!' Peter, on his way to the kitchen, remarked in no small voice, 'Yes, madam; I would see that he doesn't exert himself, not while he's carrying.'

'Oh, you witty Willie! You'll cut yourself one of

these days, with your sharp rejoinders,' David commented. Then, his hold of her tender, he led her towards the couch; and when they were seated he lowered his head on to her shoulder, and, his voice a mere whisper, he murmured, 'Oh! Hannah. Thank you. Thank you. I've longed for such a moment, yet never thought it would come about.'

More like a mother now, she put her arms about him and stroked his hair, saying, 'Well, now it has, my love, and in a way it will cement all that is between us.'

The solicitor who had dealt with the affairs of The Manor knew the situation only too well, and he, too, pointed out to David that his wife would not take this further matter lightly.

It was now three weeks since David had been informed by this man that he had had no response to two letters he had sent to Carrie. This indicated to David that she was still on her travels in America.

He had also had word from Alex to the effect that the business of the house had been settled, and that there were two letters, apparently from the solicitor, awaiting her return.

It was four days later when Alex phoned again to tell him that Carrie was home and that, to his amazement, she had taken the news of the divorce quietly; at least, seemingly so, although knowing his sister, he suggested that David be on his guard. The boys, too, he said, would be extra vigilant where she was concerned. He added that the three of them had had a wonderful time in America, and he understood that she had been on her best behaviour.

During the past weeks Hannah had had bouts of morning sickness, which meant she was unable to accompany David to work. This morning, being a Saturday, they were both at home, and happy to be so, for the scene outside the window was of winter at its worst.

It had started to snow on the Tuesday; then thawed; then froze again; but on Thursday and Friday the large snowflakes found a firm bed on the ground, and although the gritters had been out it was again lying a foot high on the edge of the pavements and had once more covered the iron steps that Peter had cleared just a couple of hours before.

The room was bright and beautifully warm, and she was seated at the small desk, which was set in front of the long window at the far end of the room, when the doorbell rang.

She realised that both David and Peter were upstairs in the bathroom attending to a drip under the washbasin, so she rose, then hesitated before going to the door. What if it were . . . ? She shook her head: well, if it was, better get it over with.

She opened the door as far as the chain would allow, and saw a young man standing on the step, covered in snow.

'Good morning,' he said.

She did not return his greeting but asked stiffly, 'May I ask what you want?'

'Yes, I . . . I'd like to see my uncle.'

'Your . . . uncle?'

'Yes, Mr Peter Miller.'

'Your uncle?'

She saw the young man smile before nodding and saying, 'Yes; I'm his nephew.'

'Oh. Oh' – her face was one broad smile now as she fumbled with the chain – 'You're young Pete?' Then the door was open and her hand was out and she was saying, 'Come in. Come in.'

She noted that he stepped sideways into the room. 'I'm soaked,' he said. 'I'll make a mess of the carpet.'

'Oh, nonsense! Here, give me your coat.'

As he handed it to her he said, 'I should have come in the back way but the snow was much thicker on the steps there.'

'Look' – she pointed towards the fire – 'go and sit down. I'll call Peter; he's upstairs with David. They've found a pipe dripping under the basin up there; I think they're enjoying themselves. Do sit down, please do. Oh, never mind your boots.' Her gaze had followed his and she had noticed immediately that he was wearing boots, not shoes; she was trying to recall something that Peter had told them about his nephew.

She ran from the room, through the kitchen and to the bottom of the stairs, where she called, 'Peter! David! We have a visitor.'

'What? Who?'

'Not for you, for Peter. It's his nephew.'

'You don't say!' And she heard David call, 'Get up out of that, it's young Pete . . . young Pete's downstairs.'

Within a few minutes Peter was at the foot of the stairs, saying, 'Young Pete here? Well, I never!'

Hannah and David followed Peter into the room, and there they witnessed the meeting between Peter and his nephew. The young man had got to his feet and instead of shaking hands they hugged as if they hadn't seen each other for years. Then, thrusting the younger man away from him, Peter turned to Hannah and said, 'I'm sorry, but this is young Pete whom you've heard me speak of, I think, madam.' Then holding his hand out towards her, he hesitated for a moment before saying, 'This is Mr David's future wife.'

Now there was a shaking of hands and cross-talk, but when Peter said to the young man, 'Come on into the kitchen and I'll hear all your news,' David said, 'He'll go no such place, and you can wait for his news. Just you get a hot drink going; he looks frozen. Sit yourself down, Pete.'

As Peter hurried towards the kitchen, David called after him, 'Hot coffee, laced, I think, should be the order of the day.'

'Just as you say, sir.'

As Hannah took a seat to the side of the couch David sat down beside the young man and said, 'Where have you come from this morning?'

'Oh, I came up from Devon yesterday; but I didn't get in until late last night, so I had to go to a B & B.'

Hannah was looking at Pete's arm, which was laid across his waist in the way a woman might have held her handbag; but both the forearm and the upper arm were foreshortened, she realised. Then she remembered: he also had a clubbed foot. Peter had told them about it, and she recalled vividly his saying, 'The gods might have partly crippled his body, but in compensation they gave him the most wonderful spirit and the most beautiful face in the world; at least, that's how I see him.'

She was looking straight at the young man's face now and realising that the skin was like alabaster. The eye sockets were beautifully shaped and the eyes were a clear grey, so light that they seemed to sparkle. His nose was straight but it appeared to end in a point. Yet it was the mouth that drew the main attention; it wasn't large and it was well shaped, but the word that came to mind was 'tender'. Yes, it was a tender-looking mouth, like that of a young boy, yet he must be well into his thirties.

David was saying, 'You're a trained nurse, then?'

'Yes; yes, that's what I am, and I'm sometimes called Sister.'

'Peter never told me. I thought you looked after the old lady with whom you'd been in service since you were young.'

'Yes, I did look after her, except during the time I did my training. I always promised that I'd go back to her after it was finished, although I didn't think she'd still be alive. But she was, and for another six years, thankfully.'

The door was pushed open and Peter entered, bearing a tray of steaming mugs together with a bottle of whisky and a bowl of cream, and he called jovially, 'Don't tell them everything; you'll only have to repeat it for me. Anyway, what's brought you this far? Three days ago you were in Falmouth.'

The young man laughed, then said, 'Well, Uncle, in another three days I'll likely be set up in York.'

'York! Why are you going to York?' asked Peter.

'Well, there's a good job going for a nurse, at a psychiatric hospital.'

'But psychiatric patients – have you any experience with them?'

Pete said, 'No, I haven't; but then they're not much different from us, are they?'

'You speak for yourself, young fellow.'

'I am, Uncle; I am.' He was smiling. 'Anyway, I've been on the phone and I've given them an exact picture of myself and what I'm capable of doing as well as what I'm not capable of doing.'

'You're too modest; there's nothing much you can't do!'

The bright face was now turned from Peter to Hannah, and the young man said, 'Isn't it wonderful to have someone to lie for you, and do it without turning a hair?' Then addressing his uncle again he said, 'Anyway, if they take me on at all it'll be on a month's trial, and that works both ways. It'll please me, because it'll be another experience; all grist to the mill.'

Peter looked at his nephew and said, 'You're not proposing to go on to York tonight, are you?'

'Oh, no. Anyway, I understand the place is a good hour's journey outside York. No; I left my luggage at the B & B. I thought I'd stay over till Monday and have a look round. I've never really seen much of London, you know. But then I didn't reckon on the snow.'

As Peter was about to say something, David cut in, 'You're not staying at any B & B. His Lordship there', he nodded towards Peter, 'has a flat upstairs and a comfortable chair-bed. I know it's comfortable because I had experience of it when we were putting this place to rights. So what I think you should do is take a taxi and get your things back here as soon as possible. What d'you say, Peter?'

'I was just about to suggest something along the same lines, sir.'

'It's most kind of you. You're sure?' The young man was appealing to Hannah now, and she replied, 'Sure? Of course I'm sure. If they hadn't suggested it, I would have done so myself.'

'Well, I'll make a bargain with you. I'll stay if I can do the cooking.'

Hannah turned a laughing face towards Peter, and he said, 'Well, it's up to you, madam; you've made the bargain. Don't blame me should you happen to be presented with some obnoxious concoction of which the only thing distinguishable would be its French name.'

'I'll risk it.' Hannah and the young man exchanged a glance that turned into a smile, then a laugh.

# Sixteen

It was Thursday evening. The snow had cleared and there was only the frozen slush left in the gutters.

Peter's kitchen was, as usual, bright and warm. He had just rolled out three separate slabs of pastry, two of which were wrapped and put in the fridge; He was sprinkling the third one with fresh almonds he had ground in the old-fashioned iron grinder attached to the end of the table when he heard what he thought was a scraping on the back door. A neighbour's tabby was in the habit of calling, to see, Peter would say, how the scrap business was proceeding. So, dusting his hands, then wiping them on a tea-towel, he went towards the door; but, on the point of opening it, he recalled the reason for the chain being on the front door and also that he did not usually have visits from the cat in the dark on a freezing night such as this. He stood quietly listening for a moment, and when he heard the sound of a foot being moved on the iron step, he called, 'Whoever's there, please go round to the front door.'

'It's me,' said a voice.

'Who's there?' called Peter.

'Me!' The voice was louder now: 'Maggie! Maggie Harper.'

'Maggie Harper?'

'Yes. Yes.'

He unlocked the door and stared down at the muffled child, thrust out his hand and pulled her indoors. Then, banging the door closed, he bent down to her, saying, 'What on earth brings you here, child?'

'I . . . I' – the lips were trembling, the head was shaking – 'I wanted to see you first, and you could tell them.'

Now the tears were pouring from her eyes and running down her nose. He said, 'Come on; get to the fire. Take your coat off first.'

As he pushed her through the kitchen into the sitting room he tugged off her coat, then her scarf, and lastly her woolly hat; but as he was about to sit her down on the couch she moved away from him, saying, 'Oh! no; she'll be in in a minute. I heard Mam say she's working and gets in . . .'

'But you want to talk to her, don't you?'

'No. N-n-n-not me. I mean, I thought that . . .'

'Now, now; stop crying. Come on, stop crying. What did you think?'

'That . . . that if I told you, you'd tell her about it. You see they . . . they don't love me any more. None of them, none of them.'

'Oh, now that's silly.'

''Tisn't. It isn't, Mr Peter. Mam and Dad don't talk in front of me like they used to, not any more.

They even don't talk to me. They speak to me but they don't talk to me. D'you know what I mean?'

Yes; yes, he knew what she meant, all right, and he could see the situation plainly, and all he could say was, 'But they do love you, Maggie.'

'Not any more. And Winnie went for me yesterday.' She choked now and rubbed her damp handkerchief around her face, before saying, 'She . . . she said that none of them would be able to come down and see Auntie Hannah any more, all because of me and . . . and my big mouth. You know . . . what I said when we were here . . . I just wanted to make you all laugh, but, as Dad said, it would need a saint not to believe that they talked like that about Auntie Hannah. That's what he said that night, and he walloped me. He's never done it before, but he did; and Mam said it wasn't before time; and then they argued, and it's been awful, awful. And now they don't speak of anything in front of me; and none of them love me, Mr Peter, not one, even John. He keeps saying I've been naughty.'

When at this stage she emitted a howl, Peter drew her close to him, saying, 'You're letting your imagination run away with you,' being sure at the same time that she wasn't imagining anything she had described. But the parents' reaction had reached a limit that was dangerous to the girl herself, and now, staring at the clock, he said, 'Well now, listen: I have a plan. They'll be here at any minute, but upstairs in my flat there's a very comfortable sitting room. Now the fire's on' – he put his head on one side and made a face – 'it's only artificial logs, but they look real. Come on upstairs and I'll explain the whole situation to your Aunt Hannah, and say how sorry you are. Then you may come down and see Mr David.'

'I don't want to see Mr David, I couldn't look at him.'

'Oh, you'll look at him, all right, or he'll look at you and want to know the reason why you're being so silly.'

'I – I – I'm not silly, Mr Peter.'

Her voice had a firm note in it now and he said, 'I'm sorry. I shouldn't have said that. You're not silly, I know you're not, Maggie, you're a very thinking little girl.'

Her voice now almost a whine, she said, 'I'll never be a little girl again.'

He grasped her arm and brought her firmly from the couch; then, picking up her wet clothes from a chair, he said, 'I'll put these in the airing cupboard, but in the meantime let's get aloft.'

Peter's sitting room was made for comfort. Two large leather club chairs were set one each side of the glowing artificial log fire. An off-white fireside rug set off an overall red carpet, and beyond the rug stood a long and low rosewood table. Here too was an upholstered folding chair that acted as a single bed. Two bookcases stood against the far wall, both with glass fronts, and between them a roll-top writing desk. There was a window in each end wall, one that looked out on to the front of the house and one to the back, which took in the main thorough-fare.

'Now, isn't this nice and cosy? But you don't want to sit in those hard leather chairs. Wait a minute!' He pushed the table to one side and drew the upholstered chair into its place. 'There now, sit in that one, it's much more comfortable.'

When she obeyed him, she sat with her hands tightly clasped between her knees. Her face was still tear-stained, but she was no longer crying. Even so, he went to the bathroom and brought back a small towel. After rubbing it round her face he said, 'There now! That feels better, doesn't it? Now I'm going to make you a nice cup of tea, and bring you a piece of my special sponge.'

'Thank you' – her lips were trembling again – 'but . . . but I couldn't eat anything, n-n-not yet.'

'Just a cup of tea, then?' He was bending over her, and she looked up into his face and whispered, 'Please.'

He had reached the door when he turned and said, 'I might be a minute or two, that's if your auntie should come in; you do want me to talk to her, don't you?' She made one slow movement with her head and he said, 'Well, in the meantime, on that shelf in the corner there are some magazines and papers. Have a look through those; and I'll be back as soon as I can.'

He had just made a pot of tea when he heard the rattle of a key in the front door. This was the signal for him to take off the chain. He let Hannah and David in, both exclaiming on the weather and the intense cold: 'Oh, isn't it wonderful to be home?'

Peter was helping Hannah off with her coat

when he said, 'We have a visitor, madam.'

At this, David, who was in the act of taking off his topcoat, swung around. His face was straight and he repeated grimly, 'Visitor? Where?'

'Oh, not that kind of a visitor, sir. It's . . . it's your niece, madam, little Maggie.'

'Maggie? By herself? What on earth . . . ?'

'If you'll both come up to the fire and unfreeze, I'll give you a run-down on why she's here, then take her up a cup of tea.'

It took Peter only a few minutes to go over what Maggie had told him, but now he added, 'If I may suggest, madam, I'd go very carefully with her, because to my mind she's disturbed. You know, it's some time since the afternoon of the tea party, and apparently the fact that her father thrashed her shows what importance he put on her behaviour. She insists that she just wanted to make people laugh; but I don't think she's laughed since, madam, and she's got the idea that no one loves her, and through her parents' reaction to her this is now deeply ingrained. She was very perceptive when she told me about this – as she says, her parents . . . they speak to her, but they don't *talk* to her.'

Hannah, obviously distressed now, cupped her face in her hands as she said to David, 'I can imagine that at this moment Janie is going mad. I must phone and tell her that Maggie's here.'

It was David who said, 'I'll phone them. You go up and see her.'

But at this Peter checked them both by saying, 'If I may suggest, sir, I wouldn't talk to Maggie just yet

338

– wait until she's had a cup of tea and feels more settled. Why don't you both go and get tidied up, and I'll prepare your meal, and over it you can decide on your next move. And if you'll allow me, madam, I'll phone your sister and tell her that her daughter is here and everything is all right.'

Hannah and David exchanged a glance; then almost simultaneously turned and hurried towards their bedroom.

Peter went into the kitchen for the tray to take upstairs, and when he had placed it on a small table at Maggie's side he said, 'I've told them, and everything's going to be all right. You drink that tea, and they'll be upstairs shortly.' He smiled at her. 'Trust me; everything's going to be all right – and with your mum and dad. You'll see.'

What happened next was so sudden and un-expected, he would remember it for the rest of his life . . .

He did not take Carrie for an apparition, for she was standing there in the flesh, and for the first time in his life he was experiencing body-shuddering fear. It did not seem to have its origin in the stomach, as with most fears, but, strangely, in the very soles of his feet, for he felt as if he was about to topple over.

The next he knew was that something was happening to his heart – it seemed to be bursting through his ribs. He eventually gave vent to it through his gasping mouth, and the sound came out as a drawn-out 'Ohhhh!'

Carrie's voice, when it came to him, sounded

calm: 'You shouldn't be surprised to see me, Peter; the door was unlocked, although I could have got in anyway; I have a duplicate key,' and this she lifted up and dangled.

When his next move was to make for the door, she sprang in front of him, saying, 'Where are you going?'

'I – I', he stammered, 'was just going—'

'Yes, to tell your master he has a visitor? Well, Peter, I'm going to do it for you.'

When his hand moved swiftly to grab the rolling-pin, hers was there first, and after grasping it she thrust him backwards. Then, as he went to yell a warning, she checked it with a doubled fist to his mouth, to which he instinctively responded, as he had done years before, by kicking her in the shins.

She let out an oath, and the next minute she was grappling with him, and so fierce was her hold he had no wind with which to yell; but he was to recall making one final effort to grab the rolling-pin before it was brought down on his head.

It was as if his body had been splintered into myriad pieces, all aiming to reach the ceiling, only for them to be drawn together before dragging him down into blackness. He wasn't aware that he had slid down her body into a heap on the floor, or that she was now standing over him, prepared to strike again.

She stood for a moment, breathing heavily and looking towards the door that led into the sitting room. There was a sign of bewilderment on her face that no one had yet put in an appearance. Slowly now she approached the door.

Looking round the sitting room, her eyes focused on the tea trolley standing towards the head of the couch. Each shelf was covered by a white cloth. This brought her eyes to the far door and the bedroom, from where she could hear voices.

She was wearing a heavy dark blue overcoat. It had large flat pockets, and from one she extracted a gun. Then, holding her left arm across her waist, she laid the gun gently along it. Her finger on the trigger, she crept very quietly towards the bedroom door.

She stopped in the open doorway of the bedroom. David was standing before the dressing-table mirror, his body bent slightly forward. His upper lip was exposing his teeth and he was pressing one of them. It had been troubling him for days but the thought of the dentist had put him off. His head was moving slightly to take in the reflection of the other side of his face when his body stiffened and he muttered, 'Oh, my God! Oh, my God!' Then he swung round, his buttocks pressed tight against the edge of the dressing table, and he cried, 'Stay where you are, Hannah! Stay where you are!'

Hannah appeared at the door of the bathroom, saying, 'What did you—?' Her words were frozen and she remained rooted to the spot at the sight of the woman with a gun in her hand, who was now addressing David, saying, 'I warned you, didn't I, David, of what I'd do if ever you brought me low again? The boys got me to sign the legal separation, oh yes. If I hadn't, they would have gone their own ways. They did that for you. But they're not here now, are they? At this moment they think I'm still chatting and listening to the drivel of Aunt Amelia Goodall. They want me to keep in with her. She's very wealthy, is Aunt Amelia, and she's known as an eccentric, not mad like Mama or Eva or me. But I needn't have been like the rest; I was getting better. I knew all about myself. If you'd been patient . . . No, you were ashamed to be with me, weren't you, David? But even then I was just known as your hysterical wife, not a madwoman. I didn't show you my real side until you decided to leave me, and what did I promise you then? I ask you again, can you remember?'

David now muttered, 'Get back in the bathroom and lock the door. Do as I say.'

As Hannah made an effort to obey him she was brought to a halt by Carrie's voice. 'You move an inch and I'll shoot him. I need this to last for some time. I need recompense for what I've gone through. No one's pitied *me*. No; it's been "Poor David, poor David married to her." So I'm warning you, you blonde slut, stay where you are. I'll deal with *you* in a minute. Oh, yes, we've met before. Played your little game, didn't you, going up the street as if you didn't know him?'

With almost a jump now David sprang round and lunged at Hannah, but as he did so a high scream came from the woman and she fired the gun.

There was silence while Hannah stood gripping the stanchion of the door in terror. Then she was on her knees, holding David's bleeding body to her and crying. 'You've shot him! You've shot him, you bitch!'

'Yes; yes, I've shot him and I'll do it again.'

As Carrie pointed the gun at the prostrate body Hannah sprang from her knees and threw herself against what seemed a solid wall of bone, and the next minute the two women were struggling madly.

When the gun went off for a second time it was evident it hadn't hit Hannah, for she continued to claw at the woman's face. But her efforts were stopped when she saw the woman's hand flash up to show the blade of a knife. It was when the point pierced some part of her neck that she screamed at the top of her lungs.

And as she too slid to the ground the mad creature gripped her by the loose braids of her hair and dragged her along the floor. Then, gripping a smaller handful of the hair, she proceeded to saw it from the roots with the knife. But on finding this a slow business she got to her feet, stepped over Hannah and, avoiding David's body, examined the pieces on the glass tray of the dressing table, looking for scissors; not finding any, she paused for a moment. Then at a run she crossed the room.

When Maggie heard the first scream she had run downstairs, terrified, to find Mr Peter lying on the floor, dead, as she thought. Then there was the sound of a woman's voice yelling from another room. She stood petrified, until what sounded to her like the crack of a gun caused her to dive under the table. A minute or so later she was amazed to hear running footsteps, then, from her position under the table, to see a pair of wool-covered legs and the bottom of an open coat showing bloodstains on the bottom of a skirt.

It was when she saw one of the legs go out and kick Mr Peter, and the woman running out of the kitchen again, that Maggie had to stuff her fingers into her mouth to stop herself from screaming.

On hands and knees now, she crawled to Peter's side, and when she saw his head lift, she whimpered, 'Oh, Mr Peter. Mr Peter, you're not dead. Oh, Mr Peter; wake up, wake up properly.'

Perhaps it was the kick in the side that had brought Peter back from the black depths. He recognised Maggie and managed to whisper, 'Hide! Hide!' But her voice came to him, again appealing, 'Get up, Mr Peter, please! She's a bad woman, she's in there.' She thumbed towards the open door. Then her body seemed to collapse under the weight of Peter's hand on her shoulder as he tried to pull himself round and on to his knees.

Having got herself to her feet, she then helped Peter to his; and there he stood, leaning with his back against the table. He felt as if his head must be split in two and that he was about to fall to the ground again, but he turned and looked down on the table, to see the rolling-pin. He was quick to notice that the knife and the scissors had gone. Slowly reaching out, he pulled the rolling-pin towards him. Then, his hand on Maggie's shoulder for support, he staggered to the kitchen door, across the sitting room and to the bedroom door; there, the sight of the beautiful golden hair and the blood still oozing from Hannah's neck aroused such an anger in him that he leapt on the woman. The surprise of the attack and his weight bore her sidewards to the ground, and now they were wrestling. He had dropped the rolling-pin and it had rolled almost to Maggie's feet, as she stood pressed against the stanchion of the door and screaming at the top of her voice, 'Leave him alone!'

As the woman's hand came across Peter's body in an effort to grab the knife now lying on the floor, Maggie reacted.

Grabbing the rolling-pin, she held it in her hands and swung it into the face of the kneeling woman. There was a gasp and a cry from the woman as the blood burst from her nose and she fell backwards. Then her hand went slowly up to her face and Maggie knew that within a minute she would be on her feet and would kill her, too. Once again she gripped the rolling-pin, and this time she brought it to the side of the woman's head and had the satisfaction of seeing her fall on to her face.

'Oh, Lord! Oh, Lord! Mam! Mam!' Maggie was shouting now. Then, looking down at Peter, who was slowly pulling himself to his feet, she cried, 'Oh, Mr Peter! Mr Peter! Get up! Get up! We must get the police and the ambulance. Get up! Get up! Oh, Mam. Where's Mam?'

Peter was on his knees now and staring down at the woman lying at his side. She looked as if she had really been knocked out; but you never knew with her: she wasn't human, she was a demon. Still on his knees, he turned and looked to where David lay, his back covered with blood, and then to Hannah, pieces of her hair seemingly sticking to everything in sight. Then again he looked at the figure at his side. She wasn't dead; that was a certainty. Suddenly he pointed towards the window and said, 'Maggie; bring the cords.' She turned and quickly brought the window cord to him. He took one of the woman's arms and brought it on to her back and to Maggie he said, 'Lift her . . . her arm.'

When she had done that, he heaved a sigh and fell back on his haunches, and his head drooped before he said again, 'Maggie!'

'Yes? Yes, Mr Peter?'

'Can . . . can you make a knot?'

She had to tie the woman's hands; and yes, yes, she could make a knot, she was very good at reef knots.

As if she was handling something repulsive she bound the cord round the blood-covered wrists; she found some difficulty in making the knot, as there was a tassel on each end of the cord, but somehow she managed. She turned now and looked at Peter. His legs were now straight and his back was resting against the foot of the bed. Again he said, 'Maggie.'

Her voice a mere tremble, she answered, 'Yes, Mr Peter?'

'Do . . . do the same.' He pointed now to the other side of the window where the matching cord hung. 'Do . . . do her legs.'

She was trembling as she took the cord from the hook, but nevertheless she quickly set about repeating the process she had just finished on the woman's wrists. When this was done she turned to Peter again. But he was no longer sitting upright; his body had fallen to the side and the sight of him looking dead, like the rest of them, caused her to let out a high cry, and again she whimpered, 'Oh! Mam, Oh! Mam,' but this time she added, 'Oh! Dad.' If only her Dad were here.

She looked helplessly towards David and Hannah. He looked awful; he was covered with blood. But to her young eyes it was her Aunt Hannah who looked the worse. She must phone the police. She wiped her hands down the front of her dress; they were sticky with blood and hair.

She stood now looking at the phone; the house was very quiet; there was no one to tell her what to do; well, she knew what to do, didn't she? She was talking to herself. She must dial 999.

She lifted the phone and dialled the number. When it was answered she gave the address, then gabbled, 'Send the police, an ambulance! As soon as you can! They're all dead, except Mr Peter. I don't know about her. I hit her with the rolling-pin. Will you send somebody?'

'Your call is being attended to immediately.'

The line went dead. She turned from the table, then let out a high scream as she saw something crawling from the bedroom, but when she realised it was Mr Peter, she staggered to him, saying, 'Aah! you gave me a fright. Can't you get up?'

He did not answer but she watched him twist round and lean his back against the side of

Hannah's desk, and he gasped, 'Open the front door. Pull . . . pull the chain back, then open the front door.'

'Yes; yes, Mr Peter.'

She opened the front door, and the cold air seemed to revive her and take away the dizzy feeling that had begun to envelop her and she said, 'I must phone Mam.'

The voice at the other end of the phone said, 'Yes? Yes? Who is it?'

Maggie knew it was her mother and said, 'Listen! Mam. Listen! Bring Dad. A big woman came and she's killed Auntie Hannah and Mr David. And Mr Peter's bad.'

'Maggie! Maggie!' She straightened up at the sound of her father's voice. 'Maggie! listen quietly. Are you at your Aunt Hannah's?'

'Yes, Dad; yes. I came to tell her I was sorry, but the big woman came and shot them.' Her voice seemed to be leaving her head, for it sounded a long way off, and it was saying, 'I'm bad, Dad. I've opened the front door. And I hit her with the rolling-pin.'

The feeling was very odd, and the phone slipped from her hands and dropped on to the table. Then she was seeing a lot of policemen, and one put his arms about her. The house was full of people, and everybody was talking at once. The only comfort she had was lying next to Mr Peter on the floor and that he had hold of her hand.

# Seventeen

Hannah was feeling weary. She'd had a busy morning of examinations. First to be looked at was her neck, about which the doctor's verdict was that the slit was healing nicely. He said it had been a near thing. This was followed by an examination of her body bruises. However, the main examination had been to make sure the baby within her was still all right; it was, and that was surprising, after all she had gone through.

After the doctor had gone she must have slept for a time, but now she was lying lazily turning over the pages of a magazine when the door opened and she saw the child. It was Maggie, and yet it wasn't Maggie. The last time she had seen her she had been a pert, rosy-faced girl. But the child now walking to the side of the bed looked puny. Her face was white and drawn; her eyes looked enlarged and had a blankness in them; and she was carrying, of all things, a rolling-pin.

She knew what the child had done with the rolling-pin, and that subsequently when a policeman tried to carry her to the ambulance she had screamed for it, and one of the many men there had to bring it from the bedroom and hand it to her.

She pulled herself further up on the pillows and, holding out her hand, she said, 'Oh, my dear. My dear Maggie; how lovely to see you!'

Maggie moved up to the head of the bed now and stood mutely looking at Hannah, and when Hannah put out her hand and stroked her face Maggie made no move whatever.

Turning to the nurse, Hannah said, 'Will you leave us for a time, nurse, please?'

'Yes, of course.' Then, patting Maggie on the head, she added, 'She's a good girl.' Stooping, she looked into Maggie's face and repeated, 'You are a good girl, aren't you?'

'Sit down, Maggie.' Hannah pointed to a chair, and after a moment's hesitation Maggie pulled the chair closer to the bed and sat down, her eyes all the while on Hannah's face.

It was as Hannah went to close the magazine that Maggie's attention dropped to it, and on seeing this Hannah lifted the page, saying, 'It's a bridesmaid's dress; isn't it pretty?' and she turned the magazine towards Maggie. 'It says', she went on, 'that it has a high, ruched bodice and a long skirt dropping to silver slippers; it's crowned with a tiara of flowers matching the pale blue and rose of the gown. It's pretty, isn't it?'

Hannah's words brought Maggie's eyes from the paper up to her, and she was sure she could detect a different expression in them, and at this an idea came into her mind. Maggie had always been interested in dress, albeit more outlandish clothes than were suitable for her age, so she repeated, 'It's pretty, isn't it? It's a girl's bridesmaid's outfit, and, you know, I've been looking for something similar – although not with such a long skirt because—' She brought her upper body forward, for she could not bend her head, and cupping Maggie's face in her hands, she said, 'I was looking for something in that line because, you see, as soon as David can walk – even if he can't, he can always sit in a chair – we're going to be married, and I want a bridesmaid. Just one girl. And d'you know who that girl is?'

The rolling-pin had slid to the bedcover, and now Maggie's mouth was open, but still no sound came from it, and Hannah said, 'Give a guess. Well, who would I want for a bridesmaid but you? I know you don't like long skirts, but it could be altered.'

'Aunt . . . Hannah, b – b – bridesmaid?'

'Yes, just you. Now mind, we can't let you have a bum-freezer, not quite. This one would suit you beautifully, and it can be cut shorter.'

'Oh, Auntie Hannah.' The lids were blinking and the tears were running fast down Maggie's face, and she cried, 'She cut your hair off! And poor Mr Peter. Poor Mr Peter.' The child's head was swinging from side to side. 'I hit her with the rolling-pin.' She picked up the rolling-pin and hugged it to her again. 'And she died and I tied her up.'

'No, no; she didn't die, Maggie. She's in a hospital. She's a bad woman, but she didn't die. But you were very clever at tying her up. If you hadn't,

I understand she would have killed Mr Peter; but you saved him.'

Her head bobbing, Maggie said, 'I opened the front door, but it was so cold, very cold.'

Hannah's arm went around the child and pulled her head on to her breast, saying, 'You'll never be cold again, Maggie, never. It's all over. Everybody's all right, and all because you saved them, you and your rolling-pin.'

'I wouldn't get on the stretcher until they gave it to me. I remember that.'

'Yes, I know, they told me . . .'

At this, Maggie's crying mounted, and the door was suddenly opened, and in came Sister and a nurse, who were warned immediately by a signal from Hannah: 'It's all right,' she said, 'it's all right. We were just discussing a bridesmaid's outfit.' She nodded knowingly towards the magazine on the bed. 'You see, Maggie is going to be my bridesmaid.'

'Is that so?' The sister took it up now. 'Well, well! And I'd like to know if I'm invited to the wedding.'

'Well, we'll get out a list later on, Sister, and see.'

'And what about me?' asked the nurse, bending down to Maggie. 'I've been looking after your auntie all this time; I should get a look-in, don't you think?'

For the first time a suspicion of a smile spread across the child's face, and more than a suspicion of the old Maggie appeared as she said, 'Me mam.'

'Oh!' said the nurse now, looking at the sister. 'She's got to ask her mother who's going to be invited. Did you hear that?'

The sister had picked up the magazine and was looking at the page as she said, 'Miracles happen in the strangest ways in this hospital.'

Peter had been twice to the operating theatre. He was found to have a seeping vein at the bottom of the brain. But why, two days later, should he be taken down to the theatre again? Pete wanted to know. Of course, his enquiry of the sister about his uncle's condition had been couched more politely than that: and he was told the surgeon was reviewing what he had previously done.

The reviewing had taken place three days earlier, the day after Pete had come back from York. He had been offered a permanent position at the psychiatric hospital, but on hearing of his uncle's condition had decided to return to London until Peter was better. Now he was sitting by his uncle's bedside. Peter had been talking for some time, and was now saying, 'Look at it this way: even if mad Carrie hadn't got up to her antics, it would have made no difference to me in the long run, now would it? And as I've said, they've got a lot of friends now, both of them, but they're friends who have jobs and businesses and families of their own. They'll rally round them, but that isn't enough. They'll want someone they know to be there all the time. In the past, with David, it's been me. Although I've always called him Mr David, to him I was never just a servant, he never thought of me in that way. Now everything on my horizon is quite clear and defined because I know when the time comes you'll take over and my spirit will stay with you.'

Pete said nothing. His head was drooped deep on his chest, his hands gripped tightly between his thighs, and for a moment there was silence in the little ward. It was as if it and the occupants had been transported far away, although the atmosphere was not one of sadness but rather of resignation.

Peter dispersed the feeling by asking, 'Have you seen Miss Hannah yet?'

'Yes,' Pete muttered, 'and she's very excited; she's going to see Mr David this afternoon, and so I thought it better not to show her the cutting I took from the paper this morning. It reports that last evening a car dumped a man on the pavement outside the Wishbeck Police Station. He had been badly beaten about the face and body and was also without his trousers. At first he refused to give his name and address, but he later gave his name as Humphrey Drayton and his address as 72 Beaufort Road. He insisted that he had not recognised any of his assailants, who seemed to be three in number; nor could he give any reason why he should have been attacked.'

Pete paused, then said, 'Now what d'you make of that, Uncle?'

'Oh, I can solve that puzzle for you straight away. It's either down to madam's brother-in-law or Micky McClean. You know I'm not for violence of any kind, yet I have to say that it was deserved, well deserved. Of course, he'll never be able to prove anything, but he'll always suspect that his brother-in-law must have had a hand in this. Life is strange, isn't it, Pete?'

'Yes, Uncle, very strange. But now, if I'm to carry out your orders back at the house, I have a lot to do. I must get on with the books. Mr Gillyman told me what I must do with them, and I'm enjoying it.' He stood up, leant forward and kissed Peter on the brow before saying, 'Goodbye, Uncle.'

'Goodbye, Pete; and the gods go with you.'

David held Hannah as tightly as he could, with her lying in an awkward position half across the bed; and neither of them spoke for some time. Then when she murmured, 'Oh, David; David, my love . . . David,' he did not answer but buried his head in her shoulder for a moment before releasing her and allowing his head to drop back on to the pillow. Then she, straightening from her painful position, hitched herself further on to the bed and, taking hold of his hands, she brought them to her breast, saying, 'You're alive; we're alive.'

The seconds ticked away as their gaze held; and then he said, 'You're alive, darling; I feel only partly so, as yet.'

'Now, now!'

He drew one of his hands away from hers and pressed it across her lips, saying, 'I've done a lot of quiet thinking during the last few days – at least, since the panic settled – and I've got to talk to you about it. You see, in a way, I'm the source of all this trouble. I know now I should have fought years ago for a divorce, not just a separation, because then the boys could have had more control over her antics. They both said so the other day.' He nodded at her now, saying, 'They came in to see me, and Tony cried. He cried like a child; it was dreadful. But later, when I thought about it, I don't know whether he was crying for me or for her being locked away with the others. Max didn't cry; he blamed himself for being duped into leaving her for a time with the aunt. Anyway, it was odd. But that visit brought me out of the panic. You see, when I first came to and thought I was going to be paralysed for life I did some shouting, until Welshy took me in hand. She's the night nurse and a tough lady. She told me to shut up or she'd push me into the main ward and show me others who really had something to shout about. Before they stuck a needle into me she told me I was lucky. But, Hannah, I didn't feel lucky, because I couldn't move my limbs. But I have a little movement in my leg now, because the swelling is going down, and I know I'm lucky; at least on that side. They tell me the bullet just missed my spine and, with the nerves going awry for a time, there was a big swelling there. As it goes down I'll become more and more mobile. But it's this left hip that promises to be the stumbling block; the bone has been shattered, and it might be months before I can put my foot on the ground. And so I must talk to you, and about our lives ahead.'

Hannah held up a hand to him now, saying, 'I know what you're going to say; well, let me have my say first. I'm engaged to be married to you, and don't forget that what's inside me belongs to you too. So yes, we've got to do something about it, and soon, but not in the way you mean, waiting until you can walk, but as soon as the divorces are through. I want to be married and have a name for our child. You don't have to walk to the altar: you can go in a wheelchair.

'Now' – she touched his cheek – 'there's no way you can live in the flat again, and so other arrangements are being made.'

'Where?'

'Well, now, at the moment I can't give you an answer because I don't know myself; I only know that a group of our friends have got their heads together: Gilly and Natasha; Mrs Drayton; and Eddie and Micky. Oh, yes, Eddie and Micky, they seem to be very busy. Janie comes in somewhere; I can't guess at her role – whenever I ask she tells me to mind my own business, and yours, and not to ask questions out of place.'

'Do they realise that for a long time yet I shall have to attend hospital for therapy?'

'I suppose so.'

There was silence now as they gazed at one another. Then, as if his mind had switched away from all she had said and implied, he asked quietly, 'Have you been to see Peter?'

She nodded. 'Yes;' and he put in sharply, 'Well, how is he?'

'Oh, since his second operation he seems better than he was.' She did not go on to say what was really on her mind, that he seemed slightly odd, as though he were resigned to something; that he kept talking about Pete and what a good fellow he was. 'When he talks it's about you and how Pete will look after us both until he himself is back on his feet.'

She brought his hands up to her breast again, saying, 'We have a lot of good friends, darling. We're very lucky.'

He gave a short laugh now as he said, 'You sound like Welshy. Oh, and how's Maggie?'

'Almost herself; not quite; but I think she's beginning to enjoy her role as the saviour with the rolling-pin. She's never away from Peter for long, you know. There's no doubt about it, she did save his life.'

But as she uttered these words a startling thought struck her, for it said, At least for a time.

She stayed with David for another fifteen minutes, during which he held her close and kissed her again and again, but said very little.

When she left him, she was assailed by another odd thought: he had never mentioned her bandaged neck, although his fingers had lain gently on it; nor had he touched on the matter of her hair, which had been tidied up into a tomboyish bob. What, to her, was more serious, he had not mentioned the baby, even though she had referred to it; and she came to the conclusion that he was suffering from shock, or perhaps guilt that he had been to blame for it all.

# Eighteen

It was nine weeks later when Hannah and David saw their new home for the first time.

David's flat was now managed by Pete, who cooked, cleaned and looked after his uncle, home from the hospital. Hannah too spent a lot of her free time with Peter, for she wasn't happy about him. Although he now rarely had what appeared to be fainting fits, he was far from the old Peter she remembered. He still insisted on getting dressed every day and making her tea, if she was in; at other times he brought her a hot drink; these attentions, she knew, were made with effort, but nevertheless they gave him the opportunity to sit with her for a time and talk.

Their conversation would generally start with David's present condition: his back being much better but his hip still causing concern. It would then drift to Maggie and her insistence on spending the weekends with them, and invariably would end with the house and trying to guess where it might be and what it would look like.

Hannah felt that Peter knew more than he would acknowledge, even though she knew he could not have seen the property.

During the past few days things had been different and the excitement all round was at its height, especially with David and Hannah, for they were to see their new home on this particular Saturday morning.

She was sitting beside his wheelchair in the hospital day-room, and she was listening to him as he sang the praises of Welshy. 'She's got something, has that nurse; it's uncanny. She's the one who stopped my nightmares. I think she let me talk it out. I told her all about you and how we met on that particular Thursday and how Thursday was the only evening in the week you could get out to meet me, and, too, that you had been born on a Thursday. And I remember her quietly saying, "Thursday's child has far to go."'

He now leant forward and, cupping her face in his hands, he whispered, 'Thursday's child has far to go, but never go far from me, will you, darling? All my big talk inside my head – that I must let you live your own life and that I can't allow you to play a nurse to me because it wouldn't be fair – I know is mere empty twaddle, because, looking ahead, I'm terrified at the thought of life without you. Oh, Hannah.'

Her arms were about him and her heart was wrenched with the thought that it wasn't only his as yet useless leg that would need time for recuperation. His mind had been so shocked that he had lost a sense of his own value, part of which derived from her need of him.

'David,' she said; 'don't you know by now that I could never go on without you? I'll soon have our child and we're going to be married and whether you walk or not I want to be near you always. I want to defy fate and look down the years to where we will still be together and our children grown up. Don't you understand, I love you for so many different things and I need them all to make my life whole? So,' her eyes blinking rapidly and her lips trembling, she added, 'come on, come on, no more doubts. They're taking us to the house today. And they're so excited about it.'

The Land-Rover glided gently to a stop. Gilly got out, then handed Hannah on to the pavement.

Behind them the second car had pulled up; and the first to alight, and quickly, was Eddie, followed by Janie, Natasha and, more slowly, Mrs Drayton.

Eddie was standing at the rear of the Land-Rover, where Gilly had already opened the doors and let down a ramp. Together they then eased David's wheelchair on to the road, to hear him exclaim loudly, 'Where are we? What's all this?'

'Shut up,' ordered Gilly. 'You'll know in a minute.' Then he said to Eddie, 'You see to that fellow, will you?' and to the ladies, 'We're going in by the tradesman's entrance. There's a better view of everything from there.'

He now took Hannah's arm and led her forward; and Eddie, pushing David's wheelchair, followed, leaving the three other women to bring up the rear.

David's head was turning from side to side now. To his left was a vegetable garden, to his right a high hedge. Then he was wheeled into an open paved area.

Hannah was now by his side, and they exclaimed simultaneously, 'Oh, no! No!' and Hannah added, 'Surely this isn't the house.'

'No!' Gilly growled; 'this isn't *the* house, it's *your* house, and *your* home.'

Hannah turned, appealing to Natasha, and she, smiling, said, 'It's our wedding present to you, my dear.'

David said nothing: he was staring at what must be the back of a long, low, two-storey house, with two french windows leading on to a large lawn, and thence down to the river . . . the Thames.

In a flash he recognised where they were: this was the house Gilly had bought, and to which he had hoped to retire.

He looked from Gilly to Natasha, his head shaking. Then he said, 'No; it's too much; we couldn't . . .'

He appealed to Hannah, and she said, 'He's right; we just can't accept it.'

'Well, where do you think you're going to live?' This raucous question came from Eddie. 'Talk about lookin' a gift horse in the mouth. Oh! come on. What d'you say, Mr Gillyman?'

'I say you're right, Eddie; let's get them inside.'

Inside, David started again: 'I can't,' he said; 'we can't.' He now looked round for Hannah, who was standing by Natasha's side looking as bewildered as he was. 'You feel the same, don't you? We . . . we just can't accept.'

'For God's sake, shut up, man!' cried Gilly.

'I won't shut up.' David's voice was loud, too, almost a shout. 'You bought this house for yourselves. All right. All right, Natasha doesn't like the water, but, in the end, she would have been persuaded about it. Of course she would; of course she would.'

'No, I wouldn't, David.' Natasha was standing in front of him now. 'That's just where you're wrong. I couldn't live by a river, not if you paid me. I have a fear of water. Gilly used to make a joke of it, but recently I had to tell him the reason. I had an aunt who drowned in the river. She drowned trying to save me, and in nightmares I'm still drowning. So, there it is. And if I had told Gilly about this beforehand, naturally he wouldn't have bought the place. But he'd bought it by then, thinking that he could talk me round; and what was more,' she smiled now, 'it was a very good buy. And, you know, David, how he can't resist a bargain. Just think of the things that are packed away in the store room, all the result of his good buying.'

'Anyway, Hannah; what've you to say about this?'

'I don't know,' she said; 'I just don't know. Such generosity! Some weeks ago I felt this was an awful world populated with dreadful people; but now I know that it is a beautiful world and holds marvellous people. The words I need to thank you are not in my vocabulary. But having said that, it's a lovely house . . . but it's such a big present to accept. I mean—' She stopped and put her fingers on her eyelids, and at this Gilly went to her and said, 'Come along to the kitchen, my dear; I want to introduce you to the staff. We'll leave that stubborn-headed man of yours to make his own way.'

He inclined his head towards David who was now holding Natasha's hand. She was saying, almost in a whisper, 'Please understand, David, Gilly thinks of you as a son, so humour him in this; from now on, take it graciously. Let's go with them into the kitchen, and see the fun.'

The beautiful kitchen resounded with laughter. At the L-shaped table were standing three cooks, all of different sizes, each wearing a tall chef's hat, their white aprons enveloping them.

Peter was smiling broadly as he said to David, 'What can I do for you, sir? By the way, this is my new assistant' – he indicated Pete – 'and this', pointing to Maggie, 'is the head chef, Mademoiselle Harper.'

Maggie, who was crushing some walnuts, was aiming to maintain a prim expression and not to burst out laughing. But then they all burst into laughter when she said, '*Ici on parle français. Le livre est sur la table.*'

'And your head will be on the table in a minute,' straight away put in Janie, 'if you don't get on with your work.' Then, turning to Mrs Drayton, she said, 'It's a beautiful kitchen, isn't it?'

'Indeed. Indeed. And look at that array of goodies

over there. The sight of them is enough to give anyone an appetite.'

'Well, they're there to be eaten,' said Gilly. 'What time is lunch, Peter?'

'Give me fifteen minutes, sir; just time enough for you all to have a drink in the drawing room.'

At this, amid chatter, Natasha led the way across the hall; but at the kitchen door David drew his chair to a stop and, looking up at Peter, who was now by his side, he said, 'It's too much; I can't take it all in.'

'Accept graciously, sir,' Peter said; 'they're getting more happiness out of their giving than you can imagine. And they've spent weeks adapting it to your needs, together with Mrs Drayton and Mrs Harper; and of course Mr McClean and Mr Harper. Oh, those two have had the time of their lives. You'll see and hear all about that later. So do this, sir, please.'

In the drawing room, Hannah was delighted by the colours of both the carpet and curtains, and by the arrangement of the pieces of their own furniture.

Then, amid the chatter and laughter, as the drinks were passed round, she stood for a moment gazing out of the long open french window down to the riverbank, where she could make out a boathouse and landing. It was all so wonderful. She suddenly felt weak, and had the desire to sit down and cry.

When she turned to find Mrs Drayton at her side, she said, 'Isn't it all beautiful!'

'Yes, it is, my dear; but as I see it, it will be a form of compensation for what you have been through.

And I can promise you, you'll have a visitor now and again' – she pointed to her chest – 'if for nothing else but to sit at this very spot and contemplate the view.'

The lunch was merry and excellent. After it, there followed a concerted tour of the house. David, of course, had to keep to the ground floor; but he was amazed at his office, which had been fitted for his future employment, as Gilly's business secretary. It was adjacent to their bedroom and bathroom, and just a short corridor's length from Hannah's small private sitting room.

It was as Hannah and Janie were descending the stairs that they heard three sharp blasts from the direction of the river; everyone came crowding round the french windows in the hall, staring towards the landing stage alongside which a large motor cruiser had been moored.

As one figure after another emerged, Hannah said, 'It's Micky!'

'Yes,' David said; 'it's Micky all right; and with his entire family, if I'm not mistaken.'

'Hello! you lot,' Micky called out, as he preceded his family up the lawn.

When he reached David he thumped him on the back, saying as loudly, 'Surprise?'

'One of them,' David answered. 'What on earth are you doing with that thing on the river?'

'That thing is a cruiser, and a damn pricey one an' all . . . Hello, Mr Gillyman! Am I on time?'

'Practically on the dot, Micky. But you've missed lunch.'

'Oh; we've brought ours with us.'

'How d'you do, ladies? I've brought my tribe with me for inspection.' He now turned to the group of people standing about him. 'This is my wife, Cissie.' He nudged the plump woman to one side of him, then introduced the woman to the other side of him: 'And this is my sister, Polly.' She, who was as thin as her sister-in-law was plump, surprised everyone when she pointed at the mound which Hannah was no longer able to conceal. 'See you're in the wagon-train; how far are you gone?' she asked.

The yell that Micky let out could have been heard well down the river as he cried, 'What did I tell you about that pontoon of yours?'

'Aah! you,' his sister came back at him. 'I'm just asking. You don't mind, do you, Mrs . . . Miss? Can I call you Hannah? That's your name, isn't it?'

Hannah chuckled and said, 'Of course, of course; and I'm nearing seven months.'

'My, my!' said the irrepressible Polly. 'You're carrying high. Me, I never—'

'Frankie!' Micky now hissed towards a man standing at the back of the family crowd. 'Will you come and take over your responsibility! Shut her up, eh?'

Amid the chuckles and laughter, Gilly's voice rose, saying, 'Well, let's all go indoors and see if there's anything to drink.'

'Oh, anything to drink,' cried Micky now. 'We brought a load with us. You, Frank and Charlie, get back down there and bring the stuff up. It's all ready. And take the girls with you. Stop gaping,

Tracey; it's as if you've never seen a house before. Go on with you.'

At this Hannah exchanged a look with Natasha and Mrs Drayton and said, 'Oh, dear, are they going to stay for a meal?'

They stayed for a meal. Well, they *had* brought a case of champagne, a whole ham and tongue, lots of French bread and a huge slab of butter and an equally large block of cheese, which was supplemented by Pete and Maggie and Janie bringing the rest of the leftovers from the earlier lunch . . .

To cap it all, David was given a further treat, when the men took the sumptuously fitted forty-foot boat up the river with him at the wheel in his chair, having lifted him in bodily, chair and all, from the landing stage.

David and Hannah later agreed, as they sat in the last of the evening light, looking out across the lawn down to the river, that they would forever treasure the memory of that most extraordinary and enjoyable day.

# Nineteen

Gilly had suggested that it would be simpler if David worked from home, so on the days when he did not have to attend the hospital for physiotherapy, he sat at his desk in front of the window that looked out across the river and read manuscripts. Gilly had told him that he intended to publish more books in the future, so there would be plenty for David to do.

Now, he laid aside the manuscript he had been reading and gazed out into the twilight. Everything was still, both in and out of the house. Hannah was seeing Maggie to bed and in a short while Pete would come in and help him too. He liked Pete, but oh, how he missed Peter; he hadn't seen him for nearly a week, not since he had returned again from hospital. But that would be rectified tomorrow, for the single bed was to be brought down into the little sitting room, and Peter would be settled there. It would be easier all round, especially for Pete.

Strange about Pete turning up as he did. What would they have done without him?

He and Hannah were to be married on Thursday.

He couldn't really tell whether or not Hannah was looking forward to it; she seemed to be so tired these days, which was natural, he supposed, for the baby was due in a little over three weeks. He hoped he'd be able to drive her to the church himself, and would do so if his adapted car were delivered tomorrow, as promised, for then he would have time to get used to handling it. Oh, he'd be glad to be independent.

The door opened, and he turned to see Hannah guiding Maggie into the room. She had her arm about the girl's shoulders, and Maggie's head was deep on her chest; it was evident that she was crying.

'What's the matter? What's up?' He wheeled his chair towards them, and Hannah said quietly, 'It's all right. She doesn't want to go to bed yet, even though I told her I couldn't go to bed until I knew she was tucked up instead of sitting in the dark.'

'What's the matter, Maggie?' David put his hand out and drew the thin body towards him. And Maggie, for a moment, leant her head on his shoulder before straightening up, sniffing loudly, then spluttering into her handkerchief, 'I'm . . . I'm all right. I'm all right.'

'You're not all right if you're crying like that. What's upset you?' He reached to the side and switched on the table lamp.

Hannah sat down; then, pulling Maggie towards her, she said, 'Come on now. Come on. You can tell us what's upset you. Has Pete said anything to . . .?'

'No. No, not Pete. No.'

'Well, who? What's made you cry like this?'

The head was down when she muttered, 'Mam.'

'Your mother?' Hannah drew Maggie's face round towards her as she repeated, 'Your mother?'

'Yes. She . . . she says I've got to spend more time at home with the others, that I'm in the way here, and I know I'm not, am I?'

'Oh, no.' Both David and Hannah denied simultaneously, and David went on, 'In the way? You're a blessing! Not only in running around for us, but keeping Peter company.'

'And Peter likes you with him,' added Hannah.

'Yes; yes, he does.' Maggie was nodding now at David. 'And I must be with him. I know I must. And that's what I told Mam: Mr Peter needs me. And . . . I . . . I' – she looked from one to the other – 'I need him, for the time he's here. So, as I told her . . .'

'Well, what did she say to that?' asked Hannah.

'Oh! Auntie Hannah; you know how she goes on: she says I'm getting above meself; and who am I to say Mr Peter's going to die?' The word trailed away. The round eyes were wide. She looked quickly from one to the other again, saying, 'It . . . it slipped out. It just slipped out.'

Hannah looked at David, then back to Maggie when David's voice, very low, said, 'What makes you think Peter's going to die?'

Maggie screwed up her eyes tight, bit on her lower lip and shook her head as if in desperation as she muttered, 'He . . . he knows; we talked about it, but he made me promise, a deep promise, that I would never say anything to you.'

Hannah was staring at David now as he asked again, quietly, 'Who else knows this?'

'Pete – Pete's always known it – and . . . and Mr and Mrs Gillyman.'

Now he and Hannah were exchanging glances again, but this time they held; and David said to Hannah, 'Oh, my God! We must have been blind, unless . . . unless you knew.'

'No; no, David. I knew his condition must have been serious when he was taken into hospital again. He said they were just tests and that he was to stay in bed for a time because there was another little leak at the back of his head, and that for a time it might make him fall about again. As usual, he made a joke of it, that one day he would do so when wheeling in the tea trolley. And he'd kept on wheeling in the trolley when he was unable to do anything else.'

When David swung his chair around towards the window again and crouched forward and sat looking out into the darkened night, Maggie said, 'He says none of us must worry, particularly you and Aunt Hannah, because he'll still be here. He keeps telling me that he'll still be here.' She looked into Hannah's eyes now, saying, 'We talk, Aunt Hannah, when nobody's there. We talk a lot and . . . and I understand most of what he says. I do now, but I wouldn't have before the night . . . that awful night. I . . . I seemed to get to know him from that night in a very odd sort of way, because I know I couldn't have understood half of what he says now if it hadn't been for that night . . . I love him, Aunt Hannah. I can't help it, and I don't want to go home, because I can't bear to leave him. And it isn't the same at home any more now. It never will be.' She was crying again, but gently, the tears falling softly down her cheeks; and she wasn't the only one, for Hannah was tearful and David's eyes were moist.

Maggie began to hiccup and gulp, and then she said, 'He'll be so vexed with me if you let on. Please don't let on. Anyway, when he knows that you know he'll make it easy for you as he did for me, 'cos, as he says, we've got two bodies: the top one dies, but the other one goes on for ever, and it'll look—'

'Be quiet, Maggie.' David's tone was harsh, so much so that the girl shrank against Hannah, but when he spoke again it was softly, as he said, 'I'm sorry, Maggie. I'm sorry. But go to bed. We'll . . . we'll talk about this in the morning.'

Hannah pulled herself up heavily from the chair and she went out of the room as she had come into it, guiding Maggie by the shoulder, and repeating, 'Shush now; no more crying. Now stop it. Come along; stop crying. It'll all be put right tomorrow.'

As for tomorrow, there would be many of them before David would be himself, for he was still carrying on his shoulders the burden of all that had happened. *Alice in Wonderland* was as if it had never been, and what Hannah was living in now was real life. She imagined a few weeks ago, when she had first seen the marvellous gift of this house, that once more she was entering the strange world of Alice, but now she knew there was no such place. There was just life, and it had to be lived: the life of the body, not the quiet everlasting spirit life to which Maggie had been introduced – and much too early at that, she thought.

She was to be married on Thursday; and Gilly had told her to expect to see the long-awaited cover design for her book; that, she was happy to know, was proceeding apace. But more important – far more important – in twenty-four days' time, if things kept to order, she would give birth to a son or a daughter – *they* would have a son or a daughter. But would this go any way to make up for the loss of Peter? No, no.

They must have been blind all these weeks not to know there was something really drastic happening to the man David loved and had always looked upon as father, brother and friend. And she too could call him a dear friend. She too must have been blind, yet when she looked back to the time when his pallor and inertia had worried her, she realised that she had simply accepted his word for their cause.

How much longer would he have? She must get in touch with the hospital tomorrow. Dr Peale, their general practitioner here, hadn't voiced any undue alarm; perhaps he too had been silenced by an earnest request from Peter.

# Twenty

The wedding was a quiet affair with no echo of the gaiety of the house-warming day.

To Micky's disappointment he learnt that there was to be no honeymoon spent on his boat. After it had been explained to him, he accepted the reason, but still he wondered, and put it forward that they could have had a night or two up the river. It seemed to him, he said, that nobody wanted to use his boat. Another thing was that the only McClean who seemed to be welcome at the White House was, of all people, tactless-tongued Polly. It was she alone who had been invited to represent the family at the wedding. And even then her invitation was not official, only coming about because, as she herself said, she visited them twice a week, and Thursday happened to be one of her days. As Micky said, there might be more to Polly than met the family eye, yet he himself couldn't see it.

The only other outsiders who were invited were Welshy, David's one-time nurse, and Gerard Johnson, one of his physiotherapists, who had also helped David get used to his new vehicle.

Besides these, there were Gilly and Natasha, Janie and Eddie, and Mrs Drayton, not forgetting the bridesmaid.

At the altar rail they must have appeared a strange pair, food for a quip from Polly, for there was the groom in a wheelchair and the bride with her belly rising high. Polly did not, at the time, comment on it; but she later produced the first real laugh of the day when she said to Hannah, 'I wondered if that parson knew he was marrying a triangle, because the way you're looking now, love, it wouldn't have surprised me if you'd had it on the altar steps.' And when Hannah had replied, 'Oh, have a heart, Polly; I've got three weeks to go yet,' Polly had answered, 'You'll never make it; believe me, you'll never make it.'

Feeling as she did at this moment Hannah was inclined to agree with her . . .

Hannah was standing in the hall saying goodbye to Welshy and Mr Johnson, and it seemed a toss-up as to who was to go next, Mrs Drayton or Polly. But Mrs Drayton won. With the practice of years in boardrooms, she remained silent and smiled until the other person moved; and that other person on this occasion was Polly. She, patting Hannah gently on the cheek, said, 'Give me a ring, mind. I've told you, I can come at a moment's notice.'

'Thanks, Polly. Yes, I'll do that.' And Hannah meant this, for although she hated to admit it, even to herself, Polly was more help and comfort to her than Janie, Mrs Drayton or even Natasha.

Then it was Mrs Drayton's turn. She spoke to David first, saying, 'You will get on the phone to me, now won't you?' And David forced himself to say, jocularly, 'I'll not only do that, I'll come and fetch you.'

'Oh, that would be first-rate. First-rate.' Mrs Drayton now gave him a familiar pat on the shoulder; then, turning to Hannah, she bent over the raised mound and kissed her on the cheek.

The next to leave were Eddie and Janie, and as the two sisters embraced Hannah whispered, 'You understand now, don't you? She'll be all right. I'll see she comes home before the end of the holidays.'

'Oh, it doesn't matter. It doesn't matter any more. We both understand. Forget about that and get on with your business.' She too now patted the hump in front of her, saying, 'I'm sick of waiting.'

'So am I, Janie,' said Hannah. 'So am I.'

Then there were only Gilly and Natasha. Their goodbyes were brief: 'Have a good night. See you in the morning.'

Of course the bridesmaid had been present at the wedding, but apparently she had found little excitement in her dress, which had been shortened to just above her knees. Now she was in the kitchen helping to set the table and tray for tomorrow's breakfast and when she said, 'Well, I'll polish the glasses before you put them away,' Pete remarked, 'Don't bother tonight; I can see to them, Maggie. You go and say goodnight to the squire and then get off to bed, but' – he nodded his head at her – 'see that he cuts the cackle short tonight, will you?'

They stared at each other for a moment, and then she said, 'All right, *I'll* cut the cackle short tonight; that's what you meant, wasn't it?'

'No, no!' His voice was in earnest now; then, shrugging his shoulders, he said, 'Half and half: you two set each other off.'

They looked at each other steadily before she turned away, saying, 'Goodnight, Pete.'

And he said, 'Goodnight, Maggie. And I should have told you before, but there hasn't been time – you looked lovely this morning.'

Her lids blinked, her lips pouted, then she shrugged her shoulders, turned about and went out.

It was only ten minutes later when she went into the drawing room to say goodnight to Hannah and David. They both kissed her warmly, and when Hannah said softly to her, 'You've been wonderful. Thanks, Maggie. Thanks,' she again shrugged her shoulders and pouted her lips. Then she turned to David who, taking up Hannah's words, said, 'Yes, indeed you have been wonderful. I don't know what we're going to do without you, and I really mean that. I was saying to your aunt only yesterday, there must be some way we can wangle you to live here, because when the baby comes you'll be needed more than ever; and there are some good schools round here. We'll see what we can do' – he was nodding at her – 'because you're badly needed.'

'That's what Mr Peter—'

She stopped herself from going on, then said quickly, 'Goodnight, Uncle David,' and leaning towards him she kissed him on the cheek, and he kissed her back. Then, as she hurried from the room, she thought, Yes; that's what Mr Peter said: 'You're wanted.' And he had said it was the most important thing in the world to be wanted, and oh, she needed to be wanted. Ever since that afternoon when she'd put her foot in it and afterwards nobody had seemed to want her at all, she had known what it was not to be wanted, and the feeling was still with her.

Mr Peter knew all about being wanted. He had been wanted by Mr David, and had said he himself would have been very lonely without Mr David in his life. He had also said that Pete needed to be wanted; because he, too, was lonely inside because he hadn't been made properly. So she must always do things to make herself wanted. But what she wanted at this moment above everything and everybody was that Peter should stay alive. But he wouldn't; he would go, and what would he leave? An emptiness. He had assured her the other part of him would fill it, but she doubted it. Spirit, or whatever it was, hadn't the power to talk, and to be needed you had to talk. But he had promised her faithfully, so she must just wait and see . . .

Downstairs, two people went into Peter's bedroom and they talked far into the night. And when at last they left the bedside they both felt strangely calm; Hannah had not found the exposing of their knowledge unbearable. And later, in their wedding bed, when he began to apologise about his restricted movements, she laughed gently with him, and for an answer she snuggled her swollen stomach to him, saying, 'We are a pair, aren't we? But it won't always be like this, darling. We're alive and together. And since I've spoken to Peter I feel strangely calm.'

There was a moment's silence before David answered slowly, 'Yes. Yes, I suppose I can say I feel calm too, my darling.'

Fourteen days later, which happened to be a Thursday, Hannah gave birth to a son. He weighed seven and a half pounds and he was perfect. As for his mother, she was exhausted after eighteen hours of struggling to bring him into the world, and after seeing him in his father's arms and the wonder on his face she left herself in the hands of the nurse and the doctor and fell into a much-needed sleep.

In the background there hovered, like three good witches, as the doctor said, Mrs Drayton, Natasha and Polly; but it was Maggie, weary-eyed but excited, who was allowed to carry the baby into Peter's room and lay him in his arms. And when Peter looked down on the chubby, wrinkled face and the moving lips now demanding sustenance, a voice within him said, Now I can go and you can take over; but the voice that came from his thin lips, as he now looked at Maggie, was soft as he said, 'He's beautiful, isn't he? And you must look after him, Maggie. He'll need you. Later on, he'll need you.'

'Yes, Peter, I'll look after him.'

Then Maggie handed the child to Mrs Gillyman and the three women went quietly from the room, and Peter, taking Maggie's hand, said, 'Now go to bed; you're walking in your sleep. We'll talk in the morning.'

At this she dared to ask, 'Will we?' and he said 'Oh, yes. Oh, yes, we'll definitely talk in the morning.'

She leant forward and kissed him on the cheek; and he held her face in his hands, and when he whispered something she was sure he said, 'My little love.'

Four days later Peter left his spirit behind him and, strangely, no one cried; at least, not on that day.

THE END

**RILEY**
by Catherine Cookson

There were many who said that Riley appeared to be older than his years. He finished school at an early age, leaving a harsh childhood behind him, brimful of optimism and secure in the knowledge that his teacher, Fred Beardsley, had faith in him. Neither of them could have envisaged at the time how their lives would be intertwined.

Fred encouraged Riley, a gifted mimic, when he was offered a position at The Little Palace Theatre in Fellburn. And then Riley surprised Fred by forming a close friendship with leading lady, Nyrene Forbes-Mason, who was nurturing his burgeoning talent as an actor. What Riley hadn't told him was that he had great hopes of the relationship developing into something more.

Over the subsequent years, Fred observed with amazement Riley's rise to fame and fortune. As for his relationship with Nyrene, that did indeed change although not in the way that Riley had envisaged.

0 552 14155 0

# THE SOLACE OF SIN
## by Catherine Cookson

As soon as she saw the house on the wild moorlands near Hexham, Constance Stapleton was attracted to it. With her marriage to Jim on the brink of collapse, she had already decided to sell the large flat they shared. And a further visit convinced her that she could live quite happily at Shekinah Hall, despite its isolation and lack of basic amenities. Connie also sensed that the move would initiate the separation from Jim she knew was inevitable, especially now that her son Peter was old enough to go off to university.

Connie was told she must negotiate with Vincent O'Connor if she wanted to buy the house, although his abrupt manner and insistence that the papers must be signed the following day took her by surprise. She was to discover that mystery was a way of life for Vincent and began to rely on him increasingly as she settled into her new routine. However, when shocking revelations about the man with whom she spent so many years came to light, she realised that her life at Shekinah could be under threat . . .

'Dame Catherine has done it again . . . a rattling good story with a satisfying ending, plenty of gritty dialogue, a tricky affair of the heart, and a strong, honourable heroine'
Val Hennessy, *Daily Mail*

0 552 14583 1

# A SELECTION OF OTHER CATHERINE COOKSON TITLES AVAILABLE FROM CORGI BOOKS

| | | |
|---|---|---|
| 14624 2 | BILL BAILEY OMNIBUS | £6.99 |
| 14533 5 | THE BONDAGE OF LOVE | £5.99 |
| 14531 9 | THE BONNY DAWN | £4.99 |
| 14348 0 | THE BRANDED MAN | £5.99 |
| 14156 9 | THE DESERT CROP | £5.99 |
| 14705 2 | THE GARMENT & SLINKY JANE | £5.99 |
| 13685 9 | THE GOLDEN STRAW | £5.99 |
| 14703 6 | THE HAMILTON TRILOGY | £6.99 |
| 14704 4 | HANNAH MASSEY & THE FIFTEEN STREETS | £5.99 |
| 13300 0 | THE HARROGATE SECRET | £5.99 |
| 14701 X | HERITAGE OF FOLLY & THE FEN TIGER | £5.99 |
| 14700 1 | THE IRON FAÇADE & HOUSE OF MEN | £5.99 |
| 13303 5 | THE HOUSE OF WOMEN | £5.99 |
| 13622 0 | JUSTICE IS A WOMAN | £5.99 |
| 14702 8 | KATE HANNIGAN & THE LONG CORRIDOR | £5.99 |
| 14569 6 | THE LADY ON MY LEFT | £5.99 |
| 14699 4 | THE MALLEN TRILOGY | £6.99 |
| 13684 0 | THE MALTESE ANGEL | £5.99 |
| 12524 5 | THE MOTH | £5.99 |
| 14157 7 | THE OBSESSION | £5.99 |
| 14073 2 | PURE AS THE LILY | £5.99 |
| 14155 0 | RILEY | £5.99 |
| 14706 0 | ROONEY & THE NICE BLOKE | £5.99 |
| 14039 2 | A RUTHLESS NEED | £5.99 |
| 10541 4 | THE SLOW AWAKENING | £5.99 |
| 14583 1 | THE SOLACE OF SIN | £5.99 |
| 14683 8 | TILLY TROTTER OMNIBUS | £6.99 |
| 14038 4 | THE TINKER'S GIRL | £5.99 |
| 14037 6 | THE UPSTART | £5.99 |
| 12368 4 | THE WHIP | £5.99 |
| 13577 1 | THE WINGLESS BIRD | £5.99 |
| 13247 0 | THE YEAR OF THE VIRGINS | £5.99 |

Transworld titles are available by post from:

**Book Service By Post, PO Box 29, Douglas, Isle of Man, IM99 1BQ**

Credit cards accepted. Please telephone 01624 675137
fax 01624 670923, Internet http://www.bookpost.co.uk
or e-mail: bookshop@enterprise.net for details

**Free postage and packing in the UK.** Overseas customers: allow
£1 per book (paperbacks) and £3 per book (hardbacks).